THE WHITE CITY DIMMED

VOLUME TWO

IMRAUT

BY

HELEN QUINN

Order this book online at www.trafford.com
or email orders@trafford.com

Most Trafford titles are also available at major online book retailers.

Note for Librarians: A cataloguing record for this book is available from Library and Archives Canada at www.collectionscanada.ca/amicus/index-e.html

Printed in Victoria, BC, Canada.

ISBN: 978-1-4251-5715-9 (sc)
ISBN: 978-1-4251-5716-6 (eb)

Our mission is to efficiently provide the world's finest, most comprehensive book publishing service, enabling every author to experience success. To find out how to publish your book, your way, and have it available worldwide, visit us online at www.trafford.com

Trafford rev. 9/17/09

North America & international
toll-free: 1 888 232 4444 (USA & Canada)
phone: 250 383 6864 • fax: 812 355 4082

PART ONE

CHAPTER ONE

Connor had seen the messenger safely away, escorting him through the silent mass of the dark, deserted courtyard, the light of the lantern flickering over the cobbles. Reaching the stables, they had parted company, Connor waiting until he had heard the soft challenge and reply as the man rode out past the sentries. Then he turned to make his way indoors, walking with quiet steps along the stone-flagged passageway in order not to disturb the members of the household who should have been all abed at this late hour. Arrived at the chamber, which served equally as a study for the master of the household and as the headquarters for his company of men-at-arms, Connor entered without knocking, stopping short on the threshold for a few seconds, before stepping inside and carefully closing the door behind him. Francys was sitting at the table staring bleakly ahead and, by the light of the tabri-oil lamp nearby, Connor saw that his face was ashen.

As he approached, Francys picked up the papers lying on the table before him and handed them over without a word. Connor looked down at them curiously, then glanced up at Francys.

'Read them,' the latter said impatiently.

Taking them over to another chair, Connor sat down to read through the documents. A feeling of increasing puzzlement spread through him as he did so, for what he held was, as far as he could judge, nothing more than the usual monthly report from Artem containing news supplied by the various members of the intelligence network which he contrived to run on Francys' behalf, and there appeared to be nothing out of the ordinary in it, certainly nothing that could possibly account for Francys' odd pallor and the tension which surrounded him. Connor's brows drew together in a perplexed frown. He glanced once more at Francys, and turned over the last page ... to find a note attached, written in the personal code reserved for private communications. Was it this that Francys wanted him to read? He presumed that it must be, and accordingly scanned it quickly. A deeper frown etched his brow and he re-read the words unbelievingly.

'Menellen,

I write with some news of vital import to your personal safety. It was conveyed to me by Mikel who, you will surely agree, is a most reliable informant and unlikely to pass on false information. To ensure myself further as to its truth, I have had it checked out by others whom I knew to be in a position to do so, and have but this minute received full confirmation.

Mikel reports that there are a number of documents which have been concocted in Carakhas, purporting to be in your handwriting and containing matters of interest to people hostile to our land. I am told that they are the result of a collaboration between certain persons in Carakhas and Väst, with Krapan acting as go-between. In a week's time, these documents will travel to Väst, where they are to be used as the basis for a charge of treachery and secret dealings with the Lord of Shadowe to be brought against you. Your brother, the Lord Hadran, is the main actor in this. Neither Mikel nor anyone else has been able to discover how they will be delivered to Väst, so it will not be possible for them to be intercepted.

Menellen, if you value your life and liberty, I beg you earnestly to disappear before they come to take you. You will not be able to refute the charge - they have made certain of that. Be assured that whatever aid I can lend you is yours.

I beg to remain your faithful servant, Artem.'

Connor perused the letter a third time as if to assure himself that he had not imagined the contents. Then he slowly raised his head to look across the room at Francys. Shock robbed him at first of words to express his emotions, but as he sat there, Francys himself began to speak, haltingly:

'How could he do this to me! There must be some mistake. Hadran would never serve me such a wicked trick. Oh, I know he hates me ... but *this*! No, no, I can't believe it. Dear Sior, I am his brother, his blood brother!'

He buried his face in his hands, unable to look Connor in the eye as he wrestled with the bitter knowledge that his own family had plotted his ruin, and intended death. The older man shifted uncomfortably in his chair, hesitating to speak, yet wishing to convey his sympathy somehow but not knowing how.

Francys could not think clearly. There seemed to be a blanket of darkness over his mind. Thoughts circled and danced in a senseless jumble, unrelated to one another, but all the time coming back to the one question: how could Hadran do this to him? A feeling of desolation crept over him. If his own brother could betray him in such a fashion, whom could he trust? He felt suddenly utterly alone.

Connor became conscious of a terrible anger inside himself. He had served Francys from the day when the latter had become old enough to command, had taken care of his affairs during Francys' enforced absence as prisoner in the South and later in the Land of Shadowe, and had come to cherish a strong affection for his commander, and a correspondingly strong feeling of dislike for the elder Coras brother, whom he considered a bully and a brute. If Hadran had been at his mercy at that moment, he would have had no compunction in despatching him in the most painful fashion possible. But that was not the most important consideration at that present. His first duty was to Francys.

Rising to his feet, he approached the table and, with some slight hesitation, ventured to touch the fair man lightly on the shoulder.

'Menellen,' he said quietly.

Francys raised his head.

'Connor,' he said slowly. 'What am I to do?'

'You must get away to safety,' Connor replied firmly. 'You have a week's grace. Use it.'

Francys turned and looked at the older man.

'You would make of me an outlaw? A hunted creature, abandoned by all my friends and living only to evade the hunters?'

'Better an outlaw and alive, Menellen, than hanged for a traitor. At least you would have some hope of someday proving your innocence.'

'True ... but is it worth it? To live out my life alone, despised ...'

'Not alone,' Connor spoke resolutely. 'And not despised. Don't forget, there are those of us who know the truth - Artem, myself - we'll not desert you.'

He marked the sudden flush, the biting of the lip as Francys struggled with his emotions, and tactfully withdrew.

When he returned, bearing a jug of warmed, spiced wine, the fair man was again master of himself, and had, it appeared, been doing some thinking.

'I must leave here tomorrow,' he announced abruptly, accepting a tankard of the steaming liquid. 'It must seem, though, to the household that I have gone merely on an ordinary journey, maybe even to Väst. Once away from here, I shall have to find some means of concealing my tracks ...'

'Our tracks, Menellen', Connor interrupted.

'*My* tracks,' Francys repeated. 'I cannot in all conscience allow you to share my exile, to give up your name, your honour ... There will be a price on my head once it is known that I have escaped...'

'Then there will be one on mine also. Menellen, you cannot stop me. You may not ask me, but I shall come all the same, if I have to walk to the ends of the earth.'

'I ... What can I say to that?' Francys said with a shaky laugh. 'You have so phrased it that I cannot refuse, can I? And in truth, I would not wish to. If I must become an outlaw, as it would appear I must, I cannot think of anyone I should wish more to have by my side.'

He paused a while, then raised his head and smiled at Connor.

'So be it. Then let us drink to our new estate.'

He lifted his tankard in a toast.

'To the outlaws!'

He drank deeply, and Connor was pleased to see that he looked more alive than he had a few minutes before.

****

Hadran Coras brought his horse to a stop, motioning those behind him to do likewise. Before him lay the lands and buildings of his brother's domain and he wished to savour the moment. Then he spurred his horse down the muddy track towards the large, well-built fortified house which nestled strategically between two outlying spurs of the foothills of the Teleth Cranem. His approach had been noted, and he reached the gatehouse to find himself confronted by closed gates, and the shapes of armed men with bent bows at the arrow slits. It was no more than he would have expected. One could not fault Francys' military management, whatever else the man might be capable of.

Recognition opened the gates to him, and he rode into the

courtyard, smiling.

'Tell my brother, I want to see him,' he announced generally.

The men looked at one another, wondering at the strength of the escort which attended him. No-one made a move. At last, one man went off to fetch the second in command, since Connor had given orders earlier that morning that *he* was not to be disturbed come what may. Hurrying forward, Joclyn bowed apologetically.

'Forgive me for having kept you waiting, Menellen. What may I do for you?'

'You may fetch my brother,' Hadran said curtly, beginning to feel annoyed. 'I wish to speak with him, immediately.'

Joclyn took a deep breath.

'I'm afraid that is impossible, Menellen.'

'Why?' demanded Hadran. 'Surely he cannot be drunk at this hour?'

The men of his escort sniggered; those of the resident company bridled angrily, but did not speak. Joclyn's face reddened with the effort of restraining the comment which rose to his lips. With a shrug, Hadran dismounted, gave the reins to one of his men and turned to Joclyn.

'Come now,' he snapped. 'Take me to my brother, if he won't come out here to me.'

Joclyn retreated a step.

'Menellen, I cannot,' he protested. 'The Lord Francys is not here. He has been gone these past ten days.'

Hadran's jaw dropped and a flush of rage mantled his cheeks. He recovered himself swiftly.

'I demand to see him,' he said angrily. 'I will not be put off in this fashion. Take me to him this instant, or it will be the worse for you!'

'I assure you, Menellen, he is not here!'

'Then where is he?'

'I know not, Menellen. He did not inform me. Perhaps Drachen Marach would know...'

'And where *is* Drachen Marach?' Hadran enquired. 'Or has *he* also disappeared?'

'That I have not, Menellen,' a voice spoke from the far side of the courtyard.

Hadran jerked his head up, to see Connor Marach standing stiffly in the doorway to the main house. He strode over to him, and Connor watched him approach, willing himself not to betray anything of the fury and disgust which the elder Coras brother invoked in him. He had been expecting this and had prepared himself for the encounter.

'The Lord Francys is absent, otherwise I am sure he would be the first to welcome you,' he said without expression. 'In his absence, I am in charge, and on his behalf let me invite you to partake of refreshment ..'

He bowed.

'I need no refreshment, I thank you,' Hadran said shortly. 'I want my brother, and I want him now.'

'I regret that it is impossible to grant your request, Menellen,' Connor observed mildly. 'He left here quite ten days ago, and we have not set eyes on him since. I myself have been absent on business and have not been back many days.'

'Where did he go?' And as Connor was slow to respond, 'Come on, come on, you must know. Where did he go?'

'I believe he intended to travel to Loden, Menellen.'

'I don't believe you,' Hadran snapped. 'What should take him *there*?'

He turned to his men.

'Search this house!' he barked.

As the men of the escort dismounted, and split into groups of three or four, disappearing in various directions, it was obvious to the resident soldiers that this had been pre-arranged.

'Menellen!' Connor protested, in duty bound. 'This is outrageous! You have no right to order a search here! Have you a warrant for it?'

'No, I haven't, but I have every right to come looking for a traitor!'

At that word, a hush fell on the assembled company in the courtyard. Those of Francys' men who were within earshot stared unbelievingly at the tall, fair man who had dared to say it.

'A traitor!' gasped Connor in well simulated amazement. 'A traitor, here? Who? ...'

'Who do you think?' said Hadran impatiently. 'Do I have to spell it out? Your precious commander, my brother. Who else? Now, will you submit to a search, or do you also wish to be charged with treachery?'

'Menellen, you are welcome to search,' said Connor, affecting stupefaction and capitulating, 'but he's not here.'

The search was lengthy and thorough, and by the time Hadran was satisfied that Francys was nowhere to be found, there was not one thing left untouched. The house and barracks presented the appearance of having been hit by a sudden strong gale. Papers, books, bedding, clothes, food, all lay scattered, furniture had been overturned, presses emptied and even tapestries and draperies pulled from their moorings. Francys' men stood angrily surveying the ruins, shocked and confused, not daring to complain. Connor, it is true, had almost given way to his feelings at one point, during the ransacking of Francys' private quarters, starting towards Hadran with an expression so murderous that it was as well that the elder Coras brother was not at that moment looking in his direction. Fortunately, Joclyn, grasping him by the arm, had brought him to his senses before he could do anything irretrievable.

Finally accepting that Francys was indeed absent, Hadran collected up his escort, swung himself into the saddle and gave a curt order to depart, leaving the members of the household and garrison to clear up the mess. The journey back to Väst was one which none of his men wished to repeat. As a matter of form, Hadran sent a small party off to Loden, but he did not expect his brother to be found in that town. Somehow his devil brother had been forewarned, and if he ever found out who ...

A few days later, further unwelcome news was received in Körain. A messenger rode into the courtyard, bearing an order from the Prince of Varadil commanding the return of the garrison to the city of Väst, where they would be re-allocated to other companies, and informing of the imminent arrival of the estate's newly appointed steward. 'The property of a traitor being forfeit', muttered Connor to himself, carefully packing amongst his own belongings, with the connivance of the ever-helpful Blial, Francys' manservant, as much of Francys' personal possessions as he could possibly manage to carry away unnoticed. Temporarily without a post, there being no spare captaincy within the forces of Varadil, even had he felt able to take it, he would be travelling, with Blial, now also without employment, to his family home in the upper reaches of the Mon valley, there to face a period of depressing inaction. At least, he thought, he would not have to witness the reading of the Register in Väst, for which deliverance Sior be thanked.

The remainder of the garrison reached Väst on the very day of the reading of the Register of State Enemies, and with one accord they made their way hastily to the main square, the Palandera, from the west side of which rose the tall, many pinnacled walls of the castle. It was more usual for the Prince of Varadil to deputize his Chief Justiciar to read out the list of wrong-doers (elsewhere in towns and villages the information was displayed upon a placard and read by the elders or mayor, or anyone else with the ability to do so), but today a whisper had arisen that the Lord Telstan Coras meant to appear in person, and a considerable crowd had gathered to witness this divergence from the norm.

At length, the big solid doors at the head of the steps were opened wide. The Lord Telstan Coras stepped out into the watery sunlight, flanked by his elder son, the Lord Hadran, and his bodyguards. The face of the Prince was haggard, his age never more evident. By contrast, though suitably sober of mein, Hadran exuded an indefinable air of smug complacency.

Silence stole through the crowd as the Lord Telstan Coras slowly surveyed the upturned faces with a sombre gaze. He raised his hand, and spoke.

'My people. I have something of grave import to tell you this day ... To the great shame and dishonour of my family name, and of this Province of ours ...'

He paused, then said:

'No, no, I cannot. My son, you must speak for me.'

Hadran stepped forward eagerly.

'My father wishes you to know that my brother, the Lord Francys Coras, has been adjudged guilty of the crime of treason. He has evaded justice and gone into hiding, and the Dukrugvola has therefore declared him imrauten. Anyone who associates with him or lends him any aid whatsoever will by that act be deemed also guilty of treason and shall incur the strictest penalty. But if anyone amongst you knows of his whereabouts, there will be a reward of five thousand caldri for his capture!'

He took his father's arm.

'Come Father,' he said.

But the Lord Telstan Coras abruptly shook him off and walked forward towards the edge of the steps. He raised his arms to the sky in a threatening gesture.

'A father's curse upon this degenerate son of mine!' he cried. 'May Sior confirm it! I cast out this rotten member, this ... this thorn in my flesh! For the dishonour which he has brought upon the reputation of our honourable name, may he be forever damned!'

He swung round and disappeared within the castle doors, closely followed by Hadran, who was, with difficulty, attempting to conceal a satisfied smirk.

****

Shaking back his long black locks, the Lord of Shadowe passed a hand lightly above the dark, viscous liquid in the wide shallow bowl on the table before him and sat back. A smile curled over his lips. Rising, he stretched cramped muscles, then wandered over to the window, which faced the West. The smile grew, and finally he frankly laughed out loud as he recalled the events which he had just viewed through the medium of the bowl.

He had done it! Francys Coras now stood convicted of treason, fugitive and outlaw. That jealous fool of a brother of his had been only too easy to manipulate. *He* had wanted him dead, of course, but Rycharst had never intended such an outcome. A judicial leaking of information had ensured Francys' prior knowledge of the plot sufficiently to enable him to make his timely escape and evade pursuit. Now, Rycharst had only to wait - for surely there was nowhere else for Francys to go ...

A yawn shook the tall Lord, and with a sudden change of mood, he shook his fist towards the West and cursed aloud. Caelvorchadu - that was his ultimate goal. He could do so little without a disproportionate draining of his energies. This fettering of his powers was intolerable. He must have Caelvorchadu. Only let him break that circlet and he would be free ... free to leave this world, to take his place once more amongst the great ones who roamed the stars. But Caelvorchadu sat safely in Lôren in the keeping of the Dukrugvola and he could not come to it ... yet.

But that could wait, he decided wearily, stifling another yawn. For now, it was sufficient that he had made a start.

****

The portrait sat upon the easel in the centre of her studio. Nyandu stood and looked at it. Since the day when she had returned from Shardu, she had not brought herself to take the painting out of the press in which it had been stored. It was the information which had arrived from Lôren so unexpectedly which had sent her to this chamber. She should at this moment be standing at her father's side in the Palandera, but she could not bear to hear the words spoken out loud. Francys Coras a *traitor*? She looked at the painted representation of the fair man's face, upon which she had expended so much time and care. Was that really the face of a traitor? Desperate, haunted, knowing too much of the dark side of life ... but no, she could not believe that it was the face of a man who would betray his country. Or was that merely because, having so recently come to a realization of her love for the man, she could not endure the thought that he was unworthy of that love?

No! She would not believe *that*. She could recall the loathing with which he had spoken to her of the Dark Lord. 'So long as there remains any strength, any breath in my body, I shall continue to oppose him, to thwart his plans in any way that I can!' Could he have changed so much in just one year?

She turned away from the painting, unable to look at that face any longer. Moving slowly across to the window, she rested her hands on the sill and gazed sightlessly at the view without. She became aware that she was crying; a silent, steady flow of tears.

Time passed. Footsteps tripped swiftly on the stairs beyond the door. There came a brisk knock, and the door opened.

'Menaïren', came the eager voice of her maid, excitement vibrating through her shrill tones. 'Menaïren, have you heard the news?!'

Nyandu forced herself to turn and smile wearily at the girl.

'Yes. I have heard.'

****

Connor tightened the straps of his saddle-bags. In an half hour, he would be off, having bade farewell to his brother and sister-in-law and his two nephews. It was time. It was best he go now, before he outstayed his welcome. He had no wish to tread on anyone's toes, and there was really no room for him in the household. Besides, as a younger son, he had always been destined for military service, and the placid pace of country life chafed him. He was not yet old enough to contemplate with pleasure a peaceful retirement.

In addition, since the day when he had parted from Francys Coras on the border of Varadil and Kirkendom, he had heard nothing of the young man. Rumours abounded, many of which he had himself helped to initiate, setting false trails to confuse any possible pursuit. He had lingered partly for this purpose, and partly because he feared that a watch might have been set upon his own movements in the hope that he might thus betray his commander. Having satisfied himself that this was not so, he now felt able to take his leave and slip away, before it occurred to someone in power to wonder what he was about.

CHAPTER TWO

Saragon shook his head irritably, then reached up a gloved hand to pull the hood further forward over his brow. The sodden folds of his cloak hung heavy about his shoulders. Rain, relentless, unceasing, lashed at the ground, scattering gouts of mud and turning ruts into rivulets beneath the horses' hooves. A far cry, he thought miserably, from the crisp, deep snow and frosty sunlight which he had left back in Vachi but a sevenday ago. Dear Sior, was it no more than that! He recalled the conversation perfectly. Seated upon the dais beside the Sar, well wrapped in warm furs, he was watching the sled races with which the people of Vachi enlivened their winter months. From personal knowledge, having been permitted to try his hand at it, he was able to appreciate the skill of the drivers, balancing astride the light sleds with their metal runners, polished and honed to deadly sharpness, guiding the pair of fleet-footed small mountain horses by means of reins in one hand and the cracking of a long, snake-like whip in the other.

In the interval between races, the Sar had turned courteously towards his guest and enquired:

'What is this I hear, Prince, of traitors in your country?'

Saragon, in the act of sipping mulled wine, choked and broke into a cough, whereat his host apologized politely for having inadvertently startled him. Once having recovered his power of speech, Saragon professed ignorance.

'Your Excellency must have better sources than I. I have heard nothing.'

'One hears news through the servants,' remarked the Sar. 'My body-servant has had leave to visit his relatives on the border with the Province of Lependom. He brings word of a great scandal ... at the time of the Register. That is the name, is it not of some festival of yours?'

Saragon nodded, intrigued.

'Does he know the names of these traitors?' he asked.

'There is only the one, I think. Yes, indeed. He is named as Francys Coras.'

For a moment, Saragon could not feel the ground beneath his feet.

Instinctively, his fingers clenched round the base of his cup. The noisy, colourful view before his eyes vanished as his mind strove to make sense of what his ears had just heard.

'No,' he said hoarsely. 'No. It can't be.'

He became aware of the Sar regarding him with some anxiety.

'My dear man, you have turned quite pale. Of course ... now I recall, he was something of a friend of yours, was he not? Was it not he who saved your Dukrugvola's life? Yes, yes. A pity ... a very great pity. He was a courageous man. I should not have thought it of him.'

He shrugged his bulky shoulders.

'What do we know always of what drives a man?' he commented rhetorically

Saragon blinked and peered through the curtain of rain. He could just make out, in the distance, the walls of the city for which he was bound. Sior be thanked. He had sent a messenger ahead to alert his household staff, and the thought of a warm fire, hot food and dry clothes was all that was keeping him going. Some half an hour later, dismounting stiffly in the courtyard of his Lôren townhouse, he gratefully embraced them all. Seated by the pleasantly roaring fire, having washed off the worst of the travel stains and clothed himself in fresh, clean, comfortable garments, a mug of hot wine in one hand and a steaming meat pie in the other, he had, for a while at least, no thought for anything further.

The following morning, rested and restored, he walked the twisty streets up towards the castle with a troubled mind. Having ascertained that the Dukrugvola was not able to see him immediately, he asked next for the Lady Menethila and was directed to the family's private parlour. Impatiently brushing aside the steward's offer to announce his arrival, Saragon bounded up the staircase and along the passage, scarcely taking note of his surroundings. He entered the room upon a hasty knock.

The parlour held two occupants. At Saragon's unexpected entrance, the younger of the two leapt to her feet in surprise, whilst the elder made a more sedate rising.

'Sharn!' Alhaîtha exclaimed in delighted tones.

For a moment she could not help the wild hope springing into her mind that he had come to declare his love for her and to ask for her hand. Of this she was swiftly disabused. According her a friendly, but unexceptionable greeting, the dark-haired man turned to the Lady Menethila, whom he found to be regarding him with compassionate eyes. She, at least, had known what had brought him thither.

'I tried to see the Dukrugvola, but he is occupied,' Saragon said, more abruptly than was usual for him. 'I must know the truth. Menaïren, when I left Vachi, I heard rumours that Francys had been denounced in the Register. Tell me, please. Is it true?'

The Lady Menethila came forward and took hold of his hands.

'My dear Sharn, I am so sorry,' she said kindly. 'Yes, it is true. He is imrauten. I am sorry you had to hear of it in such a fashion. Letters were sent to you, but it seems they never reached you.'

'Why?' he asked numbly, disregarding the latter part of her speech and caring only to know the reason for Francys' fall from grace.

It was Alhaîtha who elected to answer. Furious with him for his preoccupation with the fair man, yet again, furious with herself for having been foolish enough to imagine he had come on *her* account, she spoke bitingly.

'He is a traitor. He has been selling us all to Rycharst. There were documents ... incontrovertible proof.'

Saragon could not face her. He looked down at the Lady Menethila, an unspoken query in his grey eyes.

'I'm afraid it is so,' she said gently.

He submitted to her comforting grasp for a few moments, then quietly disengaged himself and trod stumblingly over to the window, whence he stared out unseeing at the gardens below.

'I can't believe it,' he said dully. 'Not of Francys! Not *him*!'

Memories whirled into his troubled mind.

Alhaîtha stood irresolutely, her heart pained by Saragon's evident hurt, yet still enraged by his indifference to her and his stubborn persistence in setting his friendship with that man, that *criminal*, above all else. Observing his grief, she found herself taken back to an earlier occasion some years ago, when Saragon had come to her with the news that Francys Coras had been captured by the Rarokins on the Southern border of Arami. She had not remembered the name then, nor had cause to fear it, but knowing that he must have been a friend of Saragon's, her sympathy had been roused.

For several months there had been profound silence over the fate of the unlucky youth. He had not been offered for ransom, unusually, and many people had concluded that he must have perished. Then, slowly, had come the rumours, filtering across the borders. At first they were nothing more than sly hints and veiled inferences, but soon the name of Francys Coras sounded on the lips of scandalmongers the length and breadth of the country. Gossips vied with one another in telling new and more fantastic tales until almost overnight, this little known younger son had become the subject of discussion in every salon, tavern or pothouse in the land of Karled-Dū. Although at the start few outside the Province of Varadil could recall ever having set eyes on him, very soon everybody could have recognized him, or thought they could, at first glance. Very fair, with the face of an alfëa was the description widely circulated, and rumour spoke of bitter disputes, nay even violent brawls, as wealthy and high-ranking noblemen in the Southern lands strove each to gain possession of him.

Then, into the horrified ears of the people of Karled-Dū had flowed the news that the Lord of Shadowe, travelling through the South, and setting eyes on the young man, had had him kidnapped and carried off to his fortress of Carakhas. Ripples of rumour emerged from time to time, but nothing definite was known until some four years ago, when a young man had appeared in Opel in the Province of Torano, claiming to be Francys Coras and requesting the protection of the Lord of Torano. A lucky escape, people had said, though there were a few who hinted that his return might be attributed to strategy rather than good fortune. Outraged public opinion had turned on the disparagers; now it appeared that time had vindicated them.

Saragon himself was recalling those events; the news of Francys' capture, and the long confused years which followed, when he had listened unwillingly to the scandalous tales of the alleged activities of his boyhood friend, trying to reconcile the image which emerged with his own memories. It had been immediately after the funeral of his father that the messenger had arrived with the note from the Lord Suma Pelerin of Torano. The messenger had indeed had to follow the Dukrugvola from Lôren up to Shardu, where he and his family had been staying in order to assist at the funerary rites. 'Menellen

Dukrugvola,' the note ran, 'we have in Enneth Mor a man who claims to be Francys Coras of Varadil. Since no-one amongst us knows the said Francys Coras, we are unable to verify his statement. May it therefore please you to send someone to confirm his identity....' Saragon called to mind the discussion which had taken place upon the receipt of that note. At first, the Dukrugvola had advocated informing Francys' family, but eventually the decision had been made that Saragon himself would travel to Enneth Mor to make the identification.

So Saragon had ridden in haste to the city of Enneth Mor, where he was welcomed with relief. The Lord of Torano had seemed anxious to rid himself of his 'prisoner' as swiftly as possible, and having allowed Saragon a brief period for rest and refreshment, had lost no time in suggesting that he be taken to see the young man. Even now Saragon could well remember the scene. Upon his assent, the Lord Suma had summoned his Captain of Guard and commanded him to conduct Saragon to view the prisoner.

'If he proves to be Francys Coras, he may be released forthwith,' he told Saragon fussily, 'and you and I can arrange the matter.'

Saragon accompanied the Captain down stairs and along vast stone corridors.

'Where in Sior's name have you put him?' he enquired in surprise.

'Why, Menellen, in a cell to be sure,' the man replied. 'We had no means of knowing if he spoke truth, so we must needs be cautious.'

Saragon said no more. Now that they were drawing near, he felt a knot of apprehension twisting his gut. A vague dread enveloped him as he began to recall all the rumours and stories which had come to his ears. Francys had been still on the verge of adulthood when he had seen him last, but what sort of man had he become? What would he find in that cell? He forced himself to walk naturally and not to slow down as was his inclination, and presently they arrived at a heavy door with a grate over the tiny opening at head height.

'Here we are,' announced the Captain, taking out a large bunch of keys and searching through them, much to Saragon's irritation. After a few seconds, which seemed an age to Saragon, he found the correct key and thrust it into the keyhole. It turned with a grinding noise and the door creaked open.

Saragon peered eagerly into the gloom, unable to see anything.

Stale odours wafted towards him on chilly, damp air, and he could not help wrinkling his nose in disgust. By the faint light filtering through a narrow window slit set high up in the far wall, he gradually made out a thick wooden bench and a pallet of straw in one corner, upon which sat a dim figure, cross-legged and motionless.

'For the love of Sior, give me a light!' Saragon said impatiently, turning to the Captain. 'How do you expect me to see anything in this darkness?'

There came a faint hiss of breath from the corner at the sound of Saragon's voice, and the prisoner's head came round to face his visitors. The Captain unhooked a small tabri-oil lamp from a chain on the wall and succeeded in lighting it at the third attempt. He handed it to Saragon, who raised it high and by its glow examined the occupant of the cell.

On the straw sat a thin, young man with long, straggly and unkempt fair hair, which bore traces of a brown dye. He was clad in rough peasants' clothes, and even those were filthy and torn to ribbons. The feet were bare. Saragon's eyes travelled back to the face. Eyes ringed with exhaustion, hazel eyes, blinking in the unaccustomed light, stared back with an odd expression, half defiant, half wistful, in a face smudged and bruised and unshaven, but heart-wrenchingly familiar.

For one long minute Saragon regarded the young man, not quite believing what he saw, until in the hazel eyes appeared a trace of unease and even despair, and the prisoner bent his head. This movement roused Saragon from his trance and, thrusting the lamp into the Captain's hands, he advanced into the cell.

'Francys,' he said joyfully. 'It is you! It really is you! Welcome back!'

Francys lifted his head then, a look of undisguised relief on his face. He arose and backed away from Saragon's impetuous advance.

'I thought you didn't know me,' he said simply, 'you took so long. No, don't come too close,' he added, raising a warning hand. 'I stink.'

'Don't be a fool,' returned Saragon, 'as if I'd care about *that*!'

He reached Francys and, grasping him by the shoulders, embraced him warmly on both cheeks.

'Welcome back,' he said again. 'It's so wonderful to see you.'

For the first time Francys smiled.

'Sharn,' he said, returning the embrace. 'I couldn't believe it when I heard your voice.'

He shivered involuntarily and Saragon, feeling the tremor, scrutinized him closely, noting the signs of utter exhaustion. He turned to the Captain, whom he found goggling at them from the doorway.

'Yes, Menellen,' the man said hastily, snapping to attention.

'I identify this man as Francys Coras,' Saragon said formally, 'and ask that he be released forthwith.'

The Captain bowed.

'Very well, Menellen. It shall be done. If you would care to follow me. I will send someone down to fetch him shortly.'

'No.' Saragon spoke firmly. 'He can come with us now. I'm not leaving him here a moment longer. Would you be so kind as to show us the way upstairs?'

'But ... but, Menellen, he's filthy!' the Captain protested.

'All the more reason to get him upstairs quickly,' Saragon said coolly.

He turned to Francys and said briskly:

'Come along Francys.'

Francys gazed wearily at him and muttered:

'Where to?'

'Upstairs, and then into a lovely hot bath,' Saragon told him, grinning. 'Come on.'

He escorted Francys out of the cell and together they walked along the passages and up the flights of stairs which brought them at length back to the entrance hall. Francys was limping and needed some assistance in ascending all the steps, moving slowly and in a daze of weariness. Reaching the entrance hall, Saragon confronted the Captain.

'Kindly inform the Lord Suma Pelerin that I have confirmed the identity of his prisoner and that I shall wait upon him shortly in order to sign the necessary paperwork to secure his release.'

He paused.

'I believe that a chamber has been prepared for me. Please arrange for someone to escort us there immediately and for hot water to be brought up.'

'Very good, Menellen.'

The Captain bowed, shot a disapproving glance at Francys, and disappeared down a passage.

'Stupid fool!' Saragon said viciously the moment the man had passed out of sight.

'You can't blame him,' remarked Francys peaceably. 'I'm not a pretty sight.'

'He didn't need to put you down there!'

Francys gave a faint chuckle.

'Sharn, you'd have done the same in his place!'

'I should hope that any prisoners in *my* cells are treated with somewhat more consideration than that,' Saragon rejoined tartly.

Francys smiled again at his friend. Only then, his smile fading, did he take in the significance of Saragon's attire; the grey of mourning.

'Oh, Sharn, I didn't realize... I'm sorry ... who?' he asked, gesturing towards the garments.

'My father,' Saragon told him.

'I'm sorry,' he said again, reaching out impulsively to grasp Saragon's hand.

A shudder ran through him and he swore softly. Saragon put a bracing hand under his elbow.

'Why don't you sit down?' he advised.

Francys shook his head.

'No, I'll manage. Surely they shouldn't be long now.'

He grimaced.

'If I sit down, I don't think I'll ever get up again! I'm *so* tired,' he murmured.

Fortunately, at that moment footsteps sounded in the passage and a servant in livery appeared. He bowed low to Saragon, ignoring Francys completely.

'If you will come with me, Menellen, I will conduct you to your chamber.'

His eyes flicked momentarily to Francys, and he added:

'I have ordered hot water and washing utensils to be placed there.'

'Thank you,' said Saragon.

The servant turned towards the staircase. Francys, detaching himself reluctantly from the wall, against which he had been leaning for support, stumbled and nearly fell. Saragon caught him neatly, grinned and slipped a supporting arm round his waist, and together they walked up the wide stairs behind the correct manservant,

Francys leaning ever more heavily on his friend as his strength ebbed.

'What's wrong with your leg?' Saragon asked, as the limp became more pronounced.

'I wrenched my knee.'

'How?'

'I landed awkwardly.'

More he would not say, and Saragon let the subject alone, merely remarking that he would arrange for a physician to have a look at it as soon as possible.

Arriving eventually at the chamber appointed for Saragon's use, the servant opened the door, bowed, and left them. Saragon guided his friend inside, where they discovered an inviting tub of steaming water standing in front of the hearth, with a towel and soap beside it. The bedchamber itself was comfortably furnished and pleasantly warm, in shocking contrast to the cell which they had so recently left behind.

'Right,' said Saragon firmly. 'You have a bath while I go downstairs and discuss the details with Suma. You'll have to borrow a nightshirt off me. It'll be a bit big on you, but never mind. And tomorrow, we'll have to get you some clothes. I didn't think to bring anything with me. It didn't occur to me that I'd need to.'

He looked at Francys' pale face.

'Do you think you can manage by yourself? Or would you rather I stayed to help?'

A terrible lassitude seemed to be creeping over the fair man, but he roused himself sufficiently to shake his head.

'I'll manage,' he assured Saragon faintly.

Saragon looked unconvinced.

'How long is it since you've had a proper night's sleep?' he asked.

'I've lost count,' Francys answered simply. 'But you go on, Sharn. I'll be all right.'

As Saragon still hesitated, a respectful cough sounded behind them.

'Allow me to assist,' said a voice, and a smallish, elderly man clad in the neat garments of an upper servant stepped forward to offer his arm to Francys. Saragon delivered him up, and departed downstairs to find the Lord Suma. The signing of the papers turned out to be a more lengthy matter than he had expected, since the Lord Suma insisted that he share a drink and evening meal with him before settling down to business, and it was not until some two hours later that Saragon was able to excuse himself and return upstairs, the precious order of release tucked into his belt.

Even now, after four years, the picture was as vivid in his mind as if he were there again. He had opened the door quietly and entered. Looking around for his friend, he discovered him sprawled across the big bed on top of the counterpane, fast asleep with the abandonment of utter exhaustion. The nightshirt, made for his own larger frame, had slipped off one shoulder. With his hair cropped and washed, and his face clean-shaven, Francys looked more like the youth he remembered; except that he was so painfully thin and gaunt. Saragon moved softly forwards until he stood beside the bed, looking down. Here, the changes were more visible. Although, lying as he was on his front, with his head turned to one side, it was not possible to see his face clearly, Saragon was able to note the prominence of the cheek bone, the tightness of the skin stretched taut across his jaw, and the bruising - bruises not only on the face, but equally evident on arms and legs, and no doubt, if Saragon had been able to see beneath the nightshirt, on his torso as well. All in all, the fair man looked to have been pretty thoroughly knocked about and, as Saragon noted, anger growing within him at the realization, recently at that; in other words, whilst he had been in the custody of the Prince of Torano. Saragon made a mental vow to ensure that the Dukrugvola be made aware of the treatment meted out by the Lord Suma's retainers.

He was just wondering whether to look for a blanket in one of the presses in order to cover the young man lest he become chilled when, as though he had become aware of the presence of someone nearby, Francys stirred and opened his eyes. For a split second Saragon glimpsed what, unguarded at the moment of awakening, was reflected in those hazel eyes - an instant of unfathomable horror and a desperate shocking despair. Then Francys had recognized him, and relaxed, and smiled.

Saragon traced patterns on the window-sill with one finger, the memory of that awakening fresh in his mind. The horror, the despair, *that* had been genuine, of that he had not the slightest doubt. So too had been Francys' eagerness to meet the Dukrugvola and to pass on to him all the details which he had stored up in his mind to enable the forces of Karled-Dū successfully to defeat the Lord of Shadowe and drive him from his lands. They had met in Verilith in neighbouring Arlente, Saragon having had no desire to experience the hospitality of the Province of Torano for a moment longer than was strictly necessary. He recalled the long nights which they had come to dread, when they had had to resort to drugging Francys with sleeping draughts in order to grant him at least some hours' respite from the hideous nightmares which plagued him.

No... it was unbelievable that Francys had played false. Had he been asked for *his* opinion, he would have said that Francys was the very *last* person to have betrayed his country to Rycharst. Yet, the Dukrugvola had declared him imrauten ...

Saragon swung round.

'I *must* see the Dukrugvola, ma'am', he said addressing the Lady Menethila, unconsciously seeking her understanding and approval.

She nodded.

'Yes of course.'

She made no move to detain him as he strode towards the door, but shook her head at Alhaîtha as the latter looked to be on the point of making some exclamation.

'Let him go,' she advised her quietly. 'He needs to see the evidence.'

On this occasion, Saragon was more successful. The Dukrugvola welcomed him with pleasure not unmixed with sadness.

'I can guess why you have come,' he remarked. 'A bad business, Sharn, I'm afraid.'

He sighed deeply.

'Could there not have been an error somewhere?'

The Lord Archailis shook his head.

'I have been over and over it all. I've had the papers checked and re-checked a dozen times at least. If they're forgeries, they're damned good ... too good!'

'May I see them, sir?'

'If you wish, but it won't be pleasant.'

'I need to see them.'

Wordlessly, the Dukrugvola turned and walked over to a skilfully concealed cupboard, unlocked it and extracted a thin bundle of papers. He handed them to Saragon.

'Sit down,' he advised, and Saragon did so.

The Lord Archailis returned to his desk and waited, glancing from time to time at the dark head nearby. Saragon perused the covering letter with extreme concentration. Laying it aside, he looked down at the next sheet, and could not suppress a gasp. Even though he was prepared for it, the actual sight of Francys' handwriting shocked him. A deep frown appeared on his brow as he read through the damning letters one by one. Finally, he raised his head.

'I still don't believe it,' he said abruptly. 'It may be Francys' writing, but this ...' he flicked the edges of the letters 'this is not his style. And I will never believe that he would betray us all ... to Rycharst! You saw him when he escaped from that fiend. Can you really believe that he would do anything ... *anything* at all to put himself back in his power?!'

'No, Sharn, I cannot,' the Lord Archailis said soberly. 'My memories of that time are as clear as yours, I don't doubt. But what are we to make of these letters? The hand is his. No-one can deny that. That is why I had to denounce him in the Register. I had no choice. Though, I have to admit that I was glad he managed to evade pursuit,' he added with a wry smile.

'The thought did occur that it was some monstrous plot, dreamed up mayhap by his brother. It was suspicious to my mind that Hadran should be the one to uncover the crime ... but I cannot believe that he would have the subtlety and imagination to plan such a diabolical scheme. That affair with the drugged wine was more in keeping with his character.'

Saragon froze. In that moment, certain matters suddenly became clear to him. He shifted uncomfortably in his chair.

'Ah ...' he said somewhat shamefacedly. 'You believe that *Hadran* was responsible for that?'

'Oh, I know Francys would never say who was responsible,' his liege lord explained easily. 'I respected him for that. It was obvious though that he was covering up for his brother. Who else would he have been at such pains to protect?'

Saragon grimaced to himself.

'It wasn't Hadran,' he confessed, feeling that however much he disliked Hadran Coras, in all fairness he could not allow his reputation to be blackened by something which he knew to be untrue. 'It's not important now who *was* responsible, but Hadran had no part in it.'

The Lord Archailis looked at him sharply.

'You are absolutely sure? Yes, I suppose you would know, wouldn't you. ...Not that it makes any difference to our current problems,' he added gloomily.

'No ...' Saragon had been thinking hard. 'Sir, have you not considered the most likely person, if you could call him such, to have sent these papers? Do you really think that anyone could have intercepted them in the fashion described in the covering missive without having been himself found out before he could have had the chance to collect so many? Sir, I think that behind this lies the foul hand of the Lord of Shadowe himself. I would lay you any odds you choose. It is his revenge on Francys for having escaped and for having helped to oust him from his lands. And a sweet revenge it is too, to set every hand against him ... what do you warrant that it was *he* who gave Francys sufficient warning to flee, to prolong the chase and make his suffering greater?'

'Aye,' the Dukrugvola agreed thoughtfully. 'I believe you have the right of it, Sharn.'

His face fell.

'But how do we prove it?'

Saragon rose.

'I don't know,' he said grimly, 'but before Sior, if a way exists, I'm going to find it!'

CHAPTER THREE

The Lord of Shadowe cursed softly to himself as he paced the battlements of his huge fortress, Carakhas. After yet another unproductive session with the scrying liquid, he had come outside to breathe, and to get away from the curious gaze of his courtiers. They could not understand his obsession with the fair man from Varadil. Damn it, where *was* Francys? It was weeks since he had left Körain, and Rycharst had failed to find the slightest trace of his presence anywhere. He could not be *dead*! A shudder passed through the immortal being at the thought. But no, he was certain that Francys Coras still lived. Only, *where was he?*

Many leagues distant, Connor Marach heaved a sigh of relief as the jagged towers of the ancient keep of Carledruin appeared on the horizon. It stood alone on a hilltop, surrounded by rolling plains. Fields stretched out before him, rich fields with black soil, alluvial deposits. Cattle grazed peacefully on either side of the highway. It was strange, Connor mused, that such fertile land should lie next to bare desert. He looked over to the south and tried to make out the line of the Toath Cranem. A row of trees obscured his vision, so he returned his gaze to his immediate surroundings. Arlente might be the smallest Province, but it was wealthy enough, and of course there was the lake.

Connor shook himself mentally, his thoughts turning once more to the object of his travels. As he carefully left the highway along one of the occasional narrow, winding lanes, he recollected his meeting with Artem. Having left his family home, he had made his way out of Varadil and into the neighbouring Province of Kirkendom, and had ridden by back ways up to Martle and the farm whence Artem continued to run Francys' network of secret informants. Eagerly he had pressed the man for news of their commander. Where was he? Had Artem seen him recently? How was he? And Artem had obligingly told him all that he could remember. Connor considered the words again.

'He stayed over to get the reports of the reading of the Register. The news of his father's curse hit him terribly hard. After that, he left pretty soon; said he didn't want to compromise me. I tried to keep him; I was afraid of what he might do. But I couldn't stop him going. That was beginning of arenith. Mid telenith, he arrived suddenly, very dirty and ill-clad, and starving. I gave him food and shelter for a couple of days and then he went off again. He wouldn't say much, but I believe he'd been travelling in the Toath Cranem.'

'The Toath Cranem!' Connor had exclaimed, amazed. 'But how could he survive in there? It's bare of everything!'

'I don't know. But I'm certain he'd been there.'

'And where is he now?'

'I have no idea. I believe he has made a shelter of sorts in Carledruin. You might try there.'

Which was how Connor came to be on the way to that ruined place. He had accepted food and blankets from Artem and had given him a promise to keep in touch. Now, here he was, weary and depressed, but not without a slight tingling of excitement too, concealing his tracks, dodging passers-by, not knowing whether he had been outlawed or not, but expecting sombrely that he had, and wondering what he would find ahead, and wondering too what he would do if he did not find Francys at this place.

A glance at the sky above caused Connor to swear viciously. If he did not hurry, he would be overtaken by the night, and by the looks of it, by snow as well. How much further would he have to travel? He had reached the edge of the moorlands and empty plains which immediately surrounded the fortress. No-one farmed too close to the ruins. Rather, the place was feared and avoided; a good choice for a hide-away. No-one knew what sorcery might still remain around the ancient towers, for they had stood in their dilapidated condition for as long as local folk could remember, and they equated them in their minds with the Toath Cranem. Therefore, the ruins rose from an untended wilderness of long grass, moorland plants and small trees. Here and there clumps of larger trees grew; birches, elders, beech, oak and caelin. A stream splashed down from the hill, pouring forth from a long unused culvert which had once supplied water to the fortress.

Connor shivered both from cold and apprehension. But still he pressed forward. Artem had been so sure that Francys was here, and if Francys could brave the ill reputation of Carledruin, so could he. So he came at length to the outer wall, as dusk was falling and the first soft flakes began to drift through the air. Dismounting, he led his horse to a gap in the crumbling curtain wall. A wide courtyard met his gaze, once evidently paved, but now mostly weed-covered. The stable block was miraculously almost intact, save for some gaping holes in the roof at one end, and he went over to it. Straw covered the floor at the better end, and there were bales of hay and sacks of oats. Evidently someone was living there, though the main building looked desolate and still.

Stabling his horse, Connor entered the darkening keep. He began an investigation, treading warily to avoid unexpected holes. The main hall was open to the sky and plants had grown across the floor, some even hanging from cracks in the walls. Other parts of the building looked to be in better condition, particularly the corner towers, and it was in one of these, ascending the twisting staircase, that Connor came upon a chamber which was actually furnished, albeit meagrely. A straw pallet lay upon a roughly-fashioned low bedstead in an alcove to one side of the fireplace. A table stood nearby, a cup and plate set neatly upon its surface. Candles had been placed in the wall-sconces, and in the grate a fire was laid. He looked around. Whoever it was who was using the place had been careful to leave no trace of his identity.

Connor stiffened suddenly. Hooves clattered on stone outside. He strode hastily to the narrow window, but his sense of direction had deserted him, and he looked out fruitlessly onto the countryside beyond the wall. Carefully he made his way to the door and crept down the stairs. He stopped for a moment to listen, but could hear nothing. Connor took one more step, his muscles tensed. It was dark now at the base of the tower and he could see nothing, and he was unarmed. He essayed another, stealthy step. There was a sudden movement and Connor was flung against the wall, a hand on his shoulder and a knife blade pressed to his throat. He choked.

'Who are you? What are you doing here?' a voice demanded sharply, a voice that Connor knew extremely well.

He relaxed in the other's grasp and said mildly:

'They always said you could see in the dark, like a cat ...'

The hand and knife were abruptly removed.

'Connor!' Francys exclaimed incredulously.

'The very same, Menellen.'

There was a scrape of flint on a tinder-box and Francys lit the primitive torch which he had fixed up on the wall. It flickered dangerously, but remained alight, and in its glow the two men regarded one another. Francys was warmly clad in drab but well-made garments, cloaked. Traces of snow lay on the cloak and his hair was damp. A beard of a few days' growth glinted in the torchlight, half shielding a series of scratches which ran down one cheek as though a huge paw had swiped at him, which was, in fact, the case. Lines of fatigue showed in his face and he looked a little dazed, but after a few seconds a smile spread slowly over his features and he walked forward to embrace the older man.

'Con!' he said again, in a voice that sounded as if he was not quite sure whether he might not be merely dreaming.

Connor looked into Francys' face, grinning broadly.

'Aye, Menellen, 'tis I,' he returned. 'Come to join you, as I said I would.'

'I knew there was someone here; I saw your horse,' Francys continued, almost as if Connor had not spoken. 'You should have said something, Con. I could have killed you!'

He shook his head.

'I can't believe it.'

Then, pulling himself together with a visible effort:

'Well come on then, we'd best get the horses seen to and our gear unpacked before nightfall.'

He turned and strode through the doorway into the yard, his cloak swirling in the draught. Connor followed him across to the stable block. Outside it was not quite dark, but the snow was falling more steadily. When Connor entered the stables, he found that Francys had lit a couple of torches and was unsaddling Melisor, his big black stallion. Working companionably side by side, they groomed and fed their mounts, as they had many times in the past, before gathering up the baggage and carrying it over the slippery stones into the tower and up to the furnished chamber.

'Just dump your bags down anywhere for now,' Francys directed. 'I'll get the fire going.'

He knelt beside the fireplace and soon managed to get the sticks ablaze. As soon as he was sure that it would not go out, and shivering a little, he stood up.

'That should warm us up a bit,' he said. 'Are you hungry, Con?'

'Hungry! I could eat an ox!' Connor exclaimed, grinning at the young man in the flickering torchlight.

'I haven't got an ox, unfortunately. Meat is one thing I lack. But I do have some bread and cheese, and you're welcome to as much of that as you like. Also I have oatmeal, so we can have oatcakes, or perhaps porridge ...'

'I'll make it, Menellen,' offered Connor immediately. 'If you'll show me where everything is. You leave it to me.'

He ventured to touch Francys on the arm.

'Menellen, your clothes are quite damp. You oughtn't to stay in them or you'll catch yourself a chill. Why don't you change whilst I'm cooking?'

Francys gave a crow of laughter.

'How I've missed your scolds,' he commented wickedly. 'But perhaps I haven't any others? Have you thought of *that*?'

'Then take them off and wrap yourself in a blanket.'

Francys raised his hands.

'I give in, I give in,' he said, laughing. 'I'll change ... after I've got you some water for the porridge. But what about you, Con? Aren't you wet?'

'I arrived just before the snow. I'm fine.'

Connor busied himself with the meal, unpacking the saddle-bag that Francys had indicated held his provisions, and setting a pan of water to boil. He also unpacked the remainder of his own rations, which included a portion of hard spicy sausage. Stirring in the oatmeal and concentrating on banishing the lumps, he could hear the soft sounds of Francys moving around behind him. The fire flickered and smoked as the wind blew down the flue and howled about the window shutters. He tossed a couple more logs on the fire and held his hands to the warmth. Then a hand on his shoulder caused him to look up. Francys had changed into serviceable woollen hose and shirt, topped by a thick, fur-lined jacket. Over his arm lay a cloak.

'Here,' he said. 'Put this on. You look cold.'

As he took it, Connor saw that it too was lined with fur.

'Where did this come from?' he asked.

'It was a present,' Francys said briefly. 'Is the porridge ready?'

'Yes.'

Connor turned back to the fire.

'Have you something to put it in?'

In response, Francys produced a couple of pottery bowls and held them out whilst Connor poured the steaming porridge into them. He was grateful for the cloak and could feel the added warmth already.

Sitting down on either side of the fireplace, they began to eat hungrily, blowing on the hot porridge to cool it sufficiently so as not to burn themselves. Bread, cheese and sausage they shared equally between them, Francys exclaiming appreciatively at the taste of the sausage. Then, rising to his feet, he went to rummage amongst his baggage and returned with a wineskin. Pouring each a generous measure, he lifted his cup in a silent salute before taking a deep swallow.

'I suppose Artem told you where to find me,' he remarked at length, eyeing Connor over the rim of his cup. 'Did he give you any messages for me?'

'Yes, Menellen. I have them here.'

'You can leave them on the table. I'll read them in the morning.'

He took another swallow of his wine.

'I can't tell you how glad I am to see you,' he confessed impulsively.

'And *I* to see *you*, Menellen,' responded Connor, moved.

Francys held up a restraining hand.

'And that's another thing,' he said. 'No more 'Menellen', please. I have no title now, nor any status. I am imrauten, and you I suppose will be also, once word gets round of your disappearance! If we are to be equally outcast, we ought at least to be so as equals.'

He picked up the wineskin and refilled both cups.

'Let's drink to it.'

And afterwards:

'Now, tell me Con what's been happening since I last saw you.'

Connor completed his recital and sat back, leaning against the wall, gazing across at the shadowed figure of the young man, who, head bent, was swishing the dregs of wine about in his cup. He cleared his throat and Francys looked up, startled, then smiled. Emboldened, Connor spoke:

'Won't you tell me what *you've* been doing, Men ... er, Francys? How did you come by those nasty scratches, which are bleeding a bit by the way?'

'Damn,' said Francys.

He put his hand up to his cheek and felt the wounds.

'So they are, but not much. It'll stop soon. I had a slight tussle with a palianca this morning. Fortunately, it came off worst.'

'What, in the name of Sior, is a palianca?'

'A large cat-like creature, with tawny fur spotted with black. It hunts by night, and has some very nasty habits.'

'Where on earth did you meet a creature like that? Not in Arlente surely?'

'No, no. It inhabits the Toath Cranem, though usually further to the south. I was surprised to find one so far from the centre. Perhaps they migrate in the winter.'

He spoke matter-of-factly. Connor stared at him.

'You mean you really *do* travel around that wilderness? I thought no-one could survive there.'

'Oh, that's just a tale. It's superstition that keeps people away, Con, although there *are* parts that are dead, and others that are pretty unsavoury. But there's plenty of space where men *could* live, if they needed to. It's just the fact that no-one within living history *has* lived there that makes people think it's not possible.

People did live there once, you know. The towns and villages I've seen ... all of them dead ... desolate.' He shivered involuntarily. 'But Con, there are two fortresses that remain pretty much intact. In better condition by far than this place. I daresay you've been wondering where all my stuff is that you sent by Artem? It's all over at Kordren - that's the castle closest to this edge of the Toath Cranem. It's safe enough there. I couldn't leave anything like that here, you know, in case anyone happened upon it. All this,' he waved his arm around at the meagre furnishings, 'this could belong to anyone. It gives nothing away.'

He yawned.

'Oh, I've been to most places within the Toath Cranem,' he continued, reverting back to the subject. 'I'd often wondered about it. You wouldn't believe some of the astonishing things I've seen, Con. Take Teimor, for instance. Teimor, the great capital city of long ago Teimarente. Teimor, the hidden city, all complete ... A place of wonders ...'

He yawned again and rested his head on his arms, which were

clasped round his knees. After a minute or so, he raised his head.

'What was I saying?'

'You mentioned the city of Teimor,' Connor told him.

'Oh, well I wouldn't advise you to go there,' Francys murmured.

Connor gazed at him, puzzled. Francys yawned a third time and grinned drowsily at him.

'I'm almost asleep. Don't take any notice of what I've been saying. It's probably utter rubbish. I can't think straight.'

'You should go to bed, Francys.'

Francys got to his feet.

'Yes. Sorry I've only the one mattress. But you can sleep by the fire. You'll be warmer there anyway.'

'I've got my bedroll, and a couple more blankets from Artem. I'll be fine,' Connor assured him. 'But won't you be cold over there. Why don't you bring the mattress closer to the fire?'

Francys shook his head.

'No, no, I'm fine where I am.'

Working quickly, they each made up a rough bed. Then, whilst Connor carefully banked up the fire, the fair man doused the torches. They didn't linger, merely shedding belts and boots, before wrapping themselves in their covers. Francys dropped off to sleep very quickly, but the older man lay for a while listening to his companion's regular breathing, and thinking, before finally himself succumbing.

Connor woke to the cold, blueish glow of a winter morning. The fire had burnt low and the air felt icy. He sat up cautiously and grabbed a cloak to wrap round himself. Shivering a little, he glanced over to where Francys lay. The fair man was still asleep, one hand under his cheek, hair ruffled. His whole body seemed totally relaxed, and he looked disarmingly vulnerable and young. Connor was reminded that he was only twenty-four years old after all, whilst he himself touched forty. He felt terribly old.

Fearing to disturb the sleeper, he pulled on his boots, climbed carefully to his feet, and crept towards the doorway. He descended quietly to the tower entrance and set off through the freshly fallen snow towards the stables. Having satisfied himself that the horses were comfortable, he retraced his steps. At the foot of the stairs, he had noticed a pile of logs, and further away, in the shadow, a stone trough of water, now iced over. He picked up a log and found it to be dry.

'That's a mercy,' he muttered, filling his arms with wood. 'At least it should burn well enough.'

He ascended once more with his burden and set it down on the cold, stone floor. For several minutes he was occupied in building up the fire anew, coaxing the wood to burn. His efforts having secured success at last, he stood up and glanced again at Francys.

'He must have been exhausted,' he thought, 'to sleep so long. No matter. I'll leave him be a while longer.'

He took up the pan which they had used the night before and grimaced.

'Porridge again.'

He set off downstairs to the trough, where he broke the ice and filled the pan. Soon he was busy making breakfast with whatever he could find.

Francys turned over and opened his eyes. He listened confusedly to the sounds in the room, before remembrance came to him and he raised himself on one elbow. Connor heard him and turned.

'Oh, you're awake,' he grunted.

'You should have woken me earlier.'

'I didn't like to. You looked so tired. You haven't been taking proper care of yourself,' Connor said severely.

Francys laughed. He sat up and pulled on his boots, then, having risen, walked over to the window and opened the shutters. Resting his hands on the sill, he surveyed the scene.

'Quite a depth of snow,' he observed. 'And more on the way by the looks of it. We'd best get some supplies in today, in case we're snowed in for a while.'

'Come and eat first,' suggested Connor. 'And I've warmed up the last of the wine. Where do you propose to get these supplies?'

Francys came over to the fire and took the bowl which Connor held out to him. He smiled.

'I know where to go. I've been dealing with the local folk. They don't know who I am. They think I'm some sort of travelling hunter - I bring them furs, and sometimes venison and other game, if I've been lucky.'

He sat down near the fire to eat his breakfast.

'I need another horse,' he said suddenly. 'I hate having to use

Melisor to carry baggage. A good sturdy pack-horse. I'll make enquiries. We'll need something if we're going to be able to carry the supplies we'll need to tide us over the worst of the winter.'

Setting down his empty bowl, Francys stood up and stretched.

'We'd best be on our way soon, before the snow starts again.'

Buckling his belt around his waist, he slid the long knife into its sheath. Then, throwing his cloak over his shoulder, he picked up a couple of saddle-bags which had not been opened, and bent to extract a bow and quiver from beneath the bed.

'We might come across something worth catching,' he explained.

They rode out and through the heathland by devious ways that Francys knew which brought them eventually onto a rutted, muddy cart-track. He took Connor to a farm situated just beyond the village, where he was received courteously ('I'm known as Ysmalic,' he had thought to warn Connor before their arrival) and where, beneath Connor's fascinated gaze, the contents of the saddle-bags were revealed to be pelts of animals the like of which he had never seen before. In exchange for the skins, after some brisk bargaining which Francys carried out in the local dialect, they managed to obtain sacks of oatmeal, wheat-flour, root crops, a cheese and some butter, and a barrel of the farmer's home-brewed ale. Having enquired into the possibility of obtaining a horse or mule, Francys sent Connor off with the farmer's son to a neighbouring holding, with instructions to purchase the animal if it seemed good enough to him, whilst he himself went on to conduct more business elsewhere, promising to call back for his provisions later.

He had told Connor to meet him at the bathhouse, which stood near the centre of the village. When he arrived there, Connor was horrified to hear that Francys intended to patronise the place. He began to argue, but Francys cut him short by saying that he had already been there several times, and that if *he*, Connor, would rather remain dirty, he was welcome to stand outside with the horses. The fair man then vanished inside, and Connor, shrugging, reluctantly followed. It was pleasantly warm and relaxing, and Connor began to enjoy the experience, despite his initial qualms. It was evident that Francys was quite at home there and known to a number of the local habitués and, whilst inwardly deploring the risks that Francys was taking, Connor could not but admire his courage and effrontery. To know that the whole country was on the look out for him and yet to have the nerve to stroll into a place like this!

All the same, he was relieved when, clean and, in the case of Francys, shaven, they left the village with all their various purchases and set off back to Carledruin by the same circuitous route. It had begun to snow again, large, soft flakes drifting uncannily across the view. Halfway through the trees and heather, Francys put out a hand and brought Connor to a halt.

'Stay here,' he hissed. 'Hold the horses still.'

'What is it?' asked Connor in a whisper.

'Deer.'

Francys took up his bow and slithered into the undergrowth. Connor waited, controlling the horses. He could hear nothing for a while. Then there came a crashing of branches and a dull thump, followed by a stampede. A few minutes later Francys reappeared carrying his bow and smiling.

'Give me something to wrap the carcase in, Con. A sack or something.'

He disappeared again with a piece of sacking and returned presently with the dead deer over his shoulder.

'We'll have meat for a while now,' he remarked, whilst fixing the bundle onto the back of the new horse. 'I haven't had any for too long a time.'

The snow fell steadily for the remainder of the day and night, and even the following day, so that they were cooped up in their tower with little to do once the basic tasks had been completed. The room was gloomy and they were glad of the lanterns that Francys had purchased in the village, together with a stock of tallow candles. Whittling at a piece of wood, Connor contrived to make enough counters and even a couple of passable dice. With a board drawn on the table-top in charcoal, they played endless games of chance, and above all else, they talked.

Whilst they ranged over a wide variety of topics, Connor could not but note that Francys kept away from certain areas, and it was with some trepidation that, on the afternoon of their second day in the tower, he broached the subject of the future.

'Francys,' he said hesitantly, 'I hope you will not think me presumptuous, but is it not time that we should talk about the future?

You cannot surely intend to spend the remainder of your life in hiding?'

'What would you have me do?' the fair man enquired bitterly. 'Go creeping back abjectly to Rycharst and beg him to take me in?'

He uttered a harsh laugh at the sight of Connor's surprise.

'I'm not such a fool, you know, as not to have fathomed what lies behind this plot. Sior knows, I've had the time to think about it! He wants me back.'

He shuddered involuntarily.

'I'd die sooner!'

He was leaning his shoulders against the window embrasure and looking out at the floating snow-flakes, and Connor could see only his profile.

'Neither will I go into exile, to live a kind of half-life far from this country', he stated flatly. 'Despite everything, I cannot merely abandon this land to its fate.'

'I did not mean that you should leave Karled-Dū,' Connor said after a pause. 'I merely wondered what you intend to do ... what *we* could do. I cannot see you sitting back and doing nothing, and *I* certainly don't intend to do so. In your weeks here, have you not had any thoughts, made any plans?'

'Plans?' said Francys with a bitter laugh. 'Oh, yes, I have *plans*. But what can I achieve by myself? Or even with you? However much I value your support, Con, and Sior knows that I do, what can two people do on their own, especially two outlaws ...'

'Nothing, certainly, when you embrace such a defeatist attitude,' retorted Connor tartly.

Then, as Francys glared at him, stung to anger, he added mildly:

'Will you not at least describe these plans to me? There may be possibilities which you have overlooked. It is not like you to give up without some attempt to fight ...'

There was a tense silence. Connor waited for the storm to break, but it did not. Instead, Francys gave a reluctant half-smile and came away from the window, to seat himself opposite Connor at the table.

'Very well,' he agreed. 'I'll tell you what I should like to do.'

He lowered his gaze to his hands, spread on the table-top.

'Everywhere I look,' he began, speaking with painful intensity, 'everywhere I look, it seems to me that I can detect the hand of ...

Rycharst. It's like a shadow creeping insidiously over the ground, a fraction at a time, so stealthily that it escapes notice, until it's too late and the shadow covers all. How many people would believe that the increase in robbery and violence which has been plaguing the land in recent times can be traced back to *him*? But it *is* so. Through Artem I have the proofs. Much good though it does me,' he added bitterly. 'I have arranged with Artem that he is to send them to the Dukrugvola, but I don't know whether I dare to believe that he will take any action...'

He paused for a moment.

'In any event, these activities are so difficult to counter in an official manner. For me it would be easier. I am in a position to uncover these dealings. What I should like to do, had I the means, would be to organize effective counter-measures. That is partly my reason for remaining here. We are admirably positioned here, you know, Con, to maintain a watch on Harres and Krapan, and it is through those two old enemies of ours that He is operating at the present time.'

He clenched his fists unconsciously.

'He has learnt his lesson well. He is not strong enough yet to strike openly, but if He can but weaken us sufficiently by underhand means ...'

He shuddered.

'I don't think anyone in Karled-Dū can truly conceive what life would be like should He win this battle. But *I* do so know, and I'll not let it happen here if there is any means of preventing it, whatever the cost.'

He raised his head to meet Connor's eyes.

'You ask me what I want? I want revenge, Con. I want to be revenged on that demon of evil for all that He has done to me. I intend to disrupt Rycharst's plans, to thwart every desire of His in any way that I can. He has taken everything from me, and I intend to return the favour!'

Then he sighed and said more mildly:

'But how to do it? That's the question. Two people aren't going to make much of an impact, however well intentioned ...'

'Not two alone,' interposed Connor deliberately. 'You forget Artem and his network.'

'As a source of information they are invaluable, but they cannot become involved in anything more, else they endanger the whole enterprise. No, no...'

He sank his chin in his hands and looked across at Connor.

'I need men,' he said. 'What wouldn't I give to have one company of mounted soldiers!'

'Recruit one,' suggested Connor simply.

'How?' Francys asked baldly. 'There is a price on my head. How can I approach anyone and ask them to join me? It would mean certain death should they be caught. And those who are already outlawed are quite frankly not of a type that I would care to associate with ...'

'Not to mention the likelihood that they would turn you in to the authorities for the money,' Connor said thoughtfully. 'Yes, I see the problem. It's a knotty one. Hm ... well, I suppose that there could be some of your former company who'd be interested. From what I heard, their situation hasn't been particularly easy since they got split up. They've been made scapegoats for any trouble that's arisen, and I know for a fact Joclyn's been demoted merely for having been *your* officer. It might be worth sounding them out somehow. Maybe the network could help us there? Or I could slip back down into Varadil?...'

'No!' Francys interrupted sharply. 'That is not an option, Con! You'd be sticking your head into a noose ... And besides I couldn't spare you. Now that you're here, do you think I'd let you go again...

But it's an idea,' he added, sounding more cheerful. 'The person we need to speak to is Artem. He can arrange for someone to approach Joclyn, and *he* may be able to point up other suitable candidates. Yes ... It's certainly something to think about. It will need a deal of organization. We'll have to have some sort of initial meeting place - I'd not want to risk this place. Yes,' he repeated with increased vigour.

He stretched out his hand suddenly and grasped that of Connor.

'Since you've come, things no longer seem so hopeless,' he said warmly. 'Just to have company is a joy beyond words.'

Then he stood up briskly as though afraid to show any more emotion, and said hastily:

'I must go down and take a look at the stables. I fear the snow may have penetrated the roof. I'll check on the horses, and I'll bring up some more logs on my way back.'

No more was said that day, but the subject having been raised, Francys showed a willingness to discuss it in more detail. There was much to be arranged and, since the snow still held them prisoner, much time in which to make plans. But firstly, Francys insisted, as soon as they were able to travel, they would go to Kordren, returning, he remarked, with a sideways glance at Connor, in time to celebrate the Midwinter Festival with the villagers.

CHAPTER FOUR

Connor knew that he would never forget his first sight of the castle Kordren. To be sure, the entire journey was memorable in its way. It had taken them two days riding across country through the snow, with an overnight halt in one of the ruined villages that Francys had spoken about. The first surprise had been the Toath Cranem itself. No-one had had the temerity to live within sight of the place, and the approaches were therefore left deliberately to grow wild. Stands of trees interspersed with thickets of bushes served to hide it from view so that, following the winding paths made by animal feet, one came upon the edge of the Toath Cranem quite suddenly and unexpectedly, between one step and the next, as it were. What he had expected, Connor was uncertain. From Francys, he knew that it was not a barren waste, as everyone had long believed. What he saw was a tall barrier of rock rising above their heads, like cliffs over a sea-shore, grown over with a profusion of shrubs and small trees, tough grass and even, here and there, lone evergreen lebanen trees. The track upon which they rode vanished behind a rocky outcrop and he found that they were riding into a great rift between the cliffs, so narrow that he could almost have touched both sides of the great rocks had he stretched out his arms. Doggedly following his companion, he shivered a little in the chill shadow of the cliffs. The air seemed so still, so tense, almost as though it were a palpable barrier across his path.

Then he was through. He rounded the corner, and reined in involuntarily, and sat looking at the view. Beside him, Francys smiled. There before him, spread out to his gaze, lay, snow-blanched, a land equally as fair as that which he had left. Once, long ages ago, it must have been cultivated, but it had been left untouched for many generations and few traces remained of the neat field boundaries. Here and there trees rose tall amidst the tangle of what must once have been hedgerows. On the skyline he could see the skeletal limbs of a forest, and below, in a hollow, shimmered an ice-covered lake.

As he looked, the view seemed to blur and then re-form before his gaze. He rubbed his eyes.

'No. There's nothing wrong with your eyes, Con,' Francys told him, having observed the gesture and sounding slightly amused. 'It's a phenomenon of the landscape, to confuse outsiders. If you had come here without me, you would have seen naught but the desert that folk outside believe it to be. Once you know what it really looks like, it will remain that way to you each time you travel within its borders as long as you approach it with the true picture fixed in your mind's eye. If you allow yourself to be led astray, you could be lost for evermore. But we can't stay here ... We need to get as far as the old village before nightfall.'

And so saying, the fair man dug his heels into Melisor's flanks and set off down a rough track towards the snow-draped wilderness below.

But that first view, even the old village with its decaying, but still serviceable huddle of houses about an overgrown green, paled before the magnificence of the castle. Approaching from below, as it stood raised high upon a rocky promontory, framed by dripping fronds and a tracery of branches, the walls seemed to soar into the sky, massive and yet with a subtlety of design which gave the impression that they had grown as naturally out of the anchoring rock as the trees and bushes which surrounded their feet. Following behind the fair man in single file, Connor was unable to suppress a soundless whistle at the sight. A sharp turn in the path brought them out onto the main approach, a high-arched bridge spanning a precipitous drop, leading to the gatehouse and the bailey beyond. Connor's head moved slowly from side to side as he surveyed the magnificent structure upon which the depredations of time seemed to have made but little impression.

'The ancients certainly knew how to build,' he remarked, in awe. 'It wouldn't take that much work to bring it back into proper use.'

He took in the stable ranges, the outbuildings and the vast bulk of the keep.

'You and I'll be rattling around like two grains of wheat. How many do you reckon this place would accommodate? A good couple of hundred easily, I'd say, probably more like *five* hundred.'

As he ascended the steep steps into the keep, a sense of unease began to oppress him. It was all too well preserved. The great door opened silently, as though the hinges had been kept oiled - well perhaps Francys had done so. But inside he began to feel as though at any moment he would find himself coming face to face with one of those 'ancients' . It was uncanny. The place gave the impression that it had only the moment before their arrival been bustling and full of life, and that only on hearing their approach had the inhabitants hastened into hiding. Almost he could hear them. He frowned. Had it not been for Francys, he thought, he would not have had the hardihood to remain there. Look - even furniture had survived.

'Sorcery,' he muttered under his breath, instinctively making the traditional sign to ward off evil.

To his surprise, Francys grinned.

'Yes, sorcery, but nothing like the dark powers of Rycharst,' he assured the older man. 'This is the other side of the coin. Can you not feel it? This is the doing of the alwaithaes.'

He pushed open a door and motioned Connor to enter.

'And it has an added advantage,' he continued unexpectedly. 'In the Toath Cranem, I am out of *His* reach.'

****

'I cannot reach him!' The Lord of Shadowe cursed aloud. 'He has gone to the Toath Cranem! I cannot reach him!'

In an excess of fury, he whirled round, his long velvet robes flying out, and, picking up a finely decorated glass goblet from the press nearby, flung it viciously against the wall. A patterned plate followed, smashing into shards. On the servants who came running at the noise, he vented his rage further, screaming at them to 'Get out! Get out!' Then, mastering his emotions, he flung himself into his huge carven chair and sank into thought, resting his chin on one hand, brooding.

****

Saragon stared at the man who had just been shown into his office. Big and well-muscled, with greying hair and beard, his clothes unpretentious, but of good materials and cut, he was difficult to place. Respectable, used to command, Saragon thought, noting the man's self-possession - a merchant maybe? But a stranger to the Province certainly, and what could have brought such a man to Shardu on the eve of mid winter, he could not begin to imagine. He caught the man's eye, and saw that he himself was being weighed up just as keenly. With a sudden smile, he courteously bade the man welcome, sending for spiced wine and fresh-baked bread with cheese. Then, when he had seen the man amply provided with refreshment and seated comfortably, he resumed his own chair, rested his elbows on the surface of his wide desk and fixed him with an intent stare.

'Well, now,' he invited. 'Perhaps you would care to tell me who you are, and what purpose you have in coming here to see me? For you have travelled some long distance, have you not, and the matter must be something of considerable importance to bring you here at this time of the year.'

'Aye, Menellen, indeed it is.'

The man's voice was deep and mellow, and he spoke the Karleen tongue with a strong accent, which Saragon placed to one of the eastern Provinces. He waited for the man to continue, but the latter hesitated for a moment, before suddenly seeming to come to a decision.

'My name, Menellen, is Artem Radmore and I come from the Province of Kirkendom,' he revealed at last. 'The business I come upon is of a most delicate nature ...'

Saragon's grey eyes regarded him intently. The name had stirred echoes in his mind and he attempted to recall when he had heard it before.

Again, the man appeared to debate within himself. Then, his eyes never leaving Saragon's face, he reached into his belt pouch and drew out an object, which he held out towards the younger man on the palm of his hand. Saragon reached forward and took the object. It was a ring, a signet ring. He knew it. He had seen it many a time on those long fingers. Slowly he turned it about, frowning. He raised his head and looked sternly at the man opposite him.

'Where did you get this?' he demanded.

Artem nodded to himself.

'He said that you would recognize it.'

'*He* said', repeated Saragon. 'Would this be the ring's rightful owner, or some other 'he'?'

Artem looked him in the eye.

'Menellen, you may rest assured that I had that ring from the hand of he to whom it belongs, and that it was given freely, and not taken by force or by trickery,' he informed Saragon gravely.

'Then you have seen him?' the younger man asked eagerly.

Artem nodded.

'And your business? It is connected with him?'

Again, a nod.

'You have not ... you have not found proof of his innocence?' Saragon asked quickly.

Artem shook his head regretfully.

'Alas, no,' he said sadly. 'Though it would give me great joy to do so, I can assure you, Menellen.

No,' he continued. 'My business is otherwise.'

Dipping his hand again into his belt pouch, he drew out a sheaf of papers.

'You will most likely not be aware of what my connection is with your friend. I must tell you, Menellen, that I have the honour of maintaining contact on his behalf with certain ... er ... informants both within Karled-Dū and those countries which border ours, even within the Land of Shadowe itself...'

Saragon stared and smiled.

'So,' he said, 'you are the head of Francys' network of spies are you? Well, well.'

'Aye, Menellen,' the older man responded composedly, but with a faint curve of a grin. 'I was persuaded into the enterprise. And well for him that it existed, for otherwise he would not have had warning of the plot against him ...

But be that as it may, you will be wondering no doubt why I have come to you like this. You may or may not be aware that much of the information gathered by our ... network ... was passed on by the Lord Francys Coras to the Dukrugvola. Before he left to go into hiding, the Lord Francys Coras told me that he wished that information should continue to be sent to the Dukrugvola so that he should not be hampered by the lack of it. However, I was loth to take my reports straight to the Dukrugvola, for reasons that you can no doubt guess, Menellen,' he added candidly. 'For the one thing, if the Dukrugvola knew of the connection, he'd not believe the truth of them, and for another, likely I'd be tarred with the same brush and end up in gaol, or worse! So I bethought myself of you, Menellen. I know from what the Lord Francys Coras has said that you have his trust. It was a risk, even so, and I had to think long and hard before I came here, for you might have been taken in like everyone else and believe the worst of him.'

He paused momentarily.

'Menellen, I am come here to offer you the services of my contacts should you be wishful to avail yourself of them.'

He held out the papers.

'Here I have the most recent reports. Perhaps you would like to have a glance over them before you make a decision?'

To Saragon, bemusedly taking the bundle of reports and casting a swift glance over them, the remainder of the interview passed in a daze. He recalled afterwards that they had talked of little else but the man whose friendship had brought them together so strangely. Artem had related to him the story of his first encounter with the fair man, and Saragon had responded with anecdotes of his own. He had been heartened to learn that Francys was not alone in his exile, and touched by the loyalty of Connor. To have voluntarily given up everything in order to follow his commander into the dangerous, lonely life of an outlaw argued a devotion which Saragon could only admire.

The conversation having come eventually to a natural conclusion, both men rose to their feet. With the remembrance of what day it was, Saragon extended the courtesy of an invitation to remain as a guest for the mid winter celebrations, only to be informed that Artem had already secured accommodation for himself at one of the inns within the city. It would not do, he said, to set tongues wagging. Let him be taken for just another merchant hoping to obtain the business of the Prince of Sureindom. Saragon could not but see the sense of this, and made no further attempt to persuade him.

As they walked along the corridor, they became aware of a considerable bustle and noise emanating from the entrance hall, and a man-servant, making his way towards the office, greeted his Lord with relief.

'Menellen, your sister the Lady Elise and her family have but now arrived.'

Saragon grinned.

'I'm on my way,' he responded. 'Have you informed the Lady Inisia?'

'Yes, Menellen.'

'Good.'

They continued on their way, descending the flight of wide stone steps into the expanse of the hall, well lit by lanterns hanging from brackets around the walls. Of a sudden, Saragon heard a sharp intake of breath from his companion.

'Who in Sior's name is *that*?' the man asked involuntarily.

Following the direction of his glance, Saragon was himself shocked into uttering an exclamation of surprise. To his astonishment he saw a young child standing in the middle of the hall, looking around with wide-eyed wonder; a child with hair of a familiar, unmistakable fairness, and a face so like in its structure to that of his outlawed friend, that he could not help but catch his breath. But how such a creature had arrived in his hall, was a mystery to him, and he said so.

He was not long left in doubt, for even as he spoke, the Lady Elise came forward to bestow a sisterly greeting upon him, and upon noticing the object of his interest, said smilingly:

'I see that you are looking at my protégé.'

'Who is he, and where does he come from?' Saragon asked curiously.

He caught the doubtful glance that Elise directed at his companion, and continued reassuringly:

'You may speak freely. This is Artem Radmore, who has travelled from Kirkendom to bring me news. He too has an interest in whatever concerns Francys.'

The Lady Elise smiled upon the older man and expressed herself delighted to make his acquaintance.

'But, Elise,' Saragon interrupted impatiently, 'who is this child, and whence has he come? How does he come to be in your charge? Whose child is he?'

'Whose child is he? Why, Francys' of course,' she told him.

'Close your mouth, Sharn,' she added teasingly, 'before you catch flies in it.'

'But... but... Francys has never said anything about a child ...'

'Francys doesn't know,' Elise said calmly.

'Then, how ... where has he come from, and why is he here? Where is his mother?'

'I think you mean, who is his mother,' said his sister smiling wryly. 'She is a woman of the streets, as I expect you must have guessed. She had a brief liaison with Francys some years ago, from which the child resulted. She has called him Lyndan, by the way. He is extraordinarily like Francys, don't you think? Except for the eyes - they're blue.'

Saragon and Artem both glanced towards the child, who had now been approached by Elise's own son, Lucas, and his nurse.

'I don't understand how *you* come to be involved in the matter,' Saragon complained, returning his gaze to his sister's face. 'If Francys doesn't know, how do *you*?'

'Alhaîtha told me.'

'*What*!'

Saragon was dumbstruck.

'*Alie* told you?! How in Sior's name did *she* know?'

'Apparently Hadran told her, and don't ask me how *he* knew,' said Elise tartly. 'He probably made it his business to ferret out anything which might redound to Francys' discredit. It would be just like him.'

She shrugged.

'At all events, after the reading of the Register, I found myself distinctly uneasy at the thought that there was somewhere in Väst someone of Francys' blood of whose existence, and presumably location, Hadran was aware. So I sent a man to look for the child and bring him to me. He's of an age with Luc, maybe a little younger. He'll be a playmate for him. Already they get along well together...'

She turned to look at the two boys, and her gaze noted the upright, silver-haired figure of the Lady Inisia approaching from across the hall.

'There's mother. I must go and explain matters to her... Excuse me...'

She bade a hasty farewell to the Kirkendom man, and bustled away.

The two men crossed the hall towards the great doors, where they parted, Artem to descend the steep roadway down into the city, treading with thoughtful deliberation, turning over in his mind what he had seen and learned, and heartened by the discovery that he was not alone in his support for the outlawed Francys Coras. Saragon, joining the other members of his family, was soon absorbed into the excitement of the occasion, although he did manage to find an opportunity to pass on to the Lady Inisia the news which the Kirkendom man had brought. As he retired to bed that night, he spared a thought for the fair man in hiding Sior alone knew where on the eve of this traditionally family-centred festival.

****

Saragon was not alone in remembering Francys Coras. The Dukrugvola and his wife thought of the young man with compassion, envisaging him lonely and alone on this day of all days. A similar image came to torment Nyandu, obtruding painfully into the festivities and ruining any enjoyment which she might have found therein. In Väst, memory sat as an unwanted guest at the feast. No-one mentioned his name, but all there were aware of the reason for his absence, and one at least hoped that he might not have survived to see the day. Even in Carakhas the Lord of Shadowe sat and brooded at the great high table, hearkening to the noise of the celebrations and recalling other times when he had had beside him the fair figure of his lover.

And what of Francys himself?

Seated beside the huge hearth in the place of honour, a mug of the household's best ale to hand, Connor looked across at his companion opposite and smiled to himself. Who would expect to find the country's most notorious outlaw celebrating the Mid Winter Festival in the midst of a gaggle of farmers and their womenfolk? For, despite Connor's own reservations, Francys had insisted on taking up the invitation of the farmer, Marchek, and there they were, in the guise of two hunters, Ysmalic and Tamalchik, enjoying the farmer's hospitality, replete after partaking heartily of the feast prepared by the women of the household, to which they had themselves contributed a haunch of venison.

Connor took another sip of ale, and sat back. He felt himself beginning to relax in the warmth of the crackling log fire. For safety's sake, he kept a watchful eye upon the fair man, but gradually his mind wandered, and he began to marvel at the audacity and ingenuity of Francys' conduct. Posing as the hunter Ysmalic, Francys had cleverly woven snippets of the truth into his assumed identity. In order to distance himself from any suspicion of his true origin, he had claimed Aramian citizenship, though placing his home in the northern regions of the country, so as to account for his undoubted fluency in the Karleen tongue. To Connor's immense admiration, he had, it transpired, even hinted very delicately at the existence of blood ties, albeit of an illegitimate nature, between his family and that of the ruler of the neighbouring Varadil. As for his presence so far from his native hearth, that was explained very simply by a blood feud, for which he had been outlawed by his overlord; a master stroke, so Connor considered.

Later that day, the whole household erupted into the dusk-filled snow-laden landscape, well wrapped against the cold, to take part in the traditional torch-light procession about the lanes and by-ways of the village.

CHAPTER FIVE

Francys and Connor returned to the castle of Kordren on the last day of the old year, laden with supplies. Approaching the fortress up the steep causeway, Connor was conscious, as on his first visit, of a feeling that the place was not unoccupied even though their horses' hooves echoed emptily under the great archway of the gatehouse. The interior of the keep seemed less chill than he would have expected, despite the lack of fires during their absence. But when he mentioned his thoughts to his companion, Francys merely smiled.

They celebrated the Nachrachoroi, the first day of the new year, in traditional fashion, keeping a fire burning from dusk to dawn, and marking the passing of the old and the coming of the new at midnight by bowing first to the west and then to the east before draining a cup of wine and eating a piece of bread dipped in salt.

Francys was anxious to put his plans into operation, and almost as soon as the celebration of the Nachrachoroi was over, he began to prepare for the enterprise. Despite fresh falls of snow, the roads were passable with care and he determined to begin with a visit to Artem. Despite arguments, Connor was left behind at Carledruin, Francys arguing persuasively that he would be far less conspicuous a visitor on his own, than if they travelled together. In Francys' absence, Connor found time hanging heavily on his hands, and turned his mind to the task of making the ruined castle into a more habitable residence capable of accommodating the numbers which they hoped to attract, whilst still retaining from the outside an impression of dilapidation. He could not, of course, hope to accomplish a great deal on his own, but he seized upon the self-imposed task as a means of diverting his mind from the anxiety that he could not help but feel at the thought of Francys abroad in a land where at any moment he might be recognized and taken captive.

Meantime, Francys, having parted from Connor, made his way towards the town of Arlmen. In the busy market town, he had no trouble in passing unnoticed, and was able to pay a visit to his agent, leaving the black stallion Melisor in the man's charge in exchange for a mount which would be less easily recognizable, and changing his garb for that of a landowner of moderate means. The journey to Martle passed uneventfully, and, by careful planning, he arrived at the farm as dusk was falling and the farm labourers had already dispersed homewards. Approaching by way of a narrow, rutted lane running between high-banked hedgerows, he came at length to the archway set in the tall, well-made cob wall which completely enclosed the farm buildings. Generously fashioned to accommodate the heaped hay-wains, the arch soared high above his head, home to various small birds in the summer months. The heavy great doors, rarely closed, stood back against the inner walls. Francys passed through and brought his horse to a halt within the courtyard.

For a few moments he sat still upon the horse and looked about him. Before him, facing the archway, was the farmhouse, a long, low building of cob with thick walls and thatched roof. A heavy wooden door set in a thatched porch gave entrance, flanked by the shuttered windows of the main room. Wicket gates set in low walls to either side of the building led to the garden and orchard behind the house, and against the high outer walls of the courtyard there were barns, byres and stables. A prosperous, well-managed farm, the buildings well-tended and kept in good repair.

The door to the farmhouse opened suddenly and a tall figure loomed in the porch, raising a lamp to peer through the thickening dusk. At the sight of him, Francys smiled and slid quickly down from the saddle. In a couple of strides, the farmer was at his side.

'It *is* you!' the man exclaimed. 'I heard the horse and wondered if it might be you. Welcome, Menellen, welcome.'

'Yes it is I', Francys grinned cheerfully. 'It's good to see you again, Artem. May I beg a bed for the night, or have I come at an awkward time? I have something I should like to talk about with you.'

'Surely, surely,' Artem assured him heartily. 'You are welcome to stay for as long as you wish. There is no one else here save the family. Indeed,' he added, looking up at the sky, where the first stars were visible intermittently beyond the deep grey clouds gathering ominously on the horizon, 'from the look of *that*, I'd say you'd be lucky to be able to get on your way again within the next few days. It looks like snow to me. Come on in, Menellen, and I'll get Robyn to see to your horse ...'

So saying, he turned and led the way back inside, calling to his wife, and son as he did so. Francys followed, and paused on the threshold to survey the room, cosily candle-lit and warm from a vigorous fire burning in the vast fireplace which dominated one wall. As he walked forward into the centre of the room, a young man slipped past him through the open door, shutting it with a heavy thud behind him. Artem's wife, Klara, bustled forward shyly, bobbing a curtsey and beaming with delight.

'Menellen! You must be hungry with travelling all this way. Let me get you something to eat.'

She did not stay for his response, but hastened towards the kitchen to rouse Trissa the servant girl and inspect the larder. Francys turned, smiling, to Artem, who motioned him towards the fire.

'Sit down, Menellen, sit down,' he invited.

The food was soon forthcoming: fresh bread and cheese and a bowl of thick vegetable broth. Plain fare, perhaps, but tasty, and a feast indeed to a hungry man, with a good big mug of ale to wash it down. Francys bit into the crisp crust of the bread, and smiled in delight at the flavour and texture of it. Then he grimaced, but, lest his expression be misunderstood, he made haste to explain that it was the thought of Connor missing out on such delicious food that was the cause.

'The one thing we really miss is fresh bread,' he told Klara, waving the slice towards her. 'I feel rather guilty now for having left him behind!'

'Then he met up with you safely?' Artem asked.

'Oh yes. At Carledruin, where I've left him for the present.'

He smiled.

'You cannot conceive how good it was to see him,' he confessed.

He applied himself to the broth and did not speak again until he had finished his meal.

For the remainder of the evening Francys relaxed and enjoyed the ordinary conversation of a family at home, asking after the couple's other sons and their respective families; the eldest son, Adair, having wed the daughter of the neighbouring landowner and taken over that piece of land, which he now farmed with the assistance of his growing lads; and the second, Redd, who acted as his father's agent in Martle, organizing the shipping and sale of grain and other produce from the farm. He too was married, with two young daughters. Only the youngest son, Robyn, still living at home, was unwed, though a number of hints were dropped, and confirmed by the rising colour in the young man's cheeks, that this position might soon change.

Anon, bidding his host and hostess a good night, Francys retired to the small bedchamber at the back of the house which had been prepared for him, there to strip off his clothes thankfully and slip between the fresh, clean sheets, blissfully warm from the warming-pan which had been placed therein. It had been a long time since he had slept so comfortably. His last waking thought was one of guilt that he should be enjoying such comfort when Connor would be sleeping in a cold and draughty ruin, without even a proper bed.

It was not until the following evening that he was able to broach the business which had brought him thither, having spent the day out upon the land with Robyn, hunting for the pot and returning successfully with sufficient game to stock the larder for the next few days. The threatened snow held off until the late afternoon, when the clouds closed in and soft flakes began to fall, slowly at first and then more quickly, thickening into a blizzard in the early dusk. Artem came in from the barn with a white layer covering his head and shoulders even from that short walk across the farmyard. He shook his head.

'You'll not be travelling in a hurry,' he prophesied.

After supper, Francys settled with Artem at the table, a mug of ale apiece, and began to talk. Klara and Robyn had offered to move into the kitchen to allow them to discuss matters in private, but Francys would not hear of putting them out, and they sat beside the fireplace at their usual occupations, conscious of the drone of voices from the other side of the room.

'Well, you must be wondering what has brought me here,' Francys opened. 'It's nothing to do with our arrangement ... or perhaps only incidentally. Connor and I have made a plan, and I'd like to hear your opinion of it ... whether you think it's at all feasible.'

He took a swallow of ale.

'Listen,' he said. 'You know what I feel as regards the Lord of Shadowe. You above anyone know what he's doing to this land of ours. I cannot sit still and let it happen. Oh, I know at the first after I left Körain I didn't care much *what* happened. To tell the truth, I was too busy trying to survive. But I had plenty of time to think, and Connor's arrival clinched the matter for me.'

He leaned forward across the table, resting his elbows on the polished surface.

'What we want ... nay, what we intend to do is to get together a company of like-minded men and to use them to frustrate Rycharst's designs on this country. With intelligence from our sources, we could take action which would be impossible for the Dukrugvola to attempt on an official basis. But ...'

He sat back and gestured with his hands, palms upwards.

'The big problem is how do we get the sort of men we need? I am imraut. It is treason to deal with me or assist me in any way. Don't think I don't know the risks, the danger I put you and your family in every time I come here, or that I am not truly grateful to you for your courage ...'

Artem's face reddened in embarrassment.

'Well, as to that, Menellen,' he said hastily. 'You know my thoughts on the matter, so I shan't repeat them. But, I do not believe that you would find the Dukrugvola as keen as you think to lay you by the heels. I am but shortly returned myself from travelling to Shardu, where I had the honour of speaking to the Lord Saragon Cerinor.'

Francys allowed himself to be diverted.

'Did you so?' he asked. 'And how is he?'

'In good health, and convinced of your innocence, Menellen. He gave me to understand that the Dukrugvola himself does not believe in the evidence against you, but is forced into action because he can find no way to refute it. But he is not going to do anything to encourage the hunt. I passed on the information you wanted me to to the Lord Saragon, Menellen. I thought it best to use him as a go-between.'

'Yes, yes, you did well,' Francys responded absently, his thoughts on Saragon and the household at Shardu. 'I suppose the family were there for the mid-winter festival?'

'Aye, Menellen. His sister, the Lady Elise was just arriving.'

Artem, recalling the encounter, wondered whether to mention the boy, Lyndan, but decided on second thoughts that it would not be an appropriate time to inform Francys of the existence of his son, when he could have no opportunity of ever seeing the boy. Why cause him unnecessary pain? He changed the subject.

'You were saying, Menellen, about finding men to serve with you ...' he prompted.

Francys gave himself a mental shake, coming abruptly back to the present.

'Yes,' he confirmed. 'That is the problem. To undertake what we propose, we need to recruit good men, but how? I should be asking them to give up everything and set themselves under threat of execution should they be caught, and for what return? What have *I* to offer them? A life as an outlaw, exiled from their own land and families, always having to be on guard lest they, the hunters, become the hunted. Tell me, Artem,' he said dispiritedly, 'where am I likely to find such men? Connor and I, we were so excited by our plans ...'

He gave a wry smile.

'But I think we overlooked one crucial point. In the cold light of day, they begin to look rather lame.'

'Nay, Menellen. I don't think so,' Artem said encouragingly.

Then, as Francys looked enquiringly, he continued:

'I've been in touch, as you know, with various contacts in and around Varadil, among other places. I have heard what has befallen those men who used to fight under your banner. A number of them have dropped out of the army already, and I don't doubt there are many others who'd follow if they could. I daresay they'd jump at a chance to join you. There's not much else for them to do ... Hmm ...let me think ...'

He fell into thought for a while. Francys sat patiently and watched the big farmer. He respected the man's judgment. Sipping his ale, he let his mind drift for a while. The mention of Shardu had conjured up memories, too close to the surface of his waking mind for comfort. That moment in the garden with Nyandu, when he had almost given way to temptation. He could still see her in the bright sunlight. Then that dreadful night when he had tried to drown himself, only to be rescued and brought back to the castle by Saragon. A faint, mocking smile touched his lips. He had thought his problems insurmountable *then*; now that they truly were, perversely, he found himself possessed of a desire to fight back. Shaking his head at his contrariness, he took another swallow of the ale, and returned his attention to his host.

'Well, now,' Artem pronounced, having given due consideration to the matter. 'Your best bet, I believe, is to get into contact with your former Bachendar, Joclyn Pardroy. You will have heard from Connor what has befallen him...'

'Joclyn ... yes,' nodded Francys. 'We had thought of him.'

'He would be able to find out the whereabouts of others from your company without arousing too much suspicion,' Artem continued. 'As an officer, it would be natural enough for him to take an interest in what has happened to the men. If he could organize that end of it, then we could work out a way to channel the men up to wherever you want them. I can arrange contact with Bachendar Pardroy, if you tell me what you want him to be told.'

It was Francys' turn to consider.

'I need to speak to him myself,' he stated abruptly.

'No, no,' he continued, holding up a hand as Artem broke into expostulations. 'I owe it to him. He deserves that much from me. Besides, if I can convince *him,* there'll be more of a chance that *he* will be able to convince the others. If you can get a message to him to meet me ... now where would be a suitable place?'

'You will not go into Varadil, Menellen!' Artem protested in concern.

'Nay, I am not so foolhardy as *that*!' Francys retorted. 'We can ask Joclyn to come into Kirkendom. But where? He cannot come here. Ah, I have it. There is a place near the border just a calle or two east of Corin Cem where we used to hunt deer. He will remember it. There's a spring and a small valley with plenty of cover. If you can get a message to him to come there ... We'd best put it in a fashion only he would understand in case it falls into the wrong hands. Let me see ... Tell him to come to the valley where the black stag runs. Yes, that will do. He'll know what place that means.'

Artem nodded.

'I will write it, Menellen. Your hand is too well known in Varadil. It can be dispatched tomorrow. And then ...'

'And then, we wait,' Francys said with a grimace.

And wait they did. Even in his haste to translate his intentions into reality, Francys was forced to concede that it would be a seven-day at the very least before he could hope to hear that the message had been delivered, and that only if Joclyn were not difficult to locate. So he adjured himself to be patient, and in the meantime enjoyed the hospitality of his host and hostess, who would not hear of him leaving until the response had been received. In truth, with the depth of snow on the ground, it would not have been a pleasant journey and he was not unhappy at the prospect of sitting out the waiting period in comfort. His conscience continued to prick him whenever he remembered Connor, but there was nothing that he could do about the situation now, save hope that the weather was not so bad in Carledruin, and work on an apology!

Francys had insisted on doing his share of the work around the farmyard, and on the morning after his discussion with Artem, he found himself in the stable-block, grooming and mucking out the horses, in the company of Robyn. Of an age, the two men had always been on easy terms with one another, despite the difference in their situations. To Francys' surprise, that morning Robyn seemed to show signs of ill-ease which the fair man was unable to account for. On a number of occasions, he appeared to be about to speak, but whatever it was that he had intended to say was never said. Finally, resting his chin on his hands which were holding the pitchfork with which he was spreading the fresh straw, Francys fixed his eyes upon his companion and said amiably:

'Well, out with it then. Say what you want to say. I don't bite, you know!'

Robyn grinned appreciatively. Then he took a deep breath.

'Very well, Menellen. I overheard what you were saying to Father last even. I didn't set out to listen ... but you were talking loud enough to be heard.'

Francys nodded encouragingly. He began to have an inkling of what was to come.

'So?' he enquired.

'So ... I want you to take me with you when you leave.'

Mistaking the reason for Francys' silence, he said defensively:

'I'm a good shot with a bow, you know that. I can ride anything on four legs, and I can wield a sword as well as any fyrdkarl. Father made sure of *that*.'

Francys looked up, observing the man's reddened face, the awkwardness of his stance.

'I don't doubt your skill,' he said quietly. 'That's not the problem.'

Laying the pitchfork down, he gave the young man a comradely clap on the shoulder before turning away towards the partition which separated the stalls from the hay-store. Leaning against the partition and facing Robyn once more, he began to speak again.

'Listen,' he said gently. 'Do you really have any idea what you would be letting yourself in for? I am imrauten. That means I am fair game to anyone who wishes to earn himself a good reward. That means also that anyone who associates with me is equally at risk of capture and execution. Then again, life as an outlaw is no easy thing. It is living by your wits, never knowing what the next day may bring or whether you may have anything to eat or a place to lay your head for the night. And having to be always alert lest you be discovered and taken...'

'I know all that,' Robyn broke in. 'I know it won't be easy. But I want to come with you. I want to be a part of your fight against all who threaten this land. I'd be helping to keep my family safe, after all! No-one else seems like to do so,' he added with a tinge of bitterness.

Francys felt an extraordinary longing to accede to the man's request, but ...

'What about the girl you're courting? You'd have to give her up, you know, if you're to throw in your lot with mine. It would be too much of a risk, to you and to her, otherwise.'

He saw Robyn's face flush and his eyes reflect a momentary glimpse of pain. Then the young man drew himself up and met the hazel eyes of his inquisitor.

'She will understand,' he said proudly.

'But do *you*?' Francys said bluntly. 'This is not a question of being away for a few months, a year or two. If you come with me, you may never return. You would be giving her up for good, and she you. And you cannot even tell her why. No-one must know where you have gone.'

He paused.

'At that, you will be more fortunate than most,' he added. 'At least you will still have contact with your family.'

He looked at the young man gravely.

'Well?' he asked. 'Do you still feel the same? Or have you changed your mind now that you know all that it entails?'

'Menellen, I would follow you to the ends of the earth,' the young man said simply, 'If you will have me.'

Emotion threatened to overwhelm Francys for a moment and he

struggled to overcome it before walking forward and grasping Robyn by the hand.

'I doubt we'll be going *that* far,' he said drily.

'You realize, of course, the last word on this matter lies with your father,' he warned. 'I cannot go behind his back; I owe him too much for that. If he says nay, that is an end to it.'

Robyn nodded.

'I will speak to him this evening,' Francys decided.

He had not expected Robyn's proposal to be received favourably by his father. Waiting until after the evening meal had been eaten and the two women were busy in the kitchen, Francys opened the matter somewhat tentatively, worried lest Artem might mistakenly believe him to have used persuasion to lead Robyn astray. In the event, he was surprised by Artem's reaction. The farmer listened in silence, then nodded his head resignedly.

'Aye,' he said heavily. 'I had a feeling that was the way of it. But I can't say I won't miss the lad.'

Francys stared.

'You'll let him come with me?' he asked, his voice rising in astonishment.

'I can't stop him. He's of age.'

'Even so, a word from you would be sufficient to change his mind,' Francys commented. 'He holds you in deep esteem ... as he should.'

He looked slightly dazed.

'I cannot believe it. You'd entrust your son to me, an outlaw?'

'Not *just* an outlaw, Menellen,' the man rejoined. 'I know you, I trust you, I believe in what you intend to do. If Robyn wishes to help you in that, who am I to say him nay. He's not the first from our family to follow the lure of battle, and if he would make his way as a fyrdkarl, I'd liefer he did so with you, Menellen, than under the banner of our gracious Regent!'

Francys reached over to grasp the farmer's hand.

'I don't know how to thank you, Artem,' he said, his voice thick with emotion. 'Some day I hope I may repay all that you and your family have done for me.'

After that, the waiting was harder, for the success of the venture depended upon the response from Joclyn. Now, too, Francys could not suppress a feeling of guilt whenever he happened to come upon Klara, busily reviewing her son's wardrobe, sewing new garments and planning to fill the saddle-bags of both men with tasty provisions. Although she, like her husband, had declared her acceptance of Robyn's proposed departure, Francys knew that she would have given anything to make him change his mind. Robyn was both the youngest of her sons, and the only one remaining at home. It was entirely natural that she should grieve at his going, all the more since he would be setting out on a very dangerous path. Francys was acutely aware of his own responsibilities, and not a little envious of Robyn, for the contrast with his own situation could not have been more pointed.

At last, a favourable response having been received, Francys was on his way to rendevous with his former Bachendar. He had taken his leave of the family that morning, not without some sadness. There were but few places indeed, and fewer since his denunciation, where he could feel at home, and the farmhouse at Martle was one of them. But as he rode down the narrow back lanes, he felt his spirits lift. For the first time since that terrible night when his world had crumbled around him, he had something to look forward to. The snow having melted, the tracks were indescribably muddy with deep water-filled ruts from the passage of heavy carts. After his horse had slipped on a couple of occasions, Francys, cursing the treacherous conditions, reluctantly confined his attention to the roadway. He made reasonable time, and having spent the night in a barn, grateful for the warmth of the straw, reached the designated valley before sundown on the following day. There was a small hut that he recalled, if you could call hut something that was set into the rocks on two sides beneath an overhang.

Hidden almost entirely by trees in the summer, the hut was somewhat more visible at this time of year, though from a distance it appeared to be merely a heap of rocks. Francys approached with caution, leaving his horse tethered securely behind a tangle of bushes. Slipping from tree to tree, he made his way to a point where he could see the doorway. All seemed in order. He gave the pre-arranged signal and waited. Slowly, carefully, the door was opened and a man emerged, looking around himself at the small clearing. Francys waited until the man had come into the open and it was clear that he was alone, before quietly detaching himself from the landscape and strolling out onto the grass to effect the rendevous.

The movement caught Joclyn's eye, and he spun round, his face lighting with pleasure as his gaze took in the figure that he had never expected to see again.

'Menellen!' he exclaimed hoarsely. 'It is so good to see you.'

Francys wordlessly grasped the former Barchendar by the hand and clapped him heartily on the shoulder with his other hand.

'And to see *you*,' he rejoined after a pause, releasing the man.

'Do you get a fire going, while I go and reclaim my mount,' he suggested next.

By common consent, the matter which had brought them to that spot was not broached until after they had eaten and were sitting beside the hearth inside the hut. The flickering flames of the fire were the sole source of illumination, and heat. Wrapped in his thick cloak and from time to time warming his hands over the fire, Francys began to explain just exactly what he had in mind. Joclyn listened closely, nodding occasionally. As Francys finished speaking, his companion sat for a few moments in silence, thinking. He looked up.

'I'll join you and gladly, Menellen,' he told the fair man simply. 'I've nothing to stay for in Varadil, and I'd rather serve with you than any other. Now,' he continued, thinking aloud, 'you're wanting me to do your recruiting for you ... I can do that easy enough. I've a few names in mind already. But I'll need to know what to tell them, and where to send them.'

'Not here,' said Francys involuntarily, 'and not Carledruin, not at first. Later, of course, they'll have to stop over at Carledruin before being taken into the Toath Cranem ...'

'The Toath Cranem!' Joclyn exclaimed, aghast. 'You've never been *there*?!'

Francys grinned.

'It's not so bad,' he assured the man. 'We'll be very well there, trust me, and the advantage is that no-one will dare to look for us there. No,' he continued, 'we'll need somewhere to vet the recruits. Connor can meet them there and send them on to me at Carledruin.'

He fell into thought. Joclyn waited patiently until at last his commander raised his head.

'I have it!' the fair man announced. 'There is a place next the Armenet betwixt Caleth Mor and Arlmen. It's out of the way of most travellers. I'll give you directions later. Now, as to what to tell them -

you'll be recruiting mercenaries for a new company at arms. No mention of me. You don't have to be too specific, but if pressed, you can hint that it's for a big land-owner up country who wants to set up his own guard. I leave it up to you as to who you approach. I trust your judgment, Joss, but I would suggest you concentrate on those without family ties. Once they've joined the company, they won't be able to go home - it would be too risky.'

He looked gravely at his second-in-command.

'You will be taking the most risk in this enterprise,' he said soberly. 'Don't think I'm not aware of that. Don't push things. The moment you think anyone's become suspicious of you, you're to come away, no matter how few you've recruited. I don't want you endangering yourself - is that understood?! If necessary, we'll just have to find another way of getting the men.'

He stretched out his hands to the fire for a few moments.

'I don't like having to set you and Connor in danger,' he muttered. 'But there's no help for it, if we're to get anywhere with the plan. I can't be seen to move in it at all. At your end, it's purely recruitment of mercenaries. Then when they get to Connor, he will enlighten them further, and there'll be no mention of the Toath Cranem until they arrive at Carledruin - at the moment no word has leaked out as to our presence there, and I'd like it to stay that way.'

Joclyn frowned as a thought occurred to him.

'Menellen,' he ventured. 'What if anyone changes his mind once he knows of your involvement?'

Francys frowned also.

'That had occurred to me,' he confessed. 'I don't know. I'm loath to have to dispose of anyone merely because he doesn't choose to serve under me, but on the other hand, he couldn't be let go to return to Varadil until you at least had been warned and made your escape. He would endanger the whole project, and put you in risk of certain death.'

He shrugged.

'Maybe we could restrain him somehow until there was no risk? I don't know. We'd have to deal with that problem if and when we met it, I think, and just hope we don't have to. That's *your* responsibility, I'm afraid.'

He grinned.

'*You'll* be the one doing the choosing!'

Having settled the remaining details, the two men parted amicably the next morning, Joclyn returning to the city of Väst to begin his part of the enterprise, whilst Francys made his way back up towards the ruins of Carledruin and Connor. The latter could not hide his joy at seeing his commander restored to him. The period of Francys' absence had been a considerable strain upon his nerves and he had been everyday expecting to hear the dreadful news of his capture. Sallying forth from the ruined fortress to meet the fair man, he eagerly pounced upon him for news.

'Well?' he asked almost as soon as the preliminary greetings were over.

Francys smiled mischievously.

'Well,' he responded. 'Very well.'

Then:

'Let me get Melisor under cover, and I'll tell you all.'

And indeed, tell all he did.

CHAPTER SIX

A little over a month later, Francys stood high up upon the battlements of the castle of Kordren, a warm cloak pulled around him, and looked down into the courtyard below, at the bustle and din of a company at exercise. He could hardly believe it. Their plan had succeeded, and succeeded indeed beyond all expectation. A full thirty men had made the journey at Joclyn's prompting, met by Connor at the pre-arranged rendevous and directed onwards to the keep at Carledruin. Not one had backed away once the nature and purpose of the recruitment had been vouchsafed, and all, including Joclyn and the lad, Robyn, had followed Francys into the Toath Cranem without demur, to settle into the fortress of Kordren as though coming home once more. To Francys' admiration, Joclyn had even managed to obtain the services of his former cook, baker and farrier; Francys had to admit that he himself had not given any thought as to how the company would be fed and the horses cared for. They had brought with them adequate supplies, sufficient to keep them fed for a month or more, supplemented by the fruits of their hunting, and it was certainly a treat to taste fresh bread every day.

Robyn had proved himself to be a resourceful and worthy addition to their numbers. At first, Francys had worried that he might have a hard time of it, as a newcomer in a company of men who had been in service together for a number of years and were all used to one another, but the men had welcomed him into their ranks with astonishing ease. Then, too, the lad appeared to have an aptitude for command. Despite never having served in a military capacity before, he was soon able to take the lead in exercises without setting up the backs of those more experienced than himself. Artem must have done well by him, Francys thought, and must miss him sorely.

Francys descended from the battlements, making his way across the inner bailey towards the massive bulk of the keep and his apartments therein. The thought of Artem had led him on to consideration of his future plans. Now that the Company had come together, it was time to set upon the work which he had had in mind.

Whilst he was staying at the farm, Artem had mentioned reports of a band of robbers who were terrorizing the villages and hamlets in a region to the north of Arlmen. Francys had asked Artem to continue to collect information as to the probable numbers and location of the robbers, and the results of his researches now lay upon the table in Francys' chamber, awaiting his attention.

Accompanied by Connor and Joclyn, he led the way into the chamber on the first floor of the keep which he had chosen to serve as the Company's command centre, and having supplied his companions with a mug of ale apiece, sat down at the table, cradling his own mug in one hand. The roll of reports received from Artem lay sprawled across the dark wood. Sipping his ale, Francys waited patiently whilst the two men read the details provided in the reports. Then, with a feeling of anticipation which he had not experienced since the day when he had received the fateful news of his impending denunciation, he settled down to plan their campaign.

****

Nyandu peered out of the narrow window in the corner of her bedchamber which faced the sea, and sighed. It was one of those days when everything appeared dull and dirty, and a misty rain was falling, covering every surface with a patina of tiny drops. Even as she gazed, the clouds rolled in, blotting out the view beyond a mere few feet, so that she felt encased in a solitary grey-white world, bereft of colour and strangely silent. It seemed to her an apt representation of her life since the Day of the Register when she had heard the news which had branded Francys Coras a traitor.

She had no-one in whom she could confide. Her closest friend, her cousin Alhaîtha held such views about the younger son of the Prince of Varadil that it was out of the question that Nyandu could dare to breathe even the slightest indication of her own feelings for the man. None of her local friends had known Francys, and therefore believed every word that rumour and report told about him. She had thought to open her heart to her mother. She was aware that the Lady Arlindu was concerned about her, had noticed the looks which passed between her parents upon occasion; but she could not bring herself to admit to them (for of a surety anything that she told her mother would eventually come to the ears of her father) what a fool she had made of herself, falling in love with someone who not only did not reciprocate her feelings, but against whom the entire country was arrayed in dutiful anger. Nor could she confess that, despite what the world believed of him, and despite also that she had never received the slightest encouragement from him, and now never would, she continued to love the fair man with the whole of her being. She could not foresee an end to it, this pain that ached within her like an open wound. Drearily she envisaged herself at the age, say, of the Lady Inisia, her heart still in thrall, forever wanting what she could not have. She shuddered at the prospect. Then the thought came to her that perhaps the Lady Inisia would understand, would be able to help her. Maybe if she could write to her ... She took out her pen and some parchment and sat down at her writing desk.

But it proved very difficult to write. She must have commenced the letter some five or six times, but she could not seem to find the right words to express her feelings adequately. Then she began to consider whether it was a good idea after all to write to the Lady Inisia. She knew how fond the old lady had been of Francys; would it not be thoughtless of her to mention him and thus revive painful memories? And what if her letter should go astray, be read by someone other than the Lady Inisia? That could, she supposed, plunge them both into grave trouble, for surely the expression of her belief in his innocence and of her continuing love for him, could be accounted seditious by those who most believed his guilt, and might cause serious embarrassment to her father, and to Saragon, mayhap even to the Dukrugvola himself. So, she was to be debarred from writing. Yet, she felt the need to unburden herself to somebody ...

Laying down the pen, she rose to her feet and began to pace the chamber, restlessly. If only she could speak to someone. Just to be able to say those words would be such a relief. But who could she trust? To whom could she bear to admit her folly? She began to ponder the practicalities of paying a visit to the Lady Inisia in Shardu. But she could hardly arrive uninvited, and besides, what reason could she offer for wishing to make such a journey at this time of the year? No, if she were to travel to Shardu, she would become the talk of the Provinces, and everyone would be wondering what the nature of her business could be. Although, she thought, with a mischievous giggle, they might make the error of supposing that she had designs upon that extremely eligible and much sought-after bachelor, the Prince of

Sureindom. In that, they could not be further from the truth. Certainly, she was very fond of Sharn; but he was like a brother to her and would never be anything more, even if she had not already been fully aware of her cousin's profound and jealous love for the man.

She caught her breath then as an idea occurred to her of a sudden. Sharn, she could talk to Sharn. Within a fortnight, her father would be travelling to Lôren to attend one of the quarterly sessions of meetings with the Dukrugvola and others of the Princes of Karled-Dū. Doubtless the Prince of Sureindom would be of that number. By journeying to Lôren with her father, she would be able to take the opportunity of speaking to Sharn, from whom she was bound to receive a sympathetic hearing.

****

The parlour was warm and comfortable. Saragon lounged on the settle, stretching out his feet, clad in soft house shoes, towards the busy crackling fire in the hearth. One hand grasped a generous beaker of mulled ale. Beyond the door, he could hear the bustle of his household unpacking and settling into the routines of city life. They had arrived in Lôren but a scant half hour ago, to a warm welcome from the resident servants, and Saragon was not sorry to leave behind the wet and muddy roads. Travelling in winter was not something to be embarked upon with pleasure. Whereas - he shifted position slightly and took a gulp of the ale - to sit indoors by one's own hearth in idle leisure most definitely was a situation to be enjoyed.

The noise outside rose momentarily to a new intensity, attracting his attention. Before he could react any further, however, there came a knock at the parlour door, and his steward entered.

'There is a visitor to see you, Menellen,' he stated.

Saragon set down his beaker, and rose to his feet, albeit somewhat reluctantly. It would be Alhaîtha, no doubt. Though he dearly loved the girl (as a brother might), she could be most exasperating, and he wished that she could have allowed him a rather longer interval of rest before she came to demand his attention. However, since she was here ... He turned to face the girl, and checked, staring.

'Nan!'

Nyandu came swiftly across the floor.

'Sharn!' she said hurriedly. 'I'm sorry to burst in on you like this when you have only just arrived, but I must talk to you. Do you mind? Please?'

'But of course, Nan, any time,' Saragon answered genially, though somewhat perturbed by her uncharacteristic agitation. 'What is it that you want to talk about?'

He put a friendly arm round her waist and led her towards the settle, feeling her tremble in the grip of some strong emotion.

'Come and sit down in comfort', he suggested. 'But before you broach the matter, let me get you a glass of wine, and then I will listen to what you have to say without interruption.'

He walked over to the corner of the room, rummaging in the tall cupboard which stood there, and returning after a short period with a goblet filled to the brim with crimson wine.

Nyandu sipped the wine slowly, thankfully, feeling a gradual warmth spreading through her body, stilling the tremors. Then she set the goblet down beside the hearth and nerved herself to look up at Saragon, standing nearby and watching her with concerned gaze.

'What must you think of me!' she said ruefully. 'Rushing in upon you like this when you have scarce had time to relax from the journey...'

Saragon smiled gently.

'What else should I think but that you are upset over some matter, and you believe I may help. As indeed I hope I may.'

He paused.

'Well, Nan, what is it? How may I help you?'

She drew a deep breath.

'Sharn, would you mind if I asked you a question?' she asked tentatively.

'Of course not,' he assured her, wondering what was coming.

'Well ...' she hesitated still, then took the plunge. 'Do you believe that Francys Coras is a traitor?'

The question metaphorically rocked Saragon back on his heels. He looked down at the girl, brows arched in surprise and a thoughtful expression in his grey eyes. Then he smiled.

'I take it that *you* do not?'

And without waiting for her response:

'No, Nan I do not believe it. I saw him after he had escaped, remember. Even though I have seen the papers, and they *are* damning, I do not believe in them. There is something, or rather someone behind this, pulling strings, and expecting us all to jump ...'

'Rycharst'. Nyandu mouthed the word to herself, and caught Saragon nodding in agreement.

He took a sip of his ale, set the beaker back upon the mantel and turned back to his visitor.

'But what has all this to do with you, Nan? Why did you ask me that question?'

Nyandu looked up at her friend and said quietly, but with a measure of finality:

'I love him.'

'Dear Sior, what a tangle!' was Saragon's immediate mental response. Suddenly a good many things became clear to him from the previous summer. 'What a ghastly irony,' he thought. There they had been, the two of them, each in love with the other, yet each believing that the other could not possibly reciprocate. And now as if to echo his thoughts, here was Nyandu smiling ruefully up at him and saying deprecatingly:

'You don't need to say anything, Sharn. I knew it was hopeless from the start. He was never likely to return my feelings.'

It cut Saragon to the heart, and he felt a great inclination to gather her up in his arms and tell her:

'No, you're wrong, Nan. He did love you, with all his heart.'

Yet what would that solve? It would only serve to make the situation harder for Nyandu to bear, since there was now no likelihood that she would ever see the man again.

Impulsively he sat down beside her on the settle and grasped her hands in a comforting hold.

'Oh, Nan, I'm so sorry,' he said.

Nyandu essayed a tremulous smile.

'It's none of *your* fault, Sharn,' she told him quietly and with a sadness in her voice such that he inwardly cursed the day that he had invited Francys Coras to his castle in Shardu.

'I daresay I shall get over it, in time,' she added, though she did not sound as though she believed this.

'You mustn't blame yourself for anything, Sharn,' she continued after a pause. '*You* did nothing. Believe me, I didn't come here to make you feel bad. I came because ... because I wanted to be able to talk ... I had to talk to *someone* about him ... and I couldn't think of anyone else ...'

'Oh, Nan.'

He ventured to place a friendly arm around her shoulders.

'You can come and talk to me whenever you want,' he assured her, 'and I'll gladly listen.'

They sat in silence for a while, each busy with his or her own thoughts.

At this inauspicious moment, the door to the parlour opened silently. Alhaîtha stepped forward over the threshold, and stopped dead as though she had run into an invisible wall. Then swiftly she turned, and was gone, as noiselessly as she had arrived.

'I could not believe it,' Nyandu spoke at last, softly. 'When my father told me that his name was on the Register, and why, I simply could not believe it. I remembered what he had said to me once. We had been discussing what life was like under the rule of ... of Rycharst (she spoke that dreaded name hesitantly), and he said to me 'I would sooner kill every single man, woman and child in Karled-Dū with my bare hands than watch them become what those people are'. No,' she said firmly, 'no, I will never believe it, no matter what 'evidence' may be produced. I heard those words; I saw his face as he spoke them. Francys is no traitor!'

'You are not alone in that belief, Nan,' Saragon assured her. 'I too, I have my own reasons, as does your uncle ... Yes,' he continued, smiling at her start of surprise. 'The Dukrugvola, for all that he has been obliged to concede to public opinion, in private is as certain of Francys' innocence as you and I. And there are others of a like mind.'

He gave her shoulder a comforting pat and rose to his feet.

'No, Francys is not friendless, and the dearest hope of us all is that we may find a means of overturning the Justices' declaration of outlawry and of clearing the stain of treachery from his name.'

He picked up her empty goblet and in a sort of mime asked her whether she wanted any more wine. She shook her head, and he set the goblet down again, instead taking a gulp of his ale. It had cooled during their conversation, and he pulled an involuntary face at the taste.

'Not that we have made any great progress as yet, alas,' he

remarked, continuing the conversation at the point where he had left it. 'In truth, it is difficult to know where to start.'

'If I can do aught to help, Sharn, please tell me,' Nyandu said earnestly. 'Promise me you will.'

'Yes, of course, Nan', he reassured her.

She rose, content for that moment with what she had learnt. On impulse, she kissed Saragon softly on the cheek, before turning away to retrieve her cloak from the press upon which she had cast it at her entrance.

'Thanks, Sharn,' she said quietly. 'I'll leave you now to enjoy your well-earned respite.'

He smiled, and escorted her courteously to the outer door, watching her figure recede as she walked away along the street, and then vanished around the corner. Then he returned to the parlour, sombrely thoughtful.

Alhaîtha had come away from Saragon's house in a state of speechless fury. Nan! Nan, of all people! Incredulity suffused her mind. To be sure, she had wondered at her cousin's sudden resolve to visit Lôren during the most unpleasant season of the year. It seemed as though she had found out the answer. Nyandu had come to Lôren for the purpose of meeting Saragon. The scheming minx! She would not have believed it of her. Had anyone else suggested such a thing, Alhaîtha would have laughed the notion to scorn. How could Nan do this to her, knowing as she well did Alhaîtha's feelings for Saragon, her deepest desires? But there was no getting around the fact that she had seen with her own eyes Saragon's arm encircling Nyandu's shoulders. It was the ultimate betrayal.

She begrudged every moment of the wait for Nyandu to return to the castle. In her own bedchamber, she paced the floor, fuming inwardly. Her damp skirts clung and impeded her progress, and she kicked at them irritably, but made no attempt to change her clothing. She was beyond such mundane considerations. Finally, there came a timid knock at the door, and her maid entered nervously, wary of her mistress' unchancy mood and temper.

'Menaïren, the Lady Nyandu has just now come in and has gone to her chamber.'

Nyandu was standing in her shift, her maid having just lifted the damp and mud-spattered folds of her gown over her head, when the sharp rap sounded upon the door. There was no time for her even to wrap herself in a loose robe: the door was flung open without further ado. Nyandu turned, to find herself facing a raging fury who appeared to have taken on the form of her cousin.

'So this is what a betrayer looks like, is it?' hissed the apparition. 'No, no, don't move! I want to look at you.'

Alhaîtha's dark eyes surveyed her cousin from head to foot.

'So, these are the charms that have melted his heart!' she remarked bitterly. 'You must tell me how you managed it!'

Nyandu gazed at her in bewilderment.

'I beg your pardon?' she said, wondering if she had heard aright.

'I would never have believed that you would have it in you to serve me such a foul trick,' declaimed Alhaîtha, scarcely noticing that Nyandu had spoken.

'Why, Nan, why?! How *could* you?!' she spat, raging.

Nyandu drew herself up, with the innate dignity that she could assume at need.

'I have not the slightest notion of what you are accusing me,' she said mildly. 'You must know, Alie, that I would not wish to cause you injury. What is it that you believe I have done to you?'

Alhaîtha glared at her, but her cousin's calm words acted as a brake upon the flow of recriminations which poured from her lips. With an effort, she struggled to regain control of her temper. Then her feelings overcame her once more.

'What have you done!' she screeched, her features twisted with rage. 'You know full well what you've done! *I* saw you, though you didn't know I was there! How dare you stand there and deny it! I saw you with him, and his arm around you! So cosy, the two of you, side by side on the settle!

Oh, how could you Nan!' she panted furiously.

And suddenly raising her hand, she slapped Nyandu viciously across the cheek. Nyandu stood still, shocked, her own hand lifted to touch the injured cheek. Then the import of Alhaîtha's words reached her mind, and she was enlightened.

'Oh,' she exclaimed softly, then blushed as she recalled her confession to Saragon. Had Alhaîtha overheard *that*? But no, she told herself, she could not have or she would not now be accusing her, Nyandu, of stealing Saragon's affections. Alhaîtha must merely have seen and misinterpreted Saragon's gesture of sympathy.

Slowly she raised her eyes to look at her cousin. Alhaîtha was standing watching her in baffled fury. Taken aback by her own action in assaulting Nyandu, yet still overwhelmed with rage and suspicion, she was held momentarily speechless. Nyandu took advantage of this to step forward and confront her cousin in her turn.

'Alie,' she said earnestly. 'You have made a big mistake. The situation is not as you believe. Yes, I was with Sharn; that I admit. I went to see him because ... there was something I needed to discuss with him. I cannot tell you what that was,' she added hastily. 'It is a matter that involves another person, a private matter ...

And yes,' she continued steadily, holding Alhaîtha's startled gaze with her own, 'Sharn did put his arm around me ... to comfort me. I ... you see, I had become rather upset during our conversation. It was nothing ... just a sympathetic gesture on his part.

Alie.' Nyandu forced herself to put out a hand to touch her cousin on the arm. 'Listen to me. You know me; you know that I would not lie to you in such a matter. I like Sharn very much. I always have. He's a good man. But he is like a brother to me, nothing more, an older brother to whom I can turn when I need help or comfort. That's all there is between us, I swear ... Alie?'

Alhaîtha slowly lowered her gaze and Nyandu felt the stiff muscles under her fingers relax. The next moment, she was reeling backwards as her cousin cast herself into her arms in a frenzy of self-reproachful, stormy tears.

'Oh Nan, I'm sorry,' wept Alhaîtha . 'I'm *so* sorry!'

****

Francys cautiously raised his head and peered through the screen of interwoven branches of evergreen lindorn bushes which lined the bank of the river Armen. Immediately opposite, on the far side of the river, he beheld a cliff rising from a level strip of grassy land bordering the water's edge. At one end of the curved shelf, to Francys' right, the cliff closed in again, leaning out above the swirling current, clinging shrubs and trees dipping their branch tips into the water, breaking up the smooth flow and creating pockets of dark shadow into which ducks and other water-fowl retreated to rest. Up against the foot of the cliff rough wooden structures had been erected, makeshift stables and byres, from which the occasional lowing of cattle could be overheard. To the left-hand side of the grass strip, as Francys observed it, a narrow pathway curved out of sight behind a stand of small trees, the sole approach to that isolated spit of land. He looked straight ahead, and there, partially hidden by an outcropping of rock, he glimpsed the darker outline of the entrance to the cave of which he had been told. Shrubs and tall grasses grew up the cliff, shielding the cave-mouth from view from above and preventing any ingress or egress from that direction.

No-one appeared to be at home, save for the beasts under shelter. Francys glanced sideways at his companions, Connor, Joclyn and their guide, the local agent with whom they had met up earlier that day by arrangement. He was about to suggest that they withdraw, when his ear caught the sounds of voices carrying on the breeze, initially faint, but gradually growing louder, and accompanied by jingling harness. It was the robbers, returning. Suddenly they rounded the corner, and he had his first sight of the motley band.

Swaggering in high good humour, they led between them a number of ponies whose backs were piled high with plunder from their latest raid. Wine skins hung from saddles and kegs of ale were lashed on either side. With a rapidity born of experience, some began to unload their booty and stow it safely inside the cave. Others saw to the ponies, unsaddling, rubbing down and stabling them. In its way, it was an efficient operation, overseen by one man, taller than the rest, well-built and dark-haired, and with an air of leadership about him.

Francys and his companions lingered only long enough to mark the posting of a couple of the robbers as sentries beside the outcropping behind which lay the mouth of the cave. Back at the temporary camp some small distance away, sitting beside a welcoming, warming fire and nursing tankards of mulled wine, they settled down to discuss tactics. Picking up a stick, Francys quickly drew a rough map of the site in the mud.

'We attack at dawn,' he declared. 'That will give us the advantage. They'll be waking from sleep and,' he added drily, 'no doubt suffering the after-effects of their celebratory carousings! We shan't need to worry about any possibility of escape across the river - the bank where we were hidden is far too steep and undercut, and the current flows fast and deep alongside it. But we'll post a couple of archers up there. They can distract the sentries at the appropriate moment, and cover the cave mouth from there...'

He continued to propound his plan of action, inviting comment from the others, and listening attentively to any such that was forthcoming.

'To my mind, there is only one man to be wary of,' he concluded, 'their leader.'

'I know him,' Connor said unexpectedly.

The three men turned to stare at him in surprise. He made haste to elaborate.

'I thought he seemed familiar, and I've been cudgelling my brain since we left the river to try to remember where I'd seen him. It just now came to me. His name is Ragnar. He used to be Drachen in the Prince's bodyguard at Väst, till he was dismissed some two or three years since. I forget the reason.'

'That would explain the air of command,' Francys commented.

'You'd best have a care,' Connor advised him, 'and keep your face hidden. It is possible he may know you.'

Some hours later, Francys, crouching behind the branches of a small tree at the point where the path made its turn around the jutting cliff-face, shivering a little in the pre-dawn chill, reviewed his dispositions and found them to be good, or at least, he contradicted himself, as good as they might be, given that they had no knowledge whatsoever of the interior of the cave and would have to trust to luck (and the element of surprise) once they had managed to get inside. He could see the two 'sentries' fairly well by the light of their bonfire. As he had hoped, they were not taking their guard duties especially seriously, lounging at their ease, each with a tankard in one hand, and only occasionally glancing around. Clearly they were not expecting any visitors. He grinned. They would be in for a shock shortly!

The darkness was losing its depth, and the surroundings gradually sharpened into more detail. He could see the outlines of the trees now against a lightening of the sky, interspersed with pockets of deeper shadow. Faintly the river glimmered under the fading stars. It was time. He glanced to his right across the water. Now was the moment. And there, right on cue, came a thrashing amongst the bushes on the far bank. Francys smiled. The noise and movement caught the attention of the watchmen (if indeed such they could be called), bringing them to their feet. As they stood at the water's edge, peering across at the vague shadowy shapes beyond and discussing what might be the cause of the disturbance, Francys saw the two men, whom he had picked for the task, creep stealthily forward.

Then it was done. The sentries lay on the grass, neatly bound and gagged, without having uttered a sound in alarm. Francys stepped out from the trees, motioning the remainder of his company to follow, moving cautiously until all were gathered together outside the cave mouth.

'Well done lads,' he praised those who had disabled the watchmen.

Sword in one hand and covered lantern in the other, the men entered the cave, Francys taking the lead. The mouth was wide enough to permit two men to pass through side by side, and high enough that they did not have to fear that they might hit their heads on some projection. A few paces further inside and the cave widened abruptly, the walls running off into the distance dimly glimpsed by the meagre glow of a low-burning brazier in the centre. Within the confines of the cavern, the stench of the unwashed dregs of humanity who inhabited the place was well nigh unendurable.

'Faugh!'

Francys unconsciously wrinkled his nose in disgust as he gazed around in the gloom. As far as he could make out, the residents were stretched out on truckle beds ranged around the walls, whilst the floor between was an indescribable mess of stale food, dirty plates, cups, clothes, blankets and looted items carelessly discarded.

Francys waited whilst his men began to fan out towards the sides of the cave, moving slowly and carefully. His eyes, growing accustomed to the darkness, ranged the dim recesses, searching for the man who interested him most. The men were nearly all in position when a foot, treading unwarily upon an object in the darkness, caused its owner to stumble and fall across one of the recumbent bodies, dropping his lantern with a clatter and uttering a swiftly stifled oath. Stirrings were heard amongst the sleepers and Francys, realizing that to wait longer would lose them the element of surprise, with a sudden movement, unveiled his lantern, shouting:

'Now!'

Instantly a blaze of light sprang forth, blinding after the near total darkness. Setting the lanterns down, Francys' men turned their attention to the occupants of the beds, now waking startled and bleary-eyed to find themselves confronted by several inches of cold steel and stern voices demanding their surrender. Most indeed gave themselves up immediately and were summarily bound hand and foot, but some scuffles ensued nevertheless. Leaving his men to subdue the rest, Francys started forward across the floor of the cavern, skirting the brazier. Towards the rear of the cave, he had caught sight of the tall figure that he sought - the leader of the band of robbers. Creeping stealthily, he appeared to be heading for a split in the rock-wall.

'Turn back Ragnar!' Francys shouted across the echoing space between them. 'Turn back and fight like a man!

Besides,' he added, as the man halted and swung round, 'we have your back door covered. You'll not escape that way!'

Ragnar shrugged. With a swift movement he seized his sword and with a dagger in his other hand, came forward into the body of the cave to face Francys, crouching in fighting stance, every movement proclaiming his soldier past. He stared intently at Francys who advanced to meet him, and his eyes widened.

'Almost I think I know you, *Menellen,*' he said softly.

'Oh, you do?' Francys responded gently, his eyes flickering over his opponent, searching for a weak point. 'I rather think you may find you are mistaken.'

Before he had finished speaking, the other man lunged, hoping to catch him off guard, but Francys parried the stroke, and the two men began to battle in earnest, circling one another, blade clashing against blade. Dimly behind him Francys was aware of Connor's voice giving orders to clear the floor lest he be tripped up and setting the lanterns up to better illuminate the area. He was aware of nothing further, for all his senses were concentrated on the task at hand. The man was good. Francys needed every ounce of skill that he possessed to gain the advantage against Ragnar's longer reach. Inch by inch, however, he began to drive the robber back towards the rock wall, until he had him boxed into a corner, panting for breath. Francys lowered his sword point slightly.

'Do you surrender?'

Ragnar bared his teeth in a travesty of a smile.

'And if I do, you'll let me go free, to walk out of here and go wherever I choose?'

'You know I cannot do that,' Francys said quietly.

'Then what good is there in surrender? Better to die fighting than at the hands of the hangman! And perhaps I can take you with me!'

As he said that last, the robber pushed himself away from the wall and sprang forward with renewed vigour, aiming a vicious blow at the young man before him. In the nick of time, Francys threw himself to the side. His own sword caught the other man under the ribs, slicing into the stomach. Ragnar stumbled and fell, dropping his weapons and clutching at his wound with both hands. It was a mortal blow, and he knew it. Francys knelt beside the dying man. The robber turned his head.

'Well, Menellen *Imraut*,' he whispered, speaking with difficulty, 'you've done for me. You are a better man than either your brother or your father. If I had served under you, mayhap I would not have come to this.'

The breath wheezed in his throat as his lungs laboured. His hand reached out as if to grasp one of Francys'.

'Have a care to your brother,' the failing voice counselled, then there was silence.

It was later that same morning that the Mayor of the small town of Aramante downstream from the robbers' haunt was called from his noontide meal to behold an astonishing sight. Drawn up neatly beyond the town walls, outside the North Gate, stood a cavalcade of ponies roped together, each loaded with all manner of goods, and behind them a small herd of cattle, some milling around aimlessly, some settled on the ground, chewing the cud. Next to meet his eyes was a group of unkempt, rough-looking men, also roped together, and guarded by soldiers on horseback. Then, at a brief distance, he saw a further band of horsemen, led by one on a great black horse, his face obscured by a close-fitted helm, and in front of them, what appeared to be, from their clothing and accoutrements, a pair of wealthy merchants.

The Mayor turned a bewildered gaze upon the two merchants.

'Good sirs, what *is* all this?' he enquired in confusion.

The elder of the two merchants (who was in fact Connor) waved a lordly hand towards the ruffians and beasts and said magnificently:

'These are the robbers whom I believe have been preying upon your neighbours and yourselves, and their plunder. Be so good as to have them housed in your town gaol, until they can be transferred into the custody of the garrison at Arlmen, to whom we have sent word. Might I suggest also that you put the word about the neighbourhood so that those who have suffered at the hands of these robbers may come to view and reclaim what was stolen from them?'

The Mayor goggled at him, utterly taken aback.

'But ... but...' he began.

'No buts,' Connor interrupted ruthlessly. 'We have done our part; the rest is up to you.'

He turned to his companion.

'Come.'

The two seeming merchants wheeled their horses round. As they did so, the Mayor, emboldened of a sudden, surged forward.

'Stop!' he cried. 'Who *are* you? I must know who you are!'

'A well-wisher,' came the brief reply.

The cavalcade moved off, the soldiers who had been guarding the prisoners, having relinquished them into the less than kindly hands of the town militia, making haste to fall into the ranks. As they passed, their leader lent briefly out of the saddle to remark quietly, but distinctly:

'One who loves his country.'

Then they were gone.

CHAPTER SEVEN

The capture of the gang of robbers was a nine days' wonder in the locality, and from there the story spread gradually outwards as the ripples on a pond, to be followed by further tales. For Francys, wishing to capitalize upon the success of their first venture, lost no time in organizing a number of further expeditions, utilizing information provided by Artem's intelligence network. Though none of these was as flamboyant or impressive as that first undertaking, each was in its own way satisfying, and Francys was surprised to discover that he felt happy, as he had not been since the fateful day when he had received the news of his impending denunciation. Whilst he would never be able to forgive his family for their betrayal, he was free, he had his companions about him, and he was doing the work he wanted. What was more, it appeared that the news of the daring escapade with the robbers had proved an inspiration for a number of disaffected soldiers from garrisons around the Kirkendom province, who had become disillusioned with the current regime under the Regent. A flurry of messages passing between Artem and Francys resulted in the Company at Kordren being augmented gradually by ones and twos, each potential recruit having been vetted without their knowledge before any approach was made.

As each successful mission was completed, so the standing of the troop of unknown horsemen rose in the estimation of the inhabitants of the Provinces of Arlente and Kirkendom who felt the benefits of their actions. Word had begun to spread beyond the borders of the two Provinces, no doubt exaggerated and embroidered in the telling and if at the outset all that was lacking was a name, this lack was soon remedied. No-one knew whence it had first arisen - maybe one of the robbers had chanced to overhear Ragnar's last words in the cave and had passed the knowledge on - but soon a name began to sound on people's lips, a name for the leader of this strange company: 'Menel Imraut' they called him, the Lord Outlaw.

'Menel Imraut'.

The Lord of Shadowe sat on his great golden throne, chin on hand, brooding. The echoing hall was silent, empty save for that dark, contemplative figure. Even the messenger who had brought the news was gone, dismissed from the presence.

'So, he defies me!' the immortal Lord murmured, and he smiled, a slow, devilish smile which had something of a malicious sense of gloating in the tilt of his lips and the brief gleam of his white teeth. 'Well, we shall see about *that*!'

It was time, he mused, to remind certain persons of debts which they owed to him, as he settled down to lay his plans.

****

'Menel Imraut!'

Saragon was sitting in the Dukrugvola's office, goblet in hand, his head resting against the high back of his chair, his grey eyes fixed on the face of the Lord Archaïlis seated on the further side of the wide polished table. It was from his lips that the exclamation had issued. The Dukrugvola inclined his head fractionally in assent.

'You had not heard the stories then?'

'Obviously not,' Saragon responded drily. 'Might I impose on you to tell me, Sir?'

'Certainly.'

The Dukrugvola unfolded the tale of the robbers to Saragon's highly interested ears.

'That is but the first of the ventures of this company,' he concluded. 'I understand that they have continued to harry the enemies of the people of Kirkendom and Arlente, and in doing so, have won for themselves a considerable following amongst the populace in those Provinces. Little is known about the men themselves. They appear where aid is needed, and disappear again once they have rendered the assistance required. And their leader, as I have mentioned, has come to be known by that strange title.'

Saragon leant forward.

'It has to be Francys!' he asserted. 'Who else could it be? We should have known that he would not be content with skulking in hiding. And what a coincidence otherwise! Francys is outlawed and disappears into the countryside ... along with his faithful Drachen, Connor, I may remind you ... and shortly afterwards there appears a strange 'leader'. Who else is it likely to be?' he repeated.

'It certainly bears his stamp,' the Dukrugvola agreed, 'but where would he have got a company of men? The numbers vary from tale to tale, yet they must be some 20 to 30 in total... There has been nothing in the intelligence reports, even to hint at such a group being recruited ...'

'No, and that to my mind makes it more likely that it *is* Francys,' Saragon rejoined. 'Artem is unlikely to pass on any information which might lead to Francys being captured, even knowing as he does our own opinion. It would be too risky should the information fall into the wrong hands.'

He took a sip of wine. The Lord Archaïlis sighed.

'Would that we had some means of verifying these stories. I should be interested to learn more concerning the mysterious 'Menel Imraut'. But I cannot see my way to doing so without perhaps endangering Francys. If I were to send someone to investigate formally, then I should have to take official notice of whatever might be learnt, and you know as well as I, Sharn, that if it were to turn out to be Francys, whatever gallant deeds he might be accomplishing to the benefit of Karled-Dū, the sentence of the Justiciars would still stand and he would be condemned to death.'

Saragon sat for a minute or two, sipping wine, deep in thought. Then he raised his head.

'What if the someone was 'unofficial' so to speak?' he said slowly. 'Someone who could report back privately, without the matter going any further than ourselves?'

The Dukrugvola raised his eyebrows.

'You are far too well-known Sharn, as are your sympathies. You would be as good as announcing to all and sundry who you believe the man to be. No, no, that wouldn't work...'

'Not me, Sir,' Saragon responded with a faint smile. 'Nan writes that she is intending to travel through Kirkendom during the summer months. Why not use *her*?'

'Nan!'

The Dukrugvola sounded startled.

'My niece?'

'The very same.' Saragon agreed. ' I have reason to believe that she is not unsympathetic to our views on this matter,' he added carefully.

'Indeed? Hmm ...'

The Dukrugvola thought for a moment.

'But ...' he began.

'Sir, will you allow me to explain?' Saragon interposed. 'As I said, I have received a letter from Nan, who tells me that she has made up her mind to travel during the summer months this year, instead of coming to spend some time with us in Shardu as she usually does. She feels, so she says, that she is woefully ignorant of our compatriots in the eastern Provinces of Karled-Dū and wishes to remedy this fault as best she may ...'

He thought back briefly to the words that she had inscribed and which he had read but that morning. 'You could call it a pilgrimage of sorts', she had written. She had not spelt it out explicitly, but Saragon could readily understand her reluctance to grace his castle at Shardu with her presence. After the events of the previous summer, it would have become a place of exquisitely painful memories. He had found it difficult enough himself from time to time, remembering those eventful weeks.

He shook himself free of his thoughts and brought his mind back to the matter in hand.

'In truth, sir, she is the ideal person for the enterprise,' he persisted. 'Her arrangements are already in place or will be shortly. And whilst she is there, it will be entirely natural for her to take an interest in local stories. She won't have to do anything untoward, merely be herself. You know yourself what a good listener she is. If there is any truth in these tales, Nan will find it out.'

He looked across at the Dukrugvola.

'What do you say, sir? Shall we put the proposal to her?'

The Lord Archaïlis met his eyes and gave a slight shrug of the shoulders.

'Why not? Surely no harm can come to her from listening to tales.'

He gave a rueful smile.

'You know, we, that is my wife and I, had such hopes of a match between the two of them, Nan and Francys. They seemed so well suited.'

'Yes,' said Saragon quietly.

Some weeks later, Nyandu walked down the corridor with Saragon, her long skirts swishing gently.

'You say you have a proposition to put to me?' she enquired, 'You and my uncle? Does it concern...?'

'Hush,' he interrupted quickly. 'Don't speak that name here.'

'You did ask if there was anything you could do,' he reminded her.

'And you have found something?' she asked eagerly.

'If you wish to undertake it; it will be entirely your choice.'

Nyandu looked suddenly anxious.

'Sharn, my uncle does not know ... that is, you did not tell him ...'

She had stopped walking and was gazing up at him in concern. Saragon realized what it was that she had been trying to ask him and made haste to reassure her.

'My dear Nan, I would never pass on to another what has been said to me in confidence, you should know that. All that your uncle knows is that you are of the same opinion as myself in this matter, and that he can trust you.'

He came to a halt outside the Dukrugvola's office, knocked briskly on the door, and opened it, ushering Nyandu inside. Her uncle rose to greet her.

'Nan, my dear, come in, come in. Come and sit down.'

He waited until she had seated herself, offered her wine, which she refused, and then resumed his own seat.

'Has Sharn told you what this is about?' he enquired.

'No, sir, only that you have a proposal of some kind to put to me,' Nyandu answered, 'and that it relates to the journey I am undertaking. He has been very discreet.'

She turned and smiled at the dark-haired man. The Dukrugvola regarded them both gravely for a moment.

'Inside this room, we may speak freely,' he stated, 'but what is discussed here must go no further. I am sure that you understand this.'

'Of course, sir,' confirmed the girl.

'Well then, let me begin by asking you whether you have heard the tales which have been circulating in recent weeks concerning the activities of a company of horsemen in and around the Provinces of Kirkendom and Arlente, the leader of whom, it seems, the local people have dubbed 'Menel Imraut'.'

Nyandu's eyes widened in surprise but she shook her head.

'I have heard nothing of this, sir. Do you ... are you saying that this leader, this 'Menel Imraut' (she repeated the appellation doubtfully) is Francys Coras?'

'That is precisely what we do not know,' said her uncle, a trifle testily.

He briefly recounted for her edification the tales which had reached his ears. Nyandu listened intently.

When he had finished, there was a pause; then Nyandu spoke.

'What is it that you wish me to do?' she asked.

The Dukrugvola smiled at her. He motioned to Saragon, who rose and went over to a small wall cupboard from which he extracted three goblets of fine decorated, coloured glass. Pouring wine from a jug into two of them, he brought them over to the table and presented them to his two companions, before returning to collect one for himself. As he sat down, the Dukrugvola lifted his glass to him in a gesture of appreciation. Nyandu took a sip of the crimson wine, and raised her eyes once more to meet those of her uncle.

'What is it that you believe I can do for you?' she asked again.

'You are intending to travel extensively about the Province of Kirkendom, so Sharn tells me. Is that so?'

'Yes, sir.'

'You will understand that I cannot act officially in this matter. My hands are effectively tied. But I need to know, if it can be discovered, who is this 'Menel Imraut'. I need someone who has an open and valid excuse for being in the area, and who can listen to people, and encourage them to talk, without raising suspicions.'

Nyandu gave a soft gurgle of laughter.

'In short, uncle, you need a woman who can investigate all the local gossip without being thought at worst as more than a nosey-parker!'

He could not suppress a smile, but was serious again immediately.

'Will you do this for me, Nan?'

'Yes, I will,' she answered without hesitation. 'In truth, I should like to know the answer myself.'

'There is one other matter,' the Dukrugvola added.

Both Nyandu and Saragon looked enquiringly at him.

'I have been concerned for some time regarding the state of preparedness of the garrisons in Kirkendom. Rumours have circulated that they are not as well maintained as they ought to be, and that there has been some falling out between the folk living in the towns nearest the borders with Harres and Krapan and the Regent. Maybe, on your travels, when you are listening, you could investigate the truth of these rumours also?'

'Hmm,' Saragon said thoughtfully. 'Do you think it wise for Nan to go ferreting about into the affairs of Hadran Coras, sir? Should he find out, might he not be angered by the fact that you have set Nan in effect to spy on him?'

'That I leave up to Nan to decide. It will be entirely her choice whether she deems it possible or no.'

Nyandu leaned across and laid her hand gently on Saragon's as it rested on the arm of his chair.

'Don't fret, Sharn,' she said lightly. 'There is no danger of his finding out, at least whilst I am yet in the vicinity! You forget, I have been corresponding with the Lady Annis, and she assures me that Hadran never visits Caleth Mor during the month of zenna. Apparently his father insists that he celebrate Zentrana in Väst. Why else,' she added wickedly, 'do you think I would have consented to stay in the castle at Caleth Mor, when I am not off journeying around the Province?

Besides,' she continued, turning to her uncle, 'I have had a thought about how to approach this matter. I think it best that I should have some sort of official status. If I am to visit these garrisons, which I ought to do, then I shall need to be able to prove that I have your confidence, sir. And in order to preserve Hadran's dignity, I shall also inspect those garrisons in Arlente on the border with Harres. That will give me cover for pursuing my enquiries in that region with regard to 'Menel Imraut'.'

The Dukrugvola regarded her with considerable respect.

'My dear Nan, you are a genius! It shall be so. I shall give you a commission for the purpose.'

And thus it was settled. In the days that followed, Nyandu completed her preparations for departure. She had further meetings with the Dukrugvola to go over necessary details, and during the last of these, he handed to her a folded, sealed paper: the promised commission. Finally, towards the end of the month of slionith, she pronounced herself ready to set forth.

A veritable crowd assembled to see her off: the Dukrugvola and his wife, Saragon, various of her friends, and her cousin. Alhaîtha was in two minds about Nyandu's proposed expedition, being aware only of the official version of her cousin's intentions in travelling to Kirkendom. One part of her was envious, for she herself had never travelled further east than the border between her own Province of Zaleindom and neighbouring Arlente. She had not expected Nyandu to be so enterprising and it occurred to her, not altogether pleasingly, that her cousin had considerable hidden depths. That reflection was, of course, the cause of Nyandu's departure also being of some relief to Alhaîtha. Her suspicions had not been totally allayed by Nyandu's explanation, and she could not help but be aware that there was some private understanding between Nyandu and Saragon from which she was excluded. Jealousy made her glad to see her cousin leave. She hung back while leave-takings were in progress, but at the last moment, shame overcame her. Nyandu was her cousin after all, and her closest friend until recent weeks. As Nyandu turned away from the group at the foot of the steps, Alhaîtha came forward and embraced her affectionately.

The Dukrugvola watched the little procession as it passed under the great archway and turned into the street outside. Nyandu was well-protected: she was travelling with a personal bodyguard of some ten experienced fighting men, captained by a man who had been many years in the service of the Almeneth family in Meneleindom. Armed guards rode also with the baggage wains. Nonetheless, he stared after her with unease, misgivings crowding his mind. He glanced at Saragon, reading the small signs of mirroring concern.

'Sior keep her safe', he murmured softly, the words reaching Saragon's ears only. 'Surely she cannot come to any harm by listening to stories.'

Nyandu was enjoying the journey. The first part was of course familiar to her: she had travelled northward of Lôren before, along the course of the Dern, past the edges of the vast forest Kmendel, and so onward towards the mountains of Teleth Armenor, gradually raising their lofty heads above the eastern horizon. Restrained as she was by the relatively slow pace of the baggage wains, she had leisure to look about herself as she travelled and to enjoy the scenery. The weather was fair and warm, but not too hot, and the scents of flowers drifted across the roadway from the fields and grasslands on either side. Copses and occasional larger woods dotted the landscape. Winding lanes left the highway to snake towards far off clusters of villages and hamlets. From time to time they stopped to obtain refreshment at roadside inns, and to bespeak beds for the night, although they had brought with them the wherewithal to set up camp, should it be necessary, and indeed, during their crossing of the pass through the Teleth Armenor, they were glad of it. Progress was slow along the narrow track which wound through the tumbled mountain peaks, barely wide enough to permit the passage of the carts, and with a sheer drop to one side.

Once over the mountains, Nyandu was in unfamiliar territory, though to the outward eye it differed only little from the country she had left behind. The capital of Arlente, the city of Verilith, she found very beautiful and fascinating, situated as it was on the shores of a vast lake, the Oner Arle. Indeed, some parts of the city had been built out into the lake itself on platforms raised above the water. A thriving port was filled with wide-bottomed barges, sail-driven, which plied up and down the length of the lake. Some, she learnt, made the passage down the rivers Arle and Armenet, even as far as the mouth of the latter, in distant Varadil. One afternoon, she hired a small boat and had the boatman row her out into the lake, until all she could see was water about her, and distant shorelines on the horizon, the sky a vast arched ceiling overhead. Later, she stood on the wooden jetty, feeling the breeze ruffling her hair, watching the brilliant reds and oranges of a glorious sunset over the far mountains, and wishing her paints to hand.

She had, as a matter of course, made herself known to the Prince of Arlente upon her arrival, showing him the commission from the Dukrugvola and requesting his permission for her to journey freely about his domains. She had found him an intelligent and amiable man, who had seemed to feel no sense of umbrage at having his defensive dispositions inspected, and by a woman at that, but on the contrary acceded graciously to her request. He had invited her to sup with himself and his family, and during the course of the evening the conversation had turned naturally enough to the subject of all subjects that Nyandu had wished to hear about, but had not felt able to raise herself. Not altogether to her surprise, the Prince of Arlente professed himself very grateful to the unknown group of horsemen. He did not say so in so many words, but she gathered well enough from what he did say that he had no intention of enquiring into the identity of the men, or their leader, preferring to leave well alone whilst his Province benefited. Whether he had any suspicions as to the identity of the leader, she was unable to ascertain, and wisely did not press him.

It was also in Verilith that Nyandu began to employ her talents for healing, report of which was to precede her during her subsequent travels. It came about by accident rather than design, for having seen one day on her progress about the city, a young mother carrying a baby who was screaming in obvious pain, she could not forebear from approaching her to enquire whether there was ought that she could do to relieve the child. The following day it seemed that word had spread, for on stepping forth from the inn, she discovered a small group of petitioners awaiting her, and out of the kindness of her heart she stopped to assist them, and the others who came the next day, and the next.

After a little over a week in Verilith, Nyandu took to the road again. She was aware of the vast length of the Oner Arle to her north as she rode along the highway, skirting the edges of the marshland of Kem Par, though soon enough she was turning her back to the lake as the road led her southwards. Though she knew it not, she passed within a few calle of the ruined castle of Carledruin, glimpsing the top of the tower for a few moments before it disappeared again behind the closer hills. Then they were entering the grasslands upon which the herds of cattle and horses, from which the Province gained much wealth, were pastured. A spur of the Teleth Cranem, the mountain range which divided the Province of Varadil from the 'wasteland' that was the Toath Cranem, jutted northwards across their path, and the road perforce swept round its feet. At its northernmost tip the boundaries of three Provinces came together.

Nyandu reined in her horse beside the boundary stone and sat for some moments, gazing ahead. Now that she had reached this point at last, she felt almost a reluctance to go forward, to cross the border into the Province of Kirkendom. With a sense of setting in motion events which she would be powerless to halt, she gently nudged the horse's flanks and guided it over the narrow line of stones which denoted the boundary crossing in that place. She was there. Now all that lay before her was the journey via the market town of Arlmen to the capital city of the Province, Caleth Mor. After that, her mission would truly begin.

****

In his suite of rooms in the palace in his home city of Väst, Hadran Coras sat brooding. He was bored. Always at this time of year his father expected him to dance attendance, to participate in the celebration of the festival of Zentrana. Except for last year, of course, when he and his brother had been staying at Shardu with Saragon. Aye, that had been a different matter. The midsummer festival itself had been impressive, out upon the hillside, with the chanting and the fires, and that great stone circle. What followed, had been less so. He recalled walking through the fair with Alhaîtha, coming upon the gypsies dancing, and amongst them, Francys, flaunting himself, and trying to cut him, Hadran, out with Nyandu. Well, that had come to nothing in the end. *He* had seen to that! Hadran grinned. There was no way now that Francys could ever hope to wed Nyandu; she was well and truly out of his grasp.

It were a pity, thought Hadran, that his brother had, however, managed to evade capture. He should have been dead by now! As it was, these rumours had begun to pervade the land, stories about an outlaw, who had to be none other than Francys himself. He was becoming a hero of the people. It was maddening! Would he never be free of his devil brother? By Sior, he was minded to go looking for this so-called 'Menel Imraut', and expose him for what he really was, a deadly traitor. If only he knew where to look. If only his father did not expect him to celebrate Zentrana in Väst.

And now, there was Nyandu travelling to Caleth Mor and visiting the Province of which he was the Regent. Why should *he* not go to Caleth Mor? Surely his father would not expect him to remain here in Väst when he ought, in courtesy, to pay his respects to Nyandu. Yes, he should be *there*, showing her around the Province, and maybe ... maybe pressing his suit with her once more. Surely, he argued, this journey of hers, to a region where he ruled, must at the least auger some softening of her feelings towards him, of which he should be on hand to take advantage. Aye, that was the way to put it to his father... If only he could have been rid of his brother for certain, though...

A knock at the door interrupted his train of thought. The servant brought him a folded, sealed package, informing him that the messenger had not waited for a reply. Dismissing the man with a curt nod, Hadran bent his gaze to the package. A frisson of excitement ran through him. He knew the hand. By this means had he been given the evidence which had served to brand his brother a traitor throughout the land. With a feverish haste, he tore the wrapping away and scanned the contents, and smiled.

PART TWO

CHAPTER EIGHT

Beneath the dripping boughs of the pine forest of Karenath rode a solitary horseman, closely muffled in a drab cloak with the hood drawn forward over his face. He sat in the saddle wearily, with drooping shoulders and bent head, hands loosely grasping the reins, and allowed the horse to set his own pace. Low-reaching branches plucked at his hood and finally pulled it down, to reveal the unmistakable bright hair of Francys Coras, outlaw.

Feeling the drip of the unceasing rain upon his bare head, Francys reached for the hood and covered himself up again. Interrupted from his chain of gloomy thoughts, he stirred and looked around to see where he was, automatically bringing the horse to a halt. A mild curse escaped him. During the period of his reverie he had almost reached the eaves of the forest before he was aware. Although the grasslands towards which he was headed were sparsely inhabited, it behoved him to proceed with greater caution and to keep his wits about him.

As the black horse began to move forward again, Francys glanced ahead, perfunctorily, into the distance, and his hand closed on the rein, bringing Melisor to instant, well-trained immobility. Sitting like a statue, his whole awareness focussed into the one faculty, sight, he peered intently along the track. Ahead, some few hundreds of yards before him, lay the grasslands, intermittently visible between the ranks of rough pine trunks with their needled swathes of foliage and the delicate fringed silver birches, the clumps of dark brenbaran bushes with their tough, leathery leaves shaped like the head of a lance, and the tangles of bramble and fern. It was there that he had glimpsed a momentary metallic glint, he thought. Grim-faced, he strove to pierce the misty drizzle, to see through the dull deceptive light. Then, with swift decisiveness, he turned Melisor around and began to walk him quietly up the track, hoping thus to evade the attention of the concealed watchers. Black horse and brown cloak were not the easiest of objects to spot in such dim light.

A shout echoing through the trees behind him dispelled this hope, and the hiss of an arrow slicing the air, though it did not come near him, urged upon him the need for speedy action. Hastily he kicked Melisor into a gallop, leaning low in the saddle to present a smaller target. With annoyance he recalled that, in the interests of unobtrusiveness, he had given cuirass, mail and helm into Connor's charge, retaining only his weapons. Indeed, beneath the cloak, he wore no more than a shirt and thin jacket which would not afford him even the slightest protection. The wind of his passage swept back the hood of the cloak and at the sight of his fair head a chorus of shouts went up. The drumming of hooves reverberated in his wake now, thunderous, but, to his relief, the arrow-shot was not repeated. He gripped tighter against Melisor's flanks and persuaded the horse to increase his stride. The hoof-beats began to sound closer behind him. Melisor could go no faster; like his rider, he was weary. Imperceptibly he slackened with every step he took until Francys, realizing that to press on would be futile, brought him to a halt, turning at bay with the determination of fighting to the last breath. He slid the heavy sword from its sheath.

The foremost of the half dozen men who rode in pursuit pulled up hastily at a safe distance, warily eyeing the weapon. Francys surveyed him with narrowed eyes, seeking some mark of identification, but there was nothing to show whence the riders originated. They wore no colours, only ordinary riding dress. In appearance, they could have been taken for a party of huntsmen, save that Francys' sharp gaze discerned the outline of a breastplate beneath each leather jerkin. No huntsmen were these, save hunters of men, of one man.

Within a few seconds the rearmost riders had arrived and the group began to edge forward cautiously in a body, weapons unsheathed. For a moment a corner of Francys' mind commented wryly on the numbers evidently thought appropriate for the pursuit of so dangerous a criminal as he. Then his sword was weaving through the raindrops as Melisor sprang to meet them. Steel clanged on steel unavailingly, then slipped off to pierce the shoulder of a burly, dark-bearded man who disappeared with a startled oath into the confusion of thrashing equine limbs. Dripping, the blade rose again, but fell, striking dully upon the trampled earth as a staff crashing down onto Francys' wrist caused him to loose his grasp.

Swearing, Francys promptly backed Melisor off out of the fray, leaving the other horses hopelessly entangled. Bending quickly, he snatched out his knife, grimacing at the throbbing of his bruised wrist. A couple of his attackers had dismounted and, as he now advanced, attempted to rush him from either side, whilst those in front distracted his attention. But, sensing this, he spurred Melisor into rearing and striking out with heavy hooves, successfully downing one of his assailants. Confusion reigned in the shape of neighing, tossing heads, eyes rolling, and thrashing, thudding hooves, punctuated by the oaths, sharp cries and heavy breathing of the human participants. Then, his attention momentarily focussed on the plunging bodies directly before him, and concentrating upon keeping Melisor out of their way, Francys failed to notice the horse edging in from the rear, until a hard shoulder struck him sideways, unseating him and toppling him to the ground in a helpless tangle. He had the presence of mind to shield his head as he fell, but the body landing on top of him knocked all the breath from his lungs and pitched his face into the dirt and dead pine needles which littered the forest floor.

Painfully turning his head to one side, he drew in gulps of air, unable to move. The weight of a big man complete with breastplate bore down on him intolerably and the rank odour of stale sweat and bad breath impinged sickeningly on his nostrils. Through his body pressed against the ground he could feel the jarring vibrations as Melisor's hooves crashed down dangerously close by and the men fought to control him, to the accompaniment of furious exhortations from their prostrate companion. Then a sudden quiet fell over the scene, broken after a few seconds by the tramp of booted feet approaching. Legs swam into his field of vision. The weight pressing upon him vanished, and a moment or two after he felt himself seized by rough hands. He struggled against them, lashing out with his feet, but was forced to cease these exertions when one arm was pulled excruciatingly behind his back. Dragged mercilessly upright, he stood breathing heavily, his clothes disordered and muddy, the cloak wound restrictingly about him, with tangled hair and mud-streaked visage. A harsh voice summarily commanded him to hold out his hands for binding. He ignored it. A rush of air heralded the thrust of a powerful fist, just too late for him to evade the blow. It caught the side of his head, knocking him reeling, and before he could recover, the binding was effected. The leather strap cut into his wrists, so tight had it been pulled. Its further end was knotted expertly to the stirrup-leather of his captor. Then, having retrieved and stowed away his sword and knife, and assisted their wounded comrades onto their respective mounts, the remainder of the company swung briskly into the saddle.

With a jerk the journey began, far too long and every step a nightmare for Francys stumbling humiliatingly alongside the sweating flanks of the horse. His head drooped forward, the hazel eyes closing irresistibly, only to fly open again at the tug of the strap. The smell of wet horse and leather, the jingle of bridles, the soft caress of sodden grass enveloped his weary senses and to his tired mind with sudden startling clarity resurrected the appallingly similar experience of his capture by the Rarokins in the South those years before. In his dazed state the two events seemed to melt into one and it was with a feeling almost of shock that he heard his captors speaking in the tongue of Karled-Dū.

At some point, when he was not sure, the rain had drifted away, to be replaced by bright, hot sunshine which raised wisps of steam from wet garments and wet vegetation, and explored his bare skin with burning fingers. Sweat dripped down his forehead and he could not brush it away, nor reach an irritating itch on one cheek, though he could, and did, shake his head to drive away the flies which buzzed about him. His chest rose and fell laboriously and the breath hissed audibly through his clenched teeth. And whenever he missed his footing on the uneven ground, which happened increasingly often, the strain on his wrists was agonizing.

At length he became aware of a change in pace, in scents, in noises. A multitude of voices chattered unintelligibly in a dreadfully familiar dialect, greeting his arrival with whistles and coarse jeers. The horses slowed to a halt. Destination reached, he thought numbly, his senses telling him exactly where that destination had to be, whilst his mind vainly persisted in rejecting the knowledge. The end of the strap was untied from the stirrup and a sharp tug on it brought him stumbling forward further into the encampment. He tripped over a tuft of grass, to the delight of the onlookers, but was jerked roughly to his feet and thereafter grasped by the arms and marched onwards.

After a seemingly interminable perambulation about the camp-site, surely intended to complete his disorientation, he was led at last into a small open space hedged about on all sides, save for a narrow entrance, by wicker screens such as were often employed to conceal makeshift lavatory pits. There they brought him to a halt and he stood wearily between his guards, head drooping, eyes fixed dully on the grass at his feet. Above his head voices spoke.

'We have him, Menellen,' they said.

There came an indrawn hiss of satisfaction.

'So I see,' a third voice responded, the sound of which sent an involuntary shudder rippling through Francys' body. He sensed the approach and slowly, reluctantly, lifted his heavy head to look with what impassivity he could muster into the coarse, gloating face and triumphant hazel eyes of his brother.

A smile of pure delight lit Hadran's features. Deliberately he raised a hand and struck Francys brutally across the mouth. Blood welled from the split lip and Francys swayed unsteadily, held upright only by the iron grasp of the guards at his side. Hadran continued to smile.

'Payment of a debt,' he remarked unpleasantly.

Francys made no answer, nor was he capable of one. The assault upon him in the forest and the gruelling journey to the camp had leached the last reserves of energy which he possessed. The nauseating dizziness which had hung threateningly about him during the latter part of the trek now leapt to overwhelm him. Through the fog which enveloped his mind, he was vaguely aware of an order being given. The next instant he was free of restraint, the two men having stepped aside somewhere. But before the realization had fully penetrated and before he could take advantage of it in any way, he felt himself seized by cruel, clutching hands and pulled roughly into someone's arms. As he jerked his head up, fighting against the giddiness which clogged his brain, Hadran kissed him, open-mouthed and hard, forcing his lips apart and bruising them anew. Then, with an abruptness which proved too much for his weakened state, he was released. As Hadran watched, Francys stood still for a moment, too shocked to move, then his legs buckled under him and he pitched forward, instinctively throwing up his bound arms to protect his head. His brother threw back his own head and let out a shout of laughter.

Leaving the young man where he lay, Hadran strode across to the narrow opening and barked out an order to the man waiting without. Returning, he stood for a brief while in satisfied contemplation, before dropping to one knee and unceremoniously heaving the inert body onto its back. Taking out his dagger, he cut through the bonds about the wrists, noting the dark weals which they had left, and the swollen hands. Then he began methodically to strip the young man, removing and casting to one side in an untidy heap the drab cloak, thin jacket, fine white linen shirt, riding boots, breeches and underlinen, until Francys lay completely naked on the damp grass. One cause of his collapse became evident: an ugly cut across the ribs from which a thin trickle of blood flowed sluggishly, echoed by the dribble from his lip.

Hadran sat back and let his eyes wander over the slim body. He had waited so long for this, with the tantalizing image of the young man as he had glimpsed him briefly on the beach at Shardu lingering always at the edge of his memory. And in truth, Francys was an exquisite sight, with his wonderful hair spreading on the grass about his head and his skin tanned a light golden brown by the summer sun. With a tentative gesture, Hadran stretched out a hand and ran his fingers the length of Francys' torso.

Until that moment he could still have drawn back, could have curbed his desires and let the temptation pass, but that touch changed all. For a second time he pulled that body into his arms and for a second time he pressed greedy lips onto the lips of his brother. Francys stirred.

Hadran let him fall back, sat back on his heels and looked at him. Rising, he crossed to fetch the bucket of water which he had requested, sending the man away and pulling across an extra screen to block the opening. For what he had in mind to do next, absolute privacy was essential. Returning to his brother, he dashed a portion of the water into Francys' face. The shock of it restored his senses and he opened his eyes. Above him loomed, obscenely voluptuous, the face of Hadran, his brother and implacable enemy. Instinctively he shrank away, and thereby came to the discovery that he was unclothed. Recollection of Hadran's savage kiss swam into his mind. Revolted comprehension dawned in his eyes and the muscles of his face stretched taut with loathing. With desperate determination he struggled to rise, to get away.

'No!' he cried out, appalled. 'Dear Sior, no! No!'

Torn between dizziness and horror, his stomach heaved and he began to retch chokingly. Slumped on hands and knees, his back turned to that lustful face, he was violently and painfully sick, the vomit stinging his split lip and dribbling down his chin.

Hadran got to his feet and walked away to the edge of the small enclosure, waiting until Francys should have finished, and taking advantage of the latter's preoccupation to divest himself of his own clothing. Then, as Francys sat exhausted, shivering despite the hot sun, he returned, grasped him by the arms from behind and dragged him well clear of the stinking mess of vomit onto clean grass, where he dumped him down ungently. Wide hazel eyes stared up at him.

'No!' his brother whispered despairingly. 'You cannot do this.'

But Hadran merely smiled and got down onto his knees, reaching out his hands.

With a last desperate effort, Francys rolled to the side, but he could not escape. Hadran hauled him back and cuffed him savagely until he had not the energy to fight back. Urgent, covetous hands fondled his protesting body and Francys, his head swimming dizzily and ringing from the blows which Hadran had administered, and with the foul smell of his own vomit turning his stomach, was unable to withstand them. He was reduced to the sole, futile, gesture of turning his face away from Hadran's moist, lascivious mouth. The scent of his brother's lusting, sweaty flesh filled him with revulsion and it was with a faint feeling of gratitude that he surrendered to the welcome embrace of insensibility, conscious at the last moment of being turned onto his front and the weight of his brother bearing down upon him.

He never knew all that was done to him at that time, nor did he want to. His mind recoiled from the horror of what little memory he did retain, brought back time and again from merciful unconsciousness to unwished awareness, moaning, whimpering, even screaming, only to drift off once more into darkness and stupor. Eventually he was roused from his swooning state by a searing pain in his left shoulder, his whole body jerking with the shock of it. Hadran, tiring of his carnal amusement and clothed once more, had ordered, and supervised, the branding of his own initials into his brother's sensitive flesh. A stench of burnt skin hung over the small enclosure, and the wound throbbed unmercifully.

To Francys' inexpressible relief, this proved to be Hadran's final act for that evening. After directing the two men who had administered the brand to dress Francys again, Hadran retired to his well-appointed tent, where a substantial supper awaited his attention. Francys, tied to a strong post in another part of the camp-site, to which he had had to be carried, being unable to walk, with a thick anchoring rope about his waist, like a dog, huddled in a heap at its foot, half-delirious with pain and shuddering uncontrollably with disgust, feverish, and trying desperately not to think.

****

The following morning dawned clear and sunny. After a few hours, by mid-morning, the heat had already become unbearable, and the sun continued to blaze down relentlessly for the remainder of the day. Francys sat, back to his pole, considering his position. At least, it seemed, he was not to starve. An ungracious soldier had arrived around the eighth hour and, without a word, had dumped in front of him a dirty mug of ale and a hunk of coarse bread. At noon he had appeared again, this time with a bowl of stew that Francys, despite having been roused to mouth-watering hunger by the scent of its cooking, was unable to get down. Apart from those brief visits, he was left strictly alone, although he could see men moving about the camp-site.

The wound in his shoulder was oozing lymph and had begun to swell ominously. Sweat ran stickily beneath his clothes, collecting around his waist where the thick rope pressed his shirt against his skin, and he was conscious of an urgent desire to wash himself clean of all traces of Hadran's activities. Every part of his body ached, or so it seemed to him, as a result of the outrages to which he had been subjected, and at some point during the day he was sick again in reaction. An attempt to rid himself of the ropes which bound him resulted only in an attack of giddiness, obliging him to lie down for a while, closing his eyes. His sole protection from the burning rays of the sun was the cloak which had been left beside him, but that was almost useless, merely stifling him for, although it shielded his skin from direct contact with the sun's rays, it did not produce the real shade which he craved. At first, shifting inch by inch, Francys had managed to position himself so that the shadow of the post fell across his head, but this involved constant change of position as the sun moved through the sky and in the end he had given up. His throat was dry and he ached for a few drops of water, but no-one came.

At last the sun arrived in the West and began its daily

disappearance. Cooler, fresher air drifted over the land, gently touching the hot face of the captive and ruffling the fair locks. With it came also the tall, burly figure of his brother, accompanied by a couple of his men. Francys watched them come, his face, with difficulty, empty of all expression, his mind a seething mass of terror. He noted with intense misgiving Hadran's air of pleasurable anticipation and it was all he could do not to cower back at his approach. Then, as Hadran reached him, his insides turned to water and he could not move at all out of sheer paralysing panic.

At a gesture from their Commander, the two men untied the heavy coil of rope from the post and yanked Francys roughly to his feet, where he stood swaying dizzily. On unsteady legs he was led across the camp-site again, between tents and past the horse-lines, acutely conscious at every moment of his brother striding along beside him. The sense of relief which flowed over him when they arrived at one edge of the encampment where the entire complement of soldiers had been gathered into an expectant half-circle about a second wooden post, was so great that his legs very nearly gave way altogether. He had been so sure of his destination, so dreadfully, sickeningly certain.

Still in a daze, he allowed them, without putting up any resistance, to bind him to the post, upright, with his face pressed against its rough wood and his hands stretched painfully above his head. They had pulled his shirt off him and his back was bare. When he was fixed, Hadran sauntered up to him, placing himself to one side of the pole, so that Francys could just catch a glimpse of him. He was smiling again, a smile which made Francys' flesh creep.

'My very dear brother,' Hadran said fondly, unable to keep the delight which Francys' situation afforded him out of his voice. 'Someone, not a vast distance from this place, once said, as I recall, that the death of a traitor should be neither swift nor painless, so you will be happy to learn that yours will most certainly not be either. For you *are* going to die, eventually ... when I've finished with you.'

His tongue unconsciously moistened his lips and Francys, seeing it, could not suppress a shudder.

Hadran's smile grew wider.

'When I've finished with you,' he repeated, dwelling exultantly over every word, 'I intend to see you on your knees begging for mercy, which you will not receive!'

He paused to look at Francys, who said nothing. His silence

seemed to irritate Hadran.

'What? No comment?' he taunted. 'Not even one word from that honey-tongue of yours? Haven't you even one little quotation with which to dazzle us all? And you so famed for your wit! *Such* a disappointment!'

He shook his head sorrowfully. Francys gritted his teeth and turned his face as far as he could away from the big, fair man. His brother laughed and put out a hand to receive his heavy horse-whip from the Captain of the company, to whom he had entrusted it. Running the leather lovingly through his fingers, he walked round to stand behind his captive. In silence, watched by his assembled men, he raised the whip.

At the first touch of the lash Francys gave an audible gasp and shuddered convulsively, at which the spectators uttered an ironic cheer. Hadran smiled. Francys felt the leather thong curl round his shoulders and clutch at his ribs. It stung unmercifully and he bowed his head until he could rest his brow against the wooden pole, eyes closed, biting his lip to prevent himself from uttering a sound. No matter what it cost him, he was determined not to scream, to withhold that pleasure at least from his brother. His arms ached from wrist to shoulder, pulled up so high that they felt as though they had left their sockets, and the binding about his wrists was cruelly tight, restricting the flow of blood to his hands and thus benumbing them. Would that the rest of him could have fared likewise!

The whip cut into his flesh. Drops of blood flew, spattering the grass, and trickled fierily down his back. With every stroke the air, laboriously drawn in, was knocked out of his lungs, hissing through his clenched teeth, sounding preternaturally loud in the deathly quiet that had crept over the scene. It was one of a series of noises repeated over and over with monotonous regularity, and Francys began unconsciously to listen out for each one. There was the swish of the whip slicing through the air, the thud of its landing, the hiss of his breath escaping and, somewhere in the performance, a grunt from his brother. For some time there had been no sound from the spectators and Francys eventually opened his eyes briefly to see whether they were still present, or whether they might perhaps have stolen away. They had not, though had he been able to see them more clearly, he would have observed that they looked as if they wished that the latter course was open to them.

They had gathered, so they believed, to witness the just punishment of a proven criminal, and in the expectation of deriving considerable enjoyment from the spectacle of Francys Coras' discomfiture. The man was, after all, a traitor. He deserved to suffer and there seemed no reason why he should not provide them with a little entertainment as he did so. Only it had not seemed entertaining for very long and they had soon begun to regret their earlier enthusiasm. There was something somehow indecent about the spectacle, something unseemly in the expression of exultation now illuminating the features of Hadran Coras as he sent the heavy whip crashing down again and again onto his own brother's blood-drenched back with all the force of his powerful body, which had quickly deprived them of all desire, or indeed ability, to snigger or sneer, so that they stood mute and unmoving, shocked as men of their experience had no expectation of so being. It was no longer an act of justice that they were watching; it was an exhibition of merciless brutality.

Francys' earlier giddiness had soon returned, with an enhanced potency. His head pounded in a slightly out of step accompaniment to the blows of the whip, and when Hadran paused in his exertions for a few seconds in order to speak, his words seemed to reach Francys from a tremendous distance. It was only with an effort that he managed to grasp their import.

'What a pity that the Lady Nyandu cannot be here to see you now,' his brother observed mockingly. 'She wouldn't have had so very far to come after all, from Caleth Mor. Perhaps I should have sent her an invitation.'

And he laughed at the thought.

'Nyandu is in Caleth Mor'. Crazily the thought reverberated through Francys' pain-dazed brain.

'Oh Sior,' he whispered drearily, his voice too quiet to be heard even by Hadran. He had not the strength for more and shortly afterwards, he fainted, whereat the flogging stopped. For Hadran had no wish to kill his brother, yet.

Flinging down the bloody whip onto the grass, he strode forward to check that the faint was genuine before directing a couple of the men to cut the blood-stained body down. A little procession formed, with Hadran in the van, followed by the two men carrying Francys between them, his fair hair hanging down, streaked at the tips with crimson, drops of blood dripping onto the grass in a macabre trail. Passing through a gap in the assembled company, Hadran set off across the camp-site in the direction of the original wooden post to which he had intended to have his brother secured in the same manner as before. Halfway there, however, an idea suddenly formed in his mind, and he had them instead sling the young man onto a bundle of rags beside one of the wood-piles which dotted the camp. It would not after all be necessary to tie Francys up tonight; in his condition he could not possibly get very far, if anywhere at all. And in the circumstances it would be rather a nice refinement to let him believe himself free of restraint. Hadran smiled to himself as he sought out his Captain and issued certain instructions.

****

To Hadran's cost, he had badly underestimated the desperation of his brother. Francys awoke some time in the night, to the manifold protests of his numbed, bruised and battered body. It was not a pleasant awakening, and for several lengthy minutes he lay motionless, staring up at the stars high above, fighting down nausea and the urge to scream. In his clenched fists the nails dug into his palms and drew blood. He took in great shuddering gulps of air and, eventually screwing up his courage, made a cautious attempt at movement. It was imperative that he should get off his back, either by rolling over or sitting up, if that was possible. A groping hand found the pile of wood and he knew that it was. Clinging desperately to the wood, he endeavoured very carefully to lever himself up into a sitting position. Excruciating moments passed as this manoeuvre was executed, with ultimate success, and there followed a protracted period of recovery. Francys slumped against the wood-pile, face and body running with sweat, trembling from the exertion, breathing fast and audibly and biting already sore lips to stifle his groans. Tears stung his closed lids.

But once he had remained still for a while, he found that the pain was not so bad as it had been when he was lying down since there was no longer any pressure on the wounds. Encouraged, he cautiously raised his head, wincing as the tips of his blond locks brushed his shoulders, and peered into the enveloping darkness. He had already discovered that he was not bound in any way, and presently the faint light of the moon enabled him to make the equally welcome, though puzzling, discovery that he was alone, to all seeming unguarded. An unlooked-for glimmer of hope crept into his mind.

A breeze had sprung up and the shivers which it evoked reminded him that he had no shirt. A tentative hand exploring the rags upon which he had been dumped revealed another welcome fact. Someone had left a shirt, albeit tattered and dirt-encrusted, beside him. To put it on, however, was another matter altogether and it took him a goodly while to bring himself to perform the exercise, since the slightest touch upon either the raw weals which striped his back or the pulsating letters engraved into his shoulder set every nerve of his body aflame, and when at last he steeled himself to pull the crumpled linen down over his chest and back, he promptly blacked out, coming to minutes later to find himself collapsed against the wood-pile, still, mercifully, sitting up. But it was done, and when he had accomplished that, Francys decided that it was time to go.

Unbending stiff and bruised muscles and employing them took longer than he expected, and when he was eventually on his feet, he had to clutch fervently at the neighbouring wood-pile in order not to undo all his labour by falling down again. A fresh wave of dizziness assailed him, and the very idea of leaving the support of the wood-pile seemed at that moment the absolute in absurdity. Gradually, however, the dizzy spell passed and he began to feel a little more confident. Removing his hand from the safety of the wood-pile, not without an inner qualm, he took a timid step forward, and bit back an agonized yell. He halted, swaying unsteadily, two involuntary tears spilling down his cheeks. It was unbearable. It was impossible. But there was no alternative. Grimly gritting his teeth, he drove himself to try again.

He set off, orientating himself as best he could in the darkness, through the camp in search of the horse-lines. It took him a nerve-racking half hour to reach them, though they were no more than a bare hundred yards from his wood-pile, because he could only bear to take four or five steps at a time before halting to recover. Twice he stumbled against the sides of tents and once fell over a guy-rope, causing one occupant of that particular tent to stir and turn over. On his travels he also bumped into a wicker screen, which instantly recalled to his mind the horror of that first evening as a prisoner, causing him to retch, though he was not actually sick. Several times he came close to collapse and was obliged to sit down and rest before he could continue, breathing heavily and painfully. Getting to his feet again was a horrible business.

The glow of a brazier drew him eventually towards the horse-lines and he halted in the shadow of the baggage-wains grouped nearby, staring across through the rows of horses at the bright flames. He had reckoned that, even if there should prove to be no other watch about the encampment, and that would surely be criminally foolish given their proximity to the border with Harres, then at least the horses would be under guard. They were far too valuable to be left unguarded. And indeed they were not. Beside the small fire sat three men playing at cards and getting up at intervals to make a round of the lines; and they were all armed.

Francys sighed. How in the name of Sior was he to steal a horse? Or, to be precise, one particular horse, *his* horse: Melisor. Even Golgoh himself would find it difficult to extract one horse from those lines without attracting the attention of the guards. But it would have to be done. The thought of making a journey on foot was unimaginable. If he could not come by a horse, *his* horse, escape would be impossible, and he could not face another day spent in the camp. It made him shudder even to contemplate the eventuality. One more day in the full sun imagining, remembering, and wondering what new devilment Hadran would devise for his entertainment, and he would very swiftly go out of his mind. It would not take too much; just the strain of waiting for the next assault on top of the pain, both physical and mental, that he was already suffering. So he had to find Melisor. How he would manage to get him away without immediately rousing the whole camp, he did not know, but he would work that out when he came to it, when he had found the horse.

On his knees in the shadow of the wagons, he studied the movements of the men for a long, tense period, trying to judge the amount of time that would be available to him between each inspection. There were three lines of horses tethered beneath a stand of beeches and, with luck and by forcing himself on without any pauses, he might, he had to, manage to examine one before the guard came round again. Of course, there was always the risk that one of the other men, particularly he who faced the lines, might look up and see him, but that was a risk he would have to take, and anyway they seemed comfortably absorbed in their game of cards. It was a nuisance too that the shirt that he wore was white, well whitish. It might give him away in the moonlight. He considered taking it off again, but not for long.

The current round completed, the guard settled down with his companions and a fresh hand was dealt. It was now or never. Francys began to clamber clumsily to his feet, using the side of the nearest wagon as an aid. A stab of cramp shot through one leg, but he could not linger to rid himself of it, merely hoping that it would not slow him disastrously. Then, creeping as silently and as speedily as he could, he began his search, taking pains not to startle the horses into some movement or sound which would attract attention. Two rows were managed in this fashion without detection, and without any luck either, and waiting in the darkness while the watchman made his round, hands clasped over his mouth to prevent any sound escaping him, he hoped desperately that the third essay would yield the sight of that familiar black head.

It did not. Lying face down in the grass between two carts, Francys was close to acknowledging defeat and returning to his bed of rags. Aches and stabs of pain rushed to swamp his senses now that he had no hope to sustain and shield him. The craving for water, forgotten during the ordeal of movement, seized on him with a tight, relentless grip. His parched throat burnt at every shuddering breath that he took and the dampness of the dew on the blades of grass, too faint to assuage his thirst, brushed against his lips and held out a tantalizing promise. Hot tears trickled languidly into the crushed grass, leaving a salty taste behind when they chanced to touch his lips.

Then, slowly, an intense resolve was born in him. He would not give up so easily. Melisor *must* be in the camp somewhere. He had certainly been brought in and, although it was of course possible that Hadran had had him sent off elsewhere, Francys did not think that very likely. He knew his brother too well to suppose that he would deprive himself of the opportunity to gloat over such a prize. He had coveted the stallion for years. So, where then would he have had the horse stabled, if not in the horse-lines? Francys shook his head irritably, and clenched his teeth as the movement caused fresh pain to shoot through his raw shoulders. He needed Melisor. He doubted his ability to manage an unknown mount in his present condition, particularly bare-backed, as would of necessity have to be the case, since the valuable saddles and other equipment were naturally stored under cover, within the tent beside which the guards were seated. But with Melisor there would be no need for a saddle ... he hoped grimly. And besides, he had no wish to leave his beloved stallion to Hadran's tender mercies.

If only he could find him. And he would find him, he resolved purposefully, even if he had to search the whole damned camp-site, though surely that ought not to be necessary. If he put himself in Hadran's place, he should surely be able to divine where Melisor would be. He cudgelled his unwilling brain, forcing back the clouds of pain and giddiness which threatened to overwhelm him. If not in the horse-lines, then ... then there was only one other place where he would be ... and that the very last place that Francys wanted to visit.

Resignedly he waited for the guard to finish another round of inspection and once again got painfully to his feet, setting off this time in search of his brother's quarters. Since he had not observed them on any of his conscious journeys through the camp, he did not bother to retrace his steps towards the wood-pile, but turned instead in a different direction. Stumbling over tufts of grass and expecting at every moment to be heard and caught, he wandered desperately around the camp, every nerve in his body alert and signalling its disapproval. He could not comprehend the apparent lack of watchmen, though he was grateful for their absence. Finally, as the mists of despair were closing in about him, he spotted the circular tent set in the shade of one of the broad-leaved trees which dotted the area, separated from the larger, rougher accommodation of the soldiers.

He stood still for some minutes before he plucked up the courage to go forward. Warily then he crossed the open space, his legs shaking almost uncontrollably with terror as he forced himself to approach the place where his brother lay asleep, and edged round towards the rear of the tent. There, beneath the tree, in a makeshift stable, stood the black stallion alongside Hadran's own mount, which Francys only now realized had been absent from the horse-lines. Overcome, Francys must have murmured something, for Melisor pricked up his ears and uttered a delighted whinny.

For the next few moments all Francys could hear was the racing beat of his heart as he stood paralysed with dread, expecting the arrival of the guards or, worse, his brother. Long minutes passed and no-one stirred. Francys took his courage in both hands and walked across, with what speed he could muster, into the stable, where he was forced to check Melisor's display of affection lest he provoke Hadran's horse into neighing and rousing unwelcome attention, whispering firmly:

'Chente, chente, Melisor.'

Melisor, excellently trained, stood silent as Francys struggled to untie him. He was still wearing his bridle and the only piece of equipment missing was the saddle, perched on a shelf above the hay-rack. Francys, with difficulty, fetched it down and quietly but skilfully slipped it onto the stallion's back, fastening the girth. As an afterthought he investigated the lining in a certain place and found that the knife which he habitually kept concealed there had not been disturbed. He pursed his lips thoughtfully. Even more welcome was the flask of wine, half-full, which he discovered in the saddle-bag. Unstoppering it, he gulped down an appreciable amount. His throat was so dry that the muscles cringed at the touch of the liquid, but he felt a good deal better for it.

All along he had been vaguely worried by the ease with which he was able to wander the camp-site unchallenged, even contemptuous of his brother's slackness in this regard. Now, perhaps due to the effect of the wine clearing his mind, his apprehensions grew stronger, crystallized into definition by the absence of a guard over the stable housing two such valuable mounts. It smelt ominously of trickery. He had the uneasy feeling that all that he had done had been predetermined. Maybe the whinny had not awakened Hadran for the simple reason that Hadran was already awake, watching him delude himself with vain hopes of escape, waiting until he should reach the edge of freedom before stepping in. Maybe those guards by the horse-lines had not seen him merely because they had been ordered to turn a blind eye. Maybe even now they were there, in the shadows, waiting for the right moment to step out and confront him ... And maybe he was mistaken. Maybe, after all, everything was as it appeared to be. Well, there was only one way to find out ...

He backed Melisor out of the shelter, thanking Sior that Hadran's horse was placid of nature, unlikely to kick up a fuss. It was a pity that he had nothing that he could tie over Melisor's hooves to muffle the sound, but he managed at least to tie up the stirrups so that they would not jingle. With bated breath and nerves taut as a bowstring he led the black horse slowly between the tents in the opposite direction to the horse-lines, forgetting his throbbing wounds for a while as he concentrated the whole of his attention upon the task of guiding Melisor safely round barely visible ropes and other obstacles that lay in his path, terrified that someone would wake and hear the rustle of grass.

No-one, however, moved. Incredibly the open, empty plain lay before him, waiting to embrace him into its friendly contours, offering him precious freedom. Francys walked on into the darkness, ready at every moment to hear the shouts of pursuers. He led the horse as far away from the camp as he could bear to walk before he dared to mount him, an action which, after several unsuccessful attempts, he finally managed to perform. Then, clinging to the saddle-bow in order to stay on horseback, he put Melisor into a trot, pointing him eastwards by the stars, and disappeared. Behind him, in the shadows at the edge of the camp, an unseen sentry silently raised his hand in a farewell salute.

And far away in the chamber high in the tower, another silent watcher raised his head and smiled. His man had done his work well. Francys was free again, and surely this time he would have to come to Carakhas. If he had the strength ... The pure, smooth lines of Rycharst's face were twisted by a murderous rage. How dare Hadran imagine that he could lay his hands on the beloved of the Lord of Shadowe with impunity and keep him for his own pleasure! Well, he would pay for that ... surely he would pay ... and dearly.

CHAPTER NINE

Hadran stirred lazily some time after dawn, loath to leave his dream-world in which Nyandu had at last consented to his suit and where, after the betrothal ceremony had taken place, he had had the pleasure of watching, with Nyandu at his side, the slow, exquisitely painful death of his brother. He could still see the lithe, naked body writhing in the agony of its death throes. Then the delights of that body recalled themselves to his drowsing mind - the suppleness of the skin yielding to his touch. Desire flooded through him, urgent and irrepressible, and he shifted in his bed, greedily grasping at a dream figure, until his groping hand met empty mattress and he opened his eyes with a jerk.

Yawning sleepily and relaxing back onto his pillow, he began upon a review of his plans in so far as they concerned his brother. Harking back to his dreams, it now occurred to him that it might not be a very wise move to bring Francys captive to Caleth Mor, as had been his intention, particularly whilst Nyandu remained resident there. She was too tender-hearted to enjoy witnessing the death of even the most blackguardly of traitors; and he had never quite managed to rid himself of the suspicion that she was in love with his damned brother. Besides, there was always the danger that Francys might contrive, somehow, to tell tales about his treatment at Hadran's hands. No ... a better idea would be for Francys to suffer an accident along the way ... for instance, a simulated attempt at escape resulting, unavoidably, in his death ... and to have his body arrive in Caleth Mor. After all, the dead do not talk. And in the meantime ... in the meantime he still had a day or two in which to indulge his desires. He smiled. Francys could yet pleasure him a few times more before he died.

He stretched luxuriously and sat up, swinging his legs off the camp-bed. Dressing quickly, he strode out into the early sunlight. Dew glittered on each individual blade of grass and hung shimmering on the spun cobwebs with almost blinding brightness. The fresh scent of grass mingled with the smell of wood-smoke and baking bread. Hadran yawned, sniffed appreciatively, smiled and strolled round to the rear of his tent to view his new possession.

He stopped in his tracks, mouth agape, eyes staring, for one shocked moment of disbelief. Then, with a furious shout, he reduced the entire camp to instant chaos. Dropping everything, leaving breakfasts to grow cold or to burn unheeded, the men ran up, some in varying stages of dressing, fastening their hose as they came. In stunned silence they listened to the exhortations of their irate lord. Their crass stupidity in allowing such a valuable beast to wander was graphically described. The consequences, should he discover that one or other of those unfortunates to whom had fallen the lot of standing the night-watch had permitted the horse to pass the bounds of the camp-site, were made similarly plain. Finally, he issued a command:

'I want that horse back here within the next couple of hours, or I'll know the reason why! Now, get off your fat buttocks and get searching!'

In an instant, the clearing was emptied of men. Hadran swung round and had begun to walk back towards his tent, when he was struck by a sudden doubt. Perhaps he had had Melisor put into the horse-lines for some reason and had subsequently forgotten about it. He wheeled about and strode in the appropriate direction. On his way thither he came upon the wood-pile behind which, he suddenly recalled, the men had dumped his brother's insensible carcass. Smiling, he peered around the side of the heap of wood. There was no-one there. How strange! He must have been mistaken ... there were other piles of wood dotted about the camp-site. But no, there before his eyes lay the heap of rags onto which Francys had been thrown, rags splattered with the telltale stains of blood. As he pondered, footsteps approached from behind him and a tentative voice addressed him.

'Menellen,' it said miserably. 'The saddle is missing also.'

'The saddle?' thought Hadran, preoccupied with the riddle of Francys' whereabouts. 'Dear Sior! The saddle!'

Something clicked inside his brain. Intense fury flooded him. Choking on his rage, he whirled round and bellowed for his men.

Into their startled ears poured a ferocious torrent of abuse and, like reeds, they bowed before the storm. No-one, it was well-known, could manage Hadran when the rage took him, save his father. Certainly, none of his men was prepared to make the attempt. In sweating silence they listened to the harsh, discordant voice, regarding with wary eyes the flushed and furious face, and passively accepting all responsibility for Francys' escape. No matter that they had been specifically instructed to ignore any movement that Francys Coras might make, to permit him to wander as he pleased; they should have had the wits to realize that such licence would not be extended beyond the confines of the camp. The moment it had become obvious that he was capable of effecting an escape, they should have had the sense to step in to foil the attempt. One would almost have thought that the watch must all have been asleep! That everyone had been drugged into a stupor! Damn it, wasn't it obvious enough that he was to be allowed the *illusion* of freedom merely! He should never have been permitted to remove the horse from the stable, let alone ride it out of the camp! Dear Sior, did they not know who he was? Through their imbecility, they had let slip the most sought-after, treacherous villain in the entire length and breadth of Karled-Dū!... Silently, they agreed to it all.

Having at length exhausted his stock of invective, Hadran barked out a series of commands, despatching all but a mere handful of his company to search the immediate countryside, concentrating in a westward direction, whither he believed his brother to have been bound. Then, to the relief of those left behind in the camp, he retired in a mood of black fury to the shade of his tent, for the sun was already scorching.

'Damn it,' he muttered. 'He can't have got far. Even Francys must have limits.'

During the hours which followed strenuous efforts were made. The threats, hanging ominously over their heads, spurred them on to inspect every ditch, copse, bush, any thing or any place where a man might conceivably conceal himself. In addition, they set on foot exhaustive enquiries amongst the inhabitants of each village or hamlet in the region. Claiming to have heard rumours of spies from Harres being seen in the area, they searched every cottage, hut and barn and questioned anyone they met, frantic for the merest whisper of Francys' passing. But one by one they returned empty-handed, and the tension rose a notch with every such return.

Throughout, Hadran sat in his tent and brooded. The clouds of rage in his mind were beginning to disintegrate and through the rifts trickled the first drops of fear. Encouraged by the certainty that Francys had not long to live, he had allowed his lust free rein. Why should he not indeed? Within a few days Francys would be dead and no-one could possibly ever know what had taken place before his death. Why then should he hold back, when the means of release from his intolerable longing lay there before him? Indeed, once he had seen that body lying naked on the grass before him, it would have taken more self-control than he had ever possessed to have curbed the lust which had lived in him since that ill-fated evening in Lôren, and he had not attempted the feat. For the past two years he had suffered the shaming humiliation of lusting, hopelessly, after his own brother, and the consummation had been an ecstasy beyond belief. The sheer relief of it had blinded him to any sense of guilt. It had simply not occurred to him at the time that there was any cause for self-reproach.

Francys' escape cast a vastly different complexion on the whole affair. It contrived to place Hadran himself in danger. For the first time Hadran began to comprehend the precariousness of his position, and the shape in which his behaviour would appear to the dispassionate gaze of his world. Tendrils of fear wound with suffocating tightness about his quaking mind, and a sick feeling invaded the lower regions of his abdomen. Francys at liberty meant the constant, ever present threat of public exposure. He could never again be safe, for there would always exist the possibility that Francys would one day speak out and bring his world crashing about him. No matter that Francys was imrauten; if he managed merely to spread a rumour, it would be enough to bring Hadran's character into disrepute and ensure his public disgrace. He would be allowed no quarter, that was certain, after all his outspoken censure of his brother's morals and conduct. And what of that stern moralist, his father? What could he expect from *him*? The Lord Telstan Coras had vociferously condemned, furiously and disgustedly, those instances of Francys' 'depraved' tastes which had come to his notice. Francys' behaviour had been a constant source of displeasure and vexation. What then was his reaction like to be to the intelligence that his elder, favoured son had, to put it quite bluntly, brutally raped his own brother?

A cramping surge of panic overwhelmed him as he finally named his crime, and yet he felt no remorse, only a blazing resentment towards the man who had, by reason of his escape, placed him in this present nerve-racking position. Damn Francys! Damn him, damn him, damn him! Hadran was on his feet, pacing to and fro. He should have killed him that first evening. With Francys dead, no-one could ever know! In his passion he bit his lips until they bled. Suppose Francys were even now pouring out his story into some sympathetic ear. The idea so overwhelmed Hadran that his gorge rose and the sour taste of vomit spurted into his mouth.

Fortunately for the peace of mind of his men, mid-way through the afternoon a scout rode into the camp bearing a message that Francys had been traced. An outline of a man's shadow crept into the tent, and Hadran whirled round fiercely. Upon hearing the news, the haunted look vanished, to be replaced by a smile of frightening satisfaction. It seemed that a young boy out fishing early that morning had observed a large, black horse ridden by a man with fair hair. Hadran instantly ordered the camp to be struck and, leaving his Captain to see to the operation, with instructions to proceed directly to Martle, himself set off with a small body of some ten hand-picked riders to join up with the scouts.

Whilst awaiting his arrival, the scouts had managed to uncover further reports of sightings and Hadran, gratified, was able to travel a considerable distance before darkness overtook him. Even then he would have pressed on regardless, had he not been obliged to admit the possibility of straying from the trail, and he settled down instead beside a small brook where they had found crushed and broken reeds with traces of blood; the unmistakable spoor of their quarry.

****

Little though Hadran knew it, Francys had for a few hours been within his grasp. He had travelled just far enough to exchange the open grass plain for the safer maze of fields and lanes before the demands of his battered body overwhelmed him and he collapsed into a ditch, barely having the strength and presence of mind to tether his horse. He made no attempt at concealment, trusting to the cover of night and unaware that, had anyone passed by, he would have been instantly visible. Till dawn he rested there, dozing on and off, moaning from time to time as his injuries made their existence felt.

The sunlight, falling onto his back, roused him from his attempts to sleep and impressed upon him the need to move on. With daylight would come the inevitable discovery of his disappearance and he could not afford to waste the smallest particle of what little advantage he had. Stiffly he staggered to his feet and clambered, with difficulty, into the saddle. The action of moving off evoked an involuntary gasp of anguish, repeated all too often as the day wore on. In an unvarying pattern, Francys rode a few calle, then halted, rode on and halted again in a grim effort to get the better of his weakened state, and each time the moment of departure was worse than the last. The hot sun beat down on his unprotected head and blinded him with its glare. Sweat soaked the shirt and trickled irritatingly down his face and throat. The riding breeches clung clammily to his thighs. Cramp invaded his fingers as unconsciously he tightened his grip on the pommel of the saddle, lest he slip from the horse's back. In his reckless flight he could not hope to evade every inhabitant of Kirkendom and after a while he did not even bother to attempt such a hopeless feat. He was only conscious of a faint feeling of surprise that no-one tried to stop him as he passed.

Nearing the town of Martle late that night, however, he exercised more caution. He crossed the river well above the walled town and came by devious routes to the large farmhouse standing in its own fields some distance southwards of the town. It was his errand here which had brought him so unluckily into Hadran's ambush when otherwise he would by now have been safely back in Kordren.

Hitching Melisor's reins over a fence-post at the side of the yard, Francys slid out of the saddle and landed heavily and wearily, his stiff muscles objecting to the change of movement. He gritted his teeth and walked shakily towards the closed farmhouse door, where he gave a certain whistle. In answer, after a few second's pause, there came the noise of bolts being withdrawn, the door swung back, and the familiar large, well-built figure appeared on the threshold, clad in the conventional smock and leggings of the local farming community. He held up a tabri-oil lamp and examined his visitor with scrupulous care, then a slow smile spread across his features.

'Menellen!' he exclaimed warmly. 'I'm right glad to see you.'

'Well, Artem,' Francys answered with all the vigour he could muster.

He summoned a smile.

'I've come visiting. Could you see to Melisor for me, do you think? Put him in the stable, but don't unsaddle him. I won't be staying long.'

'Surely.'

Artem hastened to perform the service, and Francys stepped into the comforting warmth and light of the principal room in the farmhouse.

A few minutes later Artem returned and shut the door with care. He found that Francys had stretched out his hand and shook it heartily. Francys winced, but merely said:

'How are you keeping Artem? What sort of a harvest have you this year?'

'Good, Menellen, very good. There'll be no fear of famine *this* winter, not in these parts anyhow. Plenty of corn we've got. The hay's in already, and it looks like we'll be having a fine crop of apples for the wine. There'll be fat purses for some. But, Menellen,' he interrupted himself, remembering, 'the messenger came through two nights ago. He waited, but had to go on.'

'I know, Artem,' Francys said wearily, back to the wall. 'I was detained. Still ... he must have left something for me.'

'Aye. I've got it safe here.'

Artem produced a package from inside his shirt.

'I've been sitting up each night in case you'd mistaken the date.'

'Thanks,' Francys said absently, opening the seal on the package.

He skimmed through the information contained therein, a frown on his brow, then looked up as he felt Artem's gaze upon him.

'Yes? What is it?' he asked.

'Menellen, is there something amiss?' Artem asked, his voice roughly anxious. 'You look dreadfully ill.'

'I had a bit of a mishap,' Francys replied, firmly stifling an urge to break down in the face of such welcome sympathy. 'That's why I'm late.'

'Two days late!' thought Artem. 'Some mishap!'

'Perhaps a rest would do you good,' he suggested out loud. 'Why don't you sit down whilst you read, and I'll fetch you a drop to drink.'

Francys smiled and moved unsteadily away from the wall which he had been using for support. He stumbled and gratefully took Artem's proffered arm. As he guided him, Artem suddenly caught sight of Francys' back, and could not suppress an exclamation of horror. The shirt was streaked liberally with blood, nay nearly soaked in it.

'Menellen, you are badly hurt!' he cried.

'No!' Francys said sharply, forbiddingly.

'Your shirt is red,' protested Artem. 'Let me take a look at your back ...'

'No!' Francys snapped shortly. 'No! Leave me alone. It'll heal soon enough.'

'But, Menellen, you cannot travel in this state! It would be madness. Stay here for a few days. Let the wounds start to heal at least ...'

'No!' Francys persisted stubbornly, against all the feverish longing of his weary body. 'I cannot! I came only to collect these papers, and even so I may have brought danger upon you. I'm hunted, Artem. I don't know how much of a lead I have, but if I were to stay here, I'd bring them down upon you for certain. If I go soon, they may pass you by ...'

'It's madness,' Artem repeated. 'You look ready to faint.'

'It's only lack of food,' said Francys wearily.

'Then you'd best stop and eat before you set off again. And while you're eating, I can see to your back,' Artem said firmly. 'I have an excellent ointment ...'

Francys gave a small chuckle, and capitulated, too tired to argue any further.

'Oh very well,' he conceded. 'Damn it, I know you're longing to use it, and I'd appreciate it.'

He allowed Artem to lead him through into a small bedchamber and made no resistance, only wincing and gritting his teeth, as Artem carefully drew off the bloodied shirt. He fortunately did not see Artem's appalled expression as the latter beheld the full extent of the injuries, but suffered himself to be helped onto the narrow, low bed, where he lay face down, his head buried in his arms.

Artem left the room for a few moments, returning with an earthenware pot, clean linen and a basin of warm water. With gentle hands he began to bathe the lacerations, his thick, grey brows drawn together in a forbidding frown as he discovered how far the lash had penetrated into the skin. He chewed his lip thoughtfully, but, with infinite tact, did not attempt to question Francys. The musty, unused scent of the chamber took on a fresher quality as the steam rose slowly from the basin. At Francys' request, Artem fetched his razor and cropped the fair locks, dusty and blood-tipped, which brushed tormentingly against the raw flesh of his shoulders.

As Artem smoothed the cool cream lightly onto the whip-marks, Francys caught his breath and clenched his teeth, stiffening. Gradually, however, the soothing properties of the ointment began to assert themselves and under the comforting influence of the gentle massage Francys relaxed and drifted into sleep. Artem, observing this fact, put aside the bandages he had prepared and laid a clean sheet over the young man. Then, bringing in a stool, he sat and watched and waited. Francys slept for nearly two hours like one drugged. As he finally stirred, Artem rose and went out of the room.

Francys opened his eyes and lay for a minute or two assessing his condition. The sleep, though short, had greatly restored him and the beneficial effects of the ointment were already apparent. His back no longer felt as though it were on fire. The raging headache had almost left him, steadying to a dull murmur. Moving cautiously he sat up and then swung his legs over onto the floor. A mistake. Immediately his muscles set up an indignant protest and he closed his eyes involuntarily.

As he did so, Artem re-entered, bearing a tray upon which reposed a generous bowl of steaming barley broth and a cup of home-made wine. A hunk of fresh-baked bread and a wedge of some local cheese completed the repast. Artem caught the tail-end of Francys' grimace.

'How do you feel now, Menellen?' he enquired solicitously. 'A little refreshed?'

'Infinitely better,' Francys assured him, helping himself to the bowl. 'Your salve is a wonder-worker. What do you put in it? Horse-tail? Yarrow?'

'Those, and others too. It's an old family recipe.'

'Oh, a secret is it?' Francys managed a grin. 'Well I won't pry. Artem, how long have I been asleep?'

'About two hours, Menellen.'

'You should have woken me when you'd finished.'

'I didn't like to; you looked so worn out. But you've a full hour still at least till dawn.'

Francys ate slowly, savouring the taste of the food after his long abstinence. He glanced up under his brows at the stalwart farmer and observed remorsefully:

'You must have lost a deal of well-earned rest on my account if you've been up these last nights. I'm sorry.'

''Tis of no account,' Artem said brusquely. 'You couldn't help it.'

'No ...' murmured Francys, applying himself once more to the broth.

Artem leaned against the wall and surveyed the young man as he sat on the narrow bed, shivering a little in the cool before dawn, his bright Coras hair falling forward over his brow, part concealing the handsome face with its beautifully chiselled features; the young man who had once saved him and his family from death at the hands of a Harres raiding party and whom he had allowed to persuade him into the highly dangerous task of controlling a vast information network. He was so young still - the same age only as Artem's youngest son, Robyn. The slim torso gave him an appearance of fragility which, as Artem well knew, was very misleading. Francys Coras was a dangerous man to make an enemy of, but a good friend ... Artem smiled to himself.

Francys looked up, his fathomless eyes dark against the pallor of his face. Setting the empty bowl down on the tray which Artem had balanced upon the stool, and picking up the cup, he said:

'Come and sit down and talk to me. It's been a while since I was last here. Tell me what life is like round here at the moment.'

The man sighed. He crossed over to Francys and picked up the bandages.

'Let me fasten these,' he said and his fingers busied themselves deftly.

'All is not well,' he divulged after a few seconds in reply to Francys' request. 'Oh, I grant you the harvest is plentiful. We've no complaints on *that* score. It's the atmosphere. Folk are not happy. They're restless, jumpy. You know how it is. A rumour spreads about activity over the border and immediately there's a fear of raids and time is wasted in false alarms, and at harvest time we just can't spare the men. Those damned watchers on the border don't help either,' he added disgustedly. 'Always stirring up alarm they are!'

'You've still the garrison though?'

'Oh, aye, we've that, and much good it is too! Though it's none of *their* fault, I grant them that. They do their best, but it needs to be doubled to be of any real support; it was cut by half after the Krapan treaty, as you'll be aware. A while ago we sent to Caleth Mor asking for reinforcements.'

He snorted.

'We might just have well held our peace for all the good we got of it!'

A wealth of acid scorn poured into his voice.

"The Regent does not consider the town of Martle to stand under any threat of invasion at this time, and cannot therefore justifiably sanction the extra expense which would arise in augmenting the garrison'. He has signed an agreement with Krapan! A piece of paper! Think you that would deter the Chan for even one minute if he saw the prospect of a successful annexation? And in the meantime there is still Harres ...

The trouble is that this land is not *his* land. He has it in charge only till the little Prince comes of age. He'll get no lasting profit from it, so what cares he if the people live in fear and uncertainty ... so long as they maintain their tithes and keep him fed! Sior alone knows what sort of a state we'd be in now if it weren't for the protection *you've* been affording us ... though it's but few, and more's the pity, who know it.'

'Oh...' Francys made a gesture, waiving the compliment.

'It's got so bad recently,' Artem continued, 'that I'm seriously thinking of sending the wife up to her people in Kelethina, though whether she'd be any safer there I do not know.'

Francys seized gratefully upon the fresh topic.

'And how is your wife?' he asked. 'Here am I eating her delicious broth and never asking after her. Is she well? And are her wheat cakes still as tasty?'

'They improve every time she makes them,' Artem assured him, grinning affectionately. 'Aye, Klara's in fine health, Sior be praised.'

He paused momentarily.

'She didn't want to intrude, Menellen, but I know she'd be well pleased to see you, if you wouldn't object ...'

'Object? How could she suppose I'd object! Bring her in at once,' Francys commanded. 'There was no need for her to hide herself away. I had thought her abed.'

Artem smiled and went to the door, returning shortly with a plump, middle-aged woman, her dark hair greying, her friendly face beaming with sincere pleasure. She twisted her work-roughened hands in her hastily resumed dress and bobbed a small curtsey. Francys got to his feet and approached her.

'Nay, you shouldn't curtsey to *me*,' he rebuked her gently and bent to embrace her.

'I must ask you to excuse my appearance. I'm afraid I'm but half-clad and that half isn't so very presentable either.'

He gave a wry smile.

'Artem tells me you're keeping well. How's the elbow?'

'Oh, Menellen,' she said, flustered. 'Fancy you remembering *that*. Artem made me a potion and it hasn't given me a twinge since, Sior be thanked. But what of you, Menellen,' she continued anxiously. 'Artem said you'd been hurt, and indeed I can see that. Won't you stay with us awhile? We'd be most pleased to have you here.'

'And I would love to stay,' he said sincerely, 'but it's impossible. It's too dangerous. Artem knows why. I'm sorry Klara. Even now I've stayed too long and must be on my way.'

He sighed, lines of dejection settling over his face. Then he achieved a passable smile and said lightly:

'Though indeed the thought of your cooking is a sore temptation!'

'Well you shall take some with you,' Klara told him. 'I shall pack you up a bag. It won't take but a minute or two. If you'll just excuse me, Menellen... What a mercy I'd baked yesterday!'

She bustled out, busily deciding what would be most appreciated.

Francys watched her go, smiling. He turned to Artem.

'You'd best have a care for her, Artem. One of these days I shall be tempted into carrying her off to look after me permanently!'

Artem gave a guffaw of laughter.

'Well don't say I haven't warned you!' Francys rallied.

'By the way,' he added, 'Robyn sends his love.'

Artem's face lit up.

'How is the lad?' he asked eagerly.

'In fine fettle. I'm very pleased with him.'

He had a thought.

'I'll tell you what, next time I need a message delivered here, I'll send him along. I don't know when that'll be mind...'

'Menellen.' Artem was overcome. 'Klara will be overjoyed. She misses the lad sorely.'

'As do you, I'll be bound, however much you conceal it.'

'Aye,' Artem confessed ruefully. 'I do miss him.'

A silence fell between them, to be broken by Francys. He was beginning to feel his strength ebbing again and knew that if he did not make an effort soon, he would give way to the irresistible longing to lie down and let the consequences take care of themselves. Accordingly, he drew a deep breath and said decisively:

'I must be on my way now. Artem, would you happen to have an old cloak I might borrow? I need something to conceal these bandages, and my hair,' he added.

'Of course, Menellen. I have just the thing.'

Artem hurried out. Francys returned to the bed and sat down in rather an involuntary hurry, burying his face in his hands. He shivered and yawned uncontrollably. His thoughts, roving free of constraint, settled upon the one topic he had been trying to avoid and a small sound, much like a sob, escaped him.

'Nan,' he whispered desolately. 'Oh Nan ...'

Artem appeared in the doorway and halted, embarrassed. Francys took his hands away and looked up, the mask of anguish transmuting into his usual self-controlled expression.

'Ah, you're back. Is that it? It looks fine.'

'I'm afraid it's rather worn, Menellen.'

'Nonsense. It's just what I need.'

He rose painfully.

'There's a shirt you can have too,' Artem said, producing it. 'It'll be a mite large, but you couldn't wear that tattered thing you brought with you. And a pair of breeches that Robyn left. You're of a size with him. Now, don't argue. You need a fresh pair. You can't go about in clothes that are streaked with blood, not if you're planning *not* to attract attention!'

Francys hesitated for a second, then came across and collected the garments.

'Thank you,' he said.

He struggled out of his breeches and was obliged to accept some assistance in re-clothing himself. The shirt was indeed baggy on him, but in some ways that was better than if it had been close-fitting; cooler for one thing. He wrapped the cloak carefully about himself.

'I took the liberty of bringing Melisor round,' Artem informed him. 'And he's had a good feed, and plenty of water.'

'Thank you,' Francys replied absently.

His fingers fumbled with the clasp of the cloak. Eventually Artem, noticing his efforts, ventured to assist him. They walked out together into the courtyard where Melisor stood waiting patiently. Klara was already there, sad-faced. Francys gave her a warm hug, telling her to cheer up, before crossing to his horse. As they reached Melisor, Artem remembered something.

'Menellen, do you require a knife?'

'I have one,' Francys slid a hand beneath the saddle and produced the sharp blade, which he stuck through his belt. He turned to Artem and held out his hand.

'I don't know how to thank you. You've done so much for me this night ... I shan't ever forget it. I only hope I haven't brought trouble upon you. But if you do find yourselves in any difficulties on this, or any, account, send word to Jeff in Arlmen, and I promise you I'll come.'

His fingers tightened over Artem's for a brief moment. Guided by some impulse, Artem suddenly dropped to one knee in the dirt and pressed his lips to the slim hand.

'No!' said Francys abruptly, withdrawing his hand and raising the older man to his feet. 'You shouldn't kneel to me. It's not right. Don't forget I have no position in society any more. I am imrauten.'

His voice shook slightly.

Turning away, he put his foot in the stirrup and, with difficulty, mounted.

'There's a bag of food behind the saddle,' Artem told him hurriedly, 'and a flask of wine. Also a nose-bag for Melisor.'

Francys looked down at him.

'You think of everything,' he said. 'My thanks, Artem. Sior bless you, and Klara!'

'And you, Menellen, and you!' Artem responded fervently.

Francys smiled, gathered up the reins and turned Melisor to ride out of the yard into the ghost light of the early morning. Artem watched him out of sight, standing in the dimness of the high archway, a grim shadow falling over his features. A footfall signalled the approach of Klara, joining him there. Without speaking, he put an arm around her and continued to stare after Francys. A heavy sigh escaped him. Klara looked up at him.

'He is in danger?' she asked worriedly.

Artem nodded sombrely.

'Grave danger. He told me he was being chased. We shall probably have visitors shortly.'

'They won't find anything.'

'Not if I can help it!'

Artem drew in an unsteady breath.

'You should have seen that lad's back,' he said. 'Scare an inch of untouched skin! He'd been flogged, and cruelly at that!'

'Dear Sior! Whoever'd do such a wicked thing? Did he say?'

'Nay. He wouldn't talk, but I know for all that. It was that bastard of a brother of his; our fine Regent! By Tandar, I wish I had that brute between my hands at this moment,' he said grimly. 'It's a wonder indeed the lad managed to survive, let alone escape! Sior alone knows what will become of him... I didn't want to let him go ...'

He turned and began to walk back to the house, his wife beside him.

****

Once clear of the lane, Francys headed towards the east, rather than the westerly direction which might have been expected. That way would have been madness to attempt. The countryside between Martle and Arlmen would be alive with Hadran's men searching for him and, in case Hadran succeeded in tracing him as far as the town of Martle, as was likely, he had to give the impression that he had merely ridden through, without halting for any purpose.

After an hour in the saddle the soothing influence of Artem's ointment had quite worn off. The coarse cloth of the cloak rubbed incessantly against the shirt and by proxy against the bandages below, and these began to work loose. The sun beat down hotly, forcing him at last to doff the heavy garment despite the danger that he might be recognised, although he hoped that the cropping of his distinctive hair, and the several days' growth of beard, might alleviate the risk. Stabs of shooting fire spread throughout his body, radiating outward from his back, aggravated by the movement of the horse. The headache had re-awakened, tearing the bones apart in his head and pounding at his brain in rhythmic strokes. The thought of the day's travel ahead of him filled him with terror.

Forcing himself on until he reached a stretch of countryside which was but sparsely populated, Francys finally halted, but did not dare descend from horseback lest he find himself unable to remount. Laying his aching head forward onto Melisor's neck, he lost consciousness for a moment or two, coming to again to discover tears streaming down his face - tears of impotence, of weakness and of pain.

A few mouthfuls of wine and wheaten cake put a little more vigour into him and he eventually nerved himself to go on. With a determined effort he blanked his mind to the agony of movement and gritted his teeth to hold back the involuntary cries which pain threatened to force from him. More and more frequently throughout the long day he was obliged to stop and rest, as the level of pain crept up to the limits of his endurance. On one occasion, having been forced to dismount in order to relieve himself, he sank down onto the grass, his body shaken by dry sobs, clasping his hands over his mouth to muffle the moans which he could not longer stifle. Sweat drenched his clothes. Tears poured unheeded. It was one of the hardest moments he had ever experienced when he had to summon the resolve to get up and continue on his journey.

In spite of everything, however, he reached his objective, though his journey took him far longer than normal. Crossing the border into Krapan, he pushed on and came at length to a spot which had served him well on earlier occasions. It was a deep hollow, walled in on three sides by steep banks, with overhanging trees shielding the little valley from any passing gaze. Hitching Melisor's reins to a convenient branch close enough to the stream to permit him to drink, Francys unbuckled the roll of blankets, supplied by Artem, his fingers trembling so much that he could scarcely manage the task. His need to lie down was so overwhelming that he could hardly bear to spend the necessary time unrolling the blankets and spreading out his bed. A feeling of incredible relief filled him as at last he allowed himself to collapse, sprawling face down, burying his face in the rough material with a murmur of contentment. The night flowed over him.

CHAPTER TEN

At about the time that Francys was making his first halt of the day, his brother was waking up. Hadran impatiently ate a hasty breakfast and within a half hour had shepherded his small troop onto the trail again. It was easy work now to follow Francys. He had been seen by too many people and if there were some who declined to give any information to his pursuers, there were enough to lend them aid. The direction of Francys' flight proved a source of puzzlement to Hadran. Recalling that he had mentioned Nyandu's presence in Caleth Mor, he had at first believed that city to be his brother's goal, and he could imagine no reason for the detour to Martle, until he remembered the river.

Reaching the outskirts of the town mid-way through the morning, Hadran encountered difficulties. Francys had evidently been very circumspect in his approach and the darkness under cover of which he had arrived had prevented anyone, it seemed, from seeing him. All respectable inhabitants of Martle had been abed, and those whose nefarious enterprises had taken them abroad at that hour were not to be found. Eventually, in pursuit of his notion with regard to boats, Hadran descended upon the Grunhalle, throwing all the worthy burghers within into panic-stricken confusion, and demanded to know instantly the names and addresses of any citizens in possession of such craft. Then, brushing aside all offers of assistance, he set out to call on each owner personally. Thus, since Artem's fields bordered on the river and he frequently sent grain down to Caleth Mor by barge, Hadran came at length to visit the farmer.

In the narrow lane bordered by high hedges, Hadran spotted hoof-marks which appeared to have been recently made. There were two sets, however, one going towards the farm, one returning. Pricking his horse forward, he hurried his men into the wide cobbled courtyard. There he observed a pile of horse dung still relatively fresh, and a strange excitement seized him. Dismounting and throwing his reins to one of his company, he strode across to the farmhouse and rapped sharply on the closed door with the butt of his whip. For a tense minute or two nothing happened. Hadran shifted impatiently and raised his whip a second time, but before he could knock again, the door opened and he found himself facing a pleasantly plump countrywoman with flour-covered hands.

'Yes, what is it?' she asked.

Her eyes took in the expensive material of his garments, then travelled up to his face with its curiously familiar hazel eyes and frame of extraordinarily fair hair, and she gave a frightened gasp.

'Menellen,' she faltered, dropping a deep curtsey. 'I didn't know. Forgive me. I thought 'twas one of the hands.'

'Is your good man at home?' Hadran enquired brusquely, ignoring the apologetic twitters.

'Yes, Menellen. He's in the stables. Would you want me to fetch him?'

'No need. I am here.'

A deep voice spoke from behind Hadran. The latter swung round to find himself looking into a pair of inimical brown eyes belonging to a well-built man of his own height. The lips beneath the greying beard were pressed tight together.

'You wished to speak with me, Menellen?' Artem enquired in tones quite as brusque as Hadran's own.

He looked past Hadran to his wife and said more mildly:

'I am sure the Regent will excuse you, my dear. You should not leave your stove untended.'

Klara glanced hesitantly at Hadran, who said testily:

'Yes, you may go.'

She bobbed a curtsey and withdrew gratefully to her kitchen.

'To what do we owe this honour, Menellen?' asked Artem, after a pause, unable to keep a faint sneer out of his voice.

Hadran glanced sharply at him, but decided that he must have been mistaken.

'I am hoping that you may be of assistance to me in an important matter,' he explained, as he had so many times already that day.

'Indeed, Menellen?' Artem said politely.

Hadran's eyes narrowed. Damn it, the fellow *was* mocking him. And he had not the courtesy to invite him indoors out of the sun, standing there, legs apart, as though perfectly ready to remain so all day. He bridled.

'I am endeavouring to trace a very dangerous fugitive,' he said coldly. 'From all indications, it seems likely that he may have taken to the river in this area. You are, I understand, the owner of a barge, and it is therefore possible that he might have come this way. Have you seen any strangers here within the last day?'

'No, Menellen,' Artem replied with unimpaired tranquillity, and perfect truth. Francys, after all, was not a stranger. 'And my boat is not here at present. It has gone down to Caleth Mor with grain.'

'When did it leave?' Hadran demanded suspiciously.

'Three days ago, Menellen.'

'Have you proof of that?'

'Menellen!' Artem showed himself offended.

'I have it written in the farm books,' he disclosed grudgingly.

'I wish to see it.'

Shrugging resignedly, Artem led the Regent across the yard to a small room built onto the side of the stable-block, and there unearthed the battered volume. There, in a clear round script, was the notification of so much grain having been sent off by water to Caleth Mor. Hadran glanced at the offending entry and bit his lips with annoyance. Without thanking Artem, he walked outside and stood looking around. When the farmer joined him, he said curtly:

'You must have labourers here. How many, and where are they? I want to see them.'

Artem heaved a sigh.

'Menellen, they are busy with the harvest. It is the busiest time of the year right now.'

Privately, he was considering hastily whether it was at all possible for any one of them to have seen or heard Francys' visit. They all lived at some distance from the farmhouse and none should have been anywhere near the lane at that hour of the night. He could rule out the possibility, he thought, and brought his mind back to what Hadran was saying.

'They are some distance away, Menellen,' he said. 'If you wish them to be fetched, it will take some time.'

'Nevertheless, I wish to speak to them. You will be pleased to send for them, and at once! I haven't time to waste. And in the meantime, we should all appreciate some refreshment.'

He stalked inside through the open door before Artem could make any protest, and seated himself on the settle.

'You may bring mine here,' he announced calmly.

Artem took a deep breath, fighting down his anger.

'Very well, Menellen,' he managed to say, with some semblance of civility.

Retreating to the kitchen, he told Klara to pour out ale and take it through to Hadran and his men, whilst he himself set off to gather up his farmhands.

In the house, Hadran lounged quite at his ease. When Klara brought him the ale, he began to put questions to her, but learnt nothing. She was too nervous to unburden herself of anything more than monosyllables and showed such great concern over the possible burning of her bread that he was obliged to let her go. Draining his tankard, Hadran rose and wandered about the room, inspecting the objects therein, fingering the stoneware jugs on the mantelpiece, then returned to throw himself down on the settle once more and there, where unbeknownst to him his brother had been seated less than twelve hours before, to dream of overtaking that errant brother and having him once more within his power. His men talked amongst themselves, squatting on their haunches in the shade of the stables, discussing in lowered voices their opinions of their commander's obsessive pursuit.

The wooden clogs of the farm-workers clattered across the courtyard and advanced nervously into the oak-beamed living room of the farmhouse. Their owners stood respectfully in a loose semi-circle in front of Hadran, whilst Artem hovered in the background, seizing a moment to exchange a few words with his wife. No, no-one had seen any strangers around the farm. No-one mounted on a black horse? No, they said, shaking their heads regretfully. The only horses they had seen were the pair pulling the hay-wains. What about those hoof-marks in the lane, and the heap of fresh dung in the yard? Well, that they knew nothing about. Hoof-marks in the lane, eh? They had not noticed them. Best to ask the master about that. Though, mind, there were often hoof-marks in the lane. They were sorry they could not be more helpful. All this in broad Kirkendom dialect which was largely unintelligible to Hadran. He was forced to call in one of his men to interpret for him, not liking to trust himself to Artem's translations.

Irritably he dipped a hand into his purse and dispensed to each a bronze coin as they filed past, receiving their expressions of gratitude with impatience. When they had all gone and could be heard departing, deep in discussion, back to their labours, he looked across at Artem, whose glowering eyes he had felt fixed on him throughout the remunerations. He met the man's smouldering gaze with one of his own.

'Well?' he enquired unpleasantly. 'Perhaps we might now have the truth?'

'The truth, Menellen?' Artem feigned bewilderment. 'I have told you the truth, Menellen.'

'The hoof-marks,' said Hadran menacingly. 'I want the truth about those hoof-marks.'

'I suppose they must have been made by the horse of the man who brought me a message,' replied Artem imperturbably. 'I didn't think to mention him as he is no stranger.'

'What message?' growled Hadran.

'About the grain, Menellen.'

'Show it to me!'

'Alas, Menellen,' said Artem regretfully, 'it was a verbal message.'

Hadran rose and approached the man, staring balefully into the brown eyes level with his own. Artem stared back coolly. The tense atmosphere in the room thickened until it became almost a palpable entity as, unseen, the spectre of a fair young man arose to stand between them. To one, he presented a tempting face and the terror of public exposure; to the other, the lingering memory of a bare back dripping with blood, shreds of skin hanging appallingly, flayed by that same whip which tapped irritably against Hadran's riding boot. The silence lengthened, broken only by the breathing of the two men. Then Hadran spoke, very slowly and deliberately.

'I don't believe you,' he said. 'I think you have been lying to me, from the start. You haven't even asked the name of this fugitive, whom I am seeking, or of what like he is. You didn't need to, did you? You already knew his name. And, moreover, I think you know very well where he is. Perhaps he is even now hidden somewhere in this house.

Answer me! Is he here?! Damn you, answer me!' he snarled.

His hands came up as though to grip the farmer by the throat and choke the words out of him, but failed to quite reach him.

'Where is my brother?' he hissed. 'Where have you hidden the bastard?!'

With difficulty, and not without reluctance, Artem managed to resist an impulse to let fly at the coarse face thrust before his eyes, resisted too the impulse to fasten his own strong hands around that thick neck and squeeze it until the hazel eyes bulged, battling against his anger until the muscles in his own neck stood taut.

'I do not know what you mean,' he said at last, stubbornly.

But Hadran flung away from him to the doorway, whence he yelled across to his men.

'I want this house searched, and searched thoroughly!' he commanded.

'Menellen! This is an outrage! I must protest. You have no cause to do this,' Artem blustered, though he had been prepared for just such an outcome.

For appearance's sake, he continued to protest long and loud throughout the subsequent minutes. It was indeed a meticulous search. Each room of the house, each barn and byre, outhouse and stable, was subjected to close examination, lest Hadran should later take it into his head to accuse his men of skimping, and the contents of each turned, literally, upside-down. Every chest or press or box had its contents removed and strewn onto the floor. Blankets on beds were pulled off and the bed-linen inspected for traces of blood. Clothing was unfolded and tossed aside. Each man, upon finishing his allotted portion, reported to Hadran, lolling on the settle and observing with intense attention the expressions of Artem and his wife, who had been summoned from the kitchen once more. Artem had positioned himself beside Klara's chair and held her hand in a comforting clasp, allowing his face to express a suitable degree of apprehension amid the rage at the invasion of his privacy.

Not that all apprehension was feigned. He had spent the remainder of the night following Francys' departure destroying all traces of his visitor, burning the bloody linen in the fireplace under cover of Klara's baking. All evidence of his involvement with the information network had been concealed with practised skill. So far as he could tell, there remained nothing untoward to be discovered in the search, but there was always a possibility, of course, that he might have overlooked something, some tiny scrap of cloth maybe, the minute stain of blood, even a fair hair, that would serve to bring the suspicions simmering in Hadran's mind to boiling point.

At length, to Hadran's profound disgust, the farmhouse and its outbuildings were pronounced free of any trace of incriminating material, and however greatly he suspected the farmer of some involvement with his errant brother, he could no longer delay his empty-handed departure. He had taken the matter as far as he could, and the man was, after all, an influential member of local society, talked of with respect. He must be wary of pushing him too far, else he might find the whole of the neighbourhood ranged against him. But on the threshold he halted and glanced back towards the couple, seated together amid the chaos wrought upon their cherished possessions, hand in hand.

'Don't think you've heard the last of this!' he snarled menacingly, and strode outside.

As he turned away, Artem could no longer control himself and leapt up, but Klara gripped his hand and he did not go any further. She released him only when they had heard the sound of horses clattering out of the courtyard. Then, slowly and sadly, they began to put the house to rights, and in doing so they found one curious addition. Artem smoothed the crumpled slip of parchment and frowned in puzzlement over the brief scrawl thereon.

'Sior protect the Lord Imraut. His cause is mine.'

****

Hadran rode enveloped in fury. He had wasted time. However suspicious he might be, there had been nothing substantial found at the farm, and he was no further forward in his pursuit. Indeed, he was now behindhand, having lost the impetus. Shifting irritably in the saddle, he cursed at the heat and sweated profusely. The landscape appeared to quiver before his gaze, as if afflicted by some mad palsy. Dust mingled with the sweat, coating both horses and men with a fine powder of a reddish hue, from the underlying sandstone. Harsh, glaring light struck up from the roadway, and bounced off the stone-slabbed streets and houses of the town. Hunger grabbed at Hadran's gut, intensified upon his journey through the crowded, noisy quarter of the bazaars by appetizing scents which wafted across his path, and he came to a decision, turning into the court yard of the most imposing of the hostelries which the town possessed.

Munching his way through a succulent pot-roasted heath-hen, originally destined for another customer, washed down with a flagon of rich, crimson wine, he considered his plans and began to make his dispositions. Speed being of the essence, he would despatch the greater part of his company back to Caleth Mor, with the heavy baggage-wains, there to mount an unobtrusive watch and to prosecute enquiries throughout the surrounding villages and hamlets, whilst he himself continued the pursuit with a smaller, faster body, unencumbered by unnecessary equipment. He had managed to find one person who could give him news of Francys' progress - an early riser who had glimpsed the big, black horse on its way to the eastern bridge.

With this in mind, the two parties set off from different gates. Hadran was anxious to make up the time lost in his fruitless enquiries, but upon this side of the river he encountered equal, if not more, difficulty in finding traces of his quarry. Although the countryside immediately to the east of Martle was thickly dotted with farmsteads, the further East he travelled, the wilder grew the region and the population decreased proportionately. Arable land gave way to pasture, and that in turn to scrubland, fit only for the grazing of sheep and goats, as the land rose gradually into the outreaches of the Marte Sen and the border with Krapan. Hadran's brows twitched together more and more often as the trail led him ever eastwards. In the distance he could now see the gorse-covered, heather-purple, tree-dotted moorland which Kirkendom shared with its oft troublesome neighbour. Was his brother out upon the vast expanse? The answer was not vouchsafed to him that day, for night caught up with the small band of riders and forced a halt beside a stand of gnarled oaks and twisty cayren.

****

Francys stirred a couple of hours before dawn, waking with a groan. Making use of convenient branches, he wriggled stiffly out of his blankets and crossed painfully to the clear stream, where he knelt and splashed water over his face and shoulders. Despite the days of burning heat, the water was icy and took his breath away, but its very coldness was invigorating and aided the process of awakening. He clambered to his feet and walked across to where he had tethered Melisor. Droplets of water clung to his hair, but he paid them no attention. Exploring the saddle-bag dumped carelessly beside the tree, he extracted a hunk of wholesome pie and a slab of journey-cake, made with honey for energy, provided by Klara. Standing, leaning against the straight, smooth trunk of a birch tree, he ate greedily, absentmindedly stroking Melisor's inquisitive nose, which turned towards him. Then, having saved a portion of the cake, he offered it to the delighted horse, and patted him, smiling.

It was tempting to stay in the quiet hollow and hope that his presence would be overlooked, but Francys dared not risk it. Eventually, regretfully, he set about rolling up his bedding and fastening it onto Melisor's back, behind the saddle. Stretching was a torture to him, cracking the newly-formed scabs and setting off slow, aggravating trickles of blood. However, apart from that discomfort, the night's sleep, the longest he had had since his capture, seemed to have restored him considerably, finally banishing the throbbing ache in his head. Having filled the now-empty flask with water from the stream, he summoned the resolve to climb into the saddle and begin the long day's journey, hoping to profit from the cooler hours of the early morning.

In the half-light which precedes the dawn, the trees and squat bushes glimmered greyly, like phantoms. A breathless stillness hung over the moor, broken only by the rhythmic hoofbeats of the black horse, galloping through the gloom. Colour had been washed out of this eerie world, faded to tints of grey and black. Francys recalled the description of Verindel's journey through the spirit realm, so similar to this ghostly ride that he felt that he would not be greatly surprised to encounter the messenger in black out upon the wild moorland. Indeed, after a while, he was inclined to feel that he would even welcome the sight. The uncanny quiet beat oppressively on his nerves, and it was with a kind of grateful relief that he heard the screech of a late owl returning to its roost.

Over in the East a thin line of pale sky peeped on the horizon, merging imperceptibly into the deeper blue of the night and gradually drifting westwards. The morning star shone out brightly in contrast to the quiet fading of its fellows. From a hidden perch a lone liquid note resounded, then, after a pause, rang out a second time. It was answered by a trill which began on a low note and ran quickly up the scale, finishing off with a roguish chirp. A third voice took up the song and, as the dawn stole softly over the hills, so the volume of sound increased until it echoed and vibrated in one great chord as the first finger of sunlight pointed across the heavens.

A red glow heralded the awakening of the sun, an intense red-pink, altering gradually to orange-red like a vast fire, and in its midst the white-hot ball climbed over the horizon and mounted the pathways of the sky. Francys could not forbear to pause a while to stare in awe. A band of Krapani warriors, riding out on a raid, saw his lone figure outlined against the crimson radiance, and, believing him to be the incarnation of Trechos, their god of war, took it for a sign that Fortune rode with them. For Francys himself, the sign was more ominous, a warning of storms to come, and he was in no state to cope with inclement weather, especially on the open moor. He increased his pace apprehensively.

****

Even Hadran gazed upon the sunrise with wonder. His men, superstitious, read in it a message from the spirits, or even from Sior himself, that their pursuit of Francys Coras was resented. They crossed their fingers, spat on the ground or recited rhymes to ward off the wrath of the other world, muttering uneasily to one another, afraid of the consequences if they continued, yet unable to bring themselves to suggest to their commander that the chase be discontinued. Gloomily they ate their morning repast, cross-legged on the ground, and gloomily they readied themselves for departure. They reached the border an hour later, halting at the stone markers. Hadran looked at them and slowly smiled. Francys had gone to Krapan. He had taken refuge in hostile country.

A shout roused Hadran from his reverie. One of his men, riding around the edge of a tall clump of thick gorse bushes and shrub, had spotted movement on the heath land beyond. A small body of cavalry was approaching, he informed his commander. Alarmed, Hadran rode forward to take a look himself. Sure enough, he saw them, about a couple of dozen in number perhaps, advancing at a smart pace, business-like. The thought flitted through his mind that Francys had trapped him, and a cold anger filled him. He withdrew out of sight and considered. To retreat now, before they were seen, was a possible course of action, but could lead to their being overtaken and forced to fight perhaps in a difficult spot. On the other hand, they could themselves take the offensive. The riders were still a fair distance away. There would be time to prepare a passable ambush ... His eyes ranged the immediate area. There was plenty of cover and they had brought bows with them and arrows aplenty. He fingered his knife hilt absently. If Francys should be among those riders ... Reaching a decision, he began to bark out orders, deploying his men in the surrounding bushes, organizing the concealment of their horses behind a screen of birch and gorse. The men settled into position, unstrapping their light bows and bending them in readiness.

The Krapani riders approached the frontier without troubling to conceal their movements, for the area was lonely and uninhabited. As they drew closer, Hadran was able to see that they were well-armed, despite the lack of visible armour and protective headgear. This was no disorganized band of outlaws seizing an opportune moment, but a well-ordered, trained raiding-party. Hadran burned with fury at the sight. How, in the name of Sior, had his brother managed to raise such men? There was a price on Francys' head in Krapan nearly equalling that which had been offered by the Dukrugvola. The Chan was reportedly vociferous in his detestation of the young man and could not bear even the mention of his name, if rumour was to be believed, for he could never forget, or forgive, the humiliation of being forced to kneel in submission before him at the Court of Rycharst, in full view of the many visitors from foreign lands.

As the horsemen passed between the stones and came within bowshot, Hadran, scanning their ranks carefully for a glimpse of that fair head, gave the signal. A volley of arrows sped forth from one side of the track, throwing the horsemen into instant confusion. Voices were raised in violent imprecations. A shrill whinnying filled the air, evoking a response from the concealed mounts of Hadran's party. A couple of the raiders had fallen amongst the plunging hooves. Several others seized their own bows, and the whole group was forming itself into a tightly-packed circle when the second shower fell, from the opposite direction. Within a few seconds a further barrage followed, from the original source. Hadran's suspicions concerning the provenance of the horsemen were validated by the discovery that they were evidently wearing some form of body-armour beneath their outer garments. Even the leather of their caps, it seemed, concealed a tougher substance. Nevertheless, after the third flight of arrows had taken its toll, there were some seven men down amongst the trampling hooves, three dead and the others wounded in arm or leg. Two of their mounts had also fallen, and a couple more were disappearing down the track towards their native country.

The remaining Krapani raiders began to send stray arrows towards those bushes where they believed their attackers to be hidden. One found a mark. A groan and a crashing of branches told of the death of one of Hadran's men, and stimulated the besieged riders to further efforts. Hadran swore under his breath.

'Shoot the horses!' he ordered furiously, and ducked hastily to one side as a shaft flew with alarming accuracy straight towards his hiding-place. Sent by Francys? Hadran cursed himself for having betrayed his position. However, his men responded enthusiastically, and succeeded in unhorsing five more of the raiders. In the resulting confusion, and upon a further signal, they arose from concealment and advanced upon the raiders, long knives catching the sunlight, blindingly. In the hand-to-hand conflict which followed, Hadran fought vigorously, always seeking, searching for his brother amongst the fray.

The fierce attack discouraged the Krapani, uncertain as they were of the numbers of their unexpected assailants, and it was not long before those who were still mounted, broke ranks in disorderly retreat, leaving their less fortunate companions to extricate themselves as best they might. In the event, five prisoners were taken. Hadran attempted to question them, fiercely and eagerly, as to their possible involvement with his brother, but got little from them, save for apparently genuine protestations of outrage at the mention of the name, though he did make the interesting discovery that one of his prisoners was none other than the son of the Chan's Chief Minister. Eventually he was forced to give up the attempt, and bend his mind instead to the problem of disposing of the dead, both men and beasts, convinced that Francys was, for the present at least, out of his reach.

****

He would have been exceedingly galled to learn that Francys had merely ridden southwards over the moor and re-entered the principality of Kirkendom some ten calle or so from the point at which he had left it. It was now the third day since he had escaped, but his wounds showed no signs of healing, breaking out afresh from the constant movement. The bandages had long since come adrift and, after a vain attempt to re-fasten them, Francys had jettisoned them, thrusting the bloody cloth into an old rabbit burrow. He still retained his shirt, but with each hour that passed this soaked up ever more blood and sweat and in the hot sun it had begun to stink. The sweet, sickly smell of blood threatened at times to turn his stomach. At the shoulder the shirt stuck fast to the lymph oozing from the brand, and the back was more red and brown than white. But it kept the rougher material of the cloak off his raw skin and for this reason Francys continued to wear it. Now, too, he had the beginnings of a beard, pale against the brown of his skin. Once, when he stopped at a stream, to satisfy his craving for water, he saw his reflection, ragged, dirty and unshaven, with dark-ringed eyes large in his gaunt face.

The need for water was an irritant. He seemed to be constantly thirsty, his throat parched, and this forced him to descend from Melisor's back oftener than he would otherwise have chosen to do. The pain was another problem, exacerbated by the movement of the horse. A permanent furrow lay across his brow, and his jaw muscles ached with the strain of withholding almost irrepressible groans. It was only the horrific thoughts of what might befall him should he be caught which gave him the energy and the willpower to go on, and he fought a losing battle with the insidious weakness which worked gradually to overwhelm him.

That third night, whilst Hadran stayed in some comfort at the home of a flattered tenant farmer, Francys slept in an unmown hayfield beside a thicket of tallus trees. Here, the bad weather predicted by the burning sunrise finally caught up with him. During the night black clouds gathered with unnatural speed. The air became stifling and still, setting nerves on edge. Then, with a jagged gash of light, which momentarily illuminated the countryside, the thunderstorm declared itself. Searing rain-drops plummeted with ever-increasing velocity and the ground vibrated to the crash of thunder. Somewhere a great, old oak flared in the darkness, at the touch of a fiery finger from the sky.

Francys, awakened by the touch of the first rain-drops, had hastily moved himself and his bedding to the shelter of the thicket, huddling beneath the densest mass of branches that he could find. The shelter proved insufficient, however, and within a quarter of an hour he was soaked through, shivering violently. The lightning split the clouds, touching the tree-tops with a brief caress, dancing over the fields, pursued by the eager thunder which, try as it might, could never quite catch up. Heavy rain drummed on the hard-baked mud. There was a kind of wild, awesome splendour about the storm, a splendour which no mortal could ever capture.

Then, of a sudden, came a flash of exceptional brilliance, followed on the instant by a deafening boom. Melisor, already nervous, reared and kicked out in frantic panic. A tree crashing down nearby caused him to give a convulsive jerk, finally freeing his reins, and, sensing the lack of restraint, he dashed headlong into the night, blind with fear. Francys was too numb and too exhausted even to notice his loss. Under the hammering onslaught of the rain, he had sunk into a state of lethargy. Unable to summon the energy to seek better shelter, he lay wrapped in his cloak and sodden blankets, shielding his face from the battery.

Eventually the rain ceased and the thunder passed over. Dawn found Francys sleeping in spite of his wet clothes. The warmth of the risen sun woke him and he stirred stiffly. In the field the long grass lay flat, beaten down by the rain. The air was clear and fresh, no longer oppressive. Raindrops sparkled and glittered on twigs and the edges of grass-blades and every where looked newly-washed. The heavy scent of damp earth pervaded the atmosphere. Rousing himself with an effort, Francys made his way to the clearing where he had left Melisor, and stopped short in disbelief. The horse was gone!

For a long moment he stood still, staring unbelievingly at the empty spot, then commenced a desperate search. He called as loudly as he dared and expended a good deal of energy combing the immediate area, to no avail. Melisor had vanished.

Returning to the thicket, he sank down despondently, burying his head in his hands. With Melisor gone he had no means of transport, and since he had not taken the precaution of unsaddling the horse, he had no food or drink either, only a roll of soaking bedding and the clothes on his back. His situation seemed entirely without hope, stranded some hundred and sixty calle from base and forty calle at the least from the nearest place where he knew he could find aid. In an access of despair he cast himself down on the ground, bitter tears mingling with the mud and grass. To have come thus far only to have to let himself be hunted down...

He lay there for a long while, shivering despite the sun, barely conscious, uncaring in the depths of his despondency. Yet, gradually, he became aware of a slowly strengthening determination taking possession of his mind. To have managed to come thus far was a feat worthy of a better conclusion than this. And the thought of what Hadran might do to him should he fall into his groping hands a second time was still as horrifying as ever, and spurred him to clamber to his feet with a sudden hardening of resolve. He would not stay to submit himself to *that*. As long as he had strength, he would struggle on, and if he died from it, as he seemed like to do, then at least he would be free from Hadran's torments.

Gritting his teeth to stop them chattering, he made his scanty preparations. The blankets he discarded, not without regret, unable to carry such a weight and, breaking off a suitable length of wood to use as a staff, he climbed wearily into the lane.

The storm had proved beneficial in one way. The sun was not as scorching as it had been, and a light breeze was blowing fitfully. At first the labour of walking proved less painful than that of riding, employing different muscles, and Francys' spirits rose slightly. He found also that he was less noticeable on foot, an advantage in these fairly densely populated parts where the roads were busy with carts and pedestrians. Other travellers tended to avoid him, repelled by his dirty, bedraggled appearance and the rank odours which emanated from him, and by the flies which swarmed around him, attracted by the festering wounds. The heat caused his feet to swell and his boots, designed for riding rather than walking any great distance, became extremely uncomfortable. The only food that he had managed to obtain was fruit stolen from orchards beside the road, and the end of a stale loaf which he had come across in the dust at the roadside. Yet, despite all this, he was amazed to find that, by nightfall, he had almost reached the river, plodding mindlessly on, intent only upon keeping going until the increasing weakness of his legs forced him to seek shelter to recover.

He crossed the river early the next morning, slipping across the stone bridge with its double arch. All day he continued his journey, though the drain on his strength due to the constant battle against pain and increasing sickness manifested itself ever more plainly, limiting the distance that he was able to walk between the ever more frequent halts. His mode of progression was erratic. He stumbled along, weaving uncontrollably and drunkenly, panting with the effort. Blood trickled down his chin from bitten lips, and his sight was often obscured by involuntary tears. He had lost all ability to think coherently. He no longer remembered the reason for his journey, only that he must keep on walking, that it was vital that he should continue.

The night that followed was the worst yet. For a long time the pain would not allow him the ease of sleep, even so desperately weary as he was. His mind cleared sufficiently for him to recall the reason for his flight, but the thought of getting up the next morning was more than he could face. No-one could be expected to endure what he had and deliberately court more pain, more agony. His hand strayed to the hilt of his knife. He had the means. Why should he not take the quick way out? He was bound to die anyway. Why should it not be now, swiftly and painlessly, instead of the slow, lingering, agonizing death which faced him? Dear Sior, he had tried to kill himself before, had almost succeeded! Why now, when death was certain, did he cling to life so greedily? Why was he so reluctant to grasp the opportunity of a quick release? What a fool he was! One half of him longed for an end to it all, whilst the other half was filled with a grim, obstinate determination to live, to spite his brother who wanted him dead. He lay and argued with himself, striving desperately to gather the necessary resolve, until he slid into feverish and restless slumber, the knife remaining undrawn.

CHAPTER ELEVEN

On the morning of the sixth day following Francys' escape, Nyandu peered out of the window of her bedchamber in the fortress at Caleth Mor. Below her in the courtyard men were loading baggage onto a waggon, her baggage. The horses of her escort stood ready nearby. It was time to leave. In more ways than one, she thought with a wry smile. She had travelled the Province and seen all that she had intended. Her inspections had shown up not a few points which she thought would interest her uncle considerably. In addition, she had extended her skills as a healer liberally to those who had sought her out during her perambulation of the countryside. As for her secret agenda, she had certainly garnered a wealth of information with which to enlighten the Dukrugvola on her return, though whether it could be said to be conclusive remained to be seen. She had hopes of learning more when she journeyed northwards beyond Arlmen and into the border regions of Arlente. And, most happily of all, she had managed to avoid meeting Hadran, so far, although he was, report had it, currently on his way towards the city. Nyandu smiled to herself. Definitely it was time to leave.

Descending thoughtfully, she sought out her hostess, the Lady Annis, aunt and guardian to the heir of Kirkendom during his minority, whom she found in the hallway discussing some matter with her steward. As Nyandu left the stairs to approach her, a boy detached himself from a neighbouring doorway and rushed at her, saying breathlessly:

' Lady Nan, Lady Nan, is it true that you're leaving?'

He skidded to a halt in front of her and looked up anxiously, his straight brown fringe tumbled over his forehead, his heart-shaped face expressing trepidation.

'Do say it's not!'

Nyandu smiled down at him apologetically.

'I'm afraid it is, my love.'

The boy's face fell.

'Can you not stay longer?' he asked.

'I'm afraid not, Morla. I have to return to Lôren.'

'Can't I come with you? You said I could come and stay with you.

Can't I come now?'

'Not this time.'

Nyandu put an arm around the thin shoulders.

'Listen Morla. I have some tasks to do at this time, which means that I shall not be going straight home. But when I am back in Silmendu, I shall write to your aunt and invite you both. I promise you.'

She hugged him.

'Don't look so downcast. It shouldn't be more than a couple of months, and then you can learn to row and sail. You'll enjoy that. And you've never seen the sea... It'll be an experience for you ...'

She straightened up.

'Come now. I must bid your aunt good-bye.'

Morla remained still, blocking her path. Staring up at her intently, he said fiercely:

'I don't want you to go! I won't let you go! You're the only person who ever plays with me. You can't just go and leave me! I won't let you!'

'Morla, love, I have to go,' Nyandu explained mildly. 'There are things that I must do.'

'Then let me come with you, Lady Nan,' the boy pleaded, his brown eyes earnestly entreating. 'I won't be any trouble, honestly I won't. Oh, please, take me with you.'

'It wouldn't be practical,' she said gently. 'But you'll be able to come in a month's time. One month isn't so long ...'

'But you'll forget! Everyone always forgets about me! Please let me come with you, *please*. If you won't, I'll ... I'll run away,' he finished defiantly.

'You wouldn't do such a thing,' Nyandu countered, laughing a little.

'I would too!' he asserted.

'Where would you run to? And whatever would your aunt say? You wouldn't want to upset her so, would you?'

He fixed his eyes upon her face, unexpectedly serious.

'I'd go and join Menel Imraut,' he said solemnly, pronouncing the name lovingly. 'And Aunt wouldn't care,' he added. 'She probably wouldn't even notice I wasn't here unless Matty told her.'

This was so true that Nyandu was momentarily at a loss for words. The Lady Annis was exceedingly absentminded, especially where

Morla was concerned, consigning the boy to the company of tutors and servants. However ...

'She's very fond of you,' she said.

'She doesn't even try to understand,' he wailed desperately, tears standing in his wide eyes. 'I can't stay here ...I can't ... not if *he's* coming ...'

'He?'

'Menel Hadran Coras.'

A sudden babble of words came tumbling from his lips, revealingly.

'He's coming soon. Everyone says so, and his men are here, so he must be. I ... I don't want to see him. He frightens me. He says things and shouts at me, and makes me cry. And then he shouts even more. And Aunt doesn't even notice. She lets him do what he wants because he's the Regent. But he's *not* my guardian, even if he acts as if he is. He tells her what I am to do and she won't say no, so I have to do what he says, and I don't like him and ... Please! Take me with you! He scares me so.'

He was crying in earnest now, clearly terrified.

Nyandu looked down at the lonely little boy, and came to a decision. After all, who was she to talk, having planned her visit for a time when she could reckon on Hadran's absence, and her departure precisely at this moment because his arrival was expected.

'Very well,' she said. 'I'll speak to your aunt. If she agrees, you may come.'

He caught his breath on a sob and looked up, his face instantly transformed.

'Truly?' he breathed. 'Truly, Lady Nan?'

'Truly,' she assured him gravely. 'Now go and dry your eyes and let me have a word with your aunt.'

She gave him a gentle push and he obediently ran off, every movement showing his delight. Nyandu gazed after him and hoped she would not be obliged to disappoint him after all. Sighing, she smoothed her skirts and walked the length of the hallway towards the Lady Annis.

She was obliged to use considerable powers of persuasion, even tendering an invitation to the Lady Annis, which was declined, and explaining at some length that she would be making a stay of some couple of weeks or so in and around Arlmen, where she had business to transact. Finally, having waded patiently through all the objections and disposed of the Lady Annis' doubts as to the Lord Regent's wishes in the matter (by saying simply that he had no authority), Nyandu was at last successful in procuring her consent to the boy's departure. His old nurse, Matty, was summoned and told to pack for him and a message was conveyed to the stables requesting the immediate saddling of his pony. Morla, forcibly detained and made to change his tunic and leggings, ran excitedly hither and thither, getting under everyone's feet and chattering to anyone who would listen, more animated than he had been for many months. He visited all his particular friends amongst the servants and, lastly, his nurse, who embraced him tearfully and impressed upon him plenty of advice, which she afterwards repeated to Nyandu.

It was rather later than she had intended, therefore, when Nyandu, and Morla, together with her escort turned onto the highway beside the Armenet. Nyandu had hoped to reach a particular inn by nightfall, but she was not sure whether this would now be possible, with Morla of the party. She turned her gaze towards the boy, who had ridden forward to chat to Thadie, her Captain, an elderly soldier who had taught her to ride. She smiled. No doubt he would inveigle Thadie into telling stories of campaigns and battles. He looked so much happier already that she was glad that he had persuaded her to allow him to come. He needed affection and companionship. Poor little boy. Eight years old, and Prince of Kirkendom for six of those years, and orphaned. His mother had died in child-birth, the child still-born, but a month after the news of his father's untimely death, at the age of two and thirty, from a fever contracted on the battlefield. She could remember him vaguely: a shrewd, clever man, greatly missed and long mourned, with hair and eyes of like hue to those of Morla. The little boy had been placed in the care of his mother's elder, unwed sister, who was only too pleased to take on the task and who had, despite her absentmindedness, tried to do her best by the child. He had had toys aplenty, servants to pander to his every whim ... but no friends of his own age; a lonely existence.

Nyandu reflected that no-one seeing Morla now, could possibly believe him to be the same as that sullen, withdrawn creature who had so reluctantly suffered her presence during the first days of her sojourn in Caleth Mor; though to be sure, he had had his reasons. She recalled the scene when she had at last managed to corner him. Her friendly overtures had met with no response and finally, growing annoyed, she had turned away, saying coldly:

'Your father would be much grieved if he could see you now, so sullen and uncivil. I met him once, and he was one of the most courteous men in the whole land. He would never have treated a guest of his in such a way ...'

She was not prepared for his reaction. Like a whirlwind, he moved and was between her and the door.

'I hate you!' he burst out passionately. 'You're going to marry *him,* and I hate you!'

Nyandu was taken aback.

'But ... your father's dead,' she said in bewilderment.

'Not my *father*. The Regent,' he clarified angrily. 'Menel Hadran Coras.'

She frowned.

'Who told you that?'

'Everyone says so. That's why you're here.'

'Well, everyone is wrong,' Nyandu said crisply. 'I am not betrothed to Menel Hadran Coras, nor will I ever be!'

She had quite startled herself with the vehemence of her denial. For a few seconds, the boy stared up at her, unmoving. Then he lowered his head, abashed.

'I'm sorry, Menaïren ,' he mumbled in a low voice. 'I apologize for being rude.'

'It is no matter,' she said, smiling and holding out a hand. 'Well? Now that you know the truth, shall we cry truce and be friends?'

He looked up then and, in a sudden rush, came to her, slipping his thin little hand confidingly into hers. She drew him over to a settle, seated herself and pulled him down beside her, one comforting arm around his shoulders.

'Now, let's get acquainted,' she suggested, and so they had.

Their friendship had quickly expanded. She had taken Morla about with her, finding herself touched by his delight in even the most mundane pursuits, and had listened indulgently to his torrent of chatter. Indeed, she had garnered an unexpected harvest of information, fact and rumour intermingled, culled from his friends amongst the serving men and stable boys, and it was made rapidly apparent that the prospective Prince of Kirkendom shared his people's opinion concerning the activities of that elusive person they styled 'Menel Imraut'. The boy had spoken of him with respect and admiration. His people were, naturally, more cautious in expressing their opinions, yet in all those places where she had visited, she had picked up the same sense of affection and trust, an abiding gratitude. It was not always what was said, but rather what was *not* said that pointed the way.

Similarly, she had soon become aware that the Lord Regent was not liked in the Province. Mention Hadran's name and a coolness entered the conversation, as though there had been a mental drawing aside of clothing lest it become contaminated. In Martle, the reaction had been particularly conspicuous. She recalled one local farmer who had appeared to scrutinize her with considerable interest, and who had made no bones of his lack of respect for the Varadil man. She smiled to herself a touch wryly. She had found herself in sympathy with him, though she could not acknowledge it. It had been to her great relief that Hadran was absent from Caleth Mor at the time of her arrival, and she had every day dreaded his coming. Upon each occasion that she had made journeys outside the city, she had been relieved upon her return to find that he was not there. More recently news had reached the household that he had returned to Kirkendom from a sojourn in Väst, but to their surprise, he had not come to Caleth Mor. No-one was entirely sure where he currently was, or what matter was engrossing his attention, but Nyandu counted herself fortunate to have thus escaped his company so entirely.

The uncertain condition of the Province had impelled Nyandu to post scouts ahead to ride periodic sweeps along the highway, and it was one of those scouts who found the horse roaming free, cropping the grass beside the roadway. He led it back, and presented it to his Lady, with a brief description of its discovery. Nyandu listened courteously and looked down at the beast in silent appraisal. Abruptly she stiffened, and the colour ebbed from her face. Thadie, at her side, surveyed the horse and frowned.

'What do you think?' she asked him quietly.

'Well, Menaïren, if I had to put a name to that one, I reckon I could,' he said. 'If I'm not mistaken, that's Melisor. There couldn't be another such.'

'I think so too.'

She slid down from the saddle and tossed her reins to her Captain. Walking forward slowly, she called to the horse by name, and he turned his head and nuzzled her outstretched hand. Nyandu stroked his neck and made a swift examination. It was plain that he had not seen a stable for many days, that he had not received any grooming, and that his saddle had not been removed for some time. An exploration of the saddle-bags revealed that they were almost empty, likewise the flask, and along Melisor's back Nyandu noticed a spattering of blood which did not seem to belong to him. She ran a gentle hand down his flank and turned away to rejoin Thadie, her face serious.

'We must press on,' she said sombrely, 'but there is no harm in keeping a look out along the way for anything untoward.'

'Aye,' pronounced Thadie thoughtfully. 'There is no harm in that.'

He paused, then said carefully:

'You have our full support, Menaïren, in whatever you have a mind to do. You may be sure of that.'

He assisted her back into her saddle, and remounted. Setting off again, with Melisor led safely somewhere towards the rear, they presently met a line of wagons travelling to Caleth Mor. They rumbled past the party, their wheels raising the dust from the dry road surface in gritty clouds, axles creaking and groaning, and horses' hooves ringing on the paved stone. When they were disappearing into the distance, Morla edged his pony next to Nyandu.

'Do you think we'll find him ... you know who ... 'Menel Imraut'?' he enquired excitedly. 'It's *his* horse, isn't it? I heard them say so.'

'I don't know,' she answered soberly, her mind busy with thoughts which she could not control, wondering just what sort of disaster could have parted Francys Coras from so treasured and valuable a possession.

They passed by fields where men worked busily scything the golden wheat and rye. Narrow lanes branched off the highway, rutted and dusty, twisting away towards distantly visible villages and farmsteads. To their left a faint shimmer beyond the rows of meadows betrayed the presence of the river and, from time to time, the tops of barges could be seen, gliding slowly up or down-stream, the upward-bound vessels pulled by unseen barge-horses on the bank. The shouts of the bargees floated faintly to the ears of the travellers on the highway, when not drowned out by the noisy passage of some wheeled vehicle closer to hand. Traffic proceeding towards Caleth Mor was fairly heavy, but nothing overtook Nyandu's party in the opposite direction, although, from time to time, a cart or wagon would lumber out from one of the side-lanes, trundle ponderously for a short distance along the highway and then turn off down another such lane.

Topping a rise, they entered upon a deserted stretch of highway, wilder than previously, the land on either side of the roadway being uncultivated and dotted with clumps of bushes and stands of small trees. Some distance ahead, a figure moved slowly; one of the occasional wayfarers who tramped the roads. Shrouded in a dark cloak, despite the heat, it was impossible to tell even the sex of the figure. It appeared to be experiencing some difficulty in walking, stumbling frequently and leaning heavily upon a wooden staff, and they quickly gained upon it. The sound of their approaching hoof-beats seemed to cause alarm, for the figure turned wildly, as if seeking to flee, and then finding that it could not, shrank back towards the entangling embrace of the roadside bushes.

Her ready sympathy roused by the parlous condition of the unknown pedestrian, Nyandu gave the signal to halt, and dismounted. After a brief exchange with Thadie, who insisted on accompanying her, she advanced towards the now motionless figure. Half turned away from them, yet undoubtedly aware of their approach, they were yet unable to see its face. A certain slight movement of the right arm beneath that enshrouding cloak alerted Thadie, and he leapt forward, seizing the unseen wrist and twisting it sharply. The knife-blade flashed blindingly in the sun as it flew in an arc through the air, landing somewhere in the rough grass a few yards off. The man, for such he surely must be, had made one convulsive attempt to escape from Thadie's grasp and, failing, now subsided into immobility. In desperate, stubborn bravado, he lifted a pair of hazel eyes to meet the concerned compassionate gaze of ... Nyandu.

The shock was like a physical blow, rocking him back on his heels. Were it not for Thadie's restraining grip, he would have fallen. As it was, the staff slipped unheeded from his suddenly nerveless grasp and he staggered helplessly. Nyandu's face was white.

'Francys?' she whispered disbelievingly. 'Is it really you? How do you come to be here, dressed like a beggar and without your horse? We found Melisor wandering ...'

He stood silently, letting her words wash over him unanswered. The urge to speak to her, to beg for help was so intense that he had almost opened his mouth, when he recalled Hadran's words and resisted the compulsion. He closed his eyes, unwilling to look at what must be her triumph. If only it had not been *Nyandu*, of all people, who had finally caught him. Even Hadran would have been less unbearable.

Nyandu stepped closer. He could feel her presence battering his raw nerves, though he dared not open his eyes, and she was able to smell the sickly sweet stench of stale blood and festering wounds.

'Francys!' she said, in a tone of such horror and concern that he could not prevent himself from opening his eyes to look at her. What he discovered in her face leached from him the last reserves of will power. With a quiet sigh, he collapsed into the grass at her feet.

He came round to find himself being gently lowered into the welcoming shade beneath one of the leafy tallus trees, the arm supporting his shoulders pressing unbearably upon the raw flesh and startling an involuntary groan from between his white lips. The hazel eyes flew open, focussing dazedly upon the bearded visage of the owner of the arm, and he began to struggle feebly.

'Bide you still, Menellen,' said Thadie comfortably, laying him onto the grass. 'You're safe for the time being.'

The world turned giddily about him, and gradually steadied until he was looking at a patch of golden, star-like caelisia, raising their petals to the sunlight only inches from his face. A huge bumble-bee buzzed over him to home in on the flowers. Further away, between tall grass-stalks, he could see white vetch and the big daisies which the local people called summer stars, and beyond them the horizon of leafy bushes. It was pleasant, it was very pleasant to lie in the shade for a while ... His eyes closed wearily. Busy hands carefully unfastened the cloak and drew its folds from over him, easing its stifling weight. He heard a hiss of indrawn breath as the sweat-soaked, bloody shirt beneath was revealed.

Then, suddenly, a voice spoke nearby.

'Drachen Thadie, Lady Nan told me to bring you this ... in case he wants a drink.'

It was an absurdly young voice, surely the voice of a child. Francys frowned.

'Good lad,' said Thadie approvingly. 'I'm sure he'll be glad of it. Is the Lady Nyandu coming?'

'She says shortly.'

The boy arrived at Thadie's side and peered down over his shoulder at the man on the grass. He could not suppress a gasp of horror.

'What's the matter with him? He looks dreadfully bad!'

Francys turned his head stiffly and opened leaden lids. It *was* a child, a boy, staring with solemn, wide brown eyes, seeing a blanched, begrimed and pain-lined face with bloody, bitten lips amid a rough stubble of beard, and hazel eyes sunk deep into their sockets.

The sound of Thadie's voice caused them both to start, so absorbed were they in gazing at one another.

'Well, lad, you can give me a hand,' he directed. 'I'll just prop him up and then you can give him a drink of water.'

The movement, even as slow and careful as the Captain was, hurt Francys terribly and Morla winced in sympathy, seeing the pain reflected in his face. As the fair head lolled limply against Thadie's sturdy shoulder, Morla knelt down beside the man and solicitously raised the flask of water to his parched lips. Francys drank greedily, swallowing almost a quarter of the flask's contents, and even managed a faint smile in gratitude. Some vestige of his famous charm lingered despite his parlous condition, catching at Morla's emotions and binding the boy in thrall to him irrevocably.

The hazel eyes closed. The fair head lay heavily against the supporting shoulder, drooping slightly to one side. Beside him, Morla crouched and watched in silent fascination, and across the grass towards them came Nyandu, her arms full of salves and bandages. Her voice, as she prevailed upon the reluctant boy to rejoin the remainder of her company, at ease and enjoying an interval of rest and refreshment beside the roadway some few yards away, appeared to rouse the fair man from his lethargy. When she turned and knelt down to examine him, she found the hazel eyes fixed upon her in a stare of passionate intensity. His lips formed a word.

'No.'

Nyandu was visibly taken aback, but swiftly recovered. Taking hold of one slack wrist, she felt his pulse and frowned.

'You're burning with fever,' she said anxiously. 'What have you been doing to get yourself into this state?'

She looked towards her Captain.

'Thadie, can you lay him down so that I can take a look at his back?' she requested.

'No!'

The command from Francys halted the Captain in the act.

'No, leave me be.'

He raised fathomless eyes to meet Nyandu's gaze.

'What point is there in patching me up merely to meet the hangman's noose?' he asked deliberately, and in a tone of bleak resignation which struck Nyandu to the heart. 'I'm dying anyway. If our past friendship means anything to you, let me die in reasonable privacy, not held up to public vilification.'

Nyandu's face was as white as that of the man she faced.

'Francys!' she whispered, distressed. Then:

'Do you really imagine that I would give you up to the Authorities?'

'It *is* your duty,' he reminded her. 'I am imrauten, a traitor to my country.'

'You are *said* to be a traitor,' she corrected. 'There is a difference. And I have heard some interesting stories about your activities during my visit in Caleth Mor which paint a strange picture indeed of a 'traitor'.'

He had stiffened at the sound of the city's name, with its ever-present associations with his brother, his mind wandering into familiar territory, reviving unwanted memories which the shock of his encounter with Nyandu had caused him temporarily to forget. He forced himself, with difficulty, to concentrate on what she was saying.

'And *are* you indeed a traitor, Francys?' she was asking.

'What does it matter now?' he answered helplessly. 'In the eyes of the law, in the eyes of the world, I am ...'

'It matters to me,' Nyandu told him, 'and I think you've answered me. Now, let me see what I am to do for your back. Of course, I haven't got everything that I need, but I expect I can make do well enough until we can get you to shelter somewhere ...'

'No!'

Amongst the confusion in his mind, which threatened at every moment to overwhelm him, one fact stood clear. He had remembered the reason for his flight. Letting Nyandu's gentle remonstrances and sensible arguments wash over him unheeded, he strove to assemble his wits and to gather his strength sufficiently to make her understand the perilous situation in which he had inadvertently embroiled her.

'Nyandu,' he interrupted brusquely (even at such a time he could not permit himself to use the diminutive). 'Please listen to me.'

He drew in a deep, tremulous breath and momentarily closed his eyes against the pain which streaked through every nerve at the smallest movement.

'Leave me here,' he said abruptly, desperate to get the words out before his strength failed him.

'Go away from here and leave me! With every minute that you stay here, you are putting yourself in greater danger. Anyone could come by and see you here. Any one of your people could know me. For the love of Sior, please go! It's too late for me, but I don't want to die knowing that I have brought *you* to a traitor's death!'

'I'm not leaving you here like this,' Nyandu stated firmly. 'Do you think I could do such a thing and bear to live with myself afterwards? In any case, the risk surely isn't as great as you fear. Thadie and I alone of our company know who you are. The others have been led to believe that you are a messenger whom I was expecting to meet and who happens to have suffered an accident. And if anyone should come along and be curious enough to stop, why they can think the same thing! Who's going to recognize you in the state you're in?'

'Hadran,' he said harshly.

Then as she looked at him in astonishment, he turned his head painfully and addressed the Captain.

'Tell her she must do as I say,' he entreated. 'For her own safety.'

'Menellen,' the man said drily, 'I have no power to compel the Lady Nyandu into any action which is against her will.'

'Even to save her life!'

Feeling the strength draining from him, Francys battled frantically against the stifling, deadening cloud which seemed to be enveloping his brain, to make one last effort. Fixing his gaze as clearly as he could upon the girl's face, his surroundings a mere blur to his fading vision, he spoke urgently and distinctly.

'Hadran is on my trail. For the love of Sior, do not let him find you here ... with me!'

Darkness overwhelmed his senses. He slumped sideways, helplessly, in a swoon, and Thadie was hard put to catch him ere he fell. Laying him carefully down upon the grass, the Captain looked up across the young man's senseless form to meet Nyandu's eyes.

'His brother in pursuit? That would perhaps explain why he let Melisor go loose ... the Lord Hadran could not fail to know the horse ...'

Nyandu nodded, but said nothing. She appeared to be thinking. Finally she came to a decision.

'Thadie,' she said resolutely. 'I cannot leave him here. Not like this. It would be to administer the death penalty myself. Yet I cannot take him on to the inn at Arlennen either. For one thing, it is too far. The journey itself would be enough to kill him. For another, if Hadran really is on his trail, he would certainly overtake us before we were anywhere near the place. And even if he did not, it would only take one person along the way to recognize Francys ... Thadie, it seems to me that the only course I can take is to try to get him away somewhere safe and reasonably nearby where I can see to him properly.

No, no,' she continued, raising a hand to halt his objections. 'No. If you think about it, you must agree with me. I am the only person here who has the requisite knowledge to care for him. No-one else can do it. And *you* must take charge of the party and take them on as far as Arlmen as though I were with you. I trust you also to take care of Morla.

Oh,' she sighed. 'Perhaps it was not such a good idea to bring him along after all, but it seemed so at the time. Well, you will just have to make him mind you, and I know that you will, and wait for me in Arlmen. As soon as Francys is well enough ...' Her voice faltered momentarily at the thought that he might not recover. Resolutely she pushed the thought away. 'As soon as he is sufficiently well to be left safely, I will rejoin you.'

The Captain attempted to remonstrate, putting forward all the objections that he could find, but his Lady remained determined and in the face of her dedicated resolve, he came at last to a resigned acquiescence. Finally, shrugging his shoulders, he went off to search out from her baggage the map of the area which she had thoughtfully packed.

Left alone with Francys, Nyandu resolutely suppressed her emotions and set about trying to alleviate the discomfort of his situation as best she could. Using water from the flask, she dampened a piece of cloth and proceeded to bathe his temples and wrists, frowning anxiously at the feverish heat of his dry skin and the racing pulse. She badly wanted to examine, and treat, those festering wounds, but she acknowledged that it was more important, particularly if it were true that Hadran was in pursuit, to get him away from so public a spot. Sighing, she put out a hand and gently stroked the burning forehead, brushing to one side the pale strands of hair which had drifted across his brow.

The touch seemed to rouse him, for he stirred slightly and muttered something in his native tongue. She answered him in the same language, whereat the long-lashed lids lifted in surprise. The hazel eyes regarded her blearily.

'Nyandu?' the fair man said wonderingly, having apparently forgotten what had passed before.

'Yes. Lie still,' she said quietly.

Obediently he did so, but continued to gaze up at her as if unable to comprehend the fact of her presence.

'Nyandu,' he repeated, confirming her identity.

His eye-lids flickered restlessly. He moved his head irritably, grimaced at the pain which the movement evoked, and finally murmured fretfully that he was so thirsty.

Nyandu stooped and, carefully sliding one arm beneath his shoulders, gently raised him and supported him whilst he drank from the flask. It was the closest contact she had had with the man since that enlightening moment on that summer morning in Shardu when she had first understood that she loved him. The ends of the roughly-cropped fair hair tickled her neck. The young man's body lay heavily against hers in an intimacy that was disturbing, and heart-breaking. She loved him and she could not even tell him so, and he might die without knowing it. She must not even seem to show him any especial attention lest she arouse suspicion as to his identity. That there were curious eyes watching her actions, she could not fail to be aware. The ordinary ministrations to a man in need would pass muster, but let her but show the least sign of tenderness and tongues would soon begin to wag.

The water revived Francys sufficiently for Nyandu to feel able to unfold to him the plan of action which she had devised with Thadie. At the first she met with obstinate resistance and a reiteration of his earlier demand to be left alone, but he was too weak to hold out for very long, and by the time Thadie appeared beside them with the map, he had even consented to divulge to her the name and location of his nearest contact. Nyandu peered down at the map, which Thadie had spread out on the grass beside her, and with some difficulty calculated their current position. She proceeded to find the village that Francys had named, and traced a line with her finger between the two for Thadie's benefit. The hazel eyes followed her movements dazedly, uncomprehending. Nyandu raised her head and looked across at Thadie, then both glanced down at Francys. Again, their eyes met. Neither needed to speak, for they each knew what the other was thinking. It was a journey of some nine or ten calle, over rough tracks, and Francys liable to collapse at any moment. Still:

'I have to try,' Nyandu said eventually.

Having despatched Thadie to see to the preparations and to instruct the remainder of the company to ready themselves for imminent departure, Nyandu remained seated on the grass, silently holding the young man in her arms and mentally reviewing her arrangements. Fortunately, this would not be the first time that she had absented herself and travelled into the countryside, on instructions from the Dukrugvola, so that it was to be hoped that her current disappearance would not be thought extraordinary. It was even true that she was expecting a messenger to come to her (though not until she had reached the town of Arlmen). From her escort it would seem that she had little to fear, assuming that she could get Francys into the cart which was being readied for him without anyone recognizing him. She glanced down at the fair head and sighed. It would look very peculiar if she should try to disguise him in any way ... or herself for that matter. At least she was plainly dressed for travelling and her garb, if one discounted the quality of the cloth, might pass for that of some well-to-do farmer's wife.

She raised her head, to find Thadie approaching, with Morla at his side. *There* was another problem. She sighed again, and gestured the boy to kneel so that she could talk to him more easily. He did so, his gaze sliding off to fix itself reverently upon Francys.

'Morla, I'm afraid I must go away for a while and leave you in Thadie's charge,' Nyandu explained.

The boy nodded, his eyes flickering to her face, then back to the fair man.

'You will mind what Thadie tells you whilst I'm gone?' she continued.

'Yes, Lady Nan.'

He paused, then said in an awed whisper:

'Is it true ... is he really Menel Francys Coras?'

Nyandu felt herself stiffen in alarm, and she knew that Thadie had done likewise. Reaching out, she placed a warning finger on the boy's lips.

'Hush. You should not speak that name.'

A disturbing thought occurred to her.

'You have not told anyone else who you think he is?' she enquired anxiously.

'No. Of course not. It's a secret.'

Morla seemed affronted at the very idea.

'That's right. It is a very important secret, Morla. Remember, if anyone wishes to know, you must tell them that I met up with a messenger who was sent with news for me. Unfortunately, he had suffered an accident, but was still able to go with me to act as my guide. That is all that you know.'

He nodded solemnly and she smiled in encouragement.

'But what about his horse?' he asked suddenly.

Nyandu blinked and looked up at Thadie.

'Melisor,' she said. 'I'd forgotten about him.'

'Melisor,' murmured a husky voice, startling them all. 'I lost him ... in the storm.'

'We found him,' Nyandu told him. 'He was wandering loose along the highway, not a great distance away from here. What would you wish us to do with him? Is there somewhere we can take him?'

There was a pause, then, just as Nyandu was beginning to think that he had not understood, Francys spoke.

'There is a man in Arlmen,' he said faintly. 'Jeff ... Take him to Jeff

...’

Some further gentle questioning elicited the man’s address in Arlmen, and a password to identify Thadie as coming upon Francys’ business.

Those details settled, the moment of departure was upon them. It was found necessary to have the cart brought to Francys rather than to attempt to support him as far as the roadway. Even so, it was with some difficulty that he was assisted within, to lie grey-faced and barely conscious upon the blankets heaped therein. Nyandu, rising stiff-legged from her seated position on the grass, conferred briefly once more with her Captain, hugged Morla affectionately and finally said farewell. Then, from the driver’s seat of the wagon, she watched the cavalcade of riders and lumbering baggage-vehicles proceed upon its interrupted journey, until it passed eventually from her view. Only then did she take up the reins and set the cart in motion.

Torn between the desire to reach their destination as quickly as possible, and the need to proceed with as little jolting as could be achieved on the rough and rutted back lanes to which they were restricted, Nyandu chafed at their slow pace. From time to time she glanced back over her shoulder to check on the fair man’s condition, but beneath the shade of the tilt which had been rigged up over the body of the cart, she could not see very clearly. She thought that he was awake, and once or twice when the wheels of the cart bumped over a stone or into a rut, she heard him cry out in pain, the sound twisting into her heart like a knife-thrust. She had also not reckoned with the interest which the sight of an unknown female driving a cart, ostensibly alone, would arouse in those local countryfolk at large upon the spider’s web of back-roads beyond the highway. Necessity was, however, an excellent teacher. To all enquiry, she responded brazenly, passing herself off as an inhabitant of a neighbouring village, returning home from a trip to Caleth Mor, with her husband, who lay sick of a fever within the cart. The mention of fever proved an effective deterrent to any more inquisitive persons who might otherwise have felt inclined to take a look at the invalid, and Nyandu was able to proceed without hindrance.

In this fashion, she travelled some three or four calle, and was beginning to allow a tiny gleam of hope to lighten her mind when she became aware of a deep, deathly silence behind her. Throughout the journey she had been conscious of Francys stirring restlessly and uncomfortably, groaning and muttering in some pain-filled nightmare. Now he was still and quiet. In terror, Nyandu hauled at the reins, bringing the horse and cart to an abrupt halt. Twisting awkwardly around, she peered under the canvas, but the interior was too dim and she could not see his face. Her heart pounding frantically, she crept carefully into the body of the cart and fearfully reached for his hand. The pulse at his wrist was not longer racing, but slow, too slow. He breathed but shallowly, his chest barely rising, and he was deeply unconscious. It was, she knew, the prelude to death. In a matter of hours, unless she could quickly find a place where it would be possible for her to bestow upon him the medical attention he so desperately needed, he would be dead. Even with prompt attention, he might be already too far along that dread path to be turned back.

Nyandu crawled out from under the tilt and looked around wildly. To travel further was out of the question. Assistance, if any were to be forthcoming, would have to be sought near at hand. The lane wound downhill before her eyes, running between fragrant hedgerows towards a distantly visible collection of houses and farmsteads beside the stream. Set amid the multi-hued patchwork of fields on the edge of the village stood a small cottage, somewhat isolated from the rest, catching her gaze like a beacon. She could but try. With a small sigh, she urged the horse forward.

She approached the door with trembling limbs, her mouth unpleasantly dry. The danger of her situation was uncompromisingly clear to her. Her timid knock went unheard and, panic-stricken, she knocked again, the sound over-loud to her sensitized nerves. After some seconds, she was finally rewarded by the appearance of a large, amiable-looking countrywoman of some fifty or more years of age.

'Yes, my dear?' she enquired briskly.

Nyandu swallowed hard and moistened her dry lips.

'I am in desperate need of help,' she said, in a voice rendered husky by tension. 'My companion (she gestured towards the cart) is very sick and like to die unless he receives immediate treatment. On his behalf, I have come to beg for shelter, at least for this night ahead ...'

Her voice faded and she gazed helplessly at the woman, who was, in her turn, inspecting her with a good deal of interest, recognizing the quality in both her clothing and her person.

'Sick, you say?' she said after a pause, frowning thoughtfully. 'What ails him?'

'It is not any disease,' Nyandu assured her swiftly, perceiving the reason for her hesitation. 'You need have no fear of contagion. He has suffered an accident and lies badly hurt.'

'An accident,' the woman repeated.

Then she opened the door wide.

'Come in and welcome,' she added generously. 'He's lying in the cart, is he? You'll not be able to manage him. I'll call my Tam to bring him in ... He can look to the horse and cart too.'

She turned and called through the open doorway.

A burly young man appeared promptly, to whom she issued instructions. He strode out to the cart and, with some assistance from both Nyandu and his mother, taking great pains to be gentle, lifted Francys down. The fair head drooped heavily and the body lay slackly in the man's strong arms. Catching sight of the wan face, the woman exclaimed in concern.

'The poor lad. He looks right poorly, that he does! Put him in my chamber, Tam. The sheets are clean on today,' she assured Nyandu earnestly.

'You'll be wanting hot water, I don't doubt?' she added, turning her head to address Nyandu as the latter followed her inside. 'I'll just set a pan on the hob. You go through after Tam ...'

When Tam had deposited his burden, at her instruction, upon an old blanket laid on the floor, and retreated from the room, Nyandu stood for some moments looking down at the dirty, battered body which lay sprawled almost lifelessly at her feet. She bit her lip, and steeled herself to kneel beside him to begin the awkward task of undressing him, pulling off his boots to expose feet that were blackened with the dirt of many days' travel and reddened with sores. His breeches and underlinen followed, and finally she had to approach that terrible shirt. Untying the laces, she attempted to remove it, only to find that the cloth had become stuck, gummed to his back and shoulder by the slowly-solidifying seepings of blood and pus. Gritting her teeth, Nyandu took hold of the front of the shirt and, with an effort, ripped it apart. Then, with infinitely patient fingers, aided by application of some drops of the water which had now been provided to her, she set to work to ease the unspeakably foul, stinking material away from the unknown horrors which it concealed.

At last it was free. She threw it to one side and turned back to take her first good look at Francys' injuries. What she had expected, she knew not, but of a certainty it was not that which now met her eyes. The long lash-marks crossed his back in a lattice-work, each weal blue and black, bruised and clotted with blood. Yellow-green matter oozed from those which had begun to fester, whilst blood still flowed glisteningly from others. The rare places where the skin remained whole were reddened and tender from the chafing of the blood-caked shirt, and a line of raw blisters ran across his waist where the top of his breeches had rubbed.

With immense care and concentration, Nyandu began to sponge away the trickles of blood and to clean out the deep lacerations, meticulously ensuring that no trace of purulent matter remained. This done, she used the salves which she had brought in from the cart, spreading a layer of soothing, disinfectant ointment over the injuries and covering it with clean linen bound in place by strips of cloth.

She then turned the fair man over, carefully, cushioning the damaged back as best she could, so as to enable her to approach the ugly-looking sore on his left shoulder, wondering what manner of injury this could be. Swabbing away the dirt and lymph, she was surprised to find a curious set of scars. She had cleansed and anointed them with the disinfectant salve before the realization of the meaning of their shape penetrated her mind like a thunder-bolt. They were letters, stamped deep into the flesh; indelible initials.

'Hadran is on my trail.' She heard again Francys' desperate warning. Hadran was on his trail, having had him all too plainly within his grasp already and somehow, Sior alone knew how, lost him. She now knew beyond a doubt whose hand had inflicted those appalling wounds. The thought so nauseated her that for a few moments it was touch and go whether she might actually be sick. Eventually, however, she was successful in her struggle to compose herself and to continue with her ministrations.

When she was at length satisfied that she could do no more for Francys, she climbed stiffly to her feet, staggering with sudden cramp from the long time spent on her knees, and turned towards the door. She would need help to lift Francys onto the bed. To her surprise, the woman was there, standing silently in the doorway. As Nyandu caught her eye, she gave a little nod and advanced into the room. Without the need for speech, she assisted Nyandu to raise the limp body of the fair man and place him gently onto the big bed with its soft, feather-filled mattress and fresh-smelling linen sheets. Together they stood, side by side, staring solemnly down at the motionless form. Nyandu had bathed his face and, despite the beard, he looked very young and vulnerable. The thick fair hair spread out on the pillow, framing the white face and drawing attention to the long-lashed eyes, closed now and ringed by the dark bruising of utter exhaustion, and the half-parted lips scarcely deeper in colour than the skin which surrounded them. One arm rested above the covers, and to Nyandu's astonishment, with a sudden, impetuous movement, the woman stooped and raised the unresponsive hand to her lips in a reverent gesture.

Nyandu gazed at her wide-eyed. Her wits seemed to have become sluggish and the import of the gesture did not strike her immediately. Then she realized.

'You know him,' she said slowly, almost accusingly.

The woman smiled.

'Aye,' she answered softly. 'It is Menel Imraut.'

There was a little silence before she spoke again.

'That was no accident,' she asserted confidently, and Nyandu knew from her tone that she must have had sight of Francys' injuries.

'No,' she agreed, wearily.

Something within her broke down and she found herself standing there with tears running down her face.

'Oh Sior!' she sobbed helplessly.

Kindly arms enfolded her against an ample bosom.

'My dear ... my dear,' the woman's voice soothed compassionately.

'I was travelling to Arlmen,' Nyandu whispered brokenly, 'and I met him by the roadside, and I could not let him die. I could not let him die!'

CHAPTER TWELVE

Hadran entered the city of Caleth Mor in mellow and contented mood, well pleased with the prisoners he had captured and certain in his own mind that his brother must now be dead, lying somewhere out upon the wild tracts of the moor. No trace of the fair man had been detected since they had followed him to the border, and every day without news brought a lifting of the oppressive burden of fear from Hadran's spirits. No-one now would ever know what had taken place between the two of them during that first evening in the camp. He was free at last to begin to forget that dangerous passion which had so tainted his life. And to help him in this assay, there was Nyandu, currently resident in Caleth Mor. Her presence at this particular juncture he took to be an auspicious omen.

Setting a brisk pace, he arrived at the gates of the castle some few hours after Nyandu's company had ridden forth and within the space of a further hour, unaware of her departure, having bathed, dined and issued instructions concerning the disposition of the Krapani captives, he was approaching the parlour door with eager anticipation. Upon his entry, however, he found himself confronting merely the uninspiring sight of the Lady Annis, dozing placidly in a high-backed armchair. His entrance disturbed her slumbers and she woke with a start, rising to her feet in a flurry of dismay and apprehension, to greet him in the nervous manner which never failed to irritate him intensely. On this occasion disappointment enhanced his customary irritation and it was with but a cursory acknowledgment of her greeting that he prefaced his enquiry as to Nyandu's whereabouts.

The Lady Annis appeared distressed, unwilling to be the bearer of bad news. But there was nothing else for it; the fact of Nyandu's departure would have to be revealed. She took the plunge.

'... but a few hours hence - three or four maybe,' she disclosed reluctantly.

'Where has she gone?' he asked, illogically offended that she had not been there, awaiting his arrival, though to be sure she could have had no reason to expect it.

'To Arlmen, I believe,' the Lady Annis answered cautiously, regarding the big, fair man uneasily and hoping that he would not break out into one of his all too frequent squalls of ill-temper. She had a great dislike of emotional scenes and Hadran's outbursts in particular she found peculiarly unpleasant and often alarming. In general she preferred to avoid arousing trouble by taking the line of least resistance, acquiescing in arrangements to which she would, if the truth be known, much rather have objected.

Happily for her nerves, this time he merely grumbled.

'Whatever can have taken her to go *there*?' he complained petulantly, wandering across to the window embrasure and taking an absent-minded look at the gardens below.

'When will she be returning?'

The query was thrown over his shoulder. The Lady Annis briefly closed her eyes and mentally breathed a hasty plea to Sior, then, with a sinking heart, she disclosed the awful truth.

'I'm afraid she will not,' she said.

'What!'

Hadran swung round to stare at her, then took a step towards her.

'What do you mean?'

'She was obliged to travel into Arlente and then return to Lôren,' the Lady Annis volunteered placatingly, racking her memory to supply facts which it had, as ever, almost forgotten already. 'A message arrived from the Dukrugvola. You know she was here on his business. He wished her to return.

She's taken Morla with her on a visit,' she added quickly, out of a desire to impart all the bad news in one bout.

The import of her last words seemed to have escaped Hadran, intent as he was on expressing his dismay and annoyance at the Dukrugvola's unwitting frustration of his plans.

'One cannot ignore the Dukrugvola's commands,' he conceded grudgingly. 'But why could not Nyandu have waited till the morrow? I particularly wanted to see her.'

And he glared at the Lady Annis as if holding her personally to blame for the missed meeting.

To her immense relief, the resulting tense silence was swiftly brought to an end by the sound of hurrying footsteps in the passage, followed by a sharp knock on the door. In response to Hadran's curt command, an officer of his personal guard entered the room. From his demeanour, it was evident that he had information of importance to convey, and he crossed briskly to stand to attention before his commander, scarcely even registering the presence of the lady. Hadran scowled at him, none too pleased at the interruption.

'Well?'

'Menellen,' the man said apologetically, 'forgive me for disturbing you, but I thought that you would wish to know immediately. I have received word concerning your recent mission...'

There he glanced sidelong at the Lady Annis.

'... and the person you were seeking.'

He was conscious of a sudden, curious stillness within the room, as though someone there had experienced a moment of sheer, paralysing terror. Then it was gone. Hadran's hand rubbed the corner of his jaw, surreptitiously easing taut muscles.

'Well?' he enquired a second time.

No doubt someone had found the body. That was all.

The officer lowered his voice confidentially.

'Menellen, following your instructions, we have been maintaining a watch on the neighbourhood of the Mart and the eastern surrounds ...'

Hadran was unprepared. He had forgotten those orders, given at the time when he had harboured the notion that Francys might attempt to travel to Caleth Mor by water. As the blood drained from his face, he heard, as from a distance and with an effort, the officer's next words.

'We think we have news of the .. er ... fugitive, Menellen.'

An ungovernable rage seized Hadran. How dared they do this to him!

'Think!' he shouted furiously, causing the Lady Annis to utter a frightened cry and to seek refuge within the depths of her armchair. 'Think! Don't you *know*?'

The man proffered a sheet of parchment, a little dog-eared and grubby from its contact with several hands.

'Menellen, if you read the report, you will understand why we cannot be absolutely sure, though the likelihood is very great, very great indeed.'

Hadran snatched the parchment and unfolded it with trembling fingers.

'Menellen, I have the honour to append here the description of a man seen crossing the bridge above the city ...'

He skipped the details of date and time of day and went straight to the nub of the information.

'... *of middle height and slim build ... thought to be young, though goes slowly, leaning on a stick and unsteady of gait ... face and hair covered ... walks as a vagrant, yet clothing is too good for such, despite recent signs of rough usage ... stinks ... unknown in district ... believed to be native of Varadil as heard to talk to self in that tongue ...*'

The words paraded before Hadran's eyes, each innocuous by itself, yet with the others serving to construct a damning portrait, and when he had finished reading, an unshakeable certainty filled his mind. Francys was not dead.

Francys lived still. The room whirled violently before Hadran's eyes, and he grabbed at the nearest object, a chair-back, to keep himself upright. The whole carefully constructed edifice of complacence within his mind was crashing down around his inner being like a house of cards touched by a breath of wind. He raised his head, alarming the officer with the wildness of his expression.

'I want ten men mounted and ready to set out within a half hour,' he said brusquely. 'Not those who came in with me. I'll meet you in the courtyard.'

Then, without a word of apology or farewell for the Lady Annis, whose presence he had, in his turmoil, forgotten, he stumbled abruptly from the room, barely reaching the sanctuary of his bedchamber before he was torn by violent spasms of uncontrollable retching.

****

So it came to pass that the evening of that same day saw Hadran once more out upon the road, with an unwilling, and uneasy, pack of riders at his back and a fanatical gleam in his hazel eyes. His mood ranged from the buoyant uplifting of hope, for sure it could not be possible for Francys, on foot and injured, to outstrip the pace of a fresh horse, to the bleak depths of fury at having been tricked and the even bleaker torments of icy terror. He should have anticipated the loop that Francys had made, but he had not, and because of that Francys had slipped through his fingers.

For, even possessing as they did, a relatively detailed description of Francys as he had appeared when last sighted, it proved difficult to follow his trail. He had been seen as he crossed the river, but once into the tangle of mud-caked, winding lanes and the miscellany of fields and woodland on the western bank of the Mart, they ran up against a wall of silence. Not a single whisper of his passing came to their ears. It was as though Francys had walked along the road and suddenly, between one step and the next, vanished out of existence. Indeed, so vivid was the impression that the more superstitious amongst the men muttered darkly of spirit interference and furtively signed themselves with the protective symbol of the double triangle.

Cursing viciously, and aware of the growing dusk and the impossibility of pursuing the chase through the night, Hadran ordered a halt at the next inn, to the amazement and immense gratification of the landlord, sat down with a tankard of ale and tried to think. Suddenly he uttered a violent imprecation and crashed his fist down onto the table with such force that the tankard was sent clattering to the floor. He sprang to his feet, almost overturning both table and chair in the process, and, oblivious to everything save his tumultuous thoughts, strode furiously about the room, much to the consternation of the innkeeper, who feared for the safety of his furniture. It had to be so! That very same morning, so the Lady Annis had explained to him, Nyandu had received a message which had prompted her to set out immediately from Caleth Mor along the highway leading to Arlmen, the highway which cut directly across the route that Francys, from their meagre gleanings of intelligence, had appeared to be following. A message from the Dukrugvola, the Lady Annis had said, but had she herself actually read the message, or was she simply repeating what she had been told, by Nyandu? He had himself apprised Francys of Nyandu's presence in Caleth Mor, fool that he was, and what was more likely than that he should seek assistance from her. And what was more likely than that he would receive it? Hadran had never been able to settle satisfactorily the vexed question of the precise state of Nyandu's feelings towards his brother, but he knew her well enough to be certain that even if she hated him (which he doubted), let her but catch a glimpse of his injuries and there was nothing in the world that would prevent her from going to his aid.

Within a matter of minutes Hadran's men found themselves back in the saddle and travelling post haste back towards the city of Caleth Mor. He arrived back at the castle in a mood more foul than any his men had experienced yet. Sleep eluded him that night, tortured as he was by visions of his brother and Nyandu together, and dawn found him up and dressed, impatiently awaiting the rising of the sun so that he could set forth again.

They could not, of course, reach the town of Arlmen that day, and even with changes of horse, it was the late afternoon of the next day before Hadran was able to present himself at the door of Nyandu's lodgings, the location of which he had had no small difficulty in ascertaining. He met with a rebuff. The Lady Nyandu, it seemed, was not at home. It was not known when she would return. An hour later, two hours, then three, and the response was still the same. The Lady Nyandu was not at home.

His ready suspicions aroused, Hadran resolved to make one further visit, and to demand to speak to someone in authority, even to conduct a search of the premises if necessary. As luck would have it, as he entered the courtyard which fronted the house, having left his men waiting without, he all but ran into Thadie, returning, had he but known it, from delivering the horse, Melisor, into the hands of Francys' agent in Arlmen. Recognizing the man, Hadran peremptorily called upon him to supply the necessary information. But the Captain, though civil, was unhelpful. The Lady Nyandu was not presently at home, and he could not say when she might return. No, she had not given any indication as to her destination or the length of her proposed absence, nor was it his place to insist upon knowing. This last was not spoken aloud, but the inference was clear enough. The Lady Nyandu was not obliged to explain her actions to her household.

Defeated by the man's imperturbable politeness, Hadran was about to retire in frustrated discomfiture, when out of the corner of his eye he observed a young boy running across the courtyard towards them. An exclamation of annoyance escaped the officer, hastily stifled, and he made a quick gesture as if to halt the boy's advance. But it was too late. Hadran had identified him, taking a stride forward out of the shadow, where he had passed unnoticed.

The effect was dramatic. Morla stopped in his tracks and his face blanched. In an instant, Thadie was by his side, a comforting hand on the thin shoulder, but the boy appeared insensible to his touch, staring with fearful fascination at the tall, burly figure which loomed imperiously over him.

'And what are *you* doing here?' Hadran enquired, his harsh voice grating on the boy's nerves, and, faintly contemptuous, bringing a flush to into the pale cheeks. Morla gulped nervously, but the knowledge of Thadie's silently-encouraging presence at his side steadied him and lent him the courage to respond.

'I am travelling to Silmendu with the Lady Nyandu, sir,' he explained with unexpected dignity. 'My aunt agreed that I could go for a visit.'

'Indeed. Well, I imagine your aunt would not be happy to learn that your kind hostess appears to have abandoned you so soon in your travels ...'

'My aunt knows,' Morla said hurriedly.

Hadran's expression grew thunderous.

'Your aunt *knows*?' he repeated disbelievingly, recalling quite clearly the Lady Annis' failure to disclose this particular item of information.

Morla nodded.

'The Lady Nyandu didn't wish my aunt to be worried. She told her that she would have to go away for a few days on business.'

'Then *you* will be able to tell *me*, no doubt, where I may find the Lady Nyandu. I need to speak to her on a matter of great importance.'

Morla licked dry lips. Beside him, the Captain stood motionless and silent.

'I do not know, sir,' the boy said eventually.

The expression on Hadran's face caused the boy to shrink back in terror.

'Is this some sort of game you are playing?' the big man snarled ferociously.

He looked at Thadie. Doubtless the man was responsible. He came to a decision.

'You may go,' he said curtly. 'I wish to speak with Morla alone.'

'Menellen!' the Captain protested, standing his ground. 'In the absence of the Lady Nyandu, the boy is in my charge ...'

'Leave us!' repeated Hadran coldly and inflexibly, and there was nothing else that Thadie could do. Making an issue of it would only do more harm. Muttering a word of encouragement and patting Morla reassuringly on the shoulder, he therefore withdrew, but only far enough to comply with the letter of Hadran's command, remaining alert to intervene should such intervention prove necessary.

Left alone with the big man, Morla stared miserably at the ground and mentally braced himself against the expected attack. So tense was he that the sound of the hated voice caused him to shy like a startled pony.

'Well, now, Morla, it's just you and me, isn't it? Look up at me, Morla!'

The boy obeyed.

'You know the nature of an oath, I suppose?'

Morla nodded, his eyes large in his pale face.

'Then swear to me that what you tell me is the truth.'

'I do swear it.'

The boy's treble voice rang out firm and clear.

'So ... let's start again,' said his tormentor. 'Where is the Lady Nyandu?'

This was at least one question that Morla could answer without hesitation, for he truly did not know.

'I don't know, sir,' he said quietly.

Hadran almost ground his teeth in his rage.

'But you have just told me that the Lady Nyandu informed your aunt where she was going. How could you know that unless you were there and heard her?'

'No, no, I didn't say that,' Morla correctly timidly.

'You said your aunt knew.'

'Yes, but I didn't mean it like *that*,' the boy explained, with a sense of relief at being able to offer a piece of genuine information which yet had the merit of giving nothing away. 'The Lady Nyandu was expecting a message. She told my aunt so, and that when the message came she would have to spend some days away from her household here, on the business of the Dukrugvola. She didn't tell my aunt where she was going, because she didn't know herself, not until the messenger came.'

Hadran stood silently, frowningly considering the implications of Morla's statement. If Nyandu had been summoned away by a messenger in *Arlmen*, about whose arrival she had previously been warned, then it would seem that the message which she had received in Caleth Mor must have come genuinely from the Dukrugvola, and all his assumptions were thus based on a misapprehension. Maybe he was wrong, and his brother had not made contact with her after all. Certainly, it made no sort of sense for Francys to have taken the trouble to get a message to Nyandu in Caleth Mor, in whose neighbourhood he had last been sighted, merely in order to send her post haste to meet someone else in another town altogether and so many calle distant; and it was impossible for Francys himself to have been the person whom Nyandu was expecting to see in Arlmen, for he could not have travelled to the town in the time available. No, whatever business Nyandu was engaged upon, it clearly could not have any connection with that which most concerned *him*.

He was on the point of turning away and releasing the boy from his ordeal, to make his excuses and leave, satisfied that there was nothing here for him, yet still vaguely uneasy, when, by chance, it came to him to pose the question which altered everything.

'When did the Lady Nyandu leave?' he enquired almost idly, for he could not have been so many hours behind her and her stay in Arlmen must, therefore, have been brief in the extreme.

Morla, relaxing, was caught off guard.

'The day before yesterday,' he answered honestly, unthinking.

The next moment realization struck him and he blanched. At the same time, before he could move, Hadran's hand shot out and grabbed him roughly by the shoulder.

'The day before yesterday!' the man hissed in fury. 'The day before yesterday! You weren't even *in* Arlmen that day. You damned lying little bastard! So, the Lady Nyandu was expecting a messenger was she? A likely story! And ... now ... I want the truth!'

'It is the truth!' Morla shouted desperately, trying to get free of the iron grip. 'It is the truth! She *was* expecting a messenger. She *was*!'

He stopped abruptly, with a whimpering cry of pain, as Hadran's cruel fingers dug into his thin shoulder and shook him violently. Instantly Thadie was there, pulling the boy away from Hadran's grasp and interposing his stalwart frame firmly in Hadran's path.

'Leave the boy alone,' he commanded sternly.

The fair man uttered a snarl of rage.

'How dare you! Get out of my way!'

He made to pass, but could not. Pausing only to issue a brief instruction to Morla to go inside, the Captain interrupted the stream of invective issuing from the big man's lips, looked him coldly in the eye and said levelly:

'I think you had better leave.'

'Are you threatening me?' Hadran challenged sharply.

'No, Menellen,' Thadie rejoined, unperturbed. 'Merely stating an opinion.'

Hadran glared at him, more than half tempted to call in his own men and have the Captain arrested. Unfortunately, however, the Captain was not a native of the Province and, in view of his position within the household of the Dukrugvola's own niece, Hadran was not yet so far gone in rage that he did not realize that his arrest, without obvious and incontrovertible evidence of wrongdoing, would provoke a gigantic scandal, and even turn the tables on his captor. Moreover, his questioning of the boy had not been entirely without reward, and the knowledge gained made it imperative that he should depart from the town with the utmost haste. Every minute that he remained here was a minute lost to the pursuit.

Hadran's men did not know what to make of their commander. Like a hurricane, he swept them out of the town of Arlmen and back along the straight, wide highway towards Caleth Mor, raking the stones and verges for a sign. Again, nightfall halted their journey, but Hadran, conscious that the trail was growing ever colder, had them up and away at an early hour, cursing the overnight rainfall and the heavy flow of traffic, travelling the highway in both directions, which considerably hampered their activities. On and on he drove them, interminably, until at last one man, riding up the grass verge in an area of uncultivated shrubland, against the oncoming traffic, suddenly brought his mount to a halt and slid down from the saddle to pick up a piece of metal which had caught his eye, glinting in the sunlight from the midst of a clump of flowers. He lifted it, glanced at his find, and uttered a shout of excitement.

Hadran received the object balefully and halted to examine it. A sound like a snarl issued from his lips. He saw a dagger, or long knife, of a popular type, the blade double-edged and tapered, with a rounded hilt bound with strips of leather. Into the blade immediately below the point at which it was set into the hilt an emblem had been engraved: the initials F and C intertwined within a six-pointed star. It was a pattern with which Hadran was only too familiar. As a boy, Francys had been in the habit of drawing it on all his books. The dagger was also familiar. He had last seen it, or at any rate one very like it, concealed beneath the saddle of Francys' horse, Melisor.

****

In accordance with his custom, that morning the Lord Telstan Coras had retired to the seclusion of his study, ostensibly in order to work. Across the surface of the long oak table, almost eclipsing the gleam of the polished wood, heavy ledgers spread their pages, in vain. The neat, black-ink columns could not hold his attention. Leaning back in his magnificent carven chair, his hands lightly clasping the arms, the Lord of Varadil surrendered to reverie. The vague feeling of unease by which he had been haunted in recent days now fastened upon him with an overwhelming persuasiveness. He was conscious of an unpleasant, and unaccustomed, sensation of helplessness, a perception that events were taking place that were outwith his control, even of his understanding, as though he stood at the edge of a ring of light looking into the darkness at movements and shapes which he could not quite comprehend but which inspired in him an uncontrollable dread. The sense of foreboding was very strong.

Frowning, he took up his pen and began to bend the quill absentmindedly between his fingers. With an irritable sigh, he constrained himself to acknowledge the source of his disquiet. A little under a month since, his son, his *elder* son, had against *his* wishes, set out upon a journey northward into Kirkendom, where he held the reins of power as Regent to the young Prince. Yet, unaccountably, Hadran had failed to arrive in the city of Caleth Mor, and that despite the reported presence there of the Lady Nyandu Almeneth, and his current location was unknown. It was not that he entertained any fears as to his son's safety; merely that it was out of character, and thereby disturbing.

The quill, bent beyond endurance, snapped suddenly with a sharp little sound. The Lord Telstan Coras laid the fragments down upon the table, then, restlessly, pushed back his chair and rose, to pace the floor. As all too frequently of late, his mind was tormented by thoughts and questions that he was loathe to consider, yet unable to evade. The stories concerning the activities of the so-called "Menel Imraut" had filtered into Varadil, as into other neighbouring provinces. He had been amongst the first to hear the whispers, initially dismissing them simply as a resurgence in these difficult times of the old heroic legends relating to the promised return of Verindel Ameanor from the Spirit Realm. The location of Menel Imraut's alleged headquarters had reinforced this supposition, for everyone knew that the Toath Cranem was inimical to man. And, beside, it *had* to be so ... for if it were not, then he, Telstan Coras, would have to admit the possibility that he had been guilty of a most grave injustice. To believe in the living presence of Menel Imraut was to cast a shadow over the validity of the evidence which had proved Francys Coras to be a traitor.

The thought of his younger son, as always, aroused in the ageing Prince of Varadil a turmoil of irreconcilable emotions. Hadran, in looks so like himself, uncomplicated, he believed he knew, at least as well as one could ever know another, but the quick-silver, unreachable Francys merely bewildered him. The charge of treason had seemed to set the seal on a life already notorious for its iniquities. His death would have served as a welcome expiation, though preferably without the ignominy of a public execution. His disappearance, on the other hand, had left his father a prey to haunting anxieties. For many months he had awaited daily the expected news of Francys' arrival in Carakhas, but it had not come. Francys, it seemed, had vanished without trace. And then had begun the whispers, the stories about the people's new hero, Menel Imraut.

He feared that he knew what had drawn Hadran away from home, and kept him from the presence of the woman he loved. Somewhere in the depths of the countryside of Kirkendom, Hadran believed he would find his brother, his traitorous brother, of whose villainy he had himself been the agent of discovery. The Lord Telstan shook his head with an irritated gesture. What *was* this? The evidence was irrefutable, no matter whose hand it was that had brought it to light...

The knock at the door came as a welcome interruption to unwelcome reflections. The Lord Telstan Coras received the proffered missive with curiosity, and waved the man away. Seated once more in the great high-backed chair, he turned the slim package over between his hands, inspecting it with a careful thoroughness before finally breaking open the indecipherable seal with which it had been fastened. The packed proved to consist of two parts: the outer covering and another paper, folded within and loosely tied with ribbon. Upon the outer parchment the message was concise, if cryptic: *'634 - slionith - 5th day. Remember!'*

The Prince of Varadil frowned, nonplussed. The significance of the date initially escaped his comprehension. *'634 - slionith - 5th day'*. Slowly his hand closed over the stark black letters, painfully obliterating their outline from his vision, as he could not from his mind. That fatal day, from which so much misfortune had flowed. In a moment of clarity, he saw how the events of that day had cruelly twisted the destiny of his younger son, lying athwart his life like a great boulder in a stream, diverting its natural course. What tragedy that the random arrows of Providence could strike so capriciously to such disastrous effect! An accident of fate had placed Francys on that day to fall victim to capture at the hands of the Rarokins, and as a consequence he had become that basest of creatures: a traitor.

Deliberately Telstan unclosed his fingers, releasing the crumpled ball of paper to drop onto the table before him. What hand had sent that strange inscription? And to what purpose? His mind troubled and uncertain, his gaze fell upon the inner, folded parchment lying forgotten and unopened. Perhaps the answer lay within? He caught it up with uncustomary fervour, pulling the ribbon free, and unfolding the leaf of parchment in haste. He almost let it slip from his fingers in amazement. Hadran's script! What devilment was this? And not of recent origin, for the parchment bore signs of age. He began to read.

With a cry of horror, the Prince of Varadil started up from his chair. The meaning of that cryptic message was now dreadfully clear. All too easily did he recognize the place whose description lay before him in Hadran's unmistakable writing.

'No!'

The protest was forced out between shaking lips.

'Not Hadran ... not my son!'

Scarcely realizing what he was doing, he walked about the room with agitated steps, his jerky movements reflecting the turmoil within his mind. Hadran, his beloved son, had delivered his own brother into captivity. That much he had to believe. Not Providence after all, but Hadran had set the young man's feet onto the downward path to life as the lover of Rycharst, and to treachery.

Bewilderment gazed blankly from the aging Prince's eyes. In one brief moment his whole world had turned itself upside down. His trusted, favoured elder son! How could he have known him so poorly, have been so blind to the bitter hatred which had festered within

Hadran's breast, a hatred so intense that it had inspired him to arrange for the deliberate ambush and capture of his own brother by enemy forces! And he, poor, foolish, doting father that he was, had taken at face value all Hadran's subsequent expressions of sorrow, and learned to revile and despise the son whose only real crime had been to exist.

Then, against all expectation, Francys had returned. What then must Hadran's feelings have been? Surely he would have been secure in the belief that he would never see his brother living again, and then suddenly that brother had reappeared. With deepening horror Telstan began to perceive whither his thoughts were leading him. He considered the years following Francys' return, the growing popularity of his younger son, culminating in his heroic rescue of the Dukrugvola during the Northern campaign, which had won for him a nationwide acclaim. How must it have galled Hadran to watch his brother's rapid rise in fortune! With the Dukrugvola's favour, to what heights might Francys not have aspired? But, instead, overnight he had become a hunted man, outcast and with a price on his head, with death his only future. And all the evidence against him, incontrovertible as it appeared, had been discovered by Hadran.

The Lord Telstan Coras stood perfectly still, staring with appalled comprehension into the abyss which his thoughts had conjured before his very feet. Had Hadran, jealous of his brother's successes, spurred on by an extreme enmity, sought to ensure his absolute destruction, encompassing not only public disgrace and ignominious death, but reaching even beyond death to stamp a lasting taint of infamy upon his memory so that his very name might never be spoken save with revulsion? As certainly as he had recognized Hadran's hand on the parchment did he now discern the truth, seeing indeed with a stark clarity, and all too much. But for some miraculous dispensation of Providence, Francys would now be dead, wrongly, unjustly condemned, to all intents and purposes a victim of assassination at the instigation of his own brother. Whereas, at great personal risk, he had in the guise of Menel Imraut proved his loyalty over and over, preferring the perilous existence of an outlaw in his own land to the safe, easy life of an exile. Whilst Hadran ... Was Hadran even at this moment hard on the trail, bent on exterminating a man whom he knew, as none other, to be entirely innocent of the charges laid against him?

Suddenly he could bear it no longer. Impelled by some vague, half-understood idea, he stumbled from the room and made his way to the apartments allotted to his elder son, alarming the servants by his wild, unseeing gaze and unsteady, agitated gait. What he was seeking there, he knew not. As he came to a halt in the centre of the main chamber, a darkness overwhelmed his senses. He felt a tightening sensation about his chest. He could not breathe ... They found him sprawled face down upon the floor, one hand clutching at his breast, the other fastened tightly about a crumpled sheet of parchment, so creased and twisted that it was impossible to decipher what was written thereon.

Consciousness returned slowly, but the Prince of Varadil was a broken man. Grey-faced and visibly aged, he seemed to have withdrawn from the world, his sole remaining emotion an intensely desperate desire to communicate with the Dukrugvola 'concerning my son.'

He lingered thus a fortnight, propped upon pillows in the splendid canopied bed, whilst his household dissolved in turmoil around him. Urgent messages despatched to Lôren and to Caleth Mor were slow of response, and it was not until the fifteenth day following his collapse that his troubled retainers were gratified by the arrival of authority in the form of Hadran Coras. Interrupted in his unsuccessful search for Francys and Nyandu, Hadran had travelled southwards in an exceedingly sour frame of mind. No more detail than the mere fact of his father's indisposition had been vouchsafed to him and he had obeyed the summons with an ill grace. But this rapidly changed to consternation at the tale unfolded to his ears and he ascended the grand staircase to his father's bedchamber with hasty steps.

Telstan opened his eyes to the sight of the burly, fair-haired man framed in the doorway. Sunlight, pouring through the wide casement, lit every detail of his features. The sick man gazed at him in silence for a moment or two, then a grimace of something like revulsion twisted the slack features, and he looked down at the bedcover.

'So blind,' he muttered harshly, 'so blind.'

Hadran crossed the floor and sank to one knee beside the bed. Misunderstanding the import of the words, he laid his hand upon that of the older man.

'Father, it's me, Hadran,' he said reassuringly.

He would have spoken further, but that the expression in his father's hazel eyes robbed him of the power of speech. Aghast, he gaped mutely as the Prince of Varadil deliberately removed his hand from the contaminating touch of the son he had so loved. With a supreme effort, Telstan raised himself up against the pillows. He seemed to gather himself together as if to face someone or something only he could see, and with the last ebbing of his strength, he spoke, more clearly and distinctly than at any time since his collapse.

'Francys, forgive me!'

A shuddering sigh passed through the straining frame, and he fell back, lifeless.

CHAPTER THIRTEEN

News of the collapse and subsequent death of Lord Telstan Coras was brought to the Dukrugvola at the castle of the Prince of Sureindom, whose guest he was at that time, together with his wife and daughter. But just returned from riding out upon the moorland beyond the city of Shardu, the Lord Archaïlis strolled with his host across the lawn towards the ancient oak, beneath which were seated the ladies of the household. Contemplating the scene before him, Saragon could not prevent himself recalling the long, hot days of the previous summer and those other guests who had been used to sit in the shade of that same tree. Momentarily the image of a fair young man seemed to flicker into being; then Saragon blinked and it was gone. The Lady Inisia, smiling up at her son, directed his attention towards the tray of cool drinks laid out on a low table nearby and, having furnished the Dukrugvola with that of his choice and himself also (the ladies having already been served), he entered into the conversation, seating himself meanwhile upon the grass midway between the Lady Menethila and Alhaîtha. The Dukrugvola, leaning against the trunk of the tree, behind his wife, raised his cup in a toast to the pleasure of the moment and the peaceful enjoyment of a respite from the cares of government.

Then came the steward treading with measured gait across the grass towards them. Saragon, seeing him, raised his brows and remarked wryly:

'I think you may have spoken too soon, sir.'

Uncoiling his long legs, he rose and advanced to meet the steward. A brief exchange ensued, concluding with the passing over of a sealed package and the departure of the steward. Saragon turned the package over in his hand, and looked towards the Dukrugvola.

'This is addressed to you, sir. Sent on from Lôren.'

The Lord Archaïlis came forward to take it from him. Frowning slightly, he broke the seal and unfolded the outer covering. Within were two letters, their seals still unbroken, written in different hands but both bearing the arms of the Province of Varadil. He glanced at Saragon.

'Indeed, it seems that I did,' he remarked, harking back to

Saragon's earlier comment.

He opened one letter and swiftly read the contents. It was brief enough.

'To the Lord Dukrugvola, greetings', he read. *'The Prince of Varadil, the Lord Telstan Coras has suffered a collapse and lies grievously ill. He wishes to communicate with you on a matter of great urgency concerning his son. May it please you, Menellen, either to come yourself or to send a trusted messenger, to ease the Prince's mind.*

Your loyal servant, and steward of Väst, Barden Mitchall.'

There was a postscript, clearly written in a hurry and intriguing in content.

'We have sent to Kirkendom for the Lord Hadran Coras, but his present whereabouts are uncertain and we know not when he may come to Väst'.

With eyebrows raised, but forbearing to comment, the Lord Archaïlis silently handed the letter to Saragon, and whilst the latter hurriedly perused it, opened the second missive. It came from Hadran himself.

'To the Lord Dukrugvola, greetings,' it began in a thick and sprawling hand. *'It is with very great sadness that I write to announce the death of my father, the Lord Telstan Coras this day past...'*

'Dear Sior!' the Dukrugvola exclaimed involuntarily. 'The Lord Telstan Coras is dead!'

The Lady Inisia looked up.

'Poor man,' she said unexpectedly. 'At last he will find peace.'

The Dukrugvola addressed his hostess.

'It seems that I am not fated to enjoy your hospitality for much longer, my dear Inisia. I must set forth tomorrow - this missive has been on its travels so long that time is now short. I'm afraid I must steal Sharn from you also. We have an investiture to attend!

But I shall leave you the company of Menethila and Alhaîtha instead,' he concluded, smiling down at them all.

Alhaîtha looked disappointed.

'Oh, but Father,' she said quickly. 'May I not travel with you? I would like to attend the investiture.

I mean no disrespect to you, Lady Inisia,' she added hastily. 'You know that I always enjoy staying here in Shardu ...'

The Lady Inisia smiled at her.

'My dear child, do not concern yourself. I know exactly what you mean.'

And Alhaîtha was suddenly rather uncomfortably sure that the Lady Inisia did indeed know that, and more than perhaps she wished her to. She flushed slightly, and turned her gaze once more to her father.

'Well, Father. May I not go with you?' She had a sudden inspiration. 'We could perhaps meet up with Nan along the way! She is in the area isn't she, after all?'

'If she has kept to her plans, she will be travelling towards the northern borders of Kirkendom and Arlente now, away from Varadil,' her father observed, with a smile.

'And I warrant that that is one investiture that she would prefer *not* to attend unless she had no choice!' interpolated Saragon, grinning.

'Please, Father,' Alhaîtha wheedled, at her most persuasive.

'Well, Alie, I won't say no,' the Dukrugvola answered, holding up a hand to stay her response. 'I must give it some thought before I decide yea or nay. I will let you know my decision this evening, how's that?'

Alhaîtha looked vaguely mutinous.

'But ...' she began.

'No buts, Alie, my dear,' said her father, preparing to walk back towards the castle with Saragon. 'Let me go and have a chat with Sharn now and I promise you'll have your answer tonight at supper.'

With that, Alhaîtha had to be content as, pouting a little with frustration, she watched the two men walk away.

Shortly thereafter, the Dukrugvola sat facing the younger man across the broad oak table in Saragon's private office. He rested his hands lightly on the polished surface and looked at Saragon. He had in recent years developed a healthy respect for the younger man's opinions, finding with pleasure someone at last with whom to share his thoughts, and from whom he might profitably seek advice. Advice was what he sorely needed at this moment, and because of the nature of the problem, Saragon was in any event the only person to whom he could speak openly.

'Well, Sharn,' he said after a pause, gesturing towards the two letters which lay between them. 'What are your thoughts on the matter? What are we to make of this first missive?'

'I hardly know, sir. The Lord Telstan Coras is dead. That's certain enough. And before he died, he suffered some sort of seizure, and sent word that he wished to speak to you 'concerning his son', but which son and what did he want to discuss?'

'I like not the postscript,' the Dukrugvola observed. 'It strikes suspicious to me. Hadran roaming around Kirkendom, his whereabouts unknown ... Now we know that the mysterious Menel Imraut, about whose identity we have our own surmise, has been making his presence felt in the area. Suppose,' he said thoughtfully, coming closer to the truth than he realised, 'that Hadran has been following some trace, some clue that might bring him to this man.'

'Or mayhap he has been dancing attendance on Nan during her travels,' suggested Saragon, with a chuckle. 'I shouldn't put *that* past him.

Still,' he added more soberly, 'at least he cannot have caught Menel Imraut, or anybody else, or he would have boasted of the fact. And we know from his letter that he is now in Väst, where he will perforce be obliged to stay at the very least until after the investiture.'

'Yes, the investiture.'

Saragon grinned.

'Will you allow Alhaîtha to accompany us, sir?'

'What are your thoughts, Sharn? Would you mind?'

The Dukrugvola looked at the other man ruefully. He was well aware of his daughter's feelings for Saragon, and in truth would have welcomed him gladly into his family, but he also knew Saragon's own feelings on the subject and was anxious not to push him into an awkward position.

'I have no strong opinion either way,' the latter said candidly. 'Yet, it might be as well to take Alie along in the party. She might serve to distract Hadran's attention for us, if need be, and her presence would perhaps provide a reassurance to the people of Varadil that the Dukrugvola values their province. We cannot afford to antagonise them in any way by showing any lack of enthusiasm for their new Prince.'

'That is well considered, Sharn. The security of our borders must always be of concern. One could not fault the Lord Telstan Coras on the manner in which he upheld the safety of the realm, whatever reservations one might have had concerning other areas of his management.

And maybe,' he added musingly, 'it is time that Alie came to know somewhat more of the realm, of which she will one day have the governance, and for the people to get to know their future Dukrugvola.'

'Sir!' protested Saragon, concerned. 'There is no reason ... you are not ...'

The Dukrugvola smiled.

'No, no,' he reassured the younger man. 'I am perfectly well, I assure you. I intend to go on for many years yet, Sior willing. Still, it would be all to the good for the people of Karled-Dū to become accustomed to her over a period of time before she takes over the role of their leader. And she is certainly old enough to wish to travel and broaden her horizons, as indeed Nan is doing. I wonder that she has not suggested it before. Well, why not let this be the first foray, eh?'

'Why not indeed? And what of the Lady Menethila, sir? Will she wish to come also?'

'I think not.'

In this he was correct. When the Dukrugvola broached the matter to his wife in the privacy of their bedchamber whilst changing for supper, the Lady Menethila immediately confirmed her intention to remain at Shardu for the present.

'We two old ladies can keep each other company', she remarked.

The Lord Archaïlis smiled at her fondly.

'Old?' he quizzed gently. 'You'll never be old to me, my love. But ... you think it's right to take Alie to Varadil?'

'Oh yes. She wouldn't want to be cooped up with us. She'd be bored here, and lonely. She misses Nan you know. They have always been very close, and with Nan off 'adventuring', Alie feels left out. Now she can be doing something too.'

She rose from her chair, where she had been tidying her hair before the mirror, and came towards her husband, slipping her arm through his.

'Let us go down and tell her the glad tidings!'

They made good time down to Lôren where Saragon, deeming it impractical to open up his town-house for a stopover of a mere couple of days, gratefully accepted an invitation to stay at the castle. Whilst Alhaîtha oversaw the packing of a suitable wardrobe for the expedition, and arrangements were set in hand for the safe transport of the Dukrugvola's regalia, the Lord Archaïlis himself took advantage of the brief return to Lôren to go through the various documents and missives awaiting his attention, which had not yet been forwarded on to him. In this manner, he came across a letter written from the Chan of Krapan, protesting in long-winded and flowery, but obviously irate terms, at the annihilation of a corps of his private fighting-men by a company of cavalry from Varadil, commanded by the Regent of Kirkendom in person. The Dukrugvola frowned, and tossed the letter over to Saragon, who happened to have entered the room at that moment. The latter scanned the epistle swiftly, and grinned.

'Well, it seems we now know what Hadran has been up to after all', he commented. 'But why? It is not like Hadran to wantonly antagonize the Chan. I thought he rather favoured an alliance with Krapan, if anything.'

'It certainly bears investigating,' agreed the Dukrugvola. 'I shall be interested to discover the detail from Hadran when we reach Väst.'

The Dukrugvola's party set out from Lôren early on the morning of the third day, travelling at a good pace. They were well-guarded. It was no small matter to take the circlet, Caelvorchadu, out upon the road where they must at all times be wary of attack; for let the agents of Rycharst only set their hands upon it, and all would be lost indeed. Yet travel it must, for it was an integral part of the ceremony of investiture, together with the two knives, the Taer elna Ancren, the knife of the oath, and the Taer elna Vordu, the knife of death. The casket containing these precious emblems of authority was strapped securely to the Dukrugvola's saddle during the day, and guarded at every rest-stop and overnight stay by one of the two bodyguards whose task it was to ensure its safety.

To Alhaîtha's regret, there was no time to spare for her to take a proper look at the countryside through which they passed, but she forbore to complain, not wishing her father, and Saragon, to feel that it would have been better had she not insisted on accompanying them. Besides, she thought, she could always take the time on her return journey and look around her at her leisure. Initially she found the pace tiring, and at the end of the first day required to be lifted from her saddle and assisted into the inn, where she was fortunate enough to enjoy a soothing soak in a bath-tub. However, she soon became accustomed to the swiftness of their progress and the regular changes of mount, which their need for haste required. Their route led them at first southwards as far as the port of Darneth, a road which she had often travelled, then east through the Province of Perendom, home to Hadran's close friend, Hethlan Lorchaset. Crossing the heather and bracken-covered rolling expanse of the Mele Sen, they rounded the tip of the mountain range of the Teleth Perineth and made for the coastal town of Der. The track led then mostly along the coast, so that they had the sea to their right, occasionally hidden by a rise in the cliffs. The Province of Perendom stretched long and narrow, squeezed between the mountains in the north and the sea to the south, and bordering Varadil in the east. Alhaîtha enjoyed the feel of the sea-breeze across her face, grateful for its soft breath as she rode under the hot sun along the seemingly endless ribbon of the highway which connected each small town like the thread of a spider's web.

As they rode, she seized the opportunity to question Saragon about their destination, only to discover that he had in fact never visited the city of Väst, his only excursion into Varadil hitherto having been in the northern region of that province some years before. The Dukrugvola proved of more use in this respect, and enlivened the ride for a while with tales of what he had seen on his last visit to the city. Saragon, listening with interest, realized with a slight shock that this last visit must have been the occasion when the Dukrugvola had travelled down to Väst with Francys, after the latter's escape from enslavement by the Lord of Shadowe. He wondered whether the Lord Archaïlis was also remembering the circumstances of his previous journey to the city, although of course he would then have been approaching it from the north rather than the west.

After they had crossed the border and had left the coast to turn inland in order to avoid the marshy delta region where the mighty river Armenet finally debouched into the sea, Saragon became noticeably more subdued. He could not help but think how different it might have been had he been approaching the great city of Väst as a welcome invitee of his friend, Francys, and not with the reluctance he now felt. He recalled that the estates that Francys had inherited from his mother lay somewhere to the north, nestling at the foot of the huge range of mountains that separated Varadil from the wastes of the Toath Cranem. So high were the greatest of the peaks of that range, that they were able to spy them far off against the horizon, standing dimly blue and purple, white headed, against the sky-line. Francys had spoken affectionately of his property at Körain, and Saragon wondered grimly what had become of it, who held it now, for of a certainty it would have been seized as forfeited lands upon the denunciation of the fair man as a traitor. He shook himself free from the gloomy thoughts which threatened to overwhelm him, and spurred his horse forward to join the Dukrugvola and Alhaîtha some little way ahead as they rode towards the wide, slow-rolling waters of the Armenet which lay across their path, crossable only by ferry at this point.

****

Those few weeks between the death of his father and the day of his own investiture as Prince of Varadil were busy ones for Hadran. His first concern had been to scotch any rumours which might have begun to circulate within the palace concerning the manner of his father's demise and its possible cause. Those of the servants who had waited upon the Lord Telstan Coras in the last days of his life, and who might have been privy to his mutterings or close enough to have overheard his last words, were granted immediate leave, on compassionate grounds. They would afterwards be encouraged to seek other employment. Gossip was actively discouraged and harsh measures taken against those who transgressed.

In truth, there was little enough leisure for the telling of tales during that time. Immediately following the old Lord's death, there were arrangements to be made for his funeral. The entire household was obliged to assume mourning livery; the body had to be washed, dressed and laid in state on a bier in the great hall so that all who wished might come to pay their respects, and the rooms which had been used by the Lord Telstan Coras be given a thorough cleansing, as was customary in the Province.

Hadran, clad in sombre grey, walking behind the bier as it was carried through the city streets on a horse-drawn cart swathed in drapes of pearl-grey silk, listened to the chanting of the priests of Sior who preceded the bier in procession, and found time for reflection. He had undertaken the last rites which the nearest relatives accord to the dead person - placing a piece of salted bread on the lips, covering the eyes with a strip of rough woollen cloth and setting a candle in one hand and a flask of water in the other, to ease the passage of the dead man to the life 'beyond'. Now came the journey to the funeral field, an area of land sited outside the city walls, where the body would be placed upon the funeral pyre. The days of its burning would be watched over by the priests, who would gather the resulting ashes and with appropriate ceremony consign them to the deeps of the ocean. (Inland, the custom was to scatter the ashes in a suitable location, usually a place with some association with the dead person).

He was at last free of his father's stern rule, although the situation was not quite as he had envisaged it in his daydreams. For one thing, he walked alone behind the bier. When he had, in the past, pictured his accession to the Princedom, he had gloried in the chance that it would provide him to underline to his brother the difference in their status. How he would be able to lord it over Francys once he became the ruler of the province! But Francys was not here to see his triumph.

That thought reminded him that Francys should not have been anywhere but in the grave. Yet he was not, and no-one knew where he was, and so long as the fair man lived on somewhere, he, Hadran, would never be safe again. The power had shifted; Hadran no longer held the upper hand, even at this moment of his ascendency. He was doomed to live ever under the threat of a hanging sword, and at any moment his brother could cut the cord and send it flashing down to pierce his heart. He could not prevent a shudder of terror from passing through his body at the notion. Those watching the procession thought that he faltered momentarily, and put it down to grief.

He pulled himself together and resumed the steady pace with which he followed the body of his late father. Francys, he reminded himself, was an outlaw. He had no standing in the land, and could not come forward to speak out against Hadran without thereby forfeiting his own life. And why should he be believed if he did so? The fear began to recede again from Hadran's mind as sense took over. Who could believe the word of a proven traitor? Might they not simply conclude that Francys was trying to impugn the honour of the man who had been instrumental in uncovering his treachery?

But, his memory reminded him, there was also Nyandu. Nyandu, with whom, if things had turned out differently, he might even now have been sharing the task of burying his father. Where *was* she? Was she with Francys somewhere, knowing all that had happened to him at his brother's hands? Or, with a spurt of desperate hope, was it true what Morla had told him, and was she even now merely travelling around in Arlente on business connected with the Dukrugvola? He *must* know! He had left a man in Arlmen with instructions to keep a watch on the household and to inform him of any sightings of the Lady Nyandu. His other desire, to search the countryside surrounding the spot on which that knife belonging to Francys had been found, had been frustrated by the requirement to return to Väst. He heaved a sigh. If his father had not been taken ill at that precise moment ... His thoughts turned then to the circumstances of that illness, which he had bullied out of the old Lord's servants, and to that strange about-turn of the Lord Telstan Coras just before he had died. What had he *known*?

The funeral over, Hadran returned to the palace to confront further difficulties in the form of a lengthy and impassioned epistle written by no less a personage than the Chan of Krapan, who had been moved to enquire in long-winded and ornate, but no less irate, terms why the Lord Hadran Coras, Regent of the Province of Kirkendom, had seen fit to attack and annihilate a corps of his private cavalry troops for no good reason and when they had, moreover, been on Krapani territory. Hadran, incensed at the Chan's presumption and, despite there being no evidence to confirm his point of view, still harbouring a conviction that the horsemen had had some connection with his brother, promptly responded at equal length and with equal irascibility. His action had been perfectly justified, he claimed, since he had been engaged in the pursuit of a very dangerous criminal and had naturally concluded that the opportune arrival of the Chan's soldiers, disguised as they were, must be linked in some way to the aforementioned malefactor. In any event, as he pointed out at length, the Chan had himself been the first to violate the agreement, both by affording asylum to the renegade Francys Coras, and in sending his horsemen into Kirkendom, for there was no denying the fact that the Province of Kirkendom was indeed their destination, even though they had not actually crossed the border at the time when they were sighted. As Regent of that Province, he, Hadran, had merely been fulfilling his duty to prevent hostile troops from entering upon the land. The letter was despatched by special messenger, bearing within the package the ransom demands in respect of the five Krapani who had been taken prisoner during the incident.

Dismissing the affair from his mind as soon as the letter had been sent, Hadran immersed himself in the preparations for his formal investiture and it was in the thick of these arrangements that the Chan's response arrived from Krapan to mar his pleasure. It came in the form of a short, concise note, which stated categorically that relations between the states of Krapan and Karled-Dū were to be considered to be at an end; that any person belonging to the state of Karled-Dū found on Krapan territory without permission of the Chan would be liable to summary execution as a spy; and, further, that any body of men bearing arms observed within the boundaries of Krapan would constitute an act of aggression, leading to an immediate declaration of war. And to underline the point, if such were necessary, the bearer of the missive was none other than the erstwhile Ambassador to the Court of the Chan, a Varadil nobleman, sent packing from Miche with his retinue, and lucky to have made the journey safely.

Thus Hadran, on the eve of his installation into the seat of power, found himself in an extremely unenviable position. Moreover, he would have to explain his actions, and those of the Chan, to the Dukrugvola in person, rather than by letter from a safe distance.

CHAPTER FOURTEEN

Saragon walked through the doorway into the bedchamber to which the steward had shown him, and stood looking about him, mopping his brow with one sleeve of his shirt. Gratefully he noted that someone had left a tray on the linen chest beside the door, with a jug of ale and a goblet. Seizing the jug, he hastened to pour himself a liberal helping, and downed most of it in one long swallow. Refilling the cup, he wandered over to the window, curious to see the view over the city. As he stood there, sipping the ale more slowly, there came a knock at the door and a couple of servants entered, bringing up his baggage. They set it down, and one man left the room. The other lingered.

'Is there aught I can do for you, Menellen?' he enquired quietly.

'No, no, thank you,' Saragon responded without looking at the man. Then something about the voice struck him as being familiar.

'Stay!' he said quickly, and turned.

'Blial!' he exclaimed in astonishment. 'I thought I recognized your voice. What in the name of all that's wonderful are *you* doing here?'

The manservant carefully closed the door.

'Can I trust you, Menellen?' he asked, then realizing what he had just said, blushed hotly and began to stammer an apology.

Saragon hastened to reassure him.

'If it has aught to do with the Lord Francys, you may speak freely to me, without fear of being denounced; I give you my word on it.'

Blial bowed his head in acknowledgment of these words.

'Well, Menellen, as you know, after the events of last arenith I was without a post. Since that time, I have managed to scrape a living, doing this and that, but I knew they were always short of men at the palace, and I thought to myself that I might as well spit two pigeons with one arrow as it were and get myself into a position where I might be of some service to my master, if you take my meaning.'

Saragon grinned.

'But how did you get them to take you on?' he enquired curiously. 'I should have thought you'd be the last person they would want to employ in this household!'

'Aye, there *was* some reluctance,' Blial conceded, 'but I put on an act and made out that I believed all the tales that were being bandied about - you'd never credit some of the stories that folks have come out with since his name was read out! Anything that could blacken his name, and someone will have told it as the honest truth! And that brother of his, aye and the father too, they never lifted a finger to stop it all. Well, if the truth be told, the old Lord, he just kept himself to himself and likely never heard any of it, but the Lord Hadran, well I wouldn't be surprised to learn that he'd made up half the stories himself!'

'Very likely,' Saragon said drily. 'I wouldn't put it past him.'

Saragon moved over to sit down on the bed and motioned to the servant to take a seat on the stool nearby.

'What do you know of the events surrounding the death of the Lord Telstan Coras?' he asked.

Some time later, Saragon knocked gently on the door of the chamber allotted to the Dukrugvola, and entered.

'I have some news which I think you will be interested to hear,' he said. 'Where do you suppose Lord Telstan was when he had the seizure?'

The Lord Archaïlis raised his head from the papers he had been studying and looked enquiringly.

'In Hadran's rooms,' the Sureindom man continued. 'It seems he had received a packet that morning, which sent him hot-foot up to Hadran's apartments. The servants found him there, slumped on the floor.'

'What was in the packet?' asked the Dukrugvola.

'A letter it's assumed. No-one knows exactly. A piece of parchment was found in Lord Telstan's clenched fist, but the contents were indecipherable. One thing is interesting though; the writing on the outer wrapper was in the same hand as that on letters previously delivered to Hadran, including one which he received only a few weeks ago which prompted him to leave Väst in haste, against the wishes of his father.'

The Dukrugvola's eyes widened.

'That *is* interesting. Well, well, Sharn, you *have* been busy. How did you manage to find out all this so quickly?'

Saragon smiled and raised his hands in a gesture of self-depreciation.

'I take no credit for it, sir. I merely had a lucky encounter. You remember Francys' manservant, Blial? He has found employment here and has been using the opportunities it affords to gather information which might be useful to his former master ... and to us,' he added with a knowing glance.

The Lord Archaïlis smiled.

'Indubitably.'

He gestured towards the papers scattered in front of him.

'I too have not been idle,' he remarked.

'So I see, sir.'

'And,' the Dukrugvola continued smoothly, ' I have arranged a meeting with Hadran privately tomorrow morning, before the investiture. I should like *you* to be there too, Sharn.'

'Hadran won't like *that*,' Saragon observed.

'He will have to put up with it nonetheless,' the Dukrugvola responded calmly. 'I want you there, as a witness if need be.'

'Very well, sir, I'll be there.'

The Lord Archaïlis smiled at him.

'It should be interesting.'

****

'*What*?!'

The two men confronted Hadran.

'The Lady Nyandu has been kidnapped,' he repeated, 'by my brother.'

The face of the Dukrugvola had blenched, he noted with satisfaction. Saragon was shaking his head.

'I don't believe it.'

Hadran looked from one to the other, slowly, savouring the moment. He had been furious (though careful not to openly display his rage) when the Dukrugvola had brought the Sureindom man into what had been intended to be a private meeting between himself and his liege-lord. Very well aware that the Dukrugvola meant to take him to task regarding the breakdown of relations with Krapan, he had no desire to be given a dressing down in the presence of Saragon Cerinor, of all people, that smug, supercilious bastard! There and then, he had decided instead to take the offensive, letting fall his statement as a bolt from the blue, with results that he found highly pleasing.

After a moment or two of silent consternation, the Dukrugvola's commonsense reasserted itself.

'If this is some sort of a jest, then it is most ill-timed,' he said sternly. 'My niece is perfectly safe and no doubt travelling through Arlente on her journey back to Lôren.'

'Are you sure of that, Menellen?' Hadran enquired. 'Have you heard from her recently?'

'I have not, nor would I expect to. Any communication will have been sent to Lôren, where she would believe me to be. But she is due to return to Lôren shortly in any event, and most likely would not have thought it necessary to write.'

'Then you would be surprised to learn that she has not been seen since she left the city of Caleth Mor, and that the members of her household have been resident in Arlmen without her for nigh on six weeks?'

The Dukrugvola raised his eyebrows. Beside him, Saragon stirred.

'And how do *you* come to know that, if indeed it is so?' he asked aggressively.

Hadran smiled sweetly at him, which made Saragon's palms itch to fetch the big fair man a crack on the jaw. He restrained himself and held his gaze levelly.

'I have had a man watching the house,' Hadran replied. 'She has not been there.'

The Lord Archaïlis was still not convinced.

'She could be travelling in Arlente still,' he observed coolly.

'Without her bodyguard, or even her maid?' Hadran enquired sarcastically. 'And having left the young boy Morla in the care of her Captain? Does this seem the sort of behaviour that Nyandu is likely to indulge in?

Besides,' he continued, in the face of their combined silence, 'Nyandu never reached Arlente. She disappeared somewhere along the highway between Caleth Mor and Arlmen.'

Saragon shook his head again.

'Nothing of what you have told us so far adds up to a kidnapping,' he said antagonistically. 'Do you know what *I* would deduce from these facts? I would imagine from my knowledge of Nan that someone stopped her on the highway to ask for her assistance,' he continued, coming closer to the truth than he suspected, 'and that she willingly agreed to give that assistance. There was no kidnapping! Why, man, I know her Captain of arms well enough. Do you really think he would offer no resistance if she was attacked? He would be dead himself before he'd let her be taken captive! No, no! If *he*'s sitting tamely in Arlmen waiting for her, it's on *her* orders, and she's off somewhere of her own free will.'

He stared challengingly at Hadran.

'Sior only knows what your game is, Hadran, but *that* story won't fadge!'

Hadran's face reddened with fury.

'What do you want?' he shouted. 'Proof?'

He reached behind him.

'There!' he said, panting with rage. 'There's your proof!'

And he cast onto the desk between them a slim, sharp dagger.

The Dukrugvola and Saragon leant forward simultaneously. Hadran's thick forefinger pointed towards an area of the blade immediately below the haft. Saragon raised his head.

'I concede that that dagger is or has been the property of Francys, but it means nothing. You could have got it from his rooms here, for all we know.'

'It was found on the highway,' Hadran insisted. 'I can bring you the man who found it.'

'That still means nothing,' Saragon declared obstinately. 'Sure it's Francys' dagger and maybe your man did find it on the highway. It could have been dropped there at any time. How can that be proof in any sense of the word that Francys has kidnapped Nan? You're dreaming Hadran! You've concocted this farcical accusation to distract attention from what *you*'ve been getting up to!...'

'How dare you!'

Hadran was on his feet like a bull about to charge.

'You're always out to get me, Saragon Cerinor! You can't bear it that your beloved Francys has been proved a traitor, can you? So you want to get your own back on me because I was the one to expose him. Nyandu *has* vanished, and I *know* it's my damned bastard of a brother who's behind it! I know it!' he spat furiously.

It was plain that he did in fact believe this.

'Now just you listen ...' Saragon began, rising from his chair, but the Dukrugvola stayed him with a hand and he subsided, reluctantly.

The Dukrugvola turned a steady gaze upon the Varadil man, under the influence of which, Hadran too slowly resumed his seat.

'Might I enquire precisely how and when you became aware of this ... situation?' the Lord Archaïlis demanded, his voice radiating icy calm belied by the flash of rage in his eyes. 'And how it comes about that you have not troubled to inform *me* before today, if, as you say, Nyandu has been missing for a month and a half?'

These questions brought Hadran up short with a jolt. In his haste to forestall the Dukrugvola's expected reprimand by imparting the most shocking news that he could provide, he had overlooked that he might be called upon to explain how he had come by the knowledge. His brain whirred at frantic speed, until at last he said slowly:

'I received information.'

'You received information,' the Dukrugvola repeated.

'Tell me, did this information come to you by way of a written note?' he asked with interest.

Hadran seized gratefully upon the prompt and agreed, only to be knocked back again by the next enquiry.

'But I understood,' the Lord Archaïlis continued smoothly, 'that you left here in response to such a message some weeks before the disappearance of Nyandu, and that your whereabouts were uncertain during that period. If you had received information that she was in danger, how is it that you did not instantly communicate this fact either to her, or by sending a message to me?'

Hadran was forced to think quickly.

'Well, it was like this,' he conceded. 'The note didn't actually state that Nyandu was in danger, else I would have taken all possible precautions on her behalf, as Regent of Kirkendom where she was staying. No, what it told me was the news that my treacherous brother had been sighted in the province. Naturally I went after him at once. I got on his trail,' he continued, adapting the truth to suit his current purpose and warming to the task, 'and it led me across Kirkendom to the border with Krapan, where we were surprised by the Krapani raiding party.'

He saw that this fact was of interest to the Dukrugvola and nodded.

'Aye ... at the time I believed ... and I have not seen any evidence since to make me change my mind on the matter ... I believed that it was set up by Francys. But anyways, the bastard wasn't with them. He'd only doubled back into Kirkendom. He must have planned it all out. I reckon he must have sent a note to Nyandu to lure her out of Caleth Mor - the Lady Annis said she'd had a message from you, but I'll warrant you hadn't sent her one! He probably told her there was some sick person needing her help. That'd bring her. I got the news she'd left Caleth Mor too late to overtake her. I was trying to find her when the news of my father's death reached me and I had to return here.'

'Ah, yes, your father,' murmured the Dukrugvola, without showing in any way whether he had accepted Hadran's story. 'I understand that he too received one of these mysterious missives from your informant.'

His knowledge of this fact clearly came as an unwelcome surprise to Hadran, who gaped at him in dismay.

'So I understand,' he replied at last, lamely. 'I did not see it myself, but I presume it must have contained the news of Nyandu's capture. Nothing else could have so overthrown my father.'

Saragon looked as though he was on the point of speaking, but at that moment there sounded a sharp rap on the door. A servant entered, deferentially reminding them that the hour of the ceremony was fast approaching. The Dukrugvola rose, gesturing to Saragon to do likewise.

'Well, Hadran, this has been a most instructive talk, but we will leave you now to prepare for your investiture. We will meet again shortly.'

He made for the door, but paused and turned.

'I must charge you not to utter even one word of your suspicions regarding my niece's current whereabouts,' he said sternly. '*I* shall deal with the matter henceforth.'

He swept from the room, closely followed by the Sureindom man, leaving Hadran, collapsed into his chair, staring after them with an expression in which mingled equal parts of fury and unease.

Saragon, striding through the corridors alongside the Dukrugvola, was unable to express his feelings adequately, given the presence of servants and others busy with last minute arrangements for the investiture.

'Whatever Hadran may say, I still do not believe it,' he stated eventually. 'He would know full well that it would be the quickest way to bring the hunt down upon himself. He would never have been so foolish!'

Inside, however, a tiny seed of doubt sprouted in his mind born of his knowledge of the love which Francys felt for Nyandu. He resolutely crushed it.

'What will you do?' he asked aloud.

The Dukrugvola glanced at him.

'For the moment, naught,' he said softly.

****

Väst was a large city bordering an inlet of the Cel Menlete upon the west side and spreading back into the countryside, edged to the south by the forest of Rue. In style it was similar to towns in nearby Arami, there having been extensive trading between the two States since time immemorial, but with its own distinctive elements. Thus, broad, paved streets lined with trees, behind which rose courtyard walls enclosing gardens and eventually the houses themselves, decorated with elaborate patterns and columns, and topped more often than not by small towers or turrets, were the rule rather than the exception, save, naturally, in the poorer areas of the city, where buildings constructed of wood and wattle and daub, crowded together in squalid narrow, winding alleys into which scarce a ray of sunlight could reach to penetrate the gloom.

The main thoroughfare and adjacent merchant quarters bore witness to the prosperity of the Province of Varadil. Shopkeepers hung their wares seductively in view, merchants, nobles and other citizens and visitors strolled along clad in good quality gowns and hose. Wagons and carts rumbled over the paving, laden with all manner of goods, exotic and ordinary: spices from Arami and farther South, wares from the foreign ships which put into the harbour, silk, timber, woollen cloth, metals, fruit, furs and meat.

In the centre of the city stood the palace, set along one length of the main square. From beyond the safety of the massive encircling wall sprang up row upon row of towers sculpted and carved into airy peaks, between which rose the steeply sloped roof of the great hall and the main body of the palace. For the purpose of the ceremony, a wooden platform had been erected, level with the top of the flight of steps which led from the square to the massive arched gateway, draped in sumptuous cloth. Already some time before the hour set for the investiture, the crowd filled the great square, pressed almost to the foot of the wooden structure, surging back and forth like a field of rye in a strong wind, and held in check by a detachment of Hadran's personal guard, ceremonially clad in scarlet surcoats emblazoned with the snarling black cat symbol of the Province. Around the edge of the square, the richer citizens had raised staging and sat in state, deriving from their higher position the benefit of the light breeze, which escaped those below. Wine and ale sellers moved amongst the crowd, dispensing liquid refreshment, whilst stalls set up in nearby streets sold fruits and pastries, and the local speciality, a form of pressed fruit puree cut into squares.

High up in one of the turrets a bell tolled out the twelve strokes of noon, and at this signal the tall bronze gates opened to reveal a procession of notables who walked slowly out onto the wooden platform and ranged themselves to each side, facing the open square, leaving a wide space in the centre. Cheers greeted them, and shouts for those amongst them who were recognized. A short moment of suspense followed. Then two servants emerged from the gates, one bearing a narrow casket of some dark metal (halain), the other a garment of rich black cloth. Taking up posts on either side of the steps, they stood to attention with their burdens. Finally, amid vociferous acclamation, the Lord Archaïlis Oneranen, Dukrugvola of the realm of Karled-Dū stepped into view, followed a pace or two behind by the Lord Hadran Coras. The Dukrugvola wore the formal robes of office: a long, sleeveless robe of white samite, emblazoned on the front with the great ring Caelvorchadu in gold, belted and with the skirts slashed to the hip, over dark hose and a fine lawn shirt with long, close-fitting sleeves. A heavy black mantle edged with sable completed his attire, and upon his head could be seen the smooth, silver-white circlet of Caelvorchadu itself. In his turn, Hadran Coras was clad only in shirt and hose and surcoat, which in his case bore the colours and crest of the Coras family.

Alhaîtha shifted very slightly as she stood beside Saragon. She had been conscious of the tension within him from the moment when he had joined her in the antechamber where the guests had congregated in readiness for the procession. Something, she surmised, had occurred to put him out of temper; something other than the mere fact of seeing Hadran succeed to the princedom, of course. Though he had smiled and spoken courteously to his fellow guests, she knew him well enough to be able to see through the mask. Now she discerned a similar tenseness in the bearing of her father. She turned her gaze towards the figure behind him. Hadran too bore the faint signs of ill-temper, coupled in his case with anxiety, which she presumed to be natural nervousness arising from the occasion. It appeared, therefore, that something had taken place between the three of them. She wished she knew what it was. Ever since her arrival, she had felt left out, on the edge of events, aware of undercurrents, but unable, despite all attempts, to discover just what was going on. She was lonely too. She was not well acquainted with the other Princes who had travelled to Väst for the investiture, most of whom were more of an age with her father. If only her cousin had been there. She had said as much to Hadran last evening, and had wondered a little at his startled reaction.

But here was her father approaching the edge of the raised stage. He raised his hand and an expectant hush settled over the crowded square, beginning with those nearest and travelling towards the far corners like a wave across a pond. Into the silence dropped the words of the Dukrugvola, measured and stately:

'I give you greetings citizens of Väst, all those of you who dwell in the Province of Varadil, and all who have travelled here to assist at this important occasion. In the name of the people of Karled-Dū, I stand here today, to carry out the commands and designs of He who rules over all men and the spirit world alike, by whose hand we are guided in our lives, Sior, Lord of All. Kush trebor vencri mire.'

He paused, then turned.

'Lord Hadran Coras, step forward.'

Hadran advanced and stood beside the Dukrugvola, facing the crowd. The Lord Archaïlis spoke to the waiting people:

'Before Sior, do you choose and take this man to rule over you, to administer your government and to dispense the justice of the Ring Caelvorchadu in this province of Varadil?'

The response was deafening. For all his failings, despite his cruel temper, Hadran was a member of the Coras family, whose name inspired the loyalty of their people as unfailingly as night followed day. Cheer after cheer spiralled upwards from the packed square, silenced only after an interval by the upraised hand of the Dukrugvola. Turning to Hadran, he continued:

'Do you, Hadran Coras, consent to enter into this high office and take up the burdens which this estate lays upon you, to bear responsibility for each person living within the boundaries of this province and to put forward your best endeavours to protect and safeguard their lands and livelihoods, to administer justice fairly without fear or favour?'

'Before Sior, I do,' the reply came directly.

'Are you also, as the chosen Prince of this Province of Varadil, prepared to bind yourself under the oath of the great circlet of Caelvorchadu and to submit yourself willingly to the authority of the Dukrugvola, whether myself or any other duly invested, on all occasions and at all times?'

'I am.'

'And do you pledge to uphold that authority to the best of your ability when the need arises?'

'I do.'

At his words, Saragon moved from his place and, approaching the servant with the casket, lifted the lid and took out from its velvet-covered interior a knife fashioned entirely of red-gold, with a thin, double-edged blade some nine inches in length, topped by a slender straight hilt set with sapphires. This was the Taer elna Ancren, the Knife of the Oath, a priceless artefact of unknown origin, reputed indeed to have come from the spirit realm. Handling it with reverence, Saragon placed the blade into the hands of the Dukrugvola, then turned again to the casket, from whence he lifted out a second knife, similar in style to the first, but wrought of the white metal thenome with a hilt bound with black leather and bearing a pale, luminous gem at the tip: the Taer elna Vordu, Knife of Death.

From his position at the side of the Dukrugvola, Hadran moved to sink down onto one knee before his liege lord, his back now to the crowded square. As he did so, Saragon stepped into the place that he had vacated, holding up the Taer elna Vordu for all to see, its blade pointing downwards. To Alhaîtha, he looked as though he would not have been sorry to have used the weapon on the man kneeling at his feet.

'Hadran Coras', said the Dukrugvola formally, 'do you now take the oath.'

Hadran reached out his right hand and placed his fingers over the golden knife offered to him. In a loud voice (in which a note of triumph was distinctly audible) he pronounced the words of the ancient oath.

'Ruath än nammen meya, Hadran Coras, lenach Telstany Corasy, prani rastery chorbe glutese stilethiny in arlethiny, nimen Sioroi, Meneloi Arachoi.'

Saragon took hold of Hadran's right forefinger and, using the very tip of the blade of the knife which he bore, nicked the skin just sufficiently to allow a drop of blood to fall onto the Taer elna Ancren as it lay across the Dukrugvola's palms. As he did so, a sigh ran through the crowd.

Now, out of the ranks of the nobility on the platform there stepped forth the Lord Hethlan Lorchaset, chosen by Hadran for this role. Taking the black garment from the second of the servants, he presented this to the Dukrugvola with a low bow. The Dukrugvola, handing the Taer elna Ancren to Saragon, shook out the folds of cloth, revealing it to be a mantle identical to that which he himself was wearing, and placed it about Hadran's shoulders, fastening it by means of a golden brooch. He then took from the Lord Hethlan a gold signet ring bearing the arms of the realm of Karled-Dū which he placed upon the ring finger of Hadran's right hand, saying as he did so:

'I hereby declare you Prince of Varadil under the authority of Sior, answerable in all your acts to Sior, Lord of All, and to me who am his representative in the realm of Karled-Dū. Welcome Hadran Coras. May you dispense your rule wisely and well.'

He raised Hadran to his feet, placing his hands on the man's shoulders and bestowing upon him the customary kiss, before turning him to face the crowded square.

'Behold the Lord Hadran Coras,' he proclaimed in ringing tones. 'Behold your new Prince.'

When at last the acclamation of the people had died down, Hadran knelt once more before the Dukrugvola, placed his two hands within those of the Lord Archaïlis, and vowed before all present the oath of allegiance as vassal to his liege lord. Then it was the turn of the officers and government officials, justiciars and commanders of the Province of Varadil to come forward to make their own promises of fealty to the newly invested Prince, and although it was true that some came reluctantly, out of deference to the family name rather than respect for the present head of that family, there were no absences; all who tradition demanded should take the oath, did so.

In the usual course of events, this marked the end of the official ceremony and the populace was then allowed to celebrate in its own style. On this day, however, as the throngs seethed and turned, ready to regale themselves with food and drink, the Dukrugvola stepped forward and made a request for silence. It came at once, a silence of surprise. To judge from his expression, which those in the front ranks could see quite clearly, the interruption was as unexpected to Hadran as to any of the spectators. He turned his head to look with puzzled and wary eyes at the Lord Archaïlis. Was he about to speak of his brother? Dear Sior, surely not! Not now!

The Dukrugvola addressed him.

'My Lord of Varadil, as we know well, you have for several years held the position of Regent for the Province of Kirkendom, during the minority of the young Prince Morla; a position which you have filled to our satisfaction. However, in view of the additional tasks which you must now undertake as you acquaint yourself with the government of this, your own Province, we have decided that it would be inconsiderate to expect you to continue to perform the duties of Regent also. The decision has been taken therefore to transfer this obligation into the capable hands of the Lord Veras Kleptal, Prince of Arlente, who has consented to accept this charge. From this date, he shall hold and defend the Province of Kirkendom on our behalf until the coming of age of the child, Morla Arkensis.'

By the time that the procession of nobles had vacated the platform and Hadran had reached the safety of his apartment, the muscles of his face were tight with the effort of holding in his temper. A false smile had transfixed his features all the while he walked beside the Dukrugvola, whilst beneath it he had seethed and raged at the humiliation dealt him by his summary dismissal from the position of Regent of Kirkendom, and in favour of that nonentity from Arlente! Of course he needed to sort out his affairs in Varadil, but that would not be such a laborious business; after all, he had always taken a close interest in his father's handling of government, encouraged to do so by his father. It was a trumped up excuse to deliver a public snub, to make him a laughing-stock. This was the Dukrugvola's revenge for the breakdown of relations with Krapan, for the accusation levelled by Hadran in his meeting that morning. Thankfully Hadran reached the sanctuary of his chamber, where he vented his spleen on the opportune target of his manservant, so that the unfortunate man trembled in his shoes and fled precipitately when released from duty.

Having divested himself of his ceremonial robes and changed into more comfortable apparel, Hadran slowly descended to the great hall to rejoin his guests for the traditional banquet. With an effort, he forced himself to greet the Lord Archaïlis with a smile, which became less forced when his eyes passed on to Alhaîtha, standing beside her father. Her congratulations were so obviously sincere, that she could not have been in on the 'plot'. Smiling at her genially, he offered her his arm, and ushered her to a seat beside his own at the high table on the dais at one end of the hall. The Dukrugvola, unavoidably, was shown to the chair at his other hand. The remaining seats were taken by other members of the nobility, Saragon, Hethlan Lorchaset, and Veras Kleptel amongst them.

The food was lavish, drink plentiful. Servants moved through the hall, bearing platters heaped with slices of meat of all kinds: beef, veal, mutton, pork, smothered in rich, spicy sauces. Vast tureens of vegetables sat heavily in the centre of the board. More exotic fare from Arami and further South also graced the tables, and there were sweet pastries, jellies and tarts to tempt the appetite. Crystal goblets emptied and filled again with regularity, the rich dark wines of the South, mellow and fragrant, slipping satisfyingly down many throats.

As custom decreed, Hadran rose to propose a toast to the Dukrugvola and the realm of Karled-Dū. The Lord Archaïlis replied with a speech of thanks, and himself toasted the new Prince of Varadil. The principal guests each received a mention, and since each person named was obliged to respond with a speech, the process was long-winded and time-consuming, not to mention hard on the stomach and head, with each toast requiring the consumption of at least half a glass of wine. It was with relief, therefore, that the guests recognized the final toast and settled down again to resume their interrupted conversations and apply themselves once more to the feast. No-one expected Hadran to remain on his feet, and it took a minute or so for people to notice and fall silent, wondering. Having collected the attention of every single person in the hall, the new

Prince of Varadil proposed an extra pledge.

'As you will all be aware,' he said harshly, 'it is my profound misfortune to be brother to one who has shown himself an avowed enemy to this land of ours and who has brought disgrace to the name I bear. Here then is my toast. I pray you all to join me in drinking to the speedy demise of this infamous traitor. May he be brought to the justice he deserves!'

He raised the goblet to his lips, quaffed the wine therein and set it down with a crash, his eyes glittering wildly.

In the subsequent hush, a few voices, notably that of Alhaîtha , could be heard repeating the toast. The majority turned towards the Dukrugvola to follow his lead, and Saragon, flushed with fury, made a movement as if to rise to his feet, but then, thinking better of it, sat back in his seat, his face set. Beside Hadran, the Lord Archaïlis rested his hands on the table and gazed impassively across the hall. He made no move to acknowledge Hadran's words, but having permitted a deathly quiet to permeate throughout the chamber for several tense minutes, he turned calmly to his neighbour, his shoulder raised to exclude his host, and tranquilly continued with what he had been saying before the interruption had occurred. A babble of noise immediately broke out as everyone hastened to cover the awkward pause.

Hadran, left ridiculously on his feet, glanced incredulously round the table, opened his mouth to speak, but did not, and finally sat down deflated and extremely disquieted. He sent a troubled glance towards the averted face of the Dukrugvola, and subsided in his chair, making no attempt to recover a normal manner, but plunging instead into panic-stricken thought.

The Lord Archaïlis was conveying an unmistakable warning that vilification of Francys Coras would not be encouraged. What did that signify? Did that mean that pursuit of Francys was no longer officially sanctioned? Was that the reason why the Regency had been taken away from him? So that he could not continue to look for his brother ... so that he would not be able to *dispose* of his brother before anyone else had a chance to question him? The thought sent a spurt of fear twisting through his guts. Surely they could not have received any communication from Francys? But no, he thought, relaxing a trifle, the Dukrugvola would have mentioned it this morning. There was no need to worry, quite yet.

For the love of Sior, why could not the bastard have died of his wounds?! Anyone else surely would have. Why must Francys live on to menace his peace of mind? Francys *must* die! In that event lay Hadran's only hope of salvation and his only means of deliverance from a burning torment. With Francys dead, nothing could ever be proved. Whatever Nyandu might have seen or heard, if indeed she had, would be worthless. With Francys dead, the terrible lust which he felt for him would plague him no more. For that evening in the camp, which was to have freed Hadran at last from his desire for his brother, had only plunged him deeper into the mire. The memory of that body clung to his senses, setting him burning with intolerable longing, and would not be dislodged. It disturbed his slumber, and sent him into the complaisant arms of courtesans in an effort to drive it out of his mind, but always at the climactic moment the haunting spectre rose up before his mind's eye to mock him. Even now, amid the raucous chatter and laughter, the clatter of cutlery and clink of glass, and the scent of the spicy dishes, if he was not careful, that image materialized before his eyes, so vividly that he was amazed that no-one else could see it. If only he knew what had become of Francys. If only he could know for certain that the man was dead!

Alhaîtha broke through his reverie with a question, and he turned to her, grateful for the distraction.

****

Someone else was also wondering about Francys Coras. Seated upon a low tabouret stool in his private apartments, Rycharst rested one elbow on his knee and his chin upon his hand and brooded. Before him stood a low rectangular table with thick, knobbed legs and upon its polished surface lay a piece of parchment rather crumpled and stained. A sigh escaped the lips of the motionless figure as his pensive gaze fell upon the parchment. What was the truth of this strange affair? His informant wrote that Hadran Coras believed his brother to have abducted the Dukrugvola's niece, she who had been travelling about the Province of Kirkendom ... the Lady Nyandu Almeneth. One white hand stole up to caress the crystal pendant in which lay imprisoned one golden strand of hair. Thoughts circled his mind confusingly. He recalled that there had been some talk of rivalry between the two Coras brothers for this girl's affections. Could it be true? Yet he was in a position to know, as few others were, the physical state of Francys as he had escaped from Hadran's clutches. Was it really possible for him, some days later, to have kidnapped a young woman from amid her bodyguard, without apparently any resistance being offered? Still, it appeared that *Hadran* believed so at any rate, and it was a fact that both Francys and the girl had not been seen since the day that she had set out from Caleth Mor.

A spasm of anguish struck him to the heart. Suppose it were true. Suppose that Francys was even now lying in this woman's arms, giving *her* the love that *he* had been denied. That he should have a rival, and a mortal at that, was not to be borne! The Lady Nyandu would soon discover that it was unwise to meddle in the affairs of one of the awaithaes, he vowed, black anger and fierce jealousy smouldering within. Francys Coras was *his*! No-one else should have him if he could not.

But he was perhaps a little hasty in his conclusions. His deep eyes contemplated the parchment again. It was not certain that she had been abducted by Francys, and even if she had been, what was to say that he had done so out of love for her. Hadran himself was said to be eager to wed her. Could not his brother have kidnapped her in order to use her as a lever in some bargain? She was, after all, heiress to the Province of Meneleindom and related to the Dukrugvola (curse the man). Maybe he planned to use her to gain his freedom? Yet it was strange, if that were the case, that he had not made any move to advance his plan.

Rycharst stirred. His hand left the crystal and rose to his mouth, where he bit the fingers absently. It was galling to know that he was in some part responsible for this present situation. All this need not have occurred had his original plan not gone sour on him. When the notion of forging documents which could be used to secure an indictment of treason against Francys had come to him, he had seen it as a means to recover his lost love. But when he had caused the fact of their existence to reach Francys' ears before the papers could be put to use against him, it had not produced the desired, the anticipated result. Francys had not fled to him. Indeed, he was further from him than ever, having gone to ground in the one area of Karled-Dū which neither Rycharst nor anyone in his service could penetrate, and from there he had contrived time and time again to frustrate Rycharst's other ambitions.

The Lord of Shadowe unfolded his legs and rose slowly to his feet. There was one way to see what Francys was doing, but it was necessary to expend a rather large amount of energy in the working of the spell and that had kept him from using it while other easier methods remained open to him. But he could endure to wait no longer; he *must* know whether the tale he had had from his informant was true. He made his way up the winding stair to the round chamber atop the highest tower, fastening the door securely behind him, though it was but very seldom that any dared to disturb him there. Donning the black robe with its arcane symbols embroidered around the hem and the edges of the sleeves, he began to prepare. Upon the circular black marble table in its exact centre he placed a wide, shallow basin. Then taking a flask from a hidden wall-cupboard, he poured into the basin a colourless liquid, filling it to the brim. Next, slipping off the pendant, he set that carefully in the space between the basin and the edge of the table nearest to himself, arranging the chain in a circle about the crystal drop. Finally, he took up a knife with a broad, double-edged blade and a hilt of ebony embossed in gold with two symbols of power. He held it over the basin and performed a series of gestures, giving himself over completely to his actions and divorcing his mind from everything save the basin and the pendant. A strange mist began to form over the liquid. The knife blade moved to inscribe a number of signs on the table, encompassing both basin and pendant. Then Rycharst completed the rite and spoke the word to set the spell to work. Instantly the room was plunged into darkness, despite the sunshine outside, and the liquid in the basin began to glow. The mist wreathed and twisted above. The Lord of Shadowe leaned forward to look into the basin, the mist cleared, and he saw.

CHAPTER FIFTEEN

Whilst the tides of gossip and intrigue flowed across the country, and Thadie waited anxiously in Arlmen, Nyandu's world had contracted into three rooms in a cottage somewhere in the vicinity of Kelethina, her energies devoted to the sole purpose of nursing Francys. In that task she received the whole-hearted assistance of the kindly Martha and her son.

The effects of the soaking he had received on the night of the storm were quickly evident in Francys. Already feverish by the time he met Nyandu, he was soon delirious and racked by rheumatic pains in his limbs. During the first few days, they often had to hold the bedclothes down as he turned restlessly and tried to throw them off, complaining that he was burning. And indeed he *was* burning, and they were constantly bathing him in cool water to try to bring down his temperature. The nightshirt was soon dispensed with because it impeded the changing of his bandages, and because within a half hour of its being put on it was already soaked with sweat. A dark mist filled his mind. He wandered down endless paths beset by nightmare creatures. And he talked, incessantly. At first it was but a whisper, but later the room rang with the sound of his husky, pain-filled voice talking first in one language, then in another, and sometimes the screaming would begin. To the watchers it very quickly became unbearable. Nyandu felt as though she were living inside a nightmare herself, sitting in the stuffy, dim-lit room, hearing hour after hour the tortured voice talking desperately, and being unable to do anything to ease his troubled mind. She could not help but listen to him, gradually piecing together from his ramblings the facts about his sojourn in Hadran's camp. Into her horror-struck ears poured the details of that first evening in the camp, the flogging and then his escape, for those were the subjects which occupied his wandering mind to the virtual exclusion of all else. Often he would believe himself to be back in the camp, or even in the great fortress of Carakhas under the dominion of the Lord of Shadowe, and he would implore them to let him go, as he had never done in reality.

One day, whilst laying him back onto the mattress after she had changed the bandages, Nyandu's hand accidentally brushed against his naked skin, barely touching him. Instantly he stiffened and opened wide, haunted eyes.

'No!' he said in a heart-wrenching whisper. 'No!'

Nyandu, realizing that in his confused state he had mistaken her for one of his phantoms, began to reassure him, but as she bent over him, the fear and revulsion in his face increased and he struggled up with a strength born of desperation, backing away from her until he had reached the wall and could go no further.

Dismayed, Nyandu tried to explain, with all the firmness she could muster.

'Francys,' she said earnestly, 'I am Nyandu. Hadran is nowhere near you. No-one wants to .... to mistreat you. You are safe here, I promise you.'

But it was in vain. Francys stared mindlessly at her, his face an almost unrecognizable mask of blind terror.

'No, no, no!' he panted over and over on a note of hysterical horror, which began in a whisper and rose to a scream. Nothing Nyandu did or said could produce any abatement of his fear. She was unable to get through to him, and her continued presence seemed only to exacerbate his condition, so that eventually, white-faced and shaking, she was obliged to retreat and leave him to the ministrations of the peasant-woman, who patiently coaxed him into quiet.

Nyandu threw herself onto the bed next door, in the room that Tam had given up for her use, and pressed her hands over her ears to shut out those dreadful screams. She felt physically sick. Later, she returned to the sickroom. Francys had asked for her, though he did not recognize her when she came; indeed, he did not appear even to see her. He would often speak her name in his delirium, and she was intrigued to notice that he called her 'Nan' as he had never done in any of his lucid conversations with her. That aroused a faint spark of hope in her heart, though later she was inclined not to think it of any particular significance, for he would as often call for Connor, his Captain, and even at times he would fancy her to be his mother, recalling perhaps some childhood illness. Then he would beg her to sing to him and as she did so, sitting by the bed and holding his hand, far away wherever he was, through whatever dark valley he stumbled, he heard her voice and responded with a smile. It was on those occasions that he was easiest to control, lying quietly and restfully, granting them a merciful hour or so of peace.

****

In the castle of Kordren, Connor was becoming anxious. Having parted from Francys on the border with Harres, he had brought the men safely back through the Toath Cranem, expecting to see his commander within a few days. Now, some two weeks later, there was still no sign of the fair man. Connor stared absently out of the window towards the expanse of meadow which edged a small lake below the castle walls, his mind busy with the problem. Distantly the thwock of arrows hitting the straw targets impinged on his hearing, and, from closer to hand arose the clashing of sword upon shield, the trampling of booted feet on stone, the grunt of effort, the hiss of breath and sharp cries of triumph which denoted the company at exercise. He shook his head. It was unlike Francys to tarry so long. He was a least a seven day overdue. There was something amiss. Connor was sure of it.

Coming to a decision, he descended to the courtyard where he stood for a while, watching the men at practice, until his eyes found the one he sought. Automatically assessing the fitness and skill of those whom he passed, Connor made his way around the edge of the wide courtyard towards his second-in-command, but that moment removing his helm and laying aside sword and shield at the conclusion of a bout of hand-to-hand combat. Signalling to him, Connor led the way into a secluded corner beside the stable-block and waited for the man to join him, still panting from his recent exertions.

'Joclyn, I'm not easy in my mind,' he confided. 'Francys should have been back here well before now. He's been gone a fortnight. That's more than sufficient time to have completed his errand. I tell you straight, I'm beginning to fear some accident has befallen him. I'm going to leave you in charge here, and go and see what I can find out.'

Joclyn nodded.

'It is indeed worrying. I think the men begin to feel uneasy about his continued absence. Where will you go?'

'I thought I'd set off by way of Carledruin, and then check the usual place for messages. If that fails, I'll try Jeff in Arlmen. He usually keeps abreast of the local news. And if *he* knows naught either, I'll risk a trip to Artem's. After all, *that's* where he was headed. If I find out aught, or I have to go further abroad, I'll get word to you.'

Joclyn thought.

'You'll go alone?'

'Aye, but I thought I'd leave a handful of the men in Carledruin, as a line of contact. I'll put Robyn in charge there. He's shaping up well and the others respect him. Let him try his hand at command for a bit ...'

Thus, some six days later, having seen to the installation of a small garrison within the ruins of Carledruin under the authority of their fledgling captain, without discovering therein any trace of their missing leader, nor any message as to his whereabouts, Connor was knocking at the door of Francys' agent in Arlmen. He had entered the town in the guise of a merchant, establishing himself at the most comfortable of the many inns with which the busy market town was provided and leaving there his bulging saddle-bags full of the pelts of the exotic animals which they hunted in the Toath Cranem, brought along for the purpose of verisimilitude. The visible relief on Jeff's face when that worthy opened the door to him, strengthened Connor's conviction that something was very badly amiss. The discovery of Melisor's presence in the stables brought his feelings of foreboding to a head and, once provided with refreshment, he could scarcely contain his questions.

He listened in bemusement to Jeff's explanation of the circumstances of Melisor's arrival.

''Twas the Captain of the Lady Nyandu's bodyguard brought him to me ... he told me some tale how they'd come upon the beast wandering upon the highway betwixt here and Caleth Mor with blood on his back ...'

Cold with horror, Connor pressed the man for more information, more detail, but there proved little enough that he could tell. It appeared that Francys himself had been seen, that he had stood in need of assistance following some sort of accident, and that he had apparently been making for the village of Kelethina.

'... but he never arrived there,' Jeff revealed, frowning. 'I sent word and I've but this day had a reply. They've not seen hide nor hair of him, and it's been more than a week now.'

There was more, he disclosed. The very same day that Melisor was brought in to him, who should have arrived in the town, but the Lord Regent, in haste. He had stayed but a few hours, and then ridden off again in a great hurry back the way he had come.

'They're saying in the town he was on the hunt,' Jeff noted, 'that he'd got news of the Lord Francys and was determined to capture him.'

Connor, who had started upon hearing the title of Francys' detested elder brother, swore comprehensively. Francys hurt and on the run with his brother on his tail - he could barely imagine a worse situation. But at least it would seem that Hadran had not yet laid hands on Francys.

'That bastard would never keep such a coup to himself,' he muttered out loud. 'He'd be boasting his cleverness to the world the minute he'd caught him.'

The following morning saw Connor back on the road. Having disposed of his merchandise to good effect, he went well supplied with provisions, despite having left the greater part of his takings in the safe-keeping of Jeff against his return. He had also, before his departure, seen to the despatch of a message destined eventually for Joclyn's eyes, merely informing the latter of Francys' disappearance and his own intended journey in pursuit. Having assumed for this occasion the dress of a reasonably prosperous farmer, Connor left his own mount in Jeff's hands and rode forth on one more appropriate to his presumed status, cursing now and again as the beast refused to respond to his wish for speed.

He made first for Kelethina in the, vain, hope that Francys might have reached that village after the negative message had been sent. At his request, feelers were sent out into the neighbourhood after any word of an injured or sick man who might have been noticed. And so it was, at length, by devious ways and occasional blind alleys, that Connor arrived at the village of Neminar wherein dwelt Martha and Tam.

****

The knock at the door came as an unwelcome intrusion from the world outside. The two women conferred anxiously. Tam was absent, busy in the fields, and they were not expecting anyone to call. The knock was repeated, and it was finally settled that Martha should open to the stranger whilst Nyandu stayed out of sight. Francys was asleep and they hoped he would remain so until after the visitor had departed.

Martha nervously swung open the thick door. Outlined against the light stood a sturdy, well-built man of above average height with greying hair and beard. His grey eyes surveyed Martha shrewdly.

'Good-day, mistress. I seek a man who lies sick or injured,' the man said gruffly. 'And I hear you have one such in your house.'

She noted from his manner of speech that he was not of the Province of Kirkendom, and the fact alarmed her.

'Nay,' she answered quickly. 'You are mistaken. There is no such man here.'

She went to close the door, but the man prevented her by putting his foot on the threshold.

'Mistress, do not send me away,' he besought her. 'I have travelled a long way to find this man, to know he is safe.'

'I tell you, there is none such in this house,' she repeated stubbornly. 'You must seek elsewhere.'

'There is nowhere else to go,' the man told her, without removing his foot. 'I have come to the end of my search.'

He changed his tactics and took what was for him a grave risk, should his information turn out to be wrong.

'Can you not at least ask him whether he knows a man named Connor Marach?' he pleaded. 'I will wait outside until you have his response.'

Martha hesitated, and as she did so, Nyandu, who had been listening from behind the door to the chamber wherein Francys lay, came forth into view. She looked towards the man on the threshold, and spoke.

'Martha, let him in,' she said quietly. 'I know this man and he is who he says he is.'

Connor started violently at the sound of her voice. He peered into the dim-lit room behind the old woman and, as Martha stood aside, strode briskly over the threshold to bring up short as he came face to face with Nyandu.

'You!' he exclaimed involuntarily.

Nyandu gave a tremulous smile. Connor recalled his manners.

'I beg your pardon,' he began, but Nyandu interrupted him.

'He is in here,' she told him, gesturing towards the room from which she had come.

Then, as Connor started forward, she laid a hand on his arm.

'I must warn you, you will find him much changed. He is very ill indeed. You must be prepared for him not to recognize you.'

Connor threw her an appalled glance, and strode quickly towards the entrance to the room which she had indicated. As he took in the man in the bed, he came to an abrupt halt. Nyandu slipped past him and went swiftly to the bedside. Francys stirred and moaned and opened his eyes. Nyandu slid an arm beneath him and raised him, setting a cup to his lips. He drank, lying passively against her, his gaze travelling vacantly around the room, obviously without any awareness of his surroundings.

'Dear Sior!' Connor ejaculated hoarsely, his face grey with shock. 'What has happened to him?'

Nyandu gently settled the young man back onto the bed and stood up. He muttered something indistinct, and she murmured reassuringly, which seemed to soothe him. She looked across at Connor.

'Come next door and I'll tell you all I know,' she said quietly. 'I'll get Martha to sit with him for a while.'

Thus Connor joined the household and took a share in the nursing of Francys, granting the two women a welcome respite. The atmosphere in the cottage was one of tense anxiety bordering at times on despair, for the young man lingered still in a state of alarming unconsciousness. Tam regularly tiptoed into the main bedchamber to enquire upon the patient's progress, only to retire disappointed and gloomy. Nyandu, pale-faced and weary, could not prevent herself from falling into despondency as the days followed one after another and the situation remained unchanging, and she found Connor a source of much needed support.

'How much longer can he continue in this manner?' she said to Connor one day as they stood beside the bed, looking down at the occupant within. 'Why doesn't the crisis come? His wounds are healing well. The rheumatic fever has almost left him. What is it that is keeping him in this state? Why does he not rouse?'

She turned to the older man, her eyes wide with fear.

'Oh, Connor,' she whispered tremblingly, 'suppose he *cannot*. How can we tell what Hadran's treatment may have done to his mind? Suppose he daren't face reality any longer. Suppose he never rouses...'

'He will come to his senses some time,' Connor reassured her confidently, though himself far from confident.

Yet the crisis still delayed. That afternoon, Nyandu sat beside the bed, watching, whilst Connor slept and Martha caught up on her baking. Francys had been much quieter that day, alarmingly so. Suddenly he moved restlessly, threw himself onto his face and began to weep. Violent, shuddering sobs shook his whole body and hot tears soaked the pillow. He gasped for breath, choking, and Nyandu hurriedly lifted him until he sat leaning against her, whereupon he buried his face in her shoulder, clutching convulsively at her arms with his long fingers. So tightly did he grip that the marks came up later as bruises. The tears streamed down his face, and his whole body jerked with the force of his sobs, his wasted muscles trembling with the exertion. Gently, automatically, Nyandu began to stroke the blond head as it lay heavily on her shoulder.

'Francys, Francys,' she murmured soothingly as if to a child.

Gradually the convulsive sobs eased and the frightening gasps gave way to deeper, regular breaths, and eventually Francys slept, his head drooping, his hands relaxing their crushing grip. The long lashes covered the tear-swollen eyes.

A terrible fear assailed Nyandu. She was afraid that this outburst might be but a last effort before his body surrendered to whatever malady it was that held him in thrall. For some time she sat there, not daring to move, until she finally understood that the long-awaited moment had arrived and that the crisis had passed. Relief poured through her in a dizzy wave, and then she dared not move in case she fainted. At last, however, she carefully laid Francys back on his pillows and went through to wake Connor.

He sprang up as soon as she touched him. Looking into her face, he guessed that something had happened and on the instant feared the worst.

'Menaïren ...' he faltered (though she had bidden him use her given name, he could not break himself of the habit). 'What is it? Is he ...?'

He could not say the word.

'No,' said Nyandu. 'No. It's over Connor. The crisis has come and gone and he is asleep. Oh Connor!'

She swayed and he caught her.

'Lie down,' he told her gently. 'It's been too much for you. You are exhausted. Lie down and get some sleep. I'll watch over him now.'

He forced her in a kindly manner to lie down in the chamber given over to her use, and waited until she had dropped off to sleep, a matter of minutes only, before going into the main bedchamber to take up position on the stool beside the bed.

Thus it was Connor who was sitting silently by the wide bed when Francys opened his eyes. Francys' gaze encountered the rough wall and roof beams, and he lay there frowning, trying to recognize them, but not succeeding. Where on earth was he? He moved his head slightly and caught sight of his arm. Sior! What had happened to him? How had he become so thin, and why did he feel so strangely weak? He could scarcely lift his hand ... An expression of puzzlement tinged faintly with unease crept over his face, to be instantly banished by relief as he turned his head and his eyes took in the familiar figure.

'Connor!' he said, with manifest satisfaction.

Connor started, then a broad smile spread itself over his features. He got down on one knee, grasping one thin hand.

'Francys!' he said joyfully, delighted to see the clear light of consciousness shining at last in the hazel eyes.

Francys smiled.

'Ah, don't be a fool, Con,' he rebuked mildly. 'There's no need for you to kneel to me.'

His gaze wandered to the rest of the chamber, examining the room with a surprised expression. He returned to Connor.

'Where are we?' he asked, his voice a low murmur. 'This isn't Kordren, or even Carledruin? What has happened? Have I had an accident?'

'Francys ...' Connor was troubled. What should he tell him? Was this a permanent loss of memory? How could he tell him about Hadran?

He hesitated, until seeing Francys' face reflect the concern in his own, he answered carefully:

'Yes, you have had an accident, and you have been very ill. When you hadn't returned, I came looking for you, and found you here.'

There befell a short silence as Francys pondered over what he had been told. Then he moved his head restlessly.

'I'm thirsty,' he said plaintively.

Connor slipped an arm behind him and lifted him so that he could drink some of the barleywater which Martha had made, then, when he had had enough, let him lie back on the pillows again.

'You mustn't try thinking about things just yet,' he advised him, adding persuasively:

'Just lie still and sleep.'

He straightened the bedclothes with a tender hand and was about to move away when Francys suddenly reached out and caught hold of him.

'Don't go away,' the young man said anxiously.

'I won't. Don't you worry about that,' Connor assured him, settling back onto the stool beside the bed.

Francys gave him a happy smile and presently closed his eyes, retaining nevertheless his hold on Connor's hand. The touch of those thin fingers moved Connor profoundly. It was a disarming and strangely childlike gesture to come from someone so self-controlled and self-reliant.

When Francys woke again about an hour later, he asked:

'How long have I been here?'

'Four weeks,' Connor replied matter-of-factly. 'Do you think you could manage some broth?'

'Four weeks!' said Francys incredulously.

He stared up intently at Connor.

'Are you sure?'

'Would I lie to you?' demanded Connor, getting to his feet.

He crossed over to the door, leaned out and conducted a low-voiced conversation with Martha. Francys lay quietly considering his newly-acquired knowledge.

'Four weeks ...' he murmured disbelievingly.

Connor returned, followed by the tall form of Martha bearing a bowl from which an appetizing smell wafted tantalizingly. Francys caught sight of the woman.

'Who's that?' he enquired with interest.

'This is Martha,' explained Connor. 'You are staying in her cottage. She has been extremely kind and generous.'

‘Oh, ‘tis the least I can do ...’ protested Martha, embarrassed.

Francys looked at her curiously.

‘We’re not with Artem then?’ he asked.

‘No,’ said Connor. ‘Let me help you up so that Martha can put some pillows for you.’

He bent over the bed and put his arms round the thin body. Francys passively allowed him to do as he wished, but turned his head to observe Martha as she carefully placed pillows and bolsters behind him. When Connor laid him back against them, he thanked her with a grateful smile, which caused the old woman to retreat precipitately from the bedchamber, sniffing and speechless.

Connor picked up the bowl and began to feed Francys with spoonfuls of the tasty broth. The young man only managed a few mouthfuls before shaking his head and lying back exhausted. A protracted silence ensued. Francys fiddled absentmindedly with the edge of the blankets, his weary brain trying to make sense of his current circumstances.

‘How did I get here?’ he asked suddenly.

‘The Lady Nyandu brought you.’

The mists cleared with startling abruptness and Francys recalled with amazing clarity the meeting on the highway. Then his mind revealed the terrible days which had preceded that meeting, and he gave a shudder. Connor, seeing shock and comprehension dawn in the hazel eyes, realized that his memory had returned. He knew not whether to be sorry or relieved.

‘I didn’t dream it then,’ Francys murmured to himself.

‘No,’ agreed Connor uncomfortably.

‘And Nyandu brought me here?’ The young man asked after a pause.

Connor nodded.

‘That was kind of her,’ Francys remarked. ‘I wish I might thank her.’

Connor smiled.

‘Well you can, when she wakes, if that’s your wish.’

‘She’s here still?’ Francys sounded surprised.

‘She stayed to nurse you,’ Connor told him. ‘And Sior be thanked that she did, else you would not now be alive. But she is sleeping at the present ...’

A voice spoke from the doorway, interrupting him.
'No, I'm not, Connor. Martha woke me.'

Francys turned his head towards the door. Nyandu stood there. At least, he thought it was Nyandu. It was her face, but she was clad in the rough serge dress of a peasant woman, with her hair loosely and hastily knotted up, her face pale and her eyes puffy from too little sleep. She returned his gaze, noting the changes in him. His face had always seemed delicate. Now, under the thick blond hair, it was thin and wan with cheek-bones protruding beneath dark-ringed eyes. His body, never over-fleshed, was painfully emaciated, the ribs clearly outlined under the skin, and on the left above the collar-bone she could make out even from where she stood the nearly healed brand mark incised into the flesh. His back, she knew, was a dreadful sight.

Francys, having reached the conclusion that it was indeed Nyandu, smiled and stretched out his hand. She came quickly to the bedside, sitting down on the edge of the bed, and put her hand in his. Francys seemed about to say something, but the effort was too much for him and all that he managed was an almost inaudible 'Nan'. The hazel eyes fixed on her face and he gazed at her as though he feared she might vanish if he looked away even for an instant. Then, soon afterwards, he drifted into slumber.

****

Francys slept a great deal to begin with. The fever had left him so weak that even eating was a trial, and to be washed totally exhausted him. Imperceptibly, however, the periods of wakefulness lengthened and he grew more alert, finding himself able to make an attempt at surveying the situation in which he was placed. The result of this consideration was a subtle rearrangement of roles between Connor and Nyandu, as the fair man contrived to so arrange matters that all the more intimate parts of the business of nursing him, such as bathing, feeding and attending to other natural and necessary functions, fell to Connor's share, which indeed left Nyandu with remarkably little to do unless she busied herself in tending to the laundry or cooking.

At first, the gradual diminishment of her duties did not cause Nyandu overmuch concern and was rather pleasant than otherwise, since it enabled her to catch up on her own lost sleep. But as she became aware that Francys was shutting her out, she felt increasingly bewildered and not a little hurt. Connor, when approached, had intimated that it might be due to simple embarrassment on Francys' part and that she should not read too much into it. Nyandu had nodded and attempted to make light of the matter, but she could not help but feel pain at the difference in his manner towards the other inmates of the cottage. Through the open door, she could hear him joking with Connor, or chatting to Martha, and even Tam, when that worthy was not too tongue-tied to speak, exercising his ready wit in a fashion that recalled to her mind the summer at Shardu. When it was her turn to sit with him, she could barely manage to win from him more than half a dozen words at a time

Connor watched her with sympathy, his observant gaze noticing the hurt in her eyes when Francys had been particularly moody and uncommunicative with her, but having discovered the cause which lay behind Francys' behaviour, he felt at a loss to make any attempt to interfere. He was now sleeping on a straw-filled mattress in the main bedchamber in case Francys should need anything during the night, since it was no longer necessary to have someone sit up at night to watch over the invalid, and it was thus that he had had the doubtful pleasure of learning Francys' secret, which now lay like a burden on his mind. He had heard the desolation in the young man's voice as he whispered Nyandu's name in the dark quiet hours of the night when he believed Connor to be asleep. It was an impossible situation, and if it helped Francys to cope with it by maintaining a distance between himself and the girl, then who was *he* to say him nay. Yet even that would not be enough in the end. Francys was still too much weakened by illness, and in the constant struggle between his heart and his brain, what harm might be caused? Certainly it would not aid his recovery. But... how was he to persuade Nyandu to leave without having to betray Francys? Connor was sure that she would refuse to go if the request appeared to emanate solely from himself, and quite rightly since he had no authority over her. But, equally, he could not appeal to her in Francys' name without the man's knowledge, and he was loth to reveal that he had overheard that which Francys supposed to have been private.

It was Francys himself who eventually solved the problem. Now that he had gained a little in strength and was beginning to regain his lost weight due to Martha's nourishing stews, Connor had started to move him to a chair near the window during the daytime. There, wearing shirt and breeches which had been procured for him by Tam on one of that worthy's regular excursions to the weekly market in Kelethina, with a blanket over his legs, his feet propped upon a stool and his head resting against a soft cushion, he watched the world beyond the confines of the cottage, and drowsed and dreamed the days away. On that particular afternoon, taking advantage of the warm sunshine, Nyandu had taken a stool outside and was sitting in the little garden not very far from Francys' window, engaged in mending one of Tam's shirts. Francys seized the opportunity afforded by her absorption in the task to lie back and contemplate her, permitting himself the luxury of admiring the play of the sunshine over her hair, and letting his eyes linger wistfully on her profile. If only, he thought idly, one could stop time. If only he could hold onto this moment for ever. Nothing else would matter; not his disastrous past; not his problematic future. There would be no Rycharst, no Hadran; only himself and Nyandu. But it could not be. Nyandu turned her head and saw him looking, and smiled, and Francys was flooded with a desperate, terrible longing, which took the breath from him, leaving him dizzy. As a wave of darkness washed across his vision, he was conscious of one thought; Nyandu must go.

He spoke to Connor that evening while they were preparing for bed.

'I want you to make arrangements for Nyandu's departure,' he announced abruptly. 'I want you to get her away from here at the earliest opportunity.'

Connor paused in the act of untying his shirt strings, and shot his commander a sidelong glance, suddenly alert.

'It's too much of a danger for her to stay here,' Francys continued stubbornly. 'And every minute that passes increases the risk of discovery.'

He was silent for a moment, before adding, with a note of desperation:

'She should never have been allowed to do this. I ought to have prevented her ...'

'I'd like to know *how*!' Connor responded roundly, interrupting to cut short the recriminations that he feared would come next. 'From what I've heard, you couldn't have restrained a mouse, let alone a grown woman, the state you were in! For the love of Sior, don't start blaming yourself for something you could do aught about. It's too late now. The deed is done!'

'I know,' Francys sighed despondently. 'But still I feel guilty over it.'

He looked at Connor, his face drawn in the lamp-light.

'I drew her into the danger in which she now stands. If any harm should come to her as a result, the responsibility would be mine. And they could trace her here at any time. Someone must be looking for her out there. She's been missing a long time,' he said grimly. 'They must be scouring the countryside for her. *Someone* must be at any rate! Sior grant it isn't my brother.'

He shuddered.

He took a deep breath and strove to sound businesslike.

'Well, we'd best work out the details. From this end, it seems easy enough. You could escort her to Kelethina, couldn't you? But what then? How is she to reappear without setting the countryside afire with speculation? And how is she to account for her disappearance? They'll be certain to question her closely, especially if my bastard of a brother has anything to do with it. But she cannot have been ill all this time ... not so suddenly, and alone ...'

He paused, then ...

'Dear Sior! Where are my wits?! She was not alone when I met her on the highway. Connor, what did she do with her escort? Where have they been all this time?'

'Sitting in Arlmen, wondering where the hell she is,' Connor replied promptly. 'You probably don't remember, or maybe she arranged it while you were senseless. She sent them on to Arlmen to give the impression that it was from that town that she had disappeared. They took Melisor with them, don't you remember? The Lady Nyandu told me you'd said to hand him over to Jeff.'

'Ah ... I remember *that*, vaguely. So they're in Arlmen. Well, that solves one problem. We could send word through Jeff and ask her Captain to meet you both in Kelethina.'

He thought for a minute or two and then asked:

'You've been out and about enough to learn the local gossip. What are they saying about her absence? Are people suspicious? What's the local opinion?'

Connor grimaced. He had foreseen this question, and was not at all sure of the reaction he was likely to provoke. However ... He shrugged.

'Rumour has it that the Lady Nyandu has been kidnapped and is being held in captivity,' he vouchsafed, watching Francys closely as he spoke.

Francys stared at him.

'Kidnapped by whom?' he enquired. 'Me?'

Connor nodded.

''Twas your brother who started the tale going,' he disclosed cautiously, eyeing Francys uneasily.

Much to his surprise, and not a little relief, Francys began to laugh, continuing until he ran out of breath and energy and then coughing painfully, the blood ebbing from his face. Connor hastened to fetch a small flask of wine, which he held to the white lips, forcing Francys to swallow a few mouthfuls. The coughing eased, Francys looked up at the older man.

'Then it's settled?' he said tensely, in a low, urgent murmur. 'You'll get word to her Captain?'

'I'll get in touch, yes,' Connor assured him.

'Thanks, Con.'

Francys gave him a grateful smile.

'And I'll speak to the Lady Nyandu,' added Connor gently.

Francys bit his lip and looked away, but said nothing further.

The following morning, Connor sat down to compose a note to Nyandu's Captain, inviting him to present himself outside a certain building in the village of Kelethina in seven days' time. That done, he steeled himself and went to find Nyandu, who was picking nuts in the orchard beyond the garden. As he approached, slowly, she heard the footfalls and looked round.

'Connor,' she said, instantly seized with anxiety. 'What is it? Am I needed? Is something wrong?'

'No, no,' Connor reassured her hastily. 'Francys is fine for the present.'

He hesitated, then said with a carefully casual air:

'I have a message here to send to your Captain, and would be glad if you could endorse it for me.'

Nyandu gave him a startled glance.

'Where is it?' she asked eventually.

With reluctance, Connor produced the paper and handed it over. Nyandu unfolded the sheet and read what he had written. He waited apprehensively, fearing the reaction. There was a pause.

'I see,' she said at last in an expressionless voice. 'Very well. I will sign it for you.'

She fell silent and turned her head away from Connor's gaze. Then she sighed deeply. Connor, prompted by an urge to ease her mind in some way, put his hand over hers and said gently, persuasively:

'Menaïren, Nyandu, you have done all that you can here. Francys is no longer in any danger that you could alleviate. Indeed, to be blunt, the danger which faces him now is more likely to result from your continued presence here. You have been absent now for several weeks. It must be only a matter of time before a search-party finds you here ... and Francys. We are incredibly lucky that it has not already arrived on our doorstep.'

'Yes,' said Nyandu. 'Yes, Connor. I do understand. I ought to have thought of that before.'

She smiled a wry, somewhat bitter smile.

'It would be a waste indeed to have brought him safely through all that fever only to see him taken into captivity and ... hanged,' she finished in a low voice.

She stooped to pick up the basket half filled with nuts.

'I'm sure you are quite capable of looking after him on your own. You almost do now, don't you. Really, I'm superfluous here now, aren't I? Very well, come in and let me sign this note of yours.'

She looked up at him and produced a smile, albeit forced.

'Don't look so nervous, Connor,' she bade him. 'Did you expect me to make a scene? You needn't worry. I understand perfectly. You've been very tactful.'

And she leant forward and kissed him softly on the cheek before turning to cross the orchard back towards the cottage. Connor's face was a fiery red as he followed her.

The message was duly delivered to its destination, and Connor received a response confirming that Thadie would be at the rendevous, and expressing his immense relief at finally having news of his errant mistress. In the same package, passed on via Jeff, was word of a more disturbing nature, which caused Connor to feel thankful that he had already arranged for Nyandu's departure. Decoded from the general cypher that they used, it read 'The old lynx is dead.' In other words, the Lord Telstan Coras had died, and Hadran had succeeded to the position of Lord of Varadil. What would happen now was anyone's guess.

CHAPTER SIXTEEN

Once the decision had been taken and the details of Nyandu's imminent departure arranged, Francys seemed to have arrived at a temporary peace of mind. He even felt able to lower his icy barriers a little and behave towards Nyandu with a greater ease than hitherto, thus permitting her to be a part of the celebration which surrounded his first attempt at walking without support. Connor, as usual, had assisted him in the task of getting dressed, and had been shocked anew at how thin the young man was, despite the weight he had gained in recent days. Francys sat on the edge of the bed. A faint frown creased his brow. Observing it, Connor said anxiously:

'Are you sure you're well enough, Francys? You could wait another day ...'

'No, Con,' Francys said firmly. 'The sooner I'm up and about, the better. If I don't start walking by myself soon, I shall forget how to!'

He held out his hand.

'Help me up, Con,' he requested, with a coaxing smile.

Connor grasped his hand and pulled him to his feet, where he stood unsteadily.

Now that he was on his feet, he felt weaker than he had expected, his muscles trembling very slightly from the effort of standing, but his resolve to try out his legs remained undaunted and, taking a deep breath, he cautiously stepped forward. At the first step, his legs buckled and he clutched desperately at Connor, hovering at his side.

'Sior!' he exclaimed with a grimace. 'It feels just as though someone has extracted the bones from my legs!'

'Let me help you,' offered Connor.

'No,' responded Francys determinedly. 'Once I get started, I shall be fine. Just let me get my breath a moment would you.'

He resolutely continued, though that resolution was sorely tried as at each step his legs threatened to give up the effort. The muscles of his face tense with the concentration required to force his reluctant limbs to obey his commands, he emerged slowly from the doorway of the bedchamber in which he had been immured for so many weeks, to the murmured exclamations of his audience.

Pausing on the threshold, he surveyed the living room with

interest, noting the wide fireplace with its invitingly warm hearth and the cauldron steaming gently, the settle nearby, the truckle bed beyond, where Tam slept, a rough wooden table with its attendant stools, and, near the door, the watching faces of Nyandu, Martha and the phlegmatic Tam, who had unexpectedly decided to assist at the occasion. With an effort, Francys summoned the energy to continue his progress and, suppressing, for the sake of the women, the epithets which rose to his lips, made his way cautiously towards the settle. Though but a few paces distant, by the time he was able to collapse onto the cushioned bench, he felt as though he had walked several calle. Exhausted, pale and breathing hard, nevertheless he flashed a triumphant smile at his audience, who responded with a cheer. The next moment, the smile vanished, as a sudden terrible cramp assailed the muscles of his calves. He uttered a gasp, closing his eyes in pain and clutching at the arm of the settle. Instantly, four worried voices chorused in enquiry, and shortly afterwards he felt strong hands begin to massage the tortured limbs. Nyandu went to rummage in the press, and returned to his side with a cup of wine, which she held to his lips, whilst Martha tenderly arranged a cushion behind his head. The cramp passed and an expression of breathless relief spread over his pale features. Francys opened his eyes and smiled down at his Captain.

'I made it,' he said with satisfaction.

'Aye,' said Connor drily. 'Obstinacy will get you everywhere.'

'Obstinacy will get you everywhere'. Francys recalled those words a couple of days later. Connor had departed some hours earlier to escort Nyandu to Kelethina. She had come to take her leave of him as he sat in the high-backed chair in his bedchamber.

'I hope that you will soon be fully recovered,' she said carefully, her voice strictly disciplined to an even tone which gave nothing away.

Francys looked up at her.

'After your excellent nursing, how can I not?' he replied courteously.

He then embarked upon a speech which he had prepared beforehand, lying sleepless through the long hours of the preceding night.

'I don't know how I can possibly repay such kindness, situated as I am, but you may be sure that I shall never forget it, and if one day I should be in a position to render you any assistance, and you should stand in need of it, do not hesitate to call on me.'

He shrugged.

'It may seem an empty promise at present, but who knows! And I do mean it; don't doubt *that*!'

He paused briefly.

'Once you were generous enough to call me a friend. The friendship seems to have been all one-sided so far, I'm afraid ...'

He extended a hand which, to his annoyance, trembled slightly.

'I must thank you for everything you have done for me. May you have a safe journey. I pray to Sior that you will not find yourself in any trouble over what you have done here.'

The touch of her hand filled him with an insane desire to insist that she stay. With a terrific effort he managed to stifle it and, in a voice made suddenly husky with emotion, he said bleakly:

'May Sior keep you safe.'

Nyandu responded correctly, repeated her wish that his health should be quickly restored, and turned away. He stared after her with stricken eyes and, as she left the room, gave an almost inaudible cry.

'Nan!' he whispered despairingly. 'Oh, Nan, don't go! Don't leave me!'

But Nyandu did not hear him and a few seconds later the sound of her voice floated in through the open door as she said her farewells to Martha, whom she embraced warmly, receiving a tearful hug in return, and to Tam, who timidly shook her hand, holding it as though he feared it might break. Connor appeared briefly in the doorway to check on Francys and to ask if there were any further instructions.

'Just keep her safe,' Francys entreated, raising fathomless eyes to his Captain's face. 'Don't let any harm befall her.'

'You may rest assured that I won't', Connor promised reassuringly. 'I'll take every care of her while she remains in my company, you know that. And try not to spend the day worrying,' he added as he was about to cross the threshold, eliciting from Francys a faint and rather bleak smile.

Francys leant his head back against the cushion and gazed moodily out of the window at the bright autumnal sunshine. It should have been raining, he thought, raining like the blinding tears which were falling in his mind. 'Obstinacy will get you everywhere'. The words echoed mockingly inside his brain. Obstinacy had got him to this place, to this moment, and how desperately he wished that it had not. Obstinacy had forced him to deny the one true desire of his heart ... Over and over he reviewed those last minutes with Nyandu, wondering if the anguish he had felt had been visible in his eyes, whether she had noticed, and hoping that she had not, that he had not made a fool of himself. For what was the use of showing how much he loved her, he thought with a bitter smile, when that love was not returned, and he was imrauten, with a darkness in his past which could never be forgotten. Yet she had braved possible death to save his life! But that meant nothing. She would not pass by anyone who needed her help, whoever they might be. That was her nature. That it had been *he* who had needed her did not signify. No doubt, had it been Hadran in his place, she would have been equally kind. All he had been in her eyes was a desperately ill fellow being who would die if she did not use her skills to save him.

A terrible feeling of desolation swept over him and he closed his eyes, unwilling to acknowledge the sunshine which seemed to mock so cruelly the dark and lonely night of his soul. Martha, entering quietly and observing him, disappeared to warm up a wholesome rabbit stew. Good food was very helpful in raising low spirits, she believed. She was well pleased to have been left in charge and was anxious that he should have no complaints to make. Setting the earthenware platters on the table, she sallied into the bedchamber once more, saying cheerily:

'I am sure you must be hungry, Menellen. Do come and eat some of my stew. I am sure it will do you good.'

Francys looked up, forced a smile, and rose stiffly from the chair, accepting her helpful hand under his elbow with an ease which surprised him, and obediently accompanied her into the living room.

The fair man had reckoned that Connor ought to be back by nightfall, but was not unduly surprised when darkness fell without a sign of him. Sitting on the settle beside the pleasantly flickering flames of a healthy fire in the wide hearth, he listened with amusement, but unruffled calm, to Martha's seemingly inexhaustible
flow of imagined horrors and accidents which might have befallen the unfortunate Captain.

'The poor man,' she exclaimed once more, after adding another log to the fire. 'He might have been set upon and robbed.'

'My dear woman,' said Francys patiently, with a twinkle in his eyes, 'Connor is more than able to take care of himself. Any robber would have an unpleasant surprise if they set upon *him*. Don't fret. He may have been delayed in Kelethina ...'

'Aye, that he might,' responded the old woman shrewdly, apparently struck by the idea. She applied herself once more to the darning of a sheet and proceeded to develop the hypothesis, chatting quite contentedly to herself without bothering to see whether Francys was listening.

'I've a fancy he might have been reluctant to part from the lady,' she said, thrusting her needle into the linen. 'And who'd be surprised at that? Such a kind girl as she is, for she *is* kind, is she not, Tam?'

She appealed to her son, sitting a little further back from the bright fire silently observing Francys, who himself stared into the flames as if seeking pictures therein.

'Aye,' Tam muttered.

'And not a bit haughty,' Martha continued, oblivious of the turmoil she was creating in Francys' mind. 'From the first she treated me like I was one of her own circle. And she wasn't a bit put out to sleep in Tam's chamber, even when she had to share with me. Thanked him very nicely she did, though it couldn't have been anything like what she was accustomed to. Turn her hand to anything she would too, for all she's the daughter of a Prince. She'd make someone a bonny wife, she would...'

She paused to negotiate a particularly complicated hole before rattling on, heedless of Francys' sudden sharp intake of breath.

'I reckon the Captain would be glad enough to take her to wed himself. Not but what he's old enough to be her father. Though there are some women who like an older man ... And I did see her kissing him in the orchard not so long back.'

She reached down for a new piece of thread. Francys, who had been listening in a state of increasing mental agitation, felt the room reel about him and closed his eyes dizzily, letting his head tilt back against the high back of the settle. A faint groan escaped him. Tam, watching closely, said reproachfully:

'There now, Mother, you've tired Menel Francys out with all your chatter. He looks fair exhausted.'

'Dear, dear,' tutted Martha anxiously, raising the candle to shed its light on Francys' face. She saw the closed eyes and pale lips, and frowned.

'Menellen,' she said humbly and self-accusingly. 'Indeed, I didn't mean to wear you out with my silly nonsense. You should have stopped me. Tam tells me I talk too much... Won't you let Tam help you to bed? And I'll just fetch the warming-pan. I am sorry, Menellen, indeed I am ...'

She sounded indeed so sorry that he was forced to make an effort and murmur that he had enjoyed her conversation, and was only rather tired from being up all day.

'To be sure, that'll be it,' she responded happily. 'Well, I'll just see to the warming-pan, and then Tam can help you to bed and you can have a good night's sleep.'

She set down her mending and bustled about her task. When she emerged from the bedchamber, it was to adjure her son to be sure to build up the fire well before he left the room.

Francys impatiently availed himself of Tam's willing though slightly clumsy aid in order to reach his bed and undress. Then, having heard the door close behind the burly man, he lay on his back and stared for a long while into the empty darkness, seeing many things. Eventually, he turned and settled himself on his side, attempting to find oblivion in the deeps of slumber. It was, however, a long time in coming, and even then he tossed and turned restlessly, dozed and woke again and again, aching for the forgetfulness of dreamless sleep, which contrived always to elude his eager grasp. Dawn found him up and dressed, seated by the window, with pale face and feverish gaze.

Martha entered the chamber tentatively, to ascertain whether he was awake and ready for breakfast. She stopped short in the doorway.

'Menellen!' she exclaimed, scandalized. 'Menellen, you should be in bed! You must be cold sitting over there. Whatever did you want to get up for like that?'

'I couldn't sleep, Martha,' said Francys wearily.

She came across and laid a toil-worn hand on his brow.

'Why, you're burning! Come, let me help you back to your bed. It won't do to be making yourself ill again, now will it? And you will do so an you stay here in the cold ...'

'I'm perfectly all right,' Francys interrupted irritably, shaking her hand off. 'You could bring me a cup of water, though. I'm thirsty.'

She hurried off to fetch it and, returning, continued to protest.

'You really ought to be abed,' she said, then as he shook his head, added persuasively:

'At the least, why not sit closer to the hearth. You must be chilled to the bone. I'll get Tam to stoke up the fire for you ...'

He continued merely to shake his head and in the end, when she persisted, snapped testily:

'For the love of Sior, leave me alone! I am not a child!'

And, recognizing defeat, Martha gave up and departed, warning him as she went that he was overtaxing his strength, a warning which she repeated in stronger terms when he failed to eat the breakfast she had carefully prepared for him, picking at it only without any appetite.

When Connor finally returned midway through the morning, Martha managed to catch him before he reported to Francys and to pour out the tale of the young man's misdoings. To her annoyance, Connor merely laughed.

'It sounds as if he's getting better.'

He opened the door to the bedchamber and paused on the threshold. Francys was sitting, head turned towards the window, motionless. A strange feeling of dread and unease crept over Connor as he looked at him, and he decided that a more formal approach might perhaps suit the young man's mood. Crossing the room, he therefore went down on one knee to announce the safe completion of his task. There was no response, and he looked up into Francys' face. The sight froze him momentarily with shock. A fell light shone from the hazel eyes, set in the midst of an expressionless mask.

Alarmed, Connor got to his feet and backed away from the dreadful gaze, meaning to call Martha to help him deal with whatever it was that was that affected the young man. But, to his horror, as he retreated Francys slowly uncoiled himself and rose from the chair. Step by step in absolute, eerie silence, as if under a trance, he followed the now-sweating Connor until they stood facing one another in the centre of the room. There, Francys put his hand to his belt and suddenly produced a glittering blade, which Connor recognized as the knife that Tam used for whittling pieces of wood.

That Connor managed to avoid the wicked blade was entirely due to the extent that illness had slowed Francys' actions. As it was, he felt the air displaced whistling past his left side. The subsequent minutes were hectic. Connor refused to turn his own knife upon the young man, and accordingly closed in with bare hands, gripping the wrist of the hand which held the weapon and trying to force it down. Despite his ill health, Francys fought with a strength which astonished Connor, acting as though possessed by some demonic force. The two men swayed back and forth, knocking over a small stool in the struggle, until at last, with an extra effort, Connor wrested the knife away and sent it flying into the corner, well out of reach. Then he released Francys and stood panting. Francys staggered backwards a couple of steps, glared at Connor and said vehemently:

'Damn you, you bastard!' before crumpling up and dropping to the floor in a senseless heap.

Aghast, Connor sprang forward, his mouth suddenly dry. On his knees, he bent over the limp form, feeling with feverish haste for the pulse in the young man's wrist. It was there, weakened, but there. Relief overwhelmed him and he knelt there for a moment unmoving. Then there came an exclamation from the doorway. He raised his head. Martha stood there, having heard the crash of the stool.

'Give me a hand, would you,' Connor requested somewhat brusquely.

Together they lifted Francys and laid him on the bed. Loosening the ties of the shirt, while Martha carefully drew off the boots, Connor spoke over his shoulder.

'Tell me, Martha, what have I done for him to fly at me with a knife?'

'Did he so? The poor lad. I expect he didn't quite know what he was doing. He's feverish again.'

'Oh, he knew all right. I only wish *I* did. I was fighting for my life!'

He looked down at the unconscious young man.

'Why?' he asked in hurt bewilderment. 'Why?'

Then, unable to bear to look at the still, pale face any longer, he turned abruptly away and left the room.

Martha settled herself comfortably in the chair and remained on watch. Francys breathed raspingly and presently became restless, moving his head irritably.

'Nan,' he muttered fretfully. 'Why did you do it?'

Opening his eyes suddenly, he struggled onto one elbow and stared wildly round the room.

'Nan,' he said desolately, 'where are you? Why do you not come?'

'Now don't you take on so,' responded Martha with comforting placidity. 'She has gone out just now.'

It was apparently a satisfactory answer, for Francys docilely permitted her to settle him back on the pillows and drifted into a deep, restorative sleep.

Some hours later, Martha having peeped in and seen that Francys was awake, Connor finally ventured back into the bedchamber, with a dish of freshly baked corn-cakes. His entrance was unusually tentative for he was not sure what form his reception might take, and after the last chaotic visit, was prepared for the worst. Advancing cautiously, he discovered to his alarm that Francys was no longer in bed, and an anxious glance around the chamber revealed the young man to be on his feet, standing beside the window, leaning against the frame. He set the dish down safely on the hearth and trod warily across the room until he had a clear view of the young man. Francys was half-turned towards the window, gazing blindly into space, but Connor was able to see his face, and the sight caused him to stop in his tracks, appalled. Guard dropped for once, the face expressed all the emotions that were normally concealed behind the mask of self-control; a visual projection of the emotions that Connor had heard expressed in the deep of the night when Francys had believed his companion asleep. A flicker of fear passed through Connor's body and impulsively he moved forward, reaching out to grasp one of the unresponsive hands. At his touch, Francys seemed to come back from the hell inside his mind. His eyes turned and focussed on the worried, bearded face of his Captain.

'Con,' he said wretchedly. 'Oh Sior, Con. I tried to kill you.'

He broke down suddenly, turning his face away, leaning his forehead against the window frame, his shoulders shaken by sobs. Connor set a strong, friendly arm about him, holding him compassionately as he wept helplessly, unable to halt the storm of tears. Then, as suddenly as he had begun, Francys regained control over himself. Connor, sensing the withdrawal, hurriedly removed his arm and stepped back a pace. The young man remained as he was for a few seconds, breathing heavily, before slowly turning round, his face flushed with embarrassment.

'I'm sorry,' he said after an awkward pause. 'My nerves must be out of order, I think.'

'Well,' responded Connor reasonably, ' you have been very ill, so it isn't surprising. And after what Martha was telling me, I'm even less surprised. You've been overtaxing yourself. Come and sit by the fire before your legs decide they've had enough.'

Francys managed a faint grin and leant appreciatively on the arm he was offered, saying nothing further until he had reached the chair and was settled into it.

Then there was nothing else for it. He steeled himself to look up into the older man's grave face, noticing the puzzled expression in the grey eyes as they rested on him, and the wariness behind the man's seemingly relaxed stance. He took a firm hold on himself.

'I tried to kill you,' he said once more.

Connor shifted uneasily.

'Don't you wonder why?'

'Naturally,' Connor said at last.

'You can't think of a reason?'

'I wish I could, for it would make it more bearable,' said Connor bluntly. 'But I'm damned if I can.'

The hazel eyes fixed on his with feverish intensity.

'Are you in love with the Lady Nyandu?' Francys asked abruptly, his voice harsh, grating.

Connor gave a grunt of surprise, taken aback.

'I want an answer,' Francys said slowly and distinctly, his hands clenching over the arms of the chair, knuckles whitened.

'Tell me!' he demanded peremptorily. 'Damn you, tell me!'

Connor stirred.

'No,' he said quietly, but firmly. 'I'm fond of her ... very fond of her in fact, but not in the way you mean. It's just, if I'd ever had a daughter, she's the way I'd have liked her to be.'

Another pause ensued before Francys could pluck up the courage to voice the other question, and he uttered it in tones so husky and taut that Connor did not at first take in its meaning.

'Does *she* love you?'

When the import penetrated his brain, Connor's head jerked up swiftly and he stared at Francys with eyes that blazed in utter disbelief. A picture rose involuntarily and unchecked before his mind's eye, of Nyandu when the moment of parting had arrived. She had ridden to Kelethina in a mood of comparative cheerfulness, chatting easily enough. But, as she had said her farewell to him, as he, in truth treating her like a daughter, had folded her in a warm embrace, then the tears had come, silently enveloping her features, and she had beseeched him in a faltering voice, saying:

'Write to me Connor. Promise me you will write to me. Tell me how he is and what he does. I cannot let him slip back into obscurity. Please, Connor, if you can, send me word from time to time. I can't bear to lose him again.'

'Dear Sior!' he exclaimed forcefully. 'Whatever put such a ridiculous idea into your head?! Of course she doesn't! Nor is she like to.'

'Martha said she saw her kissing you,' Francys said tiredly, his gaze dropping wearily.

'And you immediately leapt to the conclusion that I was trying to cheat you behind your back!' Connor responded angrily. 'After all the years you've known me, you believed I'd do a thing like *that*! Dear Sior, if your opinion of me is that low, it's a wonder you want me in your company at all...'

He turned away, bitterly hurt.

'No, Con, no!' Francys cried out hastily. 'No, it's not that way at all!'

He struggled to his feet and laid his hand on the older man's arm. Connor did not turn round, and tried to shrug it off.

'Con,' Francys said earnestly, 'I'm sorry. I never meant to hurt you. You know how much I value your company. Don't you remember what I said when you came to find me at Carledruin? I meant it then, and I mean it now. Of course, you wouldn't cheat me. I know that. It's just that sometimes I can't seem to think straight,' he said miserably. 'This illness ... I don't know ... it seems to somehow exaggerate things in my mind ... Oh hell, I can't explain, but I am truly sorry that I've hurt you. Please believe *that*!'

A subtle tremor had started within him. He was still too near to fever, and the day's events had used up what strength he possessed. As he stood there shivering, dismayed and distressed by the wound he had unintentionally inflicted upon the feelings of his companion, appalled at how close he had come to losing the friend who had stood by him so staunchly when all others had deserted him, he felt a stealthy creeping sensation take hold of him.

'Oh Sior,' he gasped suddenly, his hand tightening reflexively on Connor's arm. 'Con, get me a bowl or something. Quickly!'

Struck by the urgency in the man's voice, Connor threw him a glance, and made haste to comply, rushing from the room and returning in an instant with a basin which he had seized from the press next door. But he was already too late. Francys had slipped to his knees, doubling over with the force of his retching. When the first spasms were over and Francys knelt numbedly, shaking and breathing in shuddering gasps, Connor grabbed hold of him and got him back into the chair, placing the basin on his lap. The fair man nodded gratefully, then hurriedly bent over the bowl, the movement having caused a rush of nausea to overwhelm his senses.

At last the fair head lay limply against the chair-back. The eyes were closed, dark-circled and bruised. Flecks of blood stained the mouth and chin. Drained, he had not the energy even to open his eyes when Connor began to clean him up, allowing the older man to do as he wished. Then, as Connor had begun to think that the young man would drift into merciful sleep, Francys spoke, quietly, bitterly:

'I wish in Sior's name she had left me to die by the wayside.'

Connor started.

'Don't you dare to talk like that, Francys Coras!' he reprimanded sharply.

'Why not?' Francys said bleakly. 'It would have been better for all of us.'

'I doubt the Lady Nyandu would agree.'

'The Lady Nyandu stands in peril of her life, and it was I who brought her into that danger. Do you think that a fine thing to have on your conscience? And what of Martha, and Tam? Have I not also assured *them* of ignominious death should my presence here ever become known? And yourself? How many others must I bring to disaster in order to keep my worthless self alive? Rather than turning the knife on you, it would have been better had I used it on myself! I should have done so ... had I the courage ...'

'Courage! You think it brave to kill yourself do you?' snorted Connor derisively, bent on forcing Francys out of his deathly frame of mind. 'Myself, I'd say it was the act of a coward, one who is too afraid to face up to life. And you are not a coward, Francys. No-one could possibly call you *that*, who has seen what you have had to battle against. Don't give them the satisfaction of seeing you fail! Don't play into your brother's hands. It's what he wants, isn't it? You dead and no danger to him any longer. Think on *that*!'

He saw Francys begin to waver, and continued.

'How do you suppose the Lady Nyandu would feel, having risked her life to save yours, to have you fling that back in her face? To be shown that you hold her action in such small esteem that you took the first opportunity offered to negate it? Must I go to her and tell her that the man she spent all those terrible weeks nursing so tenderly has killed himself because he hadn't the guts to accept the life she had saved and didn't care enough about her to value it ...'

'No!' An agonized cry was torn from Francys' lips. 'No, not that! It isn't true! It is *because* I care that ... I have done her enough harm already. What could I do worse than hang at her heels, forever bringing her misfortune? If my death secures her safety, surely that is a worthy exchange!'

'I doubt she would see it that way,' said Connor drily. 'She wants you *alive*. Do you know what she said to me when we parted? She said 'I can't bear to lose him again.' Does that sound to you as if she'd be happy to learn of your death?'

He halted, realising that Francys was no longer listening. The young man's face was full of wonder.

'She said *that*?' he murmured disbelievingly.

'Aye,' Connor confirmed. 'She did ... and more besides. She wants you alive, Francys, as do I, as do all your men. We need you ...'

He took a chance. Dropping to one knee before the young man, he reached out and took hold of the long-fingered hands in a firm, yet compassionate, grasp.

'Francys,' he urged, willing himself to speak the words as persuasively as he might, 'Francys, give me your word that you will never again attempt to take your own life. Your word of honour...'

He knew that once given, it was not in Francys' nature to break such an oath. There was a tense silence. Connor found that he was holding his breath. Finally, Francys spoke, in a barely audible whisper, his voice husky with extreme weariness.

'You win, Con. You win. I promise ... On the great circlet Caelvorchadu ...'

CHAPTER SEVENTEEN

After parting with Connor at Kelethina, Nyandu and Thadie journeyed on to the town of Arlmen, disguised for greater safety as a farmer and his wife. Around them the sun shone and a small breeze ruffled the leaves and swept across the stubble of fields which had been in the full glory of golden ripeness when Nyandu had first set out towards her present destination, a thought which now struck her forcefully. For a period of seven weeks or so, from mid-kepre to mid-horenith, she had to all intents and purposes vanished off the face of the earth. Now she was about to reappear. Inwardly she shuddered to think what reaction she would encounter. What should she tell the Dukrugvola? He was bound to have been informed of her disappearance. Bestirring herself, she began to ask questions of Thadie (who had tactfully left her alone with her thoughts), ascertaining from him the rumours and stories surrounding her absence.

Towards late afternoon, unrecognized and almost unobserved, the counterfeit farmer and his wife insinuated themselves into the narrow, cobbled streets of the town and thence, by back-passages and alleys, to the house in which the servants waited so patiently.

The following morning, local people passing by the house were astounded to find that the courtyard, which had been more or less deserted for weeks save for occasional movement of horses and men, was of a sudden filled with bustle and noise. Horses, saddled and bridled, were led forth from the stable-block. An inquisitive dog leapt excitedly, yapping furiously and tangling with the moving figures, provoking good-humoured curses. Over on the steps, an elderly man of military bearing carefully watched the preparations, shouting orders and directing the scene with incisive gestures. A young boy appeared on the steps, chattering excitedly to the supervisor, then vanished back inside. Attracted by the activity, passers-by gradually gathered at the entrance to the courtyard, peering curiously through the archway. Speculations tossed from one inquisitive onlooker to the next like the foam of wind-swept waves.

Nyandu had decided that in order to divert attention from the interesting question of where she had been all these weeks, she would have to reappear in spectacular fashion. Accordingly, having ensured that there would be an audience, she presently laid the tips of her fingers on Thadie's attentive arm, and with Morla accompanying her on her other side, walked in a stately manner down the steps towards the waiting horses, where she received the assistance of her Captain to mount into the saddle. Once all were mounted, including Morla on his pony, Nyandu raised her hand and gave the signal. As the cavalcade wheeled and clattered through the archway, past the thronging, eager faces of the worthy citizens of Arlmen, it was to be seen that the soldiers of the lady's escort wore surcoats of a pale blue hue emblazoned with a white horse.

A startled cheer arose as realization struck home, spreading outwards and increasing in volume as it did so. Nyandu, sitting straight and tense, relaxed slowly, and acknowledged the greetings of the crowd with a wave and a smile, signing to Morla to do likewise. Amid applause, they passed into the main street, which they found also packed. People jostled one another for a glimpse of the lady who had apparently vanished so mysteriously, and had now reappeared in equally mysterious guise. A few older worthies recalled the legends of Verindel's visit to the spirit realm. Was not the fabled Cavern of Kandringeddan said to be located in the heights of the Teleth Cranem? Others ran alongside the party. Shopkeepers stood behind their wares, arms folded, doing no business whilst the spectacle passed by. Their apprentices were lost to them for the remainder of the morning, and many were the pickpockets and sneak-thieves who took advantage of the unexpected attraction of Nyandu's ride through the streets to pinch the purses or shopwares of fascinated spectators. In the midst of the throng stood a young man of dark complexion, dressed in the garb of a metal-worker. No sooner had Nyandu disappeared from sight, then he strode briskly towards the nearest inn and arranged the despatch of an urgent message.

Nyandu and her escort left the town by the northern gate and proceeded at a leisurely pace. Having talked it over with Thadie during the journey from Kelethina, she had determined to continue with the task of inspecting the watch-towers along the border with Harres. It would not be a lengthy diversion and at least she would have the satisfaction of having completed the assignment entrusted to her by the Dukrugvola. She also elected to take Morla. He deserved to join the excursion; besides, he stuck so close to her side, that it would have been nigh impossible to leave him behind; and she was glad of his innocent, merry chatter to lighten the low spirits with which she was afflicted. They were to spend a little over a week on the trip, before returning to Arlmen for a few days to prepare for the journey back to Lôren, and her uncle.

Meantime, a messenger was hastening southwards down endless lengths of highway towards the city of Väst and the new Prince of Varadil. Hadran, having bade a thankful farewell to his guests, was beginning to relax into the security of his elevated situation. He could not, of course, forgive the Dukrugvola for the humiliation of having the Regency of Kirkendom taken away from him in public, let alone the snub at the feast, but for the moment he was quite content to settle down and occupy himself with mundane tasks of government. Until, that was, a slip of parchment was placed in his hands, and he read thereon the unsettling news that the Lady Nyandu had surfaced from whatever place of concealment in which she had spent the past weeks.

Instantly the inner conflict reawakened. Nyandu might be perfectly innocent of any connection with Francys; her absence might be attributable to all manner of cause; but he had to know for certain, from her own lips. Mustering a small corps of his personal guard, Hadran took brusque leave of his household, before setting off at a punishing speed. Demanding regular supplies of fresh horses, and forcing his men on, he made the journey in record time, riding in to Arlmen late in the evening of the sixth day. The hour was too late to disturb Nyandu and he was forced to commandeer accommodation for the night in the town's most prestigious inn, where he summoned his spy and learned to his satisfaction that Nyandu was in residence.

He did not sleep well that night, despite the soft mattress on the bed of the inn's largest and most comfortable chamber. For a time he paced the floor, nervously chewing his lip. For a time he stood at the window, gazing unseeingly into the silent, moonlit street. Tomorrow he would know. He would see Nyandu, and he would know. But what would he learn from her? If she had not met Francys, if her disappearance was in no way connected with his devilish brother, what then? Could he be justifiably certain that his brother was dead? Dead, in some ditch or other squalid place, no longer a threat to his security, to his peace of mind, to his life? But once before he had believed that Francys was dead. He had thought him lost forever in the South by his (Hadran's) doing, only to have to learn that he had become instead the beloved of the Lord of Shadowe. Even then, the situation was not so terrible. At least, his brother was unlikely ever to return to Karled-Dū. But then Francys had escaped, and since that time everything had gone wrong. No! Before that! It would have been better if Francys had never been born. All the old feelings of hatred and self-pity began to well up inside his mind. *That* was the point at which it had all started to go amiss. Had Francys never existed, he, Hadran, would not have had to share his mother's love, would not have had to watch the boy grow up with all the charm and gifts that he himself lacked, would not have become tantalized and ensnared by that body! He would not now be in the position in which he currently found himself. But if Francys was dead, he would be safe. He could begin again, as it were. A new beginning! No more Francys, and a new position as ruler of Varadil!

He began to pace again. But what if he saw Nyandu and she told him that she had been with his brother? What then? He refused to contemplate the abyss which opened before him at the very thought of that predicament. Snatching up the jug of ale which stood upon the press, he poured a liberal amount of the liquid into the mug nearby and downed it in one swallow. Then he made his way back to the bed, where he sprawled, tossing and turning, for the remainder of the night, until falling into an uneasy slumber towards dawn.

In consequence he arose late, bleary-eyed and irritable, finding fault with whatever did not immediately suit his temper. Having breakfasted with no great appetite, he made haste to join his men in the courtyard. It was but a short ride through the streets to the house which Nyandu had made her headquarters (passing though he knew it not the establishment of Jeff, wherein was stabled Francys' stallion, Melisor), but he chafed at the crowds who slowed his progress and got in his way. At last he came to the tall arched entrance to the courtyard and swept inside. Alas: he was too late. The place was empty and the bird had flown.

Earlier that morning, Nyandu's party had finally departed the town of Arlmen on the first stage of the return journey to Lôren, and ultimately her home in the Province of Meneleindom. They proceeded at a leisurely pace, for Nyandu was unaware of pursuit, and begrudged every calle which took her further away from Francys. Morla chattered excitedly beside her, or darted away to spend some time pestering Thadie with questions. A misty rain hung over the landscape, draping trees and bushes with light, lacy veils and soaking imperceptibly into all clothing. They had come almost halfway to the border into Arlente when one of the baggage-horses fell lame. Fortunately, they were not far from one of the occasional wayside hostelries, and Nyandu decreed a halt whilst efforts were made to obtain the services of a blacksmith from the nearest village. After consuming a light meal, she walked about the neighbouring countryside with Morla, to stretch their legs, hoods raised against the continuing drizzle, before returning to the inn, to find that the smith had finished the re-shoeing and Thadie was directing the rearrangement of the baggage.

They set off again heading in a westerly direction, with the great range of the Teleth Cranem rising above the horizon to the south-west, growing steadily taller as calle by calle they approached the border. At some point the rain ceased and a pale sun appeared, striking sparks off the raindrops hanging from the twigs and grass-stalks. The ground began to rise towards the foothills of the mountains, and the long shadow of the range crept slowly across the landscape as the sun moved across the sky.

One of the escort rode up from the rear of the cavalcade.

'Sir,' he said, addressing Thadie, who was at this time riding with Nyandu, 'there is a band of horsemen approaching at a rapid pace.'

Thadie and Nyandu looked round. Yes, though still some distance away, shapes could be discerned, growing rapidly larger. Thadie grumbled to himself:

'Just where the road narrows,' he muttered crossly.

'Best tell the men to pull in to the side and let those people pass,' he ordered brusquely.

The soldier saluted and retired to pass on the command to his companions. The baggage-wain was drawn in as far as was practicable onto the rough grass at the edge of the highway, although the steepness of the bank precluded its being able to be got quite off the roadway. Those on horseback moved into single file. A wry smile curved Nyandu's lips.

'All we need now is another wagon coming the other way,' she remarked. 'Then there would be chaos.'

The hoofbeats grew louder, pounding on the stones, but instead of sweeping past, the riders came to an abrupt halt as they reached the stationary group. With a sinking heart Nyandu recognized their leader, who had thrown back his hood. Instinctively she drew closer to Thadie, pulling her own hood further forward in an attempt to conceal her features. She was vaguely aware that Morla had given a gasp of fright and was trying to hide behind his pony, having hastily dismounted.

Hadran rode slowly forward until he was level with Nyandu.

'Menaïren, might I have speech of you?' he enquired courteously.

Nyandu considered briefly and signified consent, saying merely:

'You might have chosen a more comfortable location.'

She waited for him to state his purpose, but he glanced meaningfully at Thadie.

'It is a private matter.'

Reluctantly, she moved forward, leaving Thadie and Morla some little distance behind. She could not forebear to look back at Thadie, noting with relief that he was alert, watchful, and ready to come to her assistance at any moment, should the need arise. Hadran advanced until he was close enough to talk in a low voice, and reined in. Nyandu was acutely aware of his presence and had much ado to keep her composure.

'Yes?' she said a trifle sharply as he remained silent for a few seconds, staring at her. She stared back, seeing powerful shoulders outlined under the cloak, a well-built body, a rugged face topped by close-cropped hair of Coras gold. Her mind transposed another face in its stead, and she looked hastily away.

'Well?' she asked, as he continued to remain unspeaking. 'Am I not to know after all what it is that brings you wanting speech with me? It must have been of grave importance to have brought you all the way from Väst at such a time, where you must surely have sufficient business to be involving yourself in - for I gather that I am to congratulate you on your new status? And also to tender my condolences on the death of your father.'

'I am looking for my brother,' Hadran said, breaking his silence abruptly. 'Have you seen him?'

'No,' she replied coolly, but unable to turn her eyes to his face. 'And if you think to find him in my baggage, you are much in error.'

'It wouldn't surprise me if I did,' Hadran muttered half-audibly.

'Menellen!' Nyandu feigned outrage. 'What are you suggesting?!'

She sounded so shocked that Hadran hastily backed down.

'I did not mean to offend you,' he said as soothingly as it was in his nature to be. 'There has been word that he had gone to ground somewhere in the region of Arlmen, and I thought that you might have encountered him, or that he might have slipped among your party to avoid notice.'

His attempt at conciliation was not well-received.

'Indeed!' Nyandu responded icily, speaking loudly enough for Thadie and Morla to hear. 'Do you think that I would not have noticed his presence, or that my men would not? Or do you mean to accuse us of deliberately offering him shelter and assistance? I can assure you that all these people are well-known to me and have been in my employ for some years. Would you wish to examine them, or are you prepared to take my word that none of them is Francys in disguise?'

Morla uttered a giggle, quickly suppressed. Hadran's eyes travelled to him and back to Nyandu.

'Your word is sufficient,' he said stiffly.

'I thank you,' Nyandu said bitingly. 'And now, perhaps we may continue on our way without further interruption. I am anxious to make good progress before the light fails. Allow me to wish you a safe and swift journey home to Väst. I will bid you good day.'

She gathered up her reins. Hadran regarded her thoughtfully.

'Wait'.

She turned her head in surprise.

'Where have you been all these past weeks?' he demanded abruptly.

Nyandu froze momentarily, her fingers tightening involuntarily on the reins.

'Why should that concern *you*?' she countered cautiously.

Hadran's eyes narrowed. He noted the evasion and suspicion leapt to his mind.

'Your whereabouts were of concern to a great number of persons,' he retorted. 'You vanished seemingly off the face of the earth, giving no indication to anyone beforehand where you were going. Naturally people began to wonder what had happened to you. Did you not hear the rumours, in whatever quiet, secluded spot you had hidden yourself?'

'Rumours?'

'Following your disappearance, it was widely bruited about that you had been abducted and held captive by my delightful brother and his merry band of men. Your uncle, for one, was most upset by the report.'

Nyandu looked at the smirk on Hadran's face, at the smug set of his shoulders, and suddenly she had had enough.

'Then I am sure that you will have been swift to set his mind at ease,' she retaliated.

Then, as his brows furrowed in puzzlement, she added:

'After all, who could know better than *you* how physically impossible it would have been for Francys to do any such thing after having so recently experienced the rigours of your hospitality.'

She stared at him, her face lifted challengingly, her grey eyes blazing with unaccustomed anger, and her lips taut with a revulsion that she was unable to disguise.

The colour drained from Hadran's cheeks as the meaning of her words sunk in, and the world seemed to spin around him. His mouth felt dry. She knew! Dear Sior, she knew!

'You've seen him!' he uttered hoarsely, hardly able to speak. 'I knew it. I knew it, whatever the others said. You've spoken to him. What has he told you, the lying bastard?!'

He pushed his horse forward. The violent expression on his face alarmed Nyandu, causing her involuntarily to pull sharply on the reins of her own mount. Startled, the horse reared up abruptly, and she lost her grip and fell out of the saddle, and before anyone present knew what had happened, she lay on the stones of the roadway, senseless, having struck her head and knocked herself unconscious.

Hadran, genuinely horrified, leapt from his horse to go to her aid, but found his path blocked.

'Stand back, Menellen,' Thadie commanded grimly. 'You have done enough.'

'I did not mean her to fall!' Hadran protested indignantly.

He found himself ignored. Thadie beckoned forward two of the soldiers from the escort to stand guard over the fallen girl, beside whom knelt Morla, white with shock and fear at seeing her so suddenly prostrated, and feeling frantically for her pulse as he had watched her do back on the highway from Caleth Mor so many weeks earlier. From her seat on the baggage-cart, Nyandu's maid came running forward, proffering a flask of water and a cloth with which to bathe her mistress' temples. One of the men slipped a folded cloak under Nyandu's head.

Having set in motion the tending of his mistress, only then did Nyandu's Captain return his attention to the fair-haired man, eyeing him in a combative manner despite the disadvantage of his lesser height.

'I believe you are not welcome here,' he told Hadran bluntly. 'And the telling of this incident will not redound to your credit, should it become common knowledge. To have perpetrated an assault upon the daughter of a Prince, aye and the niece of the Dukrugvola moreover ...'

'I did *not* assault her!'

'It might appear so to other eyes, and it could be made to assume that appearance,' observed Thadie blandly.

'Damn you, are you threatening me?!' demanded Hadran fiercely, angry at himself as much as at the man standing before him.

'No Menellen,' Thadie answered suavely. 'Merely advising you that you would do well to depart before this scene is interrupted by passing traffic.'

Hadran drew in his breath, but the force of the words struck home and, clenching his fists against the rush of rage within, he flung round and strode tempestuously to his horse, calling to his men in a voice which shook from the strength of the fury and mortification burgeoning in his breast. It was clear that he could do no more here, and he had what he had come for in any event.

He rode at a reckless speed, pushing himself and his men to their utmost, as if attempting to outpace some unseen pursuer, but necessity eventually forced him to moderate his pace, for which his men were profoundly grateful. Unfortunately this allowed his thoughts to catch up with him, and what dark, gloomy thoughts they were. Yes, he had found out what he had wanted to know. Nyandu *had* seen Francys; she knew ... all. She had admitted as much. But what now? He was as helpless to do aught about the fact, as if he had never found out. He asked himself what he would have done had events turned out differently and Nyandu not been hurt. What *could* he have done? Would he have denounced her for assisting a traitor, had her arrested? But then she might have felt free to tell the world what Francys had told *her*. She would have had nothing to lose.

What would she do now? A shudder passed through the big fair man. What if she were to tell the Dukrugvola? But surely, a tiny spark of hope burned in his mind, surely she would not do so, for by so doing, she would be condemning herself as a traitor. She would have to admit to having assisted one who was under the penalty of death for treachery, and that would set her against the law also. It seemed that they were both at an impasse; she could not denounce *him* for fear of being declared a traitor and he could not denounce *her* in case she disclosed his criminal acts. They were, metaphorically, sitting at opposite ends of a weighing-beam, precariously but equally balanced, and could stay there indefinitely, so long as nothing occurred to tip the scales towards one or the other.

Much comforted by this reflection, Hadran continued on his journey. It was not until he had reached the outskirts of the city of Väst that the realization came to him that in his conversation with Nyandu, he had omitted to ascertain one very important fact: he still did not know whether Francys was alive or dead.

As soon as Hadran was on his way, Thadie got the baggage-wain back onto the highway and crossed over to where Nyandu lay. Morla looked up at him, his eyes large and frightened.

'Will she be all right?' he asked apprehensively.

'Aye, lad, there's no cause for alarm,' Thadie reassured him comfortingly, suppressing his own fears. 'We'll take her to the next inn we come to and I guarantee she'll soon be right as rain.'

He signed to the two soldiers nearby to lift the unconscious girl and carry her to the cart, where a space had been hastily contrived. Leading her horse beside his own, he brought the party safe to an inn some six calle distant, across the border in the Province of Arlente, and supervised the transference of his mistress from the cart to a soft bed, before setting himself to occupy Morla and to order the bestowal of his men.

Nyandu woke some few minutes later, much surprised to discover herself to be lying on a bed.

'Where am I?' she asked in bewilderment, observing a woman seated nearby.

'You are in the Heglos Inn, Menaïren,' the innkeeper's wife replied, bobbing her head respectfully, 'in Lindon village.'

Nyandu pondered, recollection gradually filtering in behind the pulsating ache in her head.

'Who brought me here?' she enquired. 'Are my men below?'

'Yes, Menaïren. And the boy.'

'Good,' murmured Nyandu.

She relapsed into silence, closing her eyes, and began to pass in review the conversation which had taken place between Hadran and herself, the details of which had now surfaced from her memory. Bitterly she castigated herself as the full impact of her words became clear to her. If only she had had sufficient fortitude not to let her emotions overcome her reason. Hadran now knew that she had indeed seen his brother; that she was guilty in the eyes of the law of treason, for she had not turned him in to the authorities. What would Hadran do now? Would he report her? Was she soon to hear the footfalls of the justiciars' men sent to arrest her? Was she to feel the cold metal of chains about her wrists, and worse, be made to walk the last few steps to the scaffold? A shudder ran through her at the mere thought. Surely Hadran would not be so vindictive, would he?

But then, *she* had also shown *him* that she was aware of what he had done to Francys. If he were to alert the authorities to *her* guilt, what would there be to stop her from proclaiming *his*? A faint glimmer of hope flickered within. No, she could not believe that he would be as deaf to self-preservation as that! Were it merely the flogging, then perhaps he might submit to temptation, but he could not afford for her to reveal to the world those other, more private acts to which he had subjected his brother. On the other hand, *she* could not denounce *him* for his criminal acts without revealing her own. If that would affect merely herself, she would not hesitate; she deeply desired to see him reap his just deserts. However, she knew that if she were to be arraigned as a traitor, she would be bound to bring Francys to his death also, for she knew him well enough to realize that he would deem himself to blame for her predicament. For Francys' sake then, she must conspire to cover up his brother's crime.

She sighed, and sat up.

'Would you assist me to rise?' she asked the innkeeper's wife with a pleasant smile. 'I fear I am a little dizzy still.'

The latter bustled forward helpfully and soon had Nyandu settled in a chair beside a crackling fire, a warm drink in her hand and a blanket tucked round her. She asked for Thadie and he came, accompanied by Morla, who made a dash for her, hugging her tightly and nearly upsetting the hot punch. She felt his tunic.

'Morla, my love, you must change. Your clothes are quite damp and I'd rather you didn't catch a fever. Run down and ask Sabia to bring up your bag, and mine too,' she added as he obediently made for the door. Then when he had disappeared, she looked up at her Captain.

'How do you feel now, Menaïren?' he enquired solicitously.

'My head aches vilely, which is only to be expected, and I shall have some pretty bruises by and by, but otherwise, I am well enough,' she told him. 'I must thank you for your quick thinking, and for bringing us here. Tell me, what happened after I fell?'

Thadie took a deep breath and related the exchange between himself and the Lord Hadran Coras in succinct terms and a twinkle in his eyes. Nyandu uttered a soft chuckle, then put her hand up to her brow.

'Ouch,' she said ruefully. 'That hurt. Thadie, I believe I shall stay here for the night. Indeed, I have little choice in the state I am in at present. Could you arrange accommodation for everyone, do you think?'

'Certainly, Menaïren.'

'Thank you,' she sighed and closed her eyes again, laying her head wearily, if cautiously, against the high back of the chair.

Nyandu slept deeply despite her aching head and bruises, and woke late the next morning feeling stiff, but immeasurably fresher. The pain in her head had eased to a dull murmur which she felt would not impede her travel plans. The sun was shining, and she could not help but feel a lift of the spirits. Hadran was gone back to his own affairs and would not trouble her further, at least for the present. She did not know what she would say to the Dukrugvola, but that was not an immediate problem; she could think about that at a later date. For now, all she had to do was keep an eye on Morla, and try to suppress the memories of the weeks she had lived through at Martha's cottage.

She had eaten breakfast, risen and dressed, and her maid was brushing her hair, cautiously to avoid catching the bruises which had resulted from the fall, when she heard the sounds of a party of horsemen arriving at the inn. Involuntarily she paled. With a quick gesture, she motioned to Sabia to go and look out of the window to see who it might be. The girl did so, peering down over the sill.

'Menaïren!' she gasped. 'I believe it is the Dukrugvola!'

'The Dukrugvola!' exclaimed Nyandu, turning if anything even paler.

She swayed on the stool, and the maid hurried to her side.

'Menaïren, you are unwell!'

'No, no, it's nothing.' Nyandu said quickly. 'Do go back to the window and tell me what you can see.'

But when Sabia returned to the window, it was to find that the travellers had dismounted and disappeared into the hostelry.

Sabia had finished putting up Nyandu's hair, and had settled her mistress in the big oak armchair beside the fireplace before anything further was heard about the new arrivals. A discreet knock sounded on the door and the landlady entered in a state of some excitement, clearly overawed by the company her humble inn had attracted.

'Menaïren,' she spoke from the doorway, dropping a small curtsey. 'The Lord Dukrugvola, the Lady Alhaîtha Oneranen and the Lord Saragon Cerinor are below, asking after you. The Lord Dukrugvola is wishful to know if he may see you.'

Nyandu swallowed nervously, but summoned up a smile and answered graciously:

'But of course. Let him come up.'

She waited with a pounding heart which nearly drowned out by its thudding the sound of footsteps presently approaching her door. Then the door opened, and Nyandu looked up, her throat dry, to see her uncle framed in the doorway, smiling at her warmly.

'Nan, my dear child, I am rejoiced to see you safe.' he exclaimed, striding forward with open arms.

Much encouraged, Nyandu rose and advanced to meet him. The next moment she was enfolded in an embrace as affectionate as any she had ever received from him.

'Uncle,' she said softly, leaning her head momentarily on his shoulder. The relief of being able, even if only for a brief while, to depend on someone else's strength was so overwhelming that she had perforce to blink away a couple of tears.

The Dukrugvola gently disengaged himself and looked at her closely.

‘Perhaps you should sit down,’ he suggested. ‘We heard about your accident. A nasty fall. How is your head now? You look pale, my dear.’

Nyandu gratefully acceded to his suggestion, and motioned him to seat himself also. She made haste to reassure him as to her state of health.

‘It aches abominably,’ she told him with a grimace, ‘but there’s no real damage. I shall be well enough to travel today.’

‘That is as well. This inn has not the space to accommodate us all, and I don’t mean to let you out of my sight, my dear, until we have come safely back to Lôren. But we shall not travel too far today. There is a larger establishment only a few calle further along the highway, as I recall, where I have stayed before. You may rest there a day before we continue our journey.’

He smiled at her again, but Nyandu’s thoughts had been distracted by mention of Lôren. The feeling of dread which had afflicted her earlier rose to overwhelm her again.

‘Do ... do you wish to hear my report, sir?’ she asked tentatively.

The Dukrugvola raised his eyebrows.

‘Here? No, no,’ he assured her amiably. ‘That can wait until we are in Verilith, and ensured of privacy.’

He rose.

‘I shall leave you in peace now to finish your preparations for departure. There is no need for haste. Although,’ he added with a chuckle, ‘the sooner you are ready, the sooner you can appease your cousin’s impatience to see you!’

Nyandu initially felt a sense of having had a burden lifted from her, but over the following days of their journey to the city of Verilith, she began to wish that she had after all been able to deliver her ‘report’ to her Uncle. Every calle that she travelled closer to Verilith brought with it an intensification of her fear and a corresponding increase in her desire to get the matter over with and face the consequences, whatever they might be. She had feared that Alhaîtha’s natural curiosity might be difficult to evade, but to her relief, the expected questions did not come. Whether the Dukrugvola had warned his daughter not to question Nyandu about her travels, she knew not, but she was immensely grateful to her cousin for her forbearance. In fact, Alhaîtha seemed more eager to tell Nyandu about her own experiences, and Nyandu was obliged to endure a lengthy and detailed account of Hadran's investiture as Prince of Varadil. She found it difficult at first to hear his name spoken with equanimity, knowing what she knew about him, but she supposed that she would have to get used to it. Alhaîtha's account of the feast and Hadran's abortive attempt to lead a toast to the death of his brother caused Nyandu to spend a little time pondering the implication, and she felt a tiny spark of hope light in her mind.

She found Saragon's company a boon. Not once did he refer to the secret knowledge lying between them, but she was aware of his understanding and compassion. Whenever the conversation veered towards matters which might distress her, he was there with a casual word or remark to steer it off into another direction. It was also to him that she was indebted for news of events in Caleth Mor, whence they had travelled with the new Regent, leaving him there to take over management of the Province's affairs, and their subsequent journey via Arlmen to the inn where they had found her. The Dukrugvola himself had informed Morla of the change of regency, and the boy was looking forward to meeting the family of his new guardian when they arrived in Verilith, for it transpired that the Lord Veras Kleptal had two sons and a daughter of around the same age as Morla. Nyandu wondered whether he would still wish to travel on with her when the time came to leave Verilith. Then, morbidly, she wondered whether she would even be in a position to invite him. It was with a mixture of dread and relief that she finally saw the walls of Verilith loom on the horizon.

****

They had been in Verilith for a day and a night before the Dukrugvola found the opportunity to hold his private meeting with Nyandu. The Lady of the Province had allotted him a suite of rooms including a handsome office, and it was to this chamber that he repaired with Saragon after breakfasting on the second morning.

'It is time that we heard Nyandu's report,' he observed to the younger man, who nodded. 'Would you go and bring her here?'

Saragon, understanding the Dukrugvola's unspoken intention that the Sureindom man would provide reassurance to Nyandu should she require it, obeyed with alacrity. He too was eager to hear what she had to tell and had chafed at the enforced delay.

Having ascertained from the servants that she was not within doors, Saragon's search took him out into the gardens. Following directions from a groom, he found Nyandu eventually, leaning against the balustrade on a promontory overlooking a small inlet with a curve of white sand lapped by the gentle waters of the great lake. As he walked towards her, he had the thought that he had never seen her look more beautiful, in her simple gown of grass-green wool, a russet shawl wrapped round her shoulders, and her hair touched to bright copper by the rays of the autumnal sunshine. Then, as she heard his footsteps, she turned and he saw the sadness in her eyes, the knowledge of pain, and fear. It pierced him like an arrow, and as once before, he could not help but curse that impulse of his which had led him to invite the Coras brothers to his home.

Nyandu smiled at him. Indicating the lake, she said:

'I hired a boat, you know, when I was here before, to take me out onto the lake so that all I could see was the sky and the water. It was so peaceful ...'

Saragon held out his arm and she tucked her hand through it.

'It could be arranged,' he told her. 'You could do it again.'

She shook her head as they began to walk slowly away, leaving the view behind them.

'It wouldn't be the same. Morla would probably insist on coming too, and then I would worry that he would fall overboard!'

'Where is he today?'

'With the family. They have been so welcoming to him, and it's wonderful for him to have playmates. Indeed,' she added, a trifle wistfully, 'I begin to wonder whether he will want to travel on with me, when the time comes.'

Unspoken between them was Nyandu's fear that she herself might never reach Meneleindom. Saragon sensed her nervousness and gave the hand that rested on his arm an encouraging pat.

'Your uncle is a very fair and just man,' he commented, seemingly at random.

Nyandu smiled faintly.

'I know. Thanks Sharn.'

'You're welcome!'

He opened the door and ushered her through into a corridor. In silence now they walked down the passage, ascended a flight of stairs and eventually, having traversed a further length of corridor, came to a halt outside the door to the Dukrugvola's suite.

Having permitted them to settle themselves comfortably and seen them provided with refreshment, the Dukrugvola picked up a sheaf of papers and smiled across them to Nyandu.

'My dear Nan, I must thank you for an excellent piece of work. Your report is exceptionally clear and detailed. I have had it copied and sent to the Lord Veras Kleptel at Caleth Mor, where I am sure he will take steps to act on your findings. Well done, my dear.'

He glanced at Saragon.

'This only serves to confirm how right I was to effect a change of Regent. Had I but known the parlous state of the Province's defences, I should have done it long ago. Thankfully it would appear that the rulers of Harres and Krapan are less well informed than we now are, else no doubt they would have been knocking at the gates of Caleth Mor ere now and with no-one in the Province capable of stopping them!'

'It's fortunate then that they have the Lord Imraut to protect them,' Saragon commented drily.

'Fortunate indeed', agreed the Dukrugvola. 'And that brings us to the unofficial part of our business! Confess it, Sharn, you have been on tenterhooks, waiting to know what Nan here has found out, as indeed have I!'

He turned to Nyandu.

'Well, my dear, we are in your hands.'

Nyandu looked at the two faces turned towards her, radiating suppressed excitement and hope, and wondered what to say. The image of Francys as she had seen him last burned into her mind. The silence lengthened as she struggled with her feelings, until finally, her fingers clasped tightly together in her lap, she spoke.

'Yes, you were right. Menel Imraut and Francys Coras are one and the same.'

'Yes!' Saragon punched the air with one fist.

Saragon's instinctive exclamation and gesture of triumph served to lighten the atmosphere. The Dukrugvola's solemn features creased into an affectionate smile, and Nyandu felt herself relax slightly.

'Yet another good reason to rejoice in Hadran's removal from the

Regency', her uncle remarked. 'You know, my dear Nan, he had the effrontery to suggest that Francys had kidnapped *you* and was holding you captive somewhere...'

His expression was one of mild amusement, yet Nyandu was aware of the shrewd mind behind those grey eyes scrutinizing her. An unspoken question hung in the air.

This was it. Whatever her decision was at this point, there could be no going back from it. Unconsciously she drew herself up straighter and took a deep breath.

'If anyone should be deemed guilty of abduction,' she said resolutely, inwardly pleased that her voice did not waver, 'I suppose it should be I.'

'*You* Nan?' Saragon asked, grinning. 'And who have you abducted?'

She looked steadily at him.

'Who do you think? Francys, of course.'

She had the dubious satisfaction of seeing both men rendered momentarily speechless. Then, recovering control, the Dukrugvola said quietly:

'This, I take it, concerns the period of time when you were not with your escort in Arlmen. I think that you owe us an explanation.' Nyandu looked at him.

'Indeed, sir, I know that I do, and you shall have it. But it is a lengthy story, and I must tell it in some detail, so I would entreat you to refrain from passing judgment on me until you have heard the whole ..'

'My dear, I am not an ogre. You shall have all the time you wish, and you can be sure that we will listen with interest. But before you begin, let me refill your cup. If your tale is lengthy, you will need some refreshment as you speak.'

So saying, he rose and went across to a table upon which a servant had left a jug of wine. Returning with it, he proceeded to refill the cups of each of them, setting the jug down on the desk before him in case of further need.

Nyandu took a grateful swallow of the smooth wine, composed herself as best she could, and began her story. The words came out haltingly at first, but as she involved herself in the tale, she forgot her audience and concentrated on presenting the facts to the best of her ability, and her voice grew correspondingly stronger. She retraced her steps to the day of her departure from Caleth Mor, explaining her lateness in setting forth due to the complication of Morla, and describing how it was that her path had chanced to cross with that of Francys. As briefly and unemotionally as she could manage to be, she recounted the condition in which she had found him, her decision to help him and the plan which had been evolved and carried out, the journey cross-country in the cart, the weary weeks beside the sick-bed, Connor's advent and her eventual release from the duties of a nurse. There were a number of points on which she was deliberately vague and uncommunicative, notably the exact nature of Francys' illness. Of his capture by Hadran and his experiences whilst a prisoner, she made no mention at all; those were confidences unwittingly entrusted to her, which she had no right to reveal. She also refrained from naming any persons, save for Connor (who in any event had already been declared imrauten), who had given her assistance, or the location of the village in which she had taken refuge with Francys. She would not be responsible for bringing danger upon them.

Finally she reached the end of her narrative. Raising her head, she met her uncle's gaze unflinchingly and said quietly:

'I know that by helping Francys Coras and not delivering him to justice, I am in the eyes of the world guilty of treason against our realm. I do not attempt to excuse myself or my actions, sir. I could not have left him to die by the side of the road like a stray dog. He didn't deserve *that*.'

She felt the warm pressure of Saragon's hand on her own, comforting and reassuring. Then, to her surprise, her uncle came over to her and bent to enfold her in a warm embrace. Reaching over with one arm, he hooked the chair in which he had been sitting towards him and seated himself so that he was close enough to her to retain his grasp on her hands.

'Nan, Nan,' he said chidingly. 'Do you really believe I would turn you over to the justiciars for doing what you have done? With Francys I had no choice. The letters were so compelling that the matter was out of my hands. But you know my belief in his innocence, which has only been strengthened by his actions under the cloak of his assumed identity. With the help of Sharn here, and others, I have done as much as I am able to deflect the hunt without our machinations becoming too obvious. What do you suppose was my principal object in replacing Hadran as Regent of Kirkendom?'

He chuckled.

'Much to his displeasure, I must say! And it was a stroke of luck that I had a valid excuse for doing so, with his elevation to the Princedom of Varadil.'

He sobered again.

'That was our most pressing problem - Hadran. If anyone was likely to be a threat to Francys' continuing presence in the realm, *he* was! I suppose it was only to be expected. After all, it was he who brought the proofs to the attention of the justiciars, and he has the family name to uphold. In fact,' he added, frowning, 'he even admitted to us that his absence from Varadil at the time of his father's death was due to his having received news that Francys was in Kirkendom. You remember, Sharn? He said he had got on his trail ...'

Saragon nodded.

'Sior be thanked that he had not managed to catch up with him!'

Nyandu, listening in bemusement, could not repress a shudder. If only they knew!

Saragon noticed, but misinterpreted her movement.

'At least,' he said cheerfully, squeezing her hand a second time, 'now that the Regency has been taken away from Hadran, there can be no opportunity of that occurring in the future.'

Nyandu nodded and smiled gratefully at him, making use of his intervention to collect herself and bring her feelings under control. Then she turned to her uncle.

'Sir, what ought I to say if I am asked about my absence?'

The Dukrugvola paused for a moment in thought, frowning.

'My dear girl, I do not believe there are many who are likely to presume to question you, but should anyone be so ill-mannered as to press you about the matter, I think the best solution would be for you to repeat the story you have already put out, as I understand it - that is, that whilst on your travels, you came across a sick person needing assistance and very kindly undertook to give your time and knowledge to help. It has the advantage of being true, and no doubt your modesty would preclude you from going into detail,' he added with an affectionate smile. 'No-one would expect you to laud your own good deeds!

And I do believe that it would be safest if you said no more than this even to your cousin, and your parents. There is no need for anyone outside this room to know exactly what occurred.'

'Yes, sir,' Nyandu assented readily, and with some relief.

The Dukrugvola took a swallow of wine.

'So, now we come to the final problem concerning your activities.'

He turned to Nyandu.

'There are, of course, a number of persons who know the truth about your 'missing' weeks. I propose that we take them one by one and evaluate the danger each of them might pose to you.'

Nyandu nodded in silent acquiescence.

'Good, now I believe we can discount the villagers with whom you sought shelter - they themselves have a vested interest in keeping quiet. What about the remainder of the villagers?'

'I think that if anyone had been inclined to speak out, they would have done so already,' Nyandu said consideringly. 'Besides, sir, I think you underestimate the feeling of the local people towards Francys. No-one in that district would even think of betraying the one person who has taken their part in despite of all risk to himself.'

'That's true,' admitted her uncle. 'Then that brings us to those who were with you when you met Francys on the highway. Your Captain I know. He's an honourable man and will not talk. How about your maid, and the remainder of the escort?'

'They know no more than the official version. They never saw Francys close to. All they saw was a man in need of assistance.'

The Dukrugvola nodded in his turn.

'Then - Morla,' he said slowly. 'He knows the truth does he not?'

'Yes, but he won't talk, I assure you. He has grown up in a hard school, that child,' Nyandu said sadly. 'He knows when to keep his counsel. And above all, he venerates Francys. He would not wittingly set out to cause any harm to come to *him*!'

'My dear Nan, it is not Francys we are concerned about here, it is *you*.'

Nyandu shivered.

'Yes, I know. But I do not believe Morla would betray me either, sir.'

'No, I do not believe so either, not deliberately. But, given his admiration for Francys, might there not be a risk that he could be provoked into boasting of his encounter with the man? The Lord Imraut is very much a subject of gossip. It might be very tempting to be able to say that he had actually seen him.'

'I suppose so, but all the same, sir, I believe we may have confidence in Morla keeping silent. Especially,' she added as an afterthought, 'if we tell him that by keeping silent, he will be doing Hadran a bad turn! I guarantee that not a single word of the matter will pass his lips!'

Both men smiled.

'You seem to have taken the measure of him pretty well, Nan,' observed Saragon with a quiet chuckle.

'I feel very sorry for him, poor boy. Life has not been kind to him so far.'

'Well at least that will be different now,' Saragon said encouragingly, 'with the change of guardian. Sior willing, he need only have the minimum of contact with Hadran in future, and that only on formal occasions.'

'True,' Nyandu assented, 'Sior be thanked.'

The Lord Archailis got to his feet.

'A fitting conclusion to our discussions,' he observed.

He lifted the jug of wine and proceeded to pour a quantity into each goblet.

'Before we part, let us raise our glasses in a toast,' he suggested, 'to one who remains in our thoughts!'

He raised his own.

'The Lord Imraut!' he declared, smiling, and drank.

Saragon and Nyandu echoed his words, but Nyandu, having sipped her wine, sat looking troubled.

'There is one other person who knows that I have had contact with Francys,' she said slowly, swallowing nervously.

She saw the two faces swing round to stare at her in astonishment.

'Hadran knows,' she told them.

Both men swore, involuntarily, aghast.

'I beg your pardon, Nan,' her uncle said courteously.

'If you are thinking of the claims Hadran made to us at the Investiture, those were surely nothing other than guesswork based on a few snippets of information and a desire to evade the consequences of his own actions,' Saragon offered, frowning however as he recalled the knife with Francys' initials, which Hadran had claimed to have found on the highway. 'He cannot possibly have any certain knowledge.'

'I'm afraid that he does,' Nyandu said definitely.

'How can he know?' demanded Saragon, 'and how can *you* know that he knows?'

'You recall my accident on the journey here, before you all caught up with me?'

Both men nodded.

'Hadran was present ...'

Nyandu proceeded to relate an account of her encounter with the new Prince of Varadil.

'...Unfortunately, I let myself be goaded into saying something which made it clear to Hadran that I must have spoken to Francys recently,' she concluded.

Saragon clenched his fists.

'Was Hadran responsible for your accident?' he enquired tensely.

Nyandu nodded.

'In a sense,' she said, then raised her hand to still his furious outburst. 'It was not deliberate. He did not lay a finger on me, Sharn. And,' she added, looking from one man to the other, 'you do not need to fear that he will speak out and denounce me.'

She smiled reassuringly at her companions, even while in her deepest thoughts she did not feel nearly so convinced.

'I thought you ought to be aware,' she told them.

She had expected that they would try to argue with her, would demand explanations as to why she could be sure of Hadran's silence, but to her surprise, the Dukrugvola merely said, thoughtfully:

'Forewarned is forearmed, as they say. You were right to tell us, Nan.'

Nyandu nodded.

'So I thought.'

She rose, and the two men also got to their feet.

'Then if there is nothing further that you need me for, Uncle, I shall go and spend some time with Morla.'

She allowed Saragon to escort her to the door, smiled at him warmly and left.

As Saragon turned back from closing the door, the Dukrugvola said quietly:

'That is a lady of rare courage and compassion, Sharn! I am honoured to be able to call her niece.'

Saragon, having expressed his complete agreement, could not forebear, however, to add a devout wish that Sior keep her activities secret. The Dukrugvola, echoing the thought, fixed the younger man with a solemn gaze.

'Sharn, I want you to promise me that should it be necessary for any reason ... should Nyandu find herself in any danger as a result of what she has done ... you will do all in your power to protect her and keep her safe, whatever it may take.'

Saragon gravely nodded.

'I do so promise,' he said resolutely.

CHAPTER EIGHTEEN

Nyandu's initial reaction, having closed the door upon her uncle and Saragon, was to feel a deep sense of relief. For the first time since her encounter with Francys on the highway she could relax, for she had given up the reins of responsibility into her uncle's capable hands. For sure, there remained the lingering problem of Hadran, but that was counterbalanced by her own knowledge of *his* activities. To all intents and purposes, she was safe, and so was Francys, for the time being.

Relief was, however, succeeded by an unsettling feeling of dullness and lethargy, from which she gradually descended into a dark depression which she struggled to shake off. While outwardly she made an effort to appear reasonably cheerful, she was increasingly aware of an emptiness inside. Undertaking the commission for the Dukrugvola, rescuing and nursing Francys, delivering her report to the Dukrugvola, in all these she had had a purpose to her life. Now she felt as though she had been cast adrift with no clear destination in view and the possibility of becoming becalmed indefinitely out of sight of land. Her life stretched out before her like an unending level plain, lacking any features of interest. Of course, she still had her parents, her wider family ties, her friends, Morla, but what were all of these compared to that which she might have had and now never would?

Even the necessary bustle and distraction of preparations to depart from Verilith failed to rouse Nyandu from her inner bleakness, though she almost welcomed what would normally have caused her irritation, for it brought some relative normalcy to her listless mind. The leavetakings from the family of the Prince of Arlente over and the journey begun, Nyandu was conscious of every hoofbeat of her horse taking her further from any hope of happiness and of every calle enfolding her deeper into the black smothering cloak of dejection. She was barely aware of the surrounding countryside, which had seemed so interesting to her on her outward journey, and rode for hour upon hour in silence, rousing herself only to amuse Morla as best she could. Often she pleaded the excuse of a headache, and this was not entirely untrue as by the time the company reached the border with the

Dukrugvola's own province, her head was aching almost constantly, a nagging, faintly nauseating pain. She reached Lôren in a daze, her head buzzing, beset by shivers of alternating heat and chill and aching in all her limbs.

Stumbling a little as she crossed the courtyard, Nyandu was glad to feel a hand under her elbow, steadying her. She looked up, to find Saragon regarding her with anxious concern.

'Nan, are you ill? You're shaking.'

Forcing herself to smile, she reassured him.

'It was just a stumble. I've been too long in the saddle.'

She glanced ahead and noted Alhaîtha hovering in the doorway, and circumspectly withdrew her arm from Saragon's hold.

'Let's get inside out of the cold,' she suggested.

She would have liked to stay in her bedchamber, but there were obligations to fulfil, and after washing and changing her clothes, she slowly made her way down the corridors to the family's private parlour, collecting Morla on the way so that he might be formally introduced to the Lady Menethila. Presenting Morla and afterwards seeing him supplied with biscuits and a drink helped her through the initial minutes, until she could legitimately sink into a comfortable chair and sip the wine with which her uncle had provided her. As he moved off to dispense refreshments to Saragon and Alhaîtha, Nyandu sipped the bright liquid and hoped that it might restore her sufficiently to enable her to keep going until it might be possible to slip away to her bedchamber. She was beset by waves of giddiness and as each one swept over her, she momentarily lost contact with her surroundings, the room and all in it seeming to grow faint and voices fading into the distance. Her desperate longing for peace and quiet grew with every second that passed. Resting her now-throbbing head against the chair-back, she closed heavy-lidded eyes, gritting her teeth against the shivers which continued to plague her, despite the warmth of the blazing fire in the hearth. Conversation reached her as a buzz of indistinguishable voices. The glass which she was holding shook so violently that a few drops of the ruby liquid spilt onto her gown.

A hand reached out and took it from her, and she opened her eyes to find Saragon close by, looking down at her worriedly.

'You should be in bed,' he murmured. 'You don't have to hide it now.'

She shook her head, and winced.

'I don't want to be fussed over.'

'Don't be silly,' he told her. 'You would feel much better lying down for a while.'

Obstinately she repeated her refusal and demanded the return of her glass. He gave it back to her, but she trembled too much to keep it and he removed it again.

'You can't even hold a glass!' he scolded mildly. 'You're in no fit state to be up, Nan. If you don't go off to bed this instant, I'll tell your aunt myself.'

But it was too late. The Lady Menethila's eyes rested on her niece and she gave an exclamation of concern.

'My dear Nan,' she said anxiously, 'whatever is the matter? Are you not well?'

Nyandu looked across at her and tried to smile reassuringly, but the smile would not come. Lady Menethila's expression changed to one of deeper solicitude, and she got up from her seat.

'You are certainly not well, my child,' she observed decidedly. 'You should not be up out of bed.'

'It's nothing ... just a chill.

Nyandu tried to sound convincing, but to her furious embarrassment a tear slid from the corner of one eye and ran with snail-like slowness down her cheek, succeeded by another, and another, until they spilled over in a flood which she was powerless to check.

'Nan, my poor child, don't cry!'

Her aunt knelt beside the chair and drew her into a close embrace.

'Come. Let's get you into a warm bed. You should have said that you weren't feeling well. I'll have a hot posset brewed for you and you can go to sleep. Come.'

She took hold of Nyandu's hand and helped her to her feet. There a faintness assailed Nyandu and she swayed dizzily, unable to take a step. Anxious voices surrounded her in a chorus of sympathy and concern, and she tried to answer them, only to find herself sobbing uncontrollably. Still she could not move. Strong arms suddenly seized her and swung her off her feet amid a gaggle of appreciative exclamations. She felt warm skin against her cheek and realized that she was being carried by Saragon. She looked up into his face.

'I'm sorry,' she whispered wretchedly.

'Don't be,' he responded promptly. 'My dear Nan, there is nothing I like better than holding young women in my arms! Put your arm around my neck.'

She gave a watery giggle at the first part of his speech and obeyed the second.

'That's better,' he said approvingly, and carried her off.

For more than a week Nyandu lay gravely ill, the gruelling adventures that she had undergone having taken their toll on her health. Indeed, so concerned were the Dukrugvola and his Lady that a messenger was sent post-haste to bring her mother up from Silmendu. Alhaîtha, unable to be of use in the sick-room, bent her efforts to entertaining Morla, a task fraught with difficulty as the boy was frantic with worry and insisted on frequent visits to Nyandu's bedchamber simply to check that she still lived.

Saragon, though with pressing business requiring his presence in Shardu, deferred his departure. Despite reassurance from the Dukrugvola, he could not but believe himself in part to blame for Nyandu's illness. Had he not put forward her name to the Dukrugvola in the first place, she would not have been on that highway for her fateful meeting with Francys! And Francys would undoubtedly have died, said a voice in his mind. But Nyandu might die as a result. How could he rejoice at the recovery of one at the expense of the other? And Francys might yet die, and all Nyandu's sacrifice be for naught. He spent countless hours pacing the corridors, and the paths of the castle grounds, unable to settle to anything, unaware of the jealous eyes which watched him. Only once Nyandu had been pronounced to be out of danger, did he take his leave.

His departure came as a relief to one person at least. Alhaîtha, distressed though she undoubtedly was by her cousin's collapse, could not help but feel jealous as she watched his anxious pacings, detecting more than merely the concern of a friend in his demeanour. She herself had never roused such depth of feeling in those grey eyes, she thought bitterly, though honesty compelled her to admit that she had never been in a comparable situation to that suffered by her cousin. The thought brought her up short. Nyandu might die. She might lose her dearest friend, close as the sister she had never had, and all she, Alhaîtha, had done was to begrudge her the affection and concern of Saragon, whom they had both known from the cradle! What a monster she had become! In an access of self-loathing, she flung herself ever more frantically into doing what she could to ease her cousin's sufferings, be it taking care of Morla or even volunteering to sit beside the bed upon which Nyandu lay white-faced and unresponsive.

Alhaitha's inner turmoil did not pass unnoticed, however. The Lady Menethila observed her daughter with compassion. Sitting one cold, dreary afternoon in the parlour, she broached the subject, laying down her sewing for the purpose.

'Alie, my love, you must not be so hard on yourself,' she said gently. 'We don't want you falling ill too.'

Alhaîtha looked at her mother. Suddenly she could not stop herself from blurting out what she really wanted to know.

'Mama, do you think ... is Sharn in love with Nan?'

She hung her head wretchedly.

'Oh, I'm sorry', she whispered. 'I know you must be thinking, how could she worry about such a thing when Nan might be dying ... It's just ... I can't help it. He showed such concern for her. Oh, I am a wretch! A vile wretch!' she castigated herself bitterly.

The Lady Menethila leaned forward and laid a calming hand on Alhaitha's arm.

'My dear child, do not call yourself unwarranted names. I know full well how fond you are of Nan, and how worried you are about her. You have been immensely helpful, especially with that poor boy. But that doesn't mean that you shouldn't allow yourself to think of other things without feeling disloyal.'

She paused and smiled at the young woman.

'I know that you entertain feelings for Sharn. If it will make your mind easier, then I can say with some certainty that I do not believe that he is in love with Nan. He has his own reasons for feeling concerned for her, but it is not what you might think.'

'And Nan?' Alhaîtha asked quickly. 'Does *she* love *him*?'

Her mother gave her a look that she was unable to comprehend.

'What?' she asked sharply. 'Why do you look at me like that?'

The Lady Menethila appeared to reflect for a moment, then made up her mind.

'Sharn was and is only a good friend as far as your cousin is concerned. I do not believe you need have any fears about that!'

She sighed.

'Alas, poor Nan,' she said quietly, as if to herself. 'If only things had turned out differently. We had such hopes.'

Alhaîtha stared at her mother, puzzled.

'What do you mean?' she asked. 'What hopes? If what had turned out differently?'

The Lady Menethila put up a hand to smooth back a stray strand of hair from her brow.

'Your father and I had hoped for an alliance between Nan and Francys Coras,' she disclosed.

Alhaîtha started and gazed at her mother in horror.

'Nan and *Francys*!' she exclaimed. 'No! You cannot be serious, Mama! Nan and *Francys*!'

'It seemed to be a most suitable match,' her mother replied calmly.

'But Nan could not possibly have wished to marry Francys Coras!' Alhaîtha protested.

'Really, Alie!' The Lady Menethila responded, a trifle tartly. 'Just because you harbour some prejudice against a man, does not mean that no-one else may see any good in him! Not everyone felt as you did about Francys Coras, I assure you. Indeed, I should not need to tell you that many of your friends would have leapt at the chance of a union with him!'

'Yes, but *they* are not Nan! Nan has too much sense.'

'My dear girl, when love is involved, sense very seldom enters into the equation,' the Lady Menethila commented wryly. 'Though I own I should be very relieved to learn that Nan's heart was not touched. I cannot imagine what a nightmare this past year must have been for her otherwise. In fact, it had occurred to me that that might be the underlying cause of her ill-health ...'

Alhaîtha had scarcely heard the last few words, her thoughts flying back to the summer of the previous year when they had all been staying with Saragon in Shardu. She recalled Nyandu's burgeoning friendship with Francys, the portrait episode, and Nyandu's later unexplained distancing of herself and early departure.

'I am sure you are mistaken, Mama,' she broke in suddenly. 'Nan counted Francys as a friend, certainly, but no more than that. *He* may have deluded himself that she did, but Nan made it clear enough what her feelings were - she cut short her stay in Shardu last year to get away from his attentions after all!'

The Lady Menethila looked at her sharply.

'Is that so? I was not aware of that,' she said slowly. 'You are sure that it was due to Francys that she left? Not because of Hadran?'

'Hadran? Oh no. It was *Francys* whom she wished to avoid. I thought he must have tried to seduce her,' Alhaîtha said candidly, 'but maybe he had merely proposed marriage.'

She chuckled.

'Sior, what a blow that must have been to his self-esteem!'

Her mother shook her head, a trifle sadly, but merely said quietly:

'Well, I am glad for her sake that my fears are ungrounded. I daresay this illness is simply the result of travelling in this inclement weather, and I understand that she had suffered an accidental fall from her horse ...'

She gathered her sewing and rose, stating that she must go and take her turn in Nyandu's bedchamber, and departed, leaving Alhaîtha staring thoughtfully into the fire. The discussion had raised speculations in her mind which had not occurred to her before. So, Francys Coras had been in love with her cousin. That would explain many things which had puzzled her about that sojourn in Shardu. She smiled. That was why he had been so upset when she had accused him of wishing to seduce Nyandu; perhaps even why he had drunk so much that he had ended up in the river, where he had nearly drowned! She wished she had known before. Regrettably, there seemed no possible use she could make of the knowledge at the present time, but she stored it away in her mind for future reference.

****

Nyandu came to her senses to find her mother leaning over the bed, bathing her brow with a damp cloth. Confusedly, she thought for a moment or two that she was home in Silmendu, but the chamber that she could see beyond the bed was not her own, and after a few seconds' consideration, she recognized it for the chamber that was customarily allotted to her use whenever she stayed at the Dukrugvola's residence in Lôren. She blinked, and tried to raise her hand, but it felt as leaden as a statue's and she had not the energy to lift it more than a fraction. Her movement, slight though it was, however attracted her mother's attention.

'Nan, my dear child,' she said warmly, 'you've come back to us at last. You gave us some very worrying moments, my love. Now, just lie still there and I'll fetch you some broth. You are going to need a deal of cosseting to get you on your feet again.'

Convalescence was reasonably swift, however, and Nyandu was able within a few days to stagger downstairs, with the aid of her mother, to be ensconced comfortably in a chair beside the fireplace in the parlour, a footstool under her feet and a shawl about her shoulders. She had been reunited with Morla, who, it seemed, could not stop beaming and was eager to tell her about all that had happened to him in her absence. She was gazing abstractedly in the swirling flames and listening with only half an ear to a recital of an excursion to the city market, when the door opened and glancing round idly, a much-loved and exceedingly familiar figure met her eyes.

'Father!' she cried joyfully, a smile springing to her lips, and casting aside the shawl, she struggled up to meet him.

He strode across the room and received her in his arms, planting a hearty kiss on her wan cheeks. Nyandu laid her head on his shoulder.

'Oh, Father,' she murmured, half sobbing. 'I'm so sorry.'

He stroked her loose-bound locks with a gentle hand.

'Nay love,' he said soothingly, 'don't cry. Your mother won't be very pleased with me if my arrival sends you into a decline, now will she, eh? She sent me word that you were over the worst, so I had to come up and see my girl!'

He put his hands on her shoulders and held her away from him, looking down into her face.

'You look very pale still. Perhaps you should not be on your feet. Come and sit down again.'

He led her towards the chair that she had vacated on his entry, and settled her into it.

'There now, I'll just bring us some wine, and we can have an cosy chat.'

He turned, to find Morla standing quietly nearby, observing him with an intent brown-eyed stare.

'Is this the young scallywag I am to have the pleasure of entertaining?' he enquired affably.

The solemn face lightened.

'Yes, Menellen,' Morla said huskily.

'Then we must become acquainted,' the Lord Menor proposed genially, and proceeded to do so, winning Morla's confidence with an exposition of the delights which would await him in Silmendu, and provoking Nyandu into an involuntary gurgle of laughter.

'Really, Father,' she said, amused, 'one would think you a child yourself!'

Despite her delight in being reunited with her parents, Nyandu could not feel entirely at ease. The secret of her experiences in Kirkendom could not be forgotten and hung between her and them, its existence obliging her to be careful with her words, to weigh every remark lest it reveal too much. There seemed to be so many topics to be avoided because they touched too nearly on the forbidden one, and she felt that it was wrong to have to behave in such a cautious fashion towards her parents. Their restraint was admirable, not one hint of curiosity escaping them (she wondered whether the Dukrugvola might not have had a private word with them), but she knew that they longed to learn what she had been about, and all she could tell them were a few innocuous tales about the countryside through which she had passed. When her father triumphantly produced an old and battered kaïsa board, black, green and white-squared, with the requisite number of strangely-shaped pieces carven in the forms of people and animals, she was obliged to castigate herself fiercely for feeling relieved that now she would have an excuse not to talk. Above all, she felt lonely, isolated in the midst of her family. She wished that Saragon could have remained in Lôren, so that she might have had the luxury of knowing that one person at least understood what she was feeling, but he had his own affairs to concern him and she should not begrudge him the opportunity, for he had been more than generous with his time and attention during their journey from Verilith. Besides, she would soon be going home herself to Silmendu, and life would slowly return to its normal dull routine. Perhaps in time the past months would come to feel like a dream, not real at all. In her present misery, she could only fervently hope so.

****

Saragon rested his elbows on the smooth wood of his wide desk and his chin in his hands. It was mid afternoon and the door had just closed on the back of his steward. They had worked hard, barely breaking off for the midday meal, which they had taken together in the office. Now he had leisure to sit awhile and let his thoughts stray where they might; and, as so often before, images of two people arose behind his eyes. Nyandu, he knew, was recovering, at home now with her parents in Silmendu. He had received a letter from her, the handwriting shaky but clear enough, the innocuous words hiding a deeper meaning. He would write back, of course...

But as for the other: he had heard nothing. He wished that he could have got a message to Artem requesting news, but they had agreed that it would be a one-way communication only save in the direst emergency, and this could in no way be construed as such.

Abruptly pushing the chair back, he stood up, stretching limbs that had been too long in one position, and strode from the room.

CHAPTER NINETEEN

Francys had declared himself well enough to travel, despite some reservations expressed by Connor, and was bidding an affectionate farewell to his involuntary hostess and her son. Putting his arms round the tearful old woman, he planted a hearty kiss on her lips and assured her that he would never forget her or her cottage. She had indignantly refused his tentative offer of payment for her hospitality, deeply offended that he should believe her to want it, but he had taken Tam aside privately and had come to an arrangement with him so that Martha should never want for anything that it was in his power to supply.

Connor assisted Francys into the saddle of the horse which had been hired for him in the village, and mounted his own. Both men were clad in a knee-length heavy woollen tunic, woollen jacket lined with linen, and thick, baggy breeches of peasant style. Leather boots and a sheepskin cloak with a deep hood completed their attire. It was the best that Connor had been able to do in the way of disguise. A close-fitting felt hat beneath the hood served to conceal Francys' distinctive locks, but the young man had flatly refused to do anything further to alter his appearance. Touching their heels to the horses' flanks, they started out upon the journey home to Kordren. At the corner, where the lane curved out of sight, Francys twisted in the saddle and raised a hand in a gesture of adieu to the couple standing outside the doorway to the cottage. They caught a glimpse of his bright smile, before the horses swung around the bend and he vanished out of their lives. Tears running unheeded down her wrinkled cheeks, Martha turned and walked heavily indoors, and into the main bedchamber. The room was neat and clean, and empty, desolately empty without the fair man who had lived in it for so many long weeks. Not a trace remained of his occupancy, as if the whole episode had been nothing but a vivid dream. Without the lock of blond hair which she had begged from Francys, it might indeed have been such.

The hoofbeats rang out clearly in the cold, clean air. The breath of both men and beasts rose waveringly in a thin mist before them. The chill bit at the faces of the men, and they were glad of the warmth of the horses beneath them. Under the hooves, the earth was still hard, despite the dazzling sun, which shone brightly, angled in the sky above, and in the shadows where it had failed to penetrate, the grass stalks were still edged with white crystals of frost and puddles retained their icy crust, cracking explosively if a hoof chanced to touch them. Sloping thatch roofs facing northwards showed a white sheen. Smoke from wood-fires burning in the stone hearths within rose with perfumed billows to hang in the still air. Skeletons of trees silhouetted against the fields raised gnarled branches to the sun's feeble warmth. In the hedgerows and copses birds hung from twigs and pecked briskly at the bunches of scarlet berries, chattering and scolding one another whilst the village cats stalked beneath, eyeing them greedily. Sounds carried long distances in the cold air, and voices could be heard whilst their owners were yet out of sight. The noise of wood being chopped floated to their ears with startling clarity.

The two men rode contentedly at first, savouring the day. Francys was happy to be back on a horse after the long weeks of inactivity. He seemed almost oblivious to the biting cold, gazing about him with a smile on his lips. They had purposely planned a route which would avoid most villages, circuitous though it might be, keeping to the more deserted back lanes and by-ways, well away from the perilous highway. Although their presence might be in some ways more obvious on the little-used tracks, they would stand correspondingly less chance of meeting other travellers. In this surmise, they were proved correct. In an half hour, they saw only two carts in the distance, and passed one pedlar on foot.

For the main they rode without speaking, save now and then to exchange a brief remark. Then Francys suddenly demanded:

'Tell me what's been happening in Karled-Dū, Con, over the past weeks. I feel so dreadfully ignorant, and I know you've been getting news.'

Connor turned his gaze on him, consideringly.

'Yes. I have had some tidings,' he replied.

'Then tell me,' Francys said impatiently. 'Don't hide it all from me. If I'm well enough to travel, I'm surely well enough to hear the news without falling into a fit of the vapours! I want to know what's been going on.'

'I'm only wondering where best to begin,' Connor responded mildly.

He knew very well what it was that Francys wanted to know, and could not bring himself to ask directly.

He rode on a few paces, before saying quietly:

'The Lady Nyandu has made a safe return to Lôren, and is now, I believe, at home in Silmendu.'

'Indeed? Well, that's good news anyway. I wonder how she accounted for her absence,' Francys mused.

'Artem writes that Krapan has broken all ties with us over some incident,' Connor continued hastily, feeling that it was inadvisable to let Francys dwell too long on the subject of Nyandu. 'A skirmish which occurred on the border some weeks ago. It seems that a raiding party, which contained someone with high connections to the Chan's Court, was ambushed. The Chan took umbrage and repudiated the treaty! The Ambassador brought the happy news to the Investiture, and as you can imagine the Dukrugvola was not best pleased! ...'

Connor broke off, cursing himself for his carelessness. He had not meant to mention anything which related to Hadran.

'I can imagine he would not be,' Francys commented drily.

Silence fell, broken only by the thud and clop of hooves and the creaking of leather tack. Connor was beginning to hope that Francys had not noticed his slip, when:

'The Investiture?' he queried suddenly, 'What Investiture was that?'

Connor looked down at his hands. He had hoped to keep the news from Francys yet awhile, but there was no avoiding the issue. The fair man was waiting for an answer. He looked up.

'The Investiture of your brother as Prince of Varadil,' he said slowly, levelly.

'Prince of Varadil,' Francys repeated.

The words sunk into his awareness. He frowned, and shot a glance towards his Captain.

'Are you telling me that my father has died?'

Connor nodded glumly.

'Yes ... I'm sorry.'

Francys looked down over his horse's ears.

'So Father is dead,' he said meditatively, a faint undercurrent of grief shadowing the voice. 'It seems hard to believe. He was always so vigorous. I can't recall him ever being ill.'

He glanced at Connor.

'When did this happen? How did he die?'

Connor had hoped that he would not ask, but recognized that such a hope was unrealistic. With reluctance, he answered.
'Zenith. He suffered a seizure.'

Francys digested this. A shade descended over his face.

'One more misdeed to be set at my door,' he muttered unhappily.

'That, no doubt, is as your brother would like to have it,' Connor responded, 'but the tale I heard was somewhat different. *I* heard that your father died asking your forgiveness.'

'My *forgiveness*?!'

Francys' voice rose in amazement.

'My Father? But ...'

He could not continue. The notion that his father had sought absolution from *him* was so unbelievable that he could not comprehend it. Nor was Connor able to supply any reason for this remarkable volte-face.

Again they fell silent, and remained so for some time. Francys seemed deep in thought - of a certainty he had much to think on - and Connor was loth to disturb him. He concentrated instead on the road ahead, his own mind busy. Had it been wise to tell Francys now, he wondered. But then, whenever he told him, the effect would have been the same, and Francys would certainly have had something to say had he learnt that information had been withheld from him. Connor sighed. He glanced ahead, trying to calculate how much further they must travel to reach the safe house. They were riding down a winding lane with a ditch at either side of the rutted cart-track and hedgerows beyond liberally sprinkled with trees. To one side the lane widened to include a grassy bank with a stream running sluggishly behind, the bare branches of an orchard beyond. In the summer it would be a pleasant spot. Already, however, the light was beginning to fail and the cold to intensify. Connor fidgeted and wished they had been able to make better progress.

He became aware that his companion was cursing under his breath in a monotonous murmur, and turned to see what was wrong. Francys shifted in the saddle and gritted his teeth. The blood had drained from his face, to leave it pale and strained. Putting out a hand, Connor grasped Francys' reins and brought both horses to a halt. Francys raised his head, startled.

'You need a rest,' Connor elucidated. 'I don't like the look of you.'

Francys attempted a smile, which came out more as a grimace. 'I'll be all right. We ought to get on, before the dusk falls.'

'There's no sense in pushing yourself into a collapse. Come on down and rest a while.'

Francys shrugged and slid down from the saddle. As he landed, he staggered and was grateful for Connor's hand to support him. His legs felt unpleasantly strengthless and stiff from the effort of riding. Stumbling onto the verge, he subsided thankfully onto the blanket which Connor hastily unfolded and stretched out in the shelter of the hedge. Meantime, Connor led the horses across to the stream where he tethered them securely. He was not going to risk losing them. Then, rummaging in one of the saddle-bags, he returned to Francys with a flask, kneeling beside the young man and proffering it, saying gruffly:

'Here, drink some of this. You look as though you need it.'

'Thanks,' Francys gasped.

He shivered so much that Connor had to hold the flask for him.

'Damn. I thought I could manage.'

'What's wrong?'

'My head aches abominably and it makes me feel dizzy and nauseous.'

He relapsed into silence and bent his head, closing his eyes. The only visible sign of his struggle was the clenching of cramped hands until the knuckles showed white. Otherwise he was immobility itself.

Connor surveyed him worriedly, but let him be, only fetching another blanket to wrap round the motionless figure. After a few moments' thought, he set about collecting enough wood to build a small fire. It might be a little while before Francys felt recovered sufficiently to continue, and there was no sense in risking his health. Visions of fever and the sickness of the lungs rose before him. Kneeling beside the makeshift hearth, he coaxed the flames into being. Then he waited patiently. Around them the shadows lengthened and the night approached, stealing imperceptibly upon them. Stars appeared high above them, obscured by drifting clouds, and a full moon shone out brightly. Connor muttered to himself under his breath and glanced anxiously at Francys, impatient to move on. But Francys seemed almost to have fallen into a trance, and he hesitated to disturb him, even though he knew that he ought to. He began to pace up and down, stamping his chilled feet and rubbing frozen hands together. After checking on the horses, he retired some paces down the lane and stood behind a tree to relieve himself, the warm urine steaming as it met the icy air. Then he walked back slowly. Despite the fire, Francys must be frozen, he thought anxiously. Determinedly he advanced upon the still figure. Trance or no trance, Francys was not going to sit there any longer.

As he approached, however, Francys stirred and lifted his head.

'I'm sorry, Con,' he said, smiling ruefully. 'I've delayed us longer than I ought, haven't I.'

'Oh, that's no matter, but you must be frozen solid sitting there. How do you feel now?'

'The headache's gone.'

He stretched and yawned.

'Brr ... it *is* cold. I'm so sorry, Con. You must be suffering too.'

'Not unduly. But we'd best get going ... or perhaps you'd rather have something to eat first? We've a few calle more to travel before we reach our lodging for the night, and it might put some warmth into you ...'

'Please,' said Francys, so Connor crossed over to rifle their saddle-bags, returning with bread and cheese, a couple of the wrinkled apples which some villager had given Martha as a tacit gift for her guests, and the wine flask.

Francys ate hungrily, leaning against a tree-trunk, knees bent. Connor sat down nearby to devour his own share and they passed the flask companionably back and forth between them.

'Nice of them to give us these apples,' Connor observed.

'They shouldn't have,' Francys responded in a curious tone which struck Connor unpleasantly.

'Why ever not?' he asked.

'Because I'm imrauten.'

Francys sounded harsh. Connor shot him a quick glance, but his face was hidden by shadows.

'They know how much they are indebted to you,' he said. 'Why should they not show their appreciation? You're a hero round here.'

'Hero!' exclaimed Francys scornfully.

'Yes, hero. Why not? You've kept them safe from the threat of Harres raiding parties these past several months. Naturally they're grateful. They damned well should be! It's more than that bastard of a brother of yours ever managed to do for them. Why should they heed the denunciation of you in the Register, when all that you do gives the lie to it? Actions speak louder than words!'

A wry smile twisted Francys' lips, but he made no comment and silently applied himself to the scanty meal. Connor passed him the flask and he took a few swallows of the warming wine, feeling it flow satisfyingly through his veins. The headache's depressing effect upon him lingered dully. His nerves felt as if they had been stretched taut like the strings of a lute so that a single pluck upon them would set them vibrating and jangling. A heavy weight seemed to press down on his spirits. He was still so infuriatingly weak, so dependent on others, especially the man seated beside him. A rush of self-loathing overwhelmed him.

'I don't know why you waste so much time and energy on me!' he remarked suddenly, so suddenly and unexpectedly that Connor started. 'I don't deserve it in the least.'

He uttered a bitter laugh.

'By Tandar, you must really be a glutton for punishment, Con. Look at you, forced to wait on my convenience in the freezing cold out in the wilds of nowhere, and that after spending the past weeks tending to my bodily needs at all hours of the day and night. What does it feel like to be reduced to some sort of nursemaid? Sometimes I wonder if you regret throwing in your lot with mine. I shouldn't blame you for it. Don't you ever think how much better off you'd have been had you stayed in Varadil?'

'No!' Connor said hotly. 'I have never for one minute had any regrets, nor ever will! So long as you need me, I will be here no matter what should befall us.'

Francys gazed at him long and intently.

'Why?' he asked.

Connor's own gaze dropped.

'Because,' he mumbled in embarrassment, 'because you are the person I wish to serve. It's a matter of ... of personal choice. Why do you suppose all those men came so willingly to join you in the Toath Cranem?' he continued, recovering his aplomb and speaking more easily. 'They respect you. They enjoy serving you. They have a great admiration for you. They love you.

And now,' he said briskly, getting to his feet, 'for the love of Sior, let's get on our way else we'll likely freeze to the spot!'

But Francys was not listening.
'Love ...' he murmured in a strange tone, staring ahead unseeingly. His hands clasped each other tightly around his knees, knuckles whitening. To Connor's dismay and profound annoyance, he appeared to have withdrawn completely into some world of his mind and even when the Captain ventured to shake him by the shoulder, he was unable to elicit any response. Swearing choicely, Connor began to pack away the remains of their supper and to ready the horses, hoping that Francys would soon snap out of whatever was affecting him. Returning, he blew on his cold hands and stuck them under his armpits in an effort to restore them to warmth, stamping his feet noisily and, from time to time, darting irritable glances at the young man, wondering whether they would ever reach their destination this side of midnight. But Francys was far away, beyond his reach.

'Love'. The word had torn apart the carefully erected, carefully maintained barriers in his mind and through the gap he faced an infinitely long expanse of emptiness. 'Love'. One small word to describe a boundless emotion, and one that he must never acknowledge. Even the meanest beggar could speak of love to the woman of his choice, but he, Francys Coras, was forever barred from such privilege. With all his soul, with all his mind, with all his heart and body he longed for her, for Nan, and must not tell her so. And throughout the remaining dreary years of his life, he would have to carry the burden of unspoken, unrequited love. Unrequited? Yes, of course it must be so. Despite what she had said to Connor, he could not believe that she could return his feelings. Why should she, considering what he was?

What he was. He shivered. What *was* he? The memories rushed forward eagerly, thronging into his mind, thrusting themselves onto him with irrepressible force and he surrendered to their insistent pressure. After some months of life in the South as a toy of rich men and women, he had become the lover of Rycharst, unwillingly that was true, but in the end resignedly, submitting to the Dark Lord's embraces, sharing his bed. Vice was no stranger to him. Not all the tales that had been told about him were truthful, of course, but such inventions had a wide enough basis of fact to build upon. And after his escape, stripped of all respect for himself by the attentions of Rycharst, he had flung himself headlong into creating the reality of what he saw in his mind and what the public expected of him. Uncaring, he had lent himself to anyone who asked, had graced the beds of people he had never met before or since, had abused his body, while chaining up his mind behind an impenetrable wall, unreachable and, he had hoped, untouchable. For he had been proud of that mind. He had cultivated and encouraged it, trying to keep it separate from his physical body, because it alone had not betrayed him. For the flesh which had, nothing could be too bad. His name had become a by-word for scandal and he had been content to have it so, had even derived a sort of savage pleasure from the fact ... until it was too late. Until he had woken up to find that he had laid himself open to the attentions of such as Lord Elguin, until he had taken from himself all right to self-respect, until even his own brother dared to treat him as a common whore ... He had driven himself until, arrived at an intolerable pitch of disgust, he could no longer sustain his role; and he had come to Lôren resolved to put an end to all that side of his life.

But it was too late to resurrect respect. He was indelibly branded as a monster of vice. The normal entitlements of a member of society were no longer his. He had forfeited his rights, could never ask any decent woman to be his wife. But this would not have bothered him; he had had no intention of feeling anything more than mere friendship for anyone. It was too painful to allow oneself the luxury of emotions, and he had determined never to permit himself to feel anything ever again. So, of course, he had proceeded to fall desperately in love.

Nan. What must *she* think of him? What benefit had his love ever bestowed upon *her*? All he had done over and over since the day he had met her was to impose on her friendship. He had embroiled her in actions that might cost her her life should they ever become known. How could he be fool enough to entertain even the slightest hope of winning her love? Knowing what she did, how could she do other than despise him? For he had in his delirium spilled the details of his treatment at Hadran's hands. Connor had let slip that fact. And he had himself told her about the episode with Lord Elguin; and the remainder of his disgraceful past was too widely known that she could not fail to know of it. And now there was the additional slur of treachery. He was imrauten. No matter that he had not deserved it.

The mere fact that he was thought capable of betraying his country was damning enough.

What was there in that wretched list of past deeds that could possibly kindle the tiniest spark of love in someone as honest, as true as Nyandu? Nothing, he thought bitterly, nothing at all. Actions speak louder than words. That was what Connor had said, and it was true. He could tell her that he was not really the monster he appeared, that his true nature revolted from the conduct that the world had witnessed. He could swear that he would be true to her for the rest of his life, and mean it, but what would his words weigh against the overwhelming evidence of his actions. Even if he should be cleared of the charge of treason and could return to society, the past would still cling and he could never ask, or expect, her hand in marriage. It would be the deepest insult he could offer her.

But what use was there in considering such a premise when there was no likelihood of his innocence being proven in any event? Nothing lay ahead in his future save emptiness, utter emptiness. The thought of it made his very soul wince. How was he going to endure it? A lifetime of exile, of dodging and hiding and running. Oh Sior, why could Nan not have left him to die there on that highway? It would have solved everything. What cruel fate had decreed their meeting? Why could he not have died before that? Why must he continue alive when he would be far better dead and in his grave? There at last there would be peace, such as he had not known since he was sixteen - almost ten years. Then at least he could do no further harm to anyone. He was like a disease which brought death to all who came too close. It was as though a curse had been laid upon him, to single him out for misfortune. All his life, it seemed, it had dogged his footsteps, waiting for opportunities to spring. What had he done which deserved that he should be denied all hope of happiness?

What was it that the Lady Inisia had said? 'Some must take the long road ...' Yes, that was it. But not so long a road surely that they spend a whole lifetime upon it and never come to the end, he thought desolately. And not bereft of even one gleam of hope to lighten the way. Surely they could not expect him to persevere when he had nothing left, nothing at all, to strive for? It was too much. He could not go on. Not now. He had neither strength nor desire. All that he longed for now was the bliss of oblivion, not to know, not to suffer any more ...

'Con,' the voice spoke suddenly, hardly above a whisper. 'Con, release me from my promise.'

At first Connor did not comprehend the import of the words, but as the realization came to him, so he felt a finger of icy horror run down his spine.

'Please,' the voice pleaded. 'Release me, Con. Let me die! Let me have peace. I cannot go on.'

For a moment, Connor felt as if he had been turned to stone. He could not move, could not speak. And the voice continued remorselessly:

'What use am I to anyone? Look at me, Con! I cannot even last out a day's ride! All I am is a burden, a curse on everyone I meet. Better to end it now before anyone else gets hurt! Please Con, I beg you! If you have any regard for me, set me free from my promise and let me make an end of it! I beg you!'

The husky whisper, shaking with emotion, died away, and Connor could move again.

'No!' he said harshly, his voice over-loud in the need to express his horror, his absolute negation of the suggestion. 'No! For the regard I bear you, Francys, I cannot! Not now ... Not ever! That is the coward's way, and you don't deserve such as end as that!'

He stopped, then continued more gently:

'You have been so very ill, Francys. You cannot expect to be fully recovered yet. This black mood will pass as your strength comes back. Believe me. You will not always feel like this.

And now, I am going to get you onto your horse and we are leaving this ill-fated spot ... Sior,' he muttered under his breath as he stamped away to collect the horses, 'if we stay here much longer, the matter will be academic as we'll have frozen to death anyhow.'

He was uncertain what his reception might be as he brought the two mounts to a halt in front of the young man, but Francys made no demur. His legs were so stiff that Connor was obliged to help him to his feet, and assist him into the saddle. Then, having bundled the blankets into a roll behind his own saddle, and safely stamped out the embers of the fire, he took hold of the reins of Francys' beast, and nudged his own into a trot, anxious to get away from that unlucky spot. Fortunately, the night was clear and the moonlight bright enough to make riding not too hazardous an enterprise. He dared not force the pace and those few calle which they had to travel to reach their lodgings seemed the longest he had ever ridden. Francys swayed exhaustedly in the saddle, and Connor was obliged to reach out from time to time to steady him, a service which was not acknowledged, for the young man appeared to have withdrawn completely from the world around him.

Arriving at length at the small cottage, Connor descended from his horse and advanced through a veranda cluttered with the tools of their host's trade - he was a cobbler - to knock in a pre-arranged signal. The door opened immediately as though the inmate had been waiting beside it, as was in fact the case. The man appeared on the threshold and glanced warily at Connor, who returned the scrutiny, seeing a shifty-eyed, plump face framed by lanky, graying hair, a figure clad untidily and none too cleanly, but well-shod. He recalled Martha's words, for it was she who had arranged their stay here and the man was her nephew. 'He's a widower,' she had explained. 'His wife died some five years since and he's lived alone since then. They had no children. Just a cat for company and his cobbler's trade to live on. But he's got a good heart. He'll take you in and welcome, though it may be none too clean ...'

The man bowed respectfully and invited Connor in.

'And your companion,' he continued, glancing across to the horses, where Francys had made no move to dismount.

'I was expecting you somewhat earlier,' he remarked next. 'I hope that you did not lose your way.'

'We were unavoidably detained,' Connor answered briefly, and returned to Francys.

'Let me help you down,' he suggested.

The young man landed tiredly on the ground, his knees bending automatically to absorb the shock of impact. Wearily he walked to the doorway with Connor following, a little like a nanny trailing a toddler. The cobbler, Clem by name, stood aside to let them pass through, bowing and smiling nervously and apologizing profusely for the lowliness and untidiness of his home.

They crossed the threshold into a low-ceilinged, dimly lit room which bore manifest traces of having been hastily swept and cleaned. A fire crackled in the wide hearth and gave out a blissful heat. In front of it lay a massive ginger cat, stretched out luxuriously. Upon hearing their entrance, it briskly gathered itself and sat up, blinking suspiciously in their direction, paws set neatly side by side as cats do, watching whilst Connor steered Francys over to the wooden settle placed near the pleasantly active fire and seated him there. It was a massive high-backed affair without even a cushion to soften the hard seat, but Francys did not seem to notice. Connor observed with concern the pinched look about the young man's face and felt his hands to see how icy they were.

Clem, having been delegated by Connor to lead the horses out of sight to the small outhouse where he housed his one milk cow, returned in haste, carrying the blankets which he had removed from behind Connor's saddle, the which he set to warm beside the hearth. In stammering tones, due to excitement, he began to enquire what the travellers would like to eat, detailing the contents of his larder, but catching sight of Francys, whom he had not seen clearly before, he fell abruptly silent and stood staring.

'It *is* he!' he exclaimed excitedly. 'It is the Lord Imraut ... in *my* house! Who would believe it!'

Connor stepped in swiftly, and drew the man aside.

'My companion,' he explained quietly, neither confirming nor denying his identification, 'is exceedingly weary, and cold. What he would appreciate above all else is a cup of spiced ale ... and you mentioned a pasty?'

'Yes, yes, sir. At once,' the man turned eagerly to the press ranged against one wall. Whilst he busied himself, Connor picked up one of the blankets which he wrapped around Francys' shoulders without saying a word.

Francys, who had been shivering despite his proximity to the fire, looked up at that and gave a slight nod. At this, the first sign to demonstrate his awareness of Connor's presence since they had left the scene of his struggle for release from the chains of life, Connor felt his spirits rise. In a more optimistic mood, he strode outside to see to the horses, exhorting his host to brisker preparations as he passed. Unsaddling the beasts, he rubbed them down with wisps of straw, whistling through his teeth. Then, having provided them with hay and water, he picked up the saddle-bags and returned indoors.

The ale arrived, steaming in earthenware tankards. Connor carried one over to Francys, whilst the cobbler followed with a dish upon which reposed a couple of very tasty-looking venison pasties. Francys' hands were so chilled still that he was unable to hold the mug, and Connor ventured to rub the icy fingers until some life had been restored to them. The young man had, however, begun to relax, to thaw, under the influence of the crackling fire, Connor noticed with relief, although the exhaustion written on his face was not encouraging. The spiced ale brought a flush to the pale cheeks and relaxed him even more, sufficiently indeed to send him to sleep where he sat. Connor, making polite conversation with his host, sitting on a stool beside the hearth, and feeding the cat with morsels from his pasty, to the accompaniment of appreciative purrs and much weaving of the furry body about his legs, observed that the cobbler's gaze was continually drawn towards the young man. He twisted round, to discover the blond head resting limply against the corner of the settle, and a smile came to his lips.

****

As dull light crept in through the crack between the shutters, Francys stirred. He found to his surprise that he was lying flat on the settle, his cloak folded beneath his head and a couple of warm blankets wrapped about him. Opening his eyes, he raised his head a little and espied Connor stretched out upon a straw mattress beside the hearth. Remembrance of the day before flooded his half-wakened mind. He heard again his words 'Release me from my promise. Let me die. Let me have peace'. A wave of misery swept over him and he closed his eyes again, laying his head back on the makeshift pillow. In his mind the path of memory opened and he travelled down it in unwilling fascination, gliding from one landmark to the next, moving ever further back in time past the hurts, the humiliations, until at last he regarded the long-ago-shattered innocence of childhood. For a minute or two he contemplated the light-hearted, hopeful boy he had once been, until the bitterness and grief grew too strong and forced him to retreat, retracing his steps, closing the door firmly behind him. He would never revive that memory again. Too much had happened since; there had been too many injuries. He bore too many unhealed wounds in his soul. Less than ten years was all that separated that boy with all the pleasures of life before him from the man he was now, doomed to face a life without purpose, without hope; a hell from which he was denied an exit, barred in by his own promise.

'Oh Sior.'

The sound escaped his lips in a low whisper, but it was enough to rouse Connor from his doze. He started up and glanced hastily towards the settle. Hearing him rise to his feet, Francys opened his eyes and said bitterly:

'So you think I need a keeper now, do you? Don't you trust me to keep my word?'

'Of course I do,' Connor said crossly, unfolding cramped limbs and rubbing cold hands together. He bent down to poke the fire into life and to cast a couple of logs onto the glowing embers. Then, with a wary glance at Francys, he went to look for their host to arrange for some breakfast. Francys remained lying on the settle for a minute or two, then decided with reluctance that he should get up, and slid out from the blankets, shivering as he met the cold air.

Breakfast was a speedy affair, no more than a bowl of porridge apiece, and a cup of ale. Making a discreet payment, the two men took leave of their host, Francys having recovered his manners sufficiently to thank the cobbler for his hospitality and to apologize for his churlish behaviour of the night before. They rode out into a world turned white overnight, the clear skies of the evening having given way to a swirl of dancing flakes. Pulling up their hoods, they turned their faces towards the town of Arlmen, squinting against the feathery snow crystals blowing into their eyes. The only sound beyond the muted clatter of the horses' hooves and chink of stirrups, was the light, thin susurration of the snow as it gently touched upon leaves of bushes and shrubs.

Connor would have started a conversation, the silence dragging on his nerves, if he could only have decided upon a safe subject, but there seemed to be pitfalls in every one. He was at a loss how to behave, having naturally enough never before found himself in quite such a situation. What *can* you talk about with a man whom you have compelled to remain alive against all his desire? It was a ticklish problem, and Francys made no attempt to ease the inevitable tension between them. He rode briskly, his manner suggesting that he was trying to outpace something dreadful, and scarcely spoke a word. When he did open his mouth, it was merely to give some order or to make some absolutely necessary observation, and once he had said his piece, he would relapse into silence, drawing away from any attempt on Connor's part to deviate from the thin line of contact which he had permitted. This time the barriers had been reinforced.

****

Some twelve days later Francys sat in his room in the old keep at Kordren. The chamber was draughty in spite of the fire burning brightly in the grate and he wore a thick, fur-lined jacket above woollen hose. Tall candles shed a glow throughout the room, flickering in the draught, sending leaping shadows across the block-stone walls and high ceiling, bringing the figures to life in the tapestries and bed-hangings. Books and papers lay scattered liberally across the polished oak table in the centre of the chamber, but Francys was seated on a low stool beside the fireplace, staring moodily into the flames. The shouts and laughter of his men echoed up the steep, winding staircase to reach his ears. He stirred irritably, propping his chin on one hand, and sighed heavily. Somewhere nearby Connor or Joclyn would be waiting, he knew, in case he should attempt anything. They had set a discreet watch on him since the minute he had returned. That first night they had even wanted to put someone to sleep in his chamber, but he had made strong objections, delivering a pithy and impassioned speech, and concluding by bolting his door against them. When, therefore, he had suffered from nightmares, as was too frequent an occurrence, and had screamed out in his sleep, the worried Captains had experienced a panic-stricken few minutes outside the locked door, unable to discover what had happened. He grimaced wryly and his thoughts moved back to the journey thither.

Constrained to carry the burden which was his life, he had not wanted to speak, to think. He was simply concerned with keeping moving so as to outpace his mind. Besides, what could he say to someone who had thwarted his one remaining desire, save bitter, hurtful things? Normal conversation was impossible when every subject seemed to carry some hidden sting to remind him of his situation. Consequently, he had resorted to keeping speech to a minimum, knowing that it would be futile to rail against his Captain and knowing also that that was what he would do if he was forced to talk.

Arrived in Arlmen, they had made their way unseen to Jeff's house and had gathered from him all the news of the town. Packages from Artem awaited him there as, more acceptably, did Melisor. The reunion with his horse had provoked Francys into the first display of pleasure that he had shown since that ghastly night. At the sound of his voice as he entered the stable, the black stallion had let out a shrill, overjoyed whinny and Francys, hastening to him, had thrown his arms about the horse's neck, resting his face against the soft, dark head, eyes closed, whispering the horse's name in a voice which betrayed his emotion. And Melisor had seemed to understand, nudging him gently as if in sympathy.

They had stayed only a day in Arlmen, being anxious to press on towards their destination. For Francys, there was mortification enough during the ensuing journey. Try as he might, he found himself unable to stay above a couple of hours at a time in the saddle, any attempt to continue longer invariably ending in an attack of giddiness and a blinding headache. To one who was accustomed to spending a whole day astride a horse with the greatest of ease, such a situation was intensely frustrating and galled him to the soul. In the beginning, he had pressed on regardless, illogically glad of the pain which blocked his thoughts, punishing himself, but eventually he was obliged to accept the necessity of resting at least a half, if not a whole, hour after every two in the saddle, fretting and fuming inwardly throughout each enforced halt and snapping peevishly at Connor when the latter failed to show the impatience he was justified in feeling.

It was not until they had reached the edge of the Toath Cranem that Connor had finally made up his mind to broach a sensitive subject; one that had been worrying him greatly. Sitting beside the camp-fire wrapped in blankets and clutching a bowl of hot soup, he remarked suddenly:

'I don't know whether you have given the matter any thought, Francys, but I fear we may have a traitor in our camp.'

Francys did not respond immediately, but sat staring into his bowl. Connor had begun to think that he had not listened, when he spoke.

'Why?' he asked, his tone cold and uninterested.

'I cannot think how else your brother could have known where to place his ambush.'

Francys took his time to respond, spooning up the last dregs of his soup.

'You forget that I was not supposed to be on that track,' he said at last. 'That I was so, was a matter entirely of chance and last minute decision. I would have been expected to be with the company.'

Connor winced at the acidic tone of the young man's voice, but merely said quietly:

'True, but it's possible that he had placed men to cover both tracks. And it might have been planned to detain you in some way, to isolate you from the rest ...'

'A most unlikely story,' Francys observed unkindly, taking a sip of wine. 'But I suppose you propose to seek out this hypothetical traitor? How are you going to set about it?'

'There are ways.'

'I'm glad you think so,' Francys rejoined sarcastically, 'since you'll be the one to use them.'

He lifted his cup and drank down the remainder of the wine therein, gazing over the rim into the fire and apparently dismissing the subject. Connor was not so eager to let it go.

'Don't you care whether there's a traitor?' he asked incredulously.

'Why should I?'

The voice conveyed a deliberate sense of boredom and Francys did not even look round.

'You're perfectly capable of dealing with the matter without my assistance.'

'Francys!' Connor exclaimed, annoyed. 'This is a serious matter! Don't you care that there may be someone in the company who could betray us all?! You must be mad! Or,' as a thought occurred to him, 'do you see it as a fine way to get what you want without having to break your word ...?'

'No!' Francys snapped furiously, turning a blazing gaze upon him. 'I have never in my life broken my word once I have given it, in any manner, and you have no right to insult me by suggesting it! Sior knows, I don't want to be here, but I gave you a promise, so I will just have to make the best of it. But I'm damned if I'll put up with gratuitous insults! Or silly imaginings either!

Yes, if you wish to know, I have considered the matter, and there are any number of ways he could have found out where I'd be. I'm damned sure it wasn't from one of the men. After all, you and I vetted them personally did we not! But if it makes you happier, by all means put your 'ways' into practice. Just so long as you don't upset the men and you don't bother *me* with the matter!'

He set his cup down and rose.

'Wake me when you want to sleep,' he said curtly and disappeared into the rough shelter which they had constructed, leaving Connor to keep watch over the fire and the horses.

Francys stirred again and got to his feet to put some more wood onto the rapidly diminishing fire, poking it into a renewal of life. Subsiding again onto the stool, he leaned forward to warm his hands at the resulting blaze. He knew that he ought to go to bed. It was late. Downstairs the noise had faded as the men retreated to their barracks, settling down for the night and leaving only a handful to stand guard. It was time for him to make a pretence at resting. Life, existence, to which he was chained by an unbreakable promise, required him to go through the motions of sleeping even though it meant lying wakeful through long, dreary hours or enduring nightmare dreams from which he would wake himself, drenched in sweat and shaking with horror. The very memory made him flinch, and the prospect of going through it all again struck dread into his heart. Damn Rycharst, he thought, and damn Hadran.

At that moment, a spark of anger was lit within him. Between them, those two had conspired to bring him to the brink of destruction. Why should he give them the gratification of success? Determination was born. It seemed that he did have a purpose in living after all - to thwart the desires of those who would rejoice at his death. If the mere act of living was a defiance, then defy them he would, and more. He would live to turn the tables. The Lord of Shadowe would come to rue the day when he had first set eyes on Francys Coras ...

But, first he must go to bed. He continued to sit on the stool irresolutely, unable to make up his mind to the action, his hands still automatically stretched out to the flames. A faint rap on his door caught his attention. It was repeated, and Connor entered, a cup in one hand. Francys turned his head quickly at the interruption and frowned. Undaunted, his Captain walked steadily across to the fireplace and halted, looking down at the young man.

'Francys,' he said coaxingly. 'I've brought you a sleeping-draught. I know you refused it before, but you cannot go on in this way. You must get some sleep or we'll have you ill again. And it will suppress those dreams,' he added persuasively. 'Won't you take it, just this once?'

Francys, on the point of delivering a sharp rebuff, hesitated and considered. At last he stood up and held out his hand.

'Very well,' he assented wearily. 'I suppose it can do no harm.'

Connor handed him the cup wordlessly and watched him drain it to the dregs. He seemed to detect a change in the young man. Some of the intolerable strain of the past days seemed to have disappeared from his expression and he seemed somehow more alive, more vital. Francys turned away to set the empty cup down on the table, then, to Connor's surprise, he spoke.

'I'm sorry, Con,' he said quietly. 'I have not treated you well these past days. I apologize.'

He walked towards the bed and began to unlace the ties of his jacket. Then, as Connor remained standing still beside the fireplace, Francys looked round and commented with a touch of irritation:

'I'm perfectly capable of putting myself to bed. You don't have to stay.'

But the tone was no longer inimical. Connor smiled and, departing obediently, was conscious of the lifting of a weight from his mind.

He returned to the room an hour later, opening the door quietly and peering cautiously round it. A candle still burned on the table, forgotten. He crept in to snuff it and took the opportunity to survey the bed. A contented smile illuminated his features and he retired downstairs to his own chamber with a tranquil mind. There would be no need for guards tonight for Francys slept, at peace under the drug's beneficial influence.

EPILOGUE

Rycharst, Lord of Shadowe stirred. Fighting against that weakness which always followed the use of his powers, he passed his hand over his heavy-lidded eyes, shook his long dark hair back over his shoulders, and sat back in his chair. With a sudden sharp movement, his hand caught the wide shallow bowl on the table before him and sent it tilting upwards, the black viscous liquid within rising like a swirl of black silk, to fall in a pattering of thick drops onto the polished surface of the wood. Seizing the goblet which had luckily escaped the shower, he downed the wine therein in one deep swallow, and hurled the empty goblet across the room. It was of no avail. Francys Coras was lost to him, safe once more in the Toath Cranem. All his plans had come to naught.

But that would not be the end. How could he accept failure, *he*, of the race of the immortals, at the hands of mere humans? No, that day *would* come when the triumph of victory would be his, and on that day those who had contrived to thwart the desires of the Lord of Shadowe would surely be required to pay for their temerity. He was no clairvoyant, but this he could predict with certainty: the greatest struggle of all was yet to begin. What lay in ahead in the future was unclear, but of a surety there would be sorrow, pain ... and death!

A slow smile curved his thin lips.

*****